HATSHEPSUT:
DAUGHTER OF AMUN

More information is available from
www.moyracaldecott.co.uk

HATSHEPSUT: DAUGHTER OF AMUN

by

Moyra Caldecott

Published by
Bladud Books

First published by Arrow Books in 1986
Electronic editions published by Mushroom eBooks 2000

This edition published in 2004 by Bladud Books,
an imprint of
Mushroom Publishing, Bath, UK
mail@mushroompublishing.com
www.mushroompublishing.com

ISBN: 1-84319-263-2

". . . May you permit me to reach the eternal sky, the country of the favoured; may I join with the august and noble spirits of the realms of the dead; may I ascend with them to see your beauty . . ."

From Spell 15, The Ancient
Egyptian Book of the Dead

Introduction

The ancient Egyptian belief system appears very confusing to us if we examine it with minds that have been conditioned to expect rational and scientific explanations for everything. But those of us who are aware that a great deal happens that is not amenable to rational and scientific explanation, have no problem in accepting the ancient Egyptian myths, not as fantasy, but as a different way of looking at reality – a way that shows up certain subtleties and complexities that we had not noticed before.

The many gods of the Egyptian pantheon are not to be regarded literally as jackal-headed, ibis-headed, ram-headed – no more than Christians are to take it literally that Christ is a lamb and the Holy Ghost is a dove.

Most people at some point in their lives feel that they have been helped by an invisible someone, and if they don't immediately dismiss the experience as not having really happened, they will acknowledge their helper by a name drawn from their culture – St. Francis, Buddha, the angel Gabriel or, if they are ancient Egyptian, Ra, Djehuti or Ptah. They will also ponder about a life after the death of the body, about that mysterious part of them that has always felt more real to them than their body. Because we have only hints and clues, but no hard and fast facts about the other world, each culture uses its own familiar images to describe it.

The ancient Egyptians saw the Duat, or other world, in images of rivers, of boats, of fields, of marshes, of deserts, and, as in their own temples, chambers and halls only entered with difficulty through heavily guarded doors. Osiris ruled as king over this world, seated in his great hall on his throne, receiving petitions and passing judgements. A giant pair of scales weighed the heart of the deceased against the feather of truth.

They saw the body as only one aspect of the living being. They believed there were at least nine aspects in all, separating out at death. Some lingered on earth if the funerary rituals and spells were performed correctly, to pass invisibly in and out of the tomb, still taking an active part in the life of the world, helping their petitioners if required to do so, and enjoying the freedom to wander where and when they pleased. Others faced the tests and trials of the Duat and

3

came at last, if "justified" or "true of voice", to live in a kind of heaven, much like this world, but better. Others passed on to even higher realms, to the stars and beyond. Which of these many parts of the individual could and would come back to earth, reincarnated, to live again in the flesh but in a different body in a different time and place, is never made clear – but that this could and did happen was part of the belief system. Many a pharaoh had "Repeater of Births" among his many titles.

An extraordinary number of people alive today believe that they once lived in ancient Egypt. The civilisation intrigues and fascinates us. The magnificence of the ruins left to us on either side of the Nile, of the art and the funerary treasures now residing in our museums, of the complex and profound mystic truths revealed to us since their hieroglyphs have been deciphered, has much to teach us. But more and more people find that intellectual interest alone cannot account for their attachment, their obsession, with a particular place and time in such a distant past. Usually these people find that any mention of anything to do with the reign of a particular pharaoh, any glimpse of a particular object from that era, gives them a shiver down the spine, almost a thrill of recognition.

A belief in reincarnation is very old and very widespread. Many civilisations past and present have held faith in it without question. An increasing number of people these days use the word "karma" from the Hindu religion, meaning the working out in a present life of some problem from a past life. The ancient Celts believed so absolutely in it that debts from one life could be paid off in another. Others, like the Christians and the Jews, have edited out the belief from the main body of dogma, but it still survives in isolated pockets of esoteric teaching.

For a long time the female pharaoh Hatshepsut has haunted me as she has haunted others. Her mortuary temple at Deir el Bahri in the western cliffs opposite modern Luxor, built to keep her memory alive forever, was defaced shortly after her death, her name obliterated and her images broken up or usurped by other pharaohs. No mortuary priests were appointed to perpetuate her cult and see that her "ka" was comfortable and nourished. In the king lists of Abydos her name is omitted as though she had never existed. Yet archaeologists have found references to her that escaped the chisels of her successor and the vandalism of time, and have built up a fairly full picture of her life.

In this novel I have used what the Egyptologists have been able to discover about her, and the texts that she herself had inscribed on obelisks and temple walls. But I have also drawn on clues and hints I have received by less orthodox means. In the end I hope the picture I have drawn of Hatshepsut will have enough of history to satisfy those who want history, and enough of the "other" to make her story relevant to those who are experiencing their own complex and difficult journey through many realms and many lives.

Those who have read my other novels, *Guardians of the Tall Stones* and *The Silver Vortex,* will be pleased to recognise Deva, daughter of Kyra, who set off from Bronze Age Britain to train as a priestess in Egypt, the land of her father. In this book she takes her ancient name Anhai.

CHAPTER 1

The boy, Men-kheper-Ra, looking small and nervous, was seated on his huge throne, almost dwarfed by it. The red crown of the Northern Territories and the white crown of the Southern, fitted together, were balanced precariously on his head. Usually they fitted snugly, but the new Master of the Royal Vestments, recently appointed by Hatshepsut, claimed that he was growing so rapidly that a larger crown was called for. This was the first time he had worn it. It was too large, too uncomfortable, and made him look ridiculous.

Hatshepsut was not yet on the other throne, and this made him uneasy. The hall was filling up with the nobles and officials. His personal attendants, those whom Hatshepsut had not replaced recently, seemed nervous too and clustered as close as they could to each other and to the stepped stone mound on which the two thrones were mounted. Why had she not joined him? Was she ill? Was he going to have to manage this whole ceremonial occasion by himself? Sweat began to trickle down his forehead. He couldn't wipe it away because already the insignia of kingship were in place and he dared not move. The crook and flail, almost too heavy for him, had to be held at just the right angle across his chest.

The foreign princes were entering now to take their places in the great hall. He tried to remember the words he had been taught to say on such occasions. He had attended many before, but Hatshepsut had always presided and his bored mind had been free to wander where it willed.

He heard a faint tinkle and jangle to one side of him and managed to move his eyes without moving his head, wondering if it were the arrival of his stepmother-aunt at last, but from the wrong direction. It was his mother, Ast, heavily overdressed in tasteless jewellery, kept just out of whisper range by protocol, trying to get nearer him to tell him not to fidget.

The most important thing in Men-kheper-Ra's life at this moment was to keep still and somehow ignore the sweat drops that were setting up an itch as they moved down his face.

Ast, satisfied that her son was now as motionless as a statue, turned her attention back to the scene before her. Light was shafting down from the high slit windows, picking out in gleams and shimmers the gold collars of the nobles and the barbaric splendours of the foreign princes. There was a continual flow of movement as each individual or group entered the hall, prostrated themselves before the child-king, and then found their correct place to stand. All eyes alternated between the empty throne and the door through which the Regent was expected to come.

Ast became more and more uneasy. She noticed that behind the colonnade that surrounded the throne chamber there seemed to be more royal guards than usual. She narrowed her eyes and strained to see who was who in the crowds. Men-kheper-Ra's own guards were not present. Why? Men-kheper-Ra's own advisors, tutors, secretaries, scribes, were not present. Why? And only a handful of his personal attendants. Suddenly Ast was very frightened indeed and wondered if her son was about to be assassinated. But surely not in front of all these foreign princes? Whatever the internal troubles of Egypt, the Pharaoh must always appear strong, authoritative, invincible to outsiders.

At last, when the suspense was becoming unbearable and the foreign princes had been kept waiting almost to the point of insult, a fanfare of trumpets announced the arrival of Hatshepsut.

In the total silence that followed the blast, she strode in with her entourage of favourite noblemen following behind.

Stunned, the crowd momentarily forgot to fall to the ground. Every eye was opened wide, every throat expelled a gasp.

The female Regent of the Two Lands was dressed as a male king, with ceremonial beard, short kilt, bare chest, royal collar and bracelets – and double crown.

Men-kheper-Ra jerked with surprise and his own crown, which Hatshepsut had arranged would be too big for him, lolled forward rakishly, but did not fall. Ast bit her lip with rage. "What a spectacle!" she thought. She had always hated Hatshepsut and now she was almost pleased the woman was making a fool of herself. Surely she would be disgraced by this, and Men-kheper-Ra called to rule alone.

But no one was protesting. No one was laughing. Each and every one was bowing to the ground as though a real pharaoh were striding through the hall.

Behind her entourage came eight priests of Amun, carrying the holy barque mounted on cedar wood poles upon their shoulders – the golden boat containing the curtained shrine of Amun.

This in itself was unusual. This was a civil occasion, and the god did not usually come to the throne room when civil matters were being conducted.

Hatshepsut mounted the steps to the throne regally, but did not sit down. She turned and stood facing the crowd.

The barque of Amun was brought to rest before her, but not lowered to the floor.

She did not give the signal for the crowd to rise, but there was scarcely a person in the hall who did not raise his or her head enough to stare, fascinated.

Hatshepsut gazed straight ahead at the curtained shrine.

Suddenly three huge golden falcons appeared, apparently from nowhere, and began to circle the hall. Round and round they went, seven times, their wings raising such a wind that every garment and wig and lock of hair began to flutter. The curtain in front of the shrine was blown aside, and from within a beam of light blazed out directly onto the body of Hatshepsut. It was as though she were transformed into gold, her slight figure expanded to tower over them. The three falcons one by one alighted on the back of her throne, also illuminated by the brilliant and eerie light. A voice boomed out. It did not seem to come from anyone in the hall, not even from the shrine. It was in the air above them, vibrating like a mighty drum-roll in their hearts.

This is my chosen one. This is the King who will return the Two Lands to my feet. Worship him, you princes, you noblemen, you farmers, servants and slaves. Write his name and his mighty deeds on everlasting stone, you scribes. Cover him with my breath of incense, you priests. Hatshepsut. Maat-ka-Ra. Horus of Pure Gold. Sovereign of the Two Lands. King of North and South. Son of the Sun. Beloved Daughter of Amun. Living in Splendour Forever.

Men-kheper-Ra's mouth was open. What did this mean?

The High Priest of Amun, who had all this while been waiting beside the golden barque, now stepped forward and took the crook and flail from the boy's nerveless fingers and placed them in the firm and confident hands of Hatshepsut, the man-woman standing in golden light.

"Rise," the mysterious voice continued. *"Sing the praises of your King."*

Trumpets sounded again, almost drowning the sound of scuffed feet as hundreds rose to stand bemused before the magnificent luminous figure in front of the throne. Lines of chantresses from the Temple of Hathor, shaking sistrums, came dancing into the hall, leading the people in praise songs for the new Pharaoh. In the excitement of the moment no one doubted that Horus, the Falcon god, himself had given her his blessing. In triple manifestation he spread his wings and circled above her head before he disappeared as mysteriously as he had come.

Many in that moment saw her as sole male King, and swore allegiance to her in their hearts, forgetting Men-kheper-Ra completely. The foreign princes looked at each other surreptitiously, wondering how this turn of events would affect their lives and the relationships of their countries with Egypt. Would a woman keep such a tight rein on them? Would they be safer from Egyptian aggression? Many of them had not seen her before, and standing as she did now in that blaze of uncanny light, she seemed a force to be reckoned with. She might well be stronger alone than she had been as Regent for that boy. They looked at the faces of the men who now gathered round her at the foot of the throne steps, at the faces of the priests who carried the shrine, and most of all at the face of Hapuseneb, the First Prophet of Amun, who had actually placed the crook and flail in her hands. They were strong faces.

Men-kheper-Ra felt foolish and frightened. What was to become of him? He turned to his mother in despair. As his eyes met hers, she forgot the danger they were in, and like an angry lioness springing to the defence of her cub, she stepped forward and accosted Hatshepsut.

"What about my son? He is the chosen heir of Aa-kheper-en-Ra!"

"Step back, woman," growled one of the guards who had silently materialised beside Hatshepsut, pointing his spear at her breast.

"Am I to be spoken to thus," Ast said haughtily, "the mother of the King?"

"Mother of the heir," Hatshepsut corrected her clearly and distinctly. "The son of Aa-kheper-en-Ra will rule at the side of my Majesty when he is a man."

Certain of Hatshepsut's advisors had counselled that it would be safer for her to have Men-kheper-Ra put to death. But she had refused.

Ast hesitated. She was alone. She could feel the whole mood of the crowd was for Hatshepsut, and everyone present in that hall that day had status and power. Hatshepsut had chosen the moment of her usurpation cunningly and well. She had already proved to be a popular and able regent, so now her claim for greater power could not easily be faulted – let alone the effect of the supernatural dramatics! But it was unnatural, against the laws of Maat, that a woman should become a man. Surely they must see that?

Ast looked around. The admiration and awe on every face was evident. She and her son seemed an absurd alternative to that magnificent golden being standing in the god's light.

9

Well, she and her son were alive. This was Hatshepsut's moment. Theirs would come.

She stepped back and muttered irritably to Men-kheper-Ra, as she passed him, that he should shut his mouth and straighten his shoulders.

The balance of power had suddenly and dramatically changed. From being a temporary regent for a young king, Hatshepsut had become a full ruling pharaoh with Men-kheper-Ra in the role of junior partner who might or might not become full pharaoh one day. Announcements to this effect were made throughout the Two Lands so that no one, however remote from Waset, could be unaware of it.

CHAPTER 2

When had it all started, this determination to be Pharaoh?

Hatshepsut remembered looking at her great-great-grandmother, the dowager Queen Aah-hetep, sitting in the shade of a sycamore tree. How could anyone be so old? Her eyes were as bright as beads, still taking everything in, her skin folded into a thousand wrinkles, papyrus thin over the stick-like body. She had buried her husband, Se-quenen-Ra, long, long ago. She had buried three pharaoh sons and her famous daughter, Aah-mes Nefertari, now worshipped as a goddess. She had buried her grandson, Tcheser-ka-Ra. Now she watched over the household of her great granddaughter, Aah-mes. There was no longer a tooth in her head, and her mouth was a thin, sunken line in the lower part of her face, but her tongue was still sharp enough to make everyone jump to do her bidding and cower when they drew her displeasure. Hatshepsut was at once frightened of her and fascinated by her. If the old creature was in a good mood she would sometimes reminisce aloud, whether anyone was there to listen or not. At five years old Hatshepsut was shrewd enough to sense that what her great-great-grandmother said was worth listening to. It was from her she got the taste for power and intrigue.

Aah-hetep had been more than her husband's queen. She had been a powerful and influential woman and her daughter, Aah-mes Nefertari, had been another. The child Hatshepsut got the impression the old lady didn't think much of her great-granddaughter, the present Queen, because she let her husband, Aa-kheper-ka-Ra – who wasn't even of the pure royal bloodline, but born of the King by the slave, Senseneb – do all the ruling. The beautiful, elegant Aah-mes seemed always to have some secret that kept her thoughts away from them all. She performed her duties admirably and no one could have faulted her, but she didn't seem really to care what happened outside the walls of her palace. Hatshepsut listened to many a grumble from the old lady that her father wasn't pure enough in blood to rule alone as Divine King, and, although the child loved him dearly, sometimes she felt ashamed of this fact about his birth and confused that it was he with whom she felt happiest.

Hatshepsut shivered, remembering how she had longed for her mother's love.

11

Once, she saw the Queen, "the God's Great Wife", "Lady of the Two Lands", "Beloved of Amun", Aah-mes, pacing the cool tiles of the courtyard slowly, evenly, her face composed, her gaze turned inward. And Hatshepsut wanted to call out to her, but she was afraid. Where had the soul of her mother gone? Her form was there – soft muslin flowing around thigh and breast, lifting and stirring in the breeze, the gold on her throat and ear and arm gleaming in the sun. But it was as though there was no one inside.

"Mother!" she felt like calling, but could not.

Hatshepsut was overwhelmed with loneliness.

"Mother!" Her whisper broke through at last and she ran, arms out, wanting her mother's warmth more than anything in the world.

Slowly the great lady's head turned. Stiffly she bent towards her daughter, her lips shaped to kiss. But the child could see that Aah-mes was not really aware of her, and that the kiss would not reach her lips. Indeed, would never reach her lips.

That day she wanted to die. It seemed to her that her mother had enough love only for her brothers and none for her.

She remembered how she then ran off and threw a ball into the air. She watched it soaring against the tremendous blue arch of the sky, amazed at the strength of her throw. It was as though, with it, she was trying to throw herself away.

"Amun, Unseen One, Rich in Names," she whispered as the ball of red and gold reached its zenith and apparently paused there as though held by an unseen hand. "Take me. Take me now. When Khnum fashioned me on his potter's wheel, why did he not fashion me a male body? Take me back into the Millions of Years. Let me sail with you in the solar barque among the Imperishable Stars!"

Her eyes were stinging and watering as she stared into the burning sky, but she refused to shut them. If anything was to happen she wanted to see it. No one was going to do anything to her without her knowing about it! Her chin was firm, her fists clenched. Was it an eternity she waited for the ball to fall – or less than a second?

It was falling and she was still as she was. Amun had done nothing in answer to her plea. She was running, a small wiry figure, her lips pressed together with anger. What was the point of having gods if they didn't answer one's prayers?

The ball was falling outside the part of the garden where she was allowed to play, but she did not hesitate to follow it. She left the smooth flagstones beside the pool and ran down the steps of the terrace beyond, past the carefully nurtured flowerbeds to the rough, wild area where the gardeners hadn't yet managed to tame the land. She forgot Amun in her attempt to find the ball. At last she saw it under a thorn bush and reached out for it. Horrified, she found herself staring into the cold, gold eyes of a cobra, her hand almost touching its mouth. She froze. Again time seemed to stand still. She couldn't move a muscle. She looked into the eyes of the cobra and knew that she was going to die. "No!" a voice seemed to scream in her heart. "No! No! No! I don't want to die. I don't want to die!" So Amun was up there, after all, smiling. He would give her what she had asked for, but she no longer wanted it. Nothing had changed. Her mother still didn't love her, her nurse was still mean to her, and she was still a skinny slip of a girl when she wanted to be powerful and masculine and great; but she didn't want to die. The dust of the earth smelled so good. It was familiar. Shameful tears filled her eyes. She felt bitter towards Amun now. She would not plead for her life as she had pleaded for her death. She had asked him for a favour and she would accept what came as a result of that request. Her hand was as still as stone. If only that voice in her heart would stop shouting "No!"

If only – if only death would be quick! She blinked her tears away, trying to get a clear view of her executioner. At last her vision cleared and she could see that the cobra was no longer there. She could see only the ball and the mark on the sand where the cobra had slithered away.

Her knees suddenly gave way under her and she collapsed on the ground, trembling. How much she wanted to live! Small and thin and female she might be, but she would show them! Ah – how she would show them!

A short while later when one brother died, and then the second, she wondered if it were her resentment that had something to do with their deaths. She wondered if Amun had understood her passionate desire to stand alone, triumphant, in the light of her mother's eyes.

And then her great-great-grandmother died – the apparently indestructible Aah-hetep finally ceased to breathe.

"Aah Aah Aah-hetep
"Aah Aah Aah-hetep
"Aah Aah Aah-hetep"

The word became meaningless as the priests intoned it. It no longer sounded like her great-great-grandmother's name. It no longer sounded like a name at all. Would the gods hear it? Would the gods take heed of it? Would they accept her great-great-grandmother? She had thought she would cheat them and live forever. Well, she had tarried so long on this earth perhaps the gods had forgotten her name.

The child Hatshepsut watched dispassionately as the procession wound into the great valley. No one would ever forget *her* name, she vowed. A solitary hawk circled unbelievably high above them. Horus. Waiting. Watching.

They were chanting her great-great-grandmother's titles now: "Divine Wife of Amun; Royal Mother; Great Royal Wife, joined to the Beautiful White Crown . . ." The list went on and on. She had lived a hundred years in that sturdy body, shrivelling at last to almost nothing. She had seen so much. Would she take the memory of it with her into the other world, the Duat?

Hatshepsut had seen the paintings and the carvings in her tomb, noted the powerful spells, the prayers, the invocations. If anyone could be protected against extinction, Queen Aah-hetep should be. "But do you *remember,*" she asked the High Priest, "when you go on that long journey, when you go through those great portals, when you cross the Fiery Lake, face the Forty-Two Assessors? When you do all those things, do you remember your life here on earth?"

He said "Yes, you do. How else would you answer faithfully and truly when you are called to account for it."

"And when you have passed through all that, and if your eternal spirit does not ride with the gods in their golden boat forever and your personal soul does not stay with you in the House of Awakening, but is sent out to be born again in another body, in another time and place, will you still remember what happened to you in this life?" she persisted anxiously.

"Nothing is forgotten. Nothing is lost. Nothing is wasted. But some things are hidden and need to be searched for. You will think that you have forgotten. But everything you will be given to do will have its roots in what you were. Your heart will remember, but you will have no words for it."

"And if they open your mouth with the stone that comes from the stars like they do to the statues in the temple and the bodies in the House of Awakening, will you then have the words to speak of it?"

"If someone is there to open your mouth – it may be so."

"And if no one is there to do it?"

"You ask too many questions, child. Go away and think about the ones I have already answered."

"When I am grown up I will train as a priest. I will learn the answers to all questions."

He laughed. The great solemn priest threw back his head and laughed! Hatshepsut flushed scarlet and bit her lip. When she grew up she would make it her business to know *everything!*

After the deaths of Aah-hetep and her sons, Aah-mes became even more remote, not only from her daughter but from most of the court. Hatshepsut turned her attention and affection more and more towards her father.

He at least seemed prepared to allow her to take the place of the sons he had lost.

When she was fourteen her father took her on a long journey throughout the Two Lands, a royal progress visiting every cult centre.

As they approached each quay, Hatshepsut stood silently beside her father at the prow of the royal boat, dressed like a boy in a white kilt, bare-torsoed, with gold on her arms and with a broad collar at her throat. Her head had been shaved and she wore the headdress of the royal heir. At fourteen her figure was slight and small beside that of her well-built father, but even so she drew the eyes of all the thousands gathered on the bank to greet them.

It was unusual for a pharaoh to bring his daughter to present to the god on such a progress through the country. Why was she dressed in male attire? Was the King trying to pass her off as his son? Was he planning to put *her* on the throne instead of one of his sons by a lesser wife? Surely the god would not allow that! There had been talk of Aa-kheper-en-Ra, son of the King by his favourite secondary wife, Mutnofre. All had assumed Hatshepsut would marry him and rule as queen.

But whatever their queries and their doubts, Pharaoh's visit was an occasion for a tremendous festival of rejoicing. Everyone who could walk had been at the riverside since before dawn, jostling for a view, and those who were infirm or ill or crippled had been carried and placed as near to the landing stage as possible. The Divine King would pass by. He would reach out his hands. Who knew what miracles would occur? Pharaoh was the channel through which the gods poured down their power on the earth. He was their instrument.

Whenever the boat was sighted the buzz of excitement rose to a crescendo, but as it came nearer the crowd fell silent and listened to the gradual swelling of the music that wafted to them over the water. Two rows of choristers, female and male, raised their voices high in praise of the great Pharaoh, while behind them the lutes wove a sweet melody, and the drum and sistrum marked the beat of oars and song.

It was all Hatshepsut could do to keep from singing herself. They visited cult centre after cult centre on their journey, but she never tired of the excitement of arrival, the feeling of being on the edge of a great adventure.

She knew her father had his reasons for introducing her to the priesthood of the various gods. He had plans for her that would need

15

their support, knowing that his son by Mutnofre would be an ineffectual and indecisive ruler. His health had never been good and his chances of a long life were small.

Hatshepsut had never been allowed into the Holy of Holies of the temples, but now she stood beside the Pharaoh, face to face with the divine beings. At first she was disappointed. When the veil was drawn back she was shocked to see that the god was no more than a statue. Then as she stood, in silence and contemplation, the significance of "the opening of the mouth" ceremony was revealed to her. The god was not the statue, and the statue was not the god! The god used the stone image of himself as he used the living image of himself as Pharaoh, so that the people might have something which they could understand. If the great spirit beings of other realms were to reveal themselves as they really were, the people would run and hide, would shut their ears and their hearts, would not understand what needed to be understood.

At Khemnu she encountered Djehuti, the god of knowledge, and his female counterpart, Seshat, she with the seven-pointed star shimmering above her head, and he with the head of the sacred ibis. As she stood in the shrine, only half listening to the words of her father and the priest, she looked at the hieroglyphs on the walls behind him. She felt she was not reading the mundane and familiar images carved by scribes and craftsmen, but was experiencing ancient and magical symbols that burned in the heart and revealed the secret thoughts of the gods. Djehuti had given language and writing to the world to increase wisdom and understanding. How sad it would be if the world misused it.

At Men-nefer, when her father momentarily drew the veil from the face of Ptah, creator-craftsman god, she thought she glimpsed a vision, a vista so magnificent that she fell on her face on the stone floor in awe and terror. She saw universes, even greater than the one she knew, being continually formed and reformed, a vast and complex pattern in continual change and motion.

The Anmutef priest in his panther skin stooped down and lifted her to her feet, but now, as she looked fearfully into the god's shrine, she saw nothing but the statue of a man grasping a sceptre of divinity firmly with both hands, gazing steadily out ahead to the horizon of the world and beyond it to whatever mysterious realms lay out of sight.

Still trembling, she forced herself to look into his eyes – and it seemed to her that he lowered his gaze for a moment and was looking deep into hers. He understood what she had experienced and was telling her not to forget it. "You cannot live with that vision," he was saying, "but you cannot live without it."

As though in a dream, she heard the words her father and the priest were intoning. Ptah was silent now. His gaze had gone back to the horizon.

"I promise," she whispered. "I'll never forget it." But already it was fading, and the sense she had had that her own life and the life of her whole land was infinitesimal compared to what lay beyond was almost gone. The sense of her father's importance and her own was reasserting itself. The god before her was no more than a being not unlike herself – perhaps a little more powerful – to be cajoled and bribed for favours.

Perhaps at Yunu, the centre of sun worship, she would experience the true nature of the god again. She both feared and desired it.

The great sun altar was open to the sky, not enclosed in the usual dark and airless sanctuary. The images of the mighty Ra in his three forms – Kheper at dawn, Ra in full power at noon, and Atum in the evening – were carved on the sides of the altar, but the god himself blazed down on their heads from above, so hot and bright that not even the First Prophet of his temple could lift his head and look at him. At the entrance to his court stood two obelisks, their tips blazing with gold.

Hatshepsut stood beside her father, feeling the heat of the paving stones burning through her sandals. Her eyes watered with the brilliance of the light reflecting off the dazzling white and gold – but she dared not move. The chief priest's invocation seemed interminable and the rows of junior priests bringing offerings and piling them up on the altar endless. She blinked away the water in her eyes and tried to ignore the sweat trickling down her body. On the stone before her she read:

I am the Eternal Spirit,
I am the sun that rose from the Primeval Waters.
My soul is god, I am the Creator of the Word . . .
I am the Creator of the Order wherein I live,
I am the Word, which will never be annihilated . . .

It was happening again! In spite of her discomfort she could feel herself leaving her body and reaching after something only her own eternal spirit could hope to understand.

Once again she had seen behind the mask of the god.

Once again the memory of it was slipping from her.

Her father touched her arm and pushed her gently forward. There were words she had to say, motions she had to make. How inadequate they seemed in the light of what she had just experienced. But it was the custom. It was what was expected. It was part of the order the god had created. She could feel the eyes of the priests upon her, watching her every move, judging whether she was worthy of the role she was destined to play. She spoke the words clearly. She made the ritual motions confidently.

"She is strong," the High Priest thought. "Her father was right about her. If she supports us, we will support her." And he accepted without hesitation the offering the King had made in her name.

In spite of Hatshepsut's expectations after the journey she had taken with her father, he declared his son by Mutnofre his heir. She was betrothed to the prince, and though the Great Royal Wife and Queen had great status and power, Hatshepsut was bitterly disappointed.

Her betrothed, Aa-kheper-en-Ra, found himself at a disadvantage in every respect in his relationship with her.

One day he stood beside her in the garden, looking down at her as she lay asleep under her favourite tree. The servants had brought out a light couch for her in the heat of the day and, after a long morning of hunting with her father in the desert, she had flung herself down to rest. He could see the air vibrating around her. She was the sort of person who walked into a room full of people and from that moment no one in the room was aware of anyone else. Beautiful women faded into the background. Men became shadows. It was not that she was so beautiful, but she gave the impression of beauty, the impression that beauty was actively being created before their eyes. Every movement of hers seemed to draw the world with it. He couldn't explain it. He had tried to resist staring at her, resenting her effect on him, but time and again he had found himself tongue-tied and awkward in her presence. He knew she half-despised him because his mind was not as quicksilver as hers, because words stuck like flies in honey to his tongue, and because no one noticed *him* the way they noticed her. He knew she had affection for him as her father's son, but never love, never respect, never admiration.

He pursed his lips. He tried to imagine taking that lion body to bed, touching that smooth feline form, feeling the powerful beat of her heart under his hand. She was lying now with only the finest film of fabric over the rise and fall of her breast, and her firm and slender thighs. With his eyes he removed the film and took a step nearer. He didn't touch her with his hands yet he could feel how it would be if he were stroking her skin, his hands following the curves of her body, his fingertips pausing on her nipples. His mouth dropped open and he could hardly breathe for the wave of desire that flooded through him. He wanted to take her now before her eyes opened. When she looked into his eyes, he knew, he would feel himself dissolving like one of those scent cones on a woman's wig. He would become nothing . . . nothing.

He took a step closer, sweat glistening on his body, his breath coming in short bursts. "One day she will lie in my bed like any other woman," he told himself. "But first, first I must conquer my fear of her. I must take her on my terms, not on hers."

The garden was deserted apart from the two of them. No breeze stirred. Flowers hung limp. The tree itself seemed to be holding its breath. With a hand that he had to force not to tremble he reached out. Even before it touched her flesh he could feel her energy almost like a physical thing, a vibrant cocoon that surrounded her. He hesitated. Would he be able to handle this woman? Would he be able to keep his own identity, his own power?

He dropped his hand and stepped back with a start. She had opened her eyes and was looking directly into his. She knew what he had been about to do, and he shrivelled under the blaze of her anger. She said nothing. She didn't move. Only her eyes saw him and everything about him.

He turned and walked away as fast as he could. The moment had gone and he was still afraid of her. "One day," he promised himself bitterly, "I will conquer her. I will reduce her! She will lie in my bed and I will be master! One day!"

He could not wait for the time he would be Pharaoh and she would have to walk behind him, head down, in humility. Sometimes he chuckled bitterly to think of it. She would never be humble – but she would have to give the appearance of humility, and that would really irk her proud spirit.

Hatshepsut propped herself up on her elbow and looked after him, amused. She tolerated his presence on formal occasions because she knew that in the eyes of the world she had to, but in private she treated him with impatience and ill-disguised contempt. Without her, he would be nothing. It was the purity of *her* royal blood from her mother, Aah-mes, that would give him the status of Pharaoh, son as he was of a non-royal mother. She found it unjust that this was the tradition, and argued against it at every opportunity until even her father, who adored her, snapped impatiently that that was the way it was and she would have to accept it. If Aa-kheper-en-Ra survived him, he would be King, and Hatshepsut would have to content herself with being the power behind the throne. If he did not survive, one of his other sons by one of his minor wives would be King, and again Hatshepsut would have to be content to be Queen. He knew the real power in the Two Lands would always be hers, and that is why he had made such a point of associating her so often with him on state occasions, but he had thought better of changing the time-honoured form of things for her. It would be too dangerous. The Two Lands were balanced precariously over the Void, and if this balance were not meticulously kept, who knew what disasters might befall.

The news of her father's death came to Hatshepsut when she was in the palace garden at Men-nefer. She had been pacing the shady paths beneath the huge sycamores since the dawn, having woken with a start from a dream of falling off a precipice, her heart pounding, knowing that something was terribly wrong. Gradually the racing of her pulse slowed down and she lay listening to the first sounds of the day, the comforting sounds of the birds that this morning brought no comfort, the distant call of the herd boys on their way to the grazing fields.

She slipped into a light robe and padded on bare feet out of the building into the garden, standing for a long time gazing at the lily buds about to open, before seeking out the avenue of sycamores.

What was wrong? She felt as though everything in the Two Lands was off balance, off course, as though it were a boat caught in a current about to be dragged down into the white water and harsh rocks of a cataract. And then she heard them, the wailing, her father's many wives raising their voices in the sound of mourning. Her father was dead.

She stood very still, and it was as though everything in existence stood still with her. It was very strange. In all the realms there was no movement. Pharaoh was dead. There was no Pharaoh to be the pivot for all the energies and forces of the many and varied realms. It was as though even the gods were dead.

Hatshepsut's skin prickled with a chill of alarm.

Could this be? Could time suddenly cease and everything be frozen in this way at the death of a Pharaoh? What an awesome responsibility!

She longed for movement, for flow and change, and life. She called out to the gods, but none came to her. And then she felt the presence of the Mysterious Unseen One, the one who for her always seemed to be more accessible than the others though, paradoxically, by his very nature should be less so. The one her people called Amun, yet for her was beyond all the naming of names.

She saw no stylised figure, no powerful and numinous being, but suddenly her fear was gone and she had a wonderful and overwhelming feeling that everything had meaning and purpose and was as it should be.

The birds were moving in the sky again, and a bee alighted on a flower. The women were still keening, but she felt detached from their sorrow. Pharaoh was dead – yet Pharaoh lived. She shivered. What now? Her father had trained her like a man for responsibility, and she knew it would be she who would wield the real power in the land, yet her role would be a subsidiary one as Great Royal Wife to the half-brother for whom she had no love and very little respect. Her father should not have died so soon – she was not ready. She was angry with him for leaving her.

Ineni, her father's favourite architect and friend, was approaching. She could see that his shoulders stooped more than usual, and his step was slow and heavy. She knew he was worrying about how he was going to tell her the news. Everyone was aware of the close relationship of father and daughter. Aa-kheper-ka-Ra had been ill more than once lately, but each bout of pain had passed, leaving him apparently as fit as he had ever been. He had left Men-nefer in good health the week before to visit the delta lands, and they had had no reports of illness.

The young girl, no longer a child, stood as still as a statue, watching the approaching figure. He reached her at last and stood looking into her eyes.

"You know?" he said.

"Yes," she replied.

He looked around, wondering who had reached her before he had.

"No one," she said quietly. "I just knew."

"You heard the women?"

"Before that."

He was not surprised. He had noticed on several occasions how her thoughts seemed to leap ahead, as though she had some private communication with the gods.

The funeral barge of Aa-kheper-ka-Ra approached the quay at Waset to the accompaniment of solemn drumming, the royal praise-singers in the prow carrying the swelling majestic hymn that was sung at the death of a pharaoh, the royal praise-singers on the land echoing the theme, chanting his names and accomplishments, preparing the gods to receive this great being into their midst. He had been embalmed at Men-nefer, his capital, but was being brought to the western mountains of Waset to be interred for eternity, the first king to choose the valley beneath the great pyramidal mountain of Meretseger for his secret resting place.

Hatshepsut stood dry-eyed and unmoving beside her half-brother, Aa-kheper-en-Ra, now King. Her mother had already passed out of this realm, but the dead king's secondary wives were making a great noise in the background. Hatshepsut bit her lip. She would have liked to sweep them all away, tossing them wailing into the desert to be swallowed up by the sand. How she hated their clinging, whining, hypocritical worship of him. He was *hers* – not theirs! How dared they pretend such grief when all they were concerned about was their status under the new regime.

Mutnofre stood a step or two behind her son – away from the other women. At least she had some dignity. Hatshepsut had always liked her more than the others. She had been her father's favourite after her own mother. Mutnofre had helped him through the loneliness after Aah-mes died and had been almost a mother to Hatshepsut – or at least as much of a mother as the independent and spiky little girl would allow. Mutnofre was on the whole uncultured, but beautiful and naturally kind. It was not she who pushed her son forward against the other claimants, but Aa-kheper-ka-Ra himself who chose him for his heir. "As long as he is married to Hatshepsut," he stipulated. "Hatshepsut must be at his side." It was possible Aa-kheper-ka-Ra chose Mutnofre's son for his very weakness, for with him Hatshepsut would be assured of a chance to use the skills he had taught her, whereas a stronger man might keep her in the background.

So here she was – at the side of Aa-kheper-en-Ra. One step behind him, in fact – and resenting it. Well, her great-great-grandmother, Aah-hetep, and her great-grandmother, Nefertari, had not been docile wives – and she would not be either.

She had not fully grasped her father's death yet. She had been so busy with matters of state and her own personal problems with her half-brother that she had hardly been alone. But now, for a moment, as the crowds and even the wailing women hushed, and the great barge slid silently into the quayside, she looked into the eyes of grief and saw her own reflection there.

That night she had a dream.

She was standing on the very lip of the cliff that overlooked the ancient temple of Mentu-hotep which nestled in against the mountainside at Serui. Far below her she could see the neat pattern of the almost ruined temple and beyond it the narrow desert plain

22

becoming suddenly and startlingly green in the irrigated fields bordering the river. Across the Nile she could see the faint outline of the great Temple of Amun at Ipet-Esut and the obelisks her father had raised. She felt that there was something she had to do. Something was expected of her. Something beyond duty.

She frowned, and forgetting where she was, took a step forward.

She began to fall. Now she was caught in the nightmare she had had the night her father died – she was falling off a precipice. And in her dream she had believed that if she reached the bottom she would not wake up. She would be dead.

"I want to live!" she cried. "Whatever I have to do —I'll do it! Just let me live!"

Suddenly she was caught in strong and powerful arms. She was safe . . . she was soaring . . . she was lifted up beyond the desert and the mountains, beyond the city with its flags fluttering above the entrance pylons of so many mighty temples.

"*You will live, my beloved,*" she heard a deep voice say, though she could not turn her head to see who spoke. "*You will live and build me a temple more beautiful than any in the world. In that temple there will be a threshold between the realms. Your step will be light, my daughter, my wife. Your step will cross that threshold with ease. You will know all there is to know in the two worlds, and you will do my work upon the earth. As a sign of your commitment to me and me alone—*"

"I'll sacrifice a hundred bulls," she interrupted, "gazelles, cranes, snow-white kids."

"*Not those, my child. Not those. That would be too easy. I ask more than that.*"

"What do you want?" she asked eagerly. "Tell me. I will sacrifice anything if I might freely cross the threshold between the realms and be with you, yet still be 'in the flesh'. I will be your right arm upon the earth! I will make you honoured above all other gods in the Two Lands!"

Although she still could not see his face, she felt that he smiled as a fond parent might smile at a favourite child.

"*Shut your eyes,*" he said quietly.

She felt that she was now standing on firm ground and that the arms of the Great Being were no longer around her.

Tentatively she opened her eyes a crack, then completely.

She was standing in a shrine dedicated to Amun, not yet built, as far as she knew. In front of her was an altar of gleaming white alabaster.

She knew that it was on this altar she must make her sacrifice.

But what? She had no priests with her, no animals to slaughter, no bowls or baskets of food. Nothing.

She was clad in a simple white sheath of linen, her feet bare, her hair unbound. On her arm she was wearing the bracelet her father had given her when she was a child as a secret pledge that she would one day rule the Two Lands. It was a fine piece of work – lapis lazuli, turquoise and carnelian set in silver, more precious than gold.

"Oh no!" she thought, as it dawned on her the mysterious god was demanding this of her. Why?

"He wants it because I don't want to give it," she thought. "He wants it because it is my promise of worldly power, my attachment to my ambition to rule the Two Lands. I have to choose between worldly power and true spiritual enlightenment."

She knew that in these crucial moments her whole life was in the balance.

"I'm not ready," she whispered. "I'm not ready."

She fingered the jewelled silver on her arm, turning it round and round. The bracelet seemed heavier than before. She turned to go, still clutching it. Then she turned back – and with a sudden impulsive gesture she tore it off her arm and laid it on the white stone altar. As she did so, a shaft of light came from above and illuminated it so vividly it seemed to dissolve . . .

Above her the winged shape of Nekhbet, the vulture, hovered, holding in her claws the circle of completion, the circle of infinity.

Hatshepsut did not look up, but turned and ran.

It seemed to her she ran down a thousand thousand white alabaster steps until . . . until . . .

She woke up, startled, in her own bed.

She knew this dream had not been like other dreams. She looked at her arm: the bracelet was not there. She leapt up and called her maids. Sleepily they came to her. They denied seeing the bracelet anywhere but on her arm. She shouted at them to search, and search they did.

"I must find it," she thought frantically. "If I don't, it means I am committed. I want more time to think. I'm not ready. Surely I've just mislaid it?"

All day the women searched, harried by an increasingly anxious and hysterical Queen.

That night it was found. One of her women who had not been at the palace that day had taken it to be repaired. The craftsman who brought it back to Hatshepsut was startled by her expression as she put it back on her arm. Was she not pleased with the workmanship?

Although she had been frightened and dismayed when she

believed she had committed herself to Amun, now that she was not committed, she was disappointed. Had the whole thing been no more than a dream, after all?

She determined then and there to build the temple Amun had asked her to build. The temple that would outshine all the temples in the Two Lands and carry her far beyond the dust and flies of this earth, beyond the Fiery Lake, beyond the Forty-Two Assessors, beyond the Seven Gates, beyond the Hall where her heart would be weighed against the feather of Maat before Osiris, beyond the stars in Ra's mystic boat.

She would record all her deeds in everlasting stone, checking and counting the processions of priests as they filled her storehouse for eternity with magical replicas of familiar things. She would carve images of her body and her soul upon the walls of his temple, so beautiful, so powerful, that, mirrored in eternity, she would live with him forever. She would write such things in stone that her name and the name of her god would never be forgotten by the thousands upon thousands of generations of people who lived after her.

Her temple would be celebrated by all who saw it.

Djeser Djeseru: Most splendid. The temple of Myriads of Years. It would be called the Great Seat of Amun, his horizon in the west. Its great door would be fashioned of black copper, inlaid with figures of electrum. All its doors would be real cedar, wrought with bronze. Its floor would be wrought with gold and silver, its beauty like the horizon of heaven. There would be a great shrine of ebony from Nubia, the stairs beneath it, high and wide, of pure alabaster from Hatnub. It would indeed be the palace of the god, his enduring horizon of eternity, wrought with gold and silver to illuminate the faces of all with its brightness.

And when this was done, Amun her Father would see that she had been faithful to him though she had also been faithful to her calling as worldly ruler of the Two Lands.

CHAPTER 3

When Hatshepsut's husband Aa-kheper-en-Ra, died after an undistinguished rule, she – sole living representative of the pure royal bloodline through Aah-mes, her mother – was made Regent for her husband's son by a lesser wife.

At first she had not disputed the role, though it irked her that she who had been behind almost every decision her husband had made, and was now openly making decisions for the Two Lands, should always stand behind the small and arrogant figure of her stepson-nephew, Men-kheper-Ra, and suffer the smirks of his mother, named Ast, most inappropriately, after the goddess Isis.

It was not long before certain shrewd and ambitious men, noting her impatience at the subordinate role she was forced to play and aware of the proud blood that flowed in her veins from the powerful princes who had seized Egypt back from the hated Hyksos after centuries of domination, began to gather at her side, waiting and watching for an opportunity of advancement.

Hapuseneb was one of these. He was Vizier of the South when she became Regent, a brilliant and reliable diplomat, an able administrator – but tired of his long sojourn in the provincial towns of uncivilised Nubia. Since her family had come to power, Waset had grown from a sleepy small town to a bustling city. Either here or Men-nefer would suit him well. But there were not many positions higher than the one he already had. He was not sure what he would ask for, or indeed that he would ask for anything at all. He knew only that with the instability caused by the death of Aa-kheper-en-Ra while his heir was still only an infant, it would be shrewd to be at the centre where decisions were being made. There would be changes – and he would be there when they happened, ready to take advantage.

A tall man with stern, aquiline features, he came upon her sitting by herself beside a lily pond in the gardens of the palace. She seemed very young and fragile as she sat on the alabaster pavement, her knees drawn up to her chin, staring thoughtfully into a blue water lily. What was she thinking? Was she afraid? She needed a strong man at her side at this time, he thought; but if she married again, all kinds of violent factions would leap into action. A woman by herself as Regent would not cause concern for the future, but with a husband who might be after ultimate power, Men-kheper-Ra and his supporters would be instantly alerted to danger and compelled to secure their claim any way they could. But would she be able to handle by herself the jockeying for power that was bound to go on after a pharaoh's death? Would she be able to see through the hypocrisy and intrigue?

"Your Majesty," he said quietly, his reflection appearing beside her own in the water. She did not turn her head but her eyes met his on the still surface.

Hapuseneb, she thought. She knew who he was, though she had never been alone with him before. She remembered thinking when he was appointed that he was a man better to have as an ally than an enemy. A strong, intelligent, ambitious man. Impressive to look at; a shrewd observer of events; decisive and quick-witted.

"If you would rather be alone . . .?" he said quietly, bowing, but she noted that in doing so he lost nothing of his own dignity.

She turned slowly and looked up at him. She could do with strong, loyal men around her now. She had grown up at her father's right hand and had seen the ruthlessness of those who struggled for power. But could she trust him? What did she know about him? She could have him investigated, of course, but such investigations never revealed what was in a man's heart.

When she stood up at full height she did not reach his shoulder, but what she lacked in height she more than compensated for in power of personality. She gazed so searchingly into his eyes, he knew he had been wrong to assume she would not be able to judge those around her shrewdly and wisely. He was surprised suddenly to feel at a disadvantage, but he did not lower his eyes. There were some things in his past he would rather keep hidden, and for a moment he wondered if she indeed had the royal cobra vision and could see into his soul. Momentarily he felt uneasy – but his long training in not showing his feelings in public served him well. He stared back into her eyes steadily with just the right degree of respect.

"I am alone, Hapuseneb," she said. "No one shares the burden of Pharaoh." He noticed she used the word for king and not for regent, and wondered if it was deliberate.

"Indeed, Majesty," he replied carefully, "but others can ease the weight of the burden."

"Could you do that, Hapuseneb?"

"Ay, your Majesty. If your Majesty would allow me."

His humility was not overdone, and yet in a lesser man it would have been.

She smiled and relaxed her scrutiny.

27

"Come," she said, "let us walk in the shade a while. Tell me about your life in the southern provinces. I don't want an official report – I have enough of those. Tell me about your thoughts and feelings and how your days pass."

There was something almost childish in the questions that followed, but he did not underestimate her. He knew his future depended on how he answered her, and suddenly he wanted very much to win her confidence.

She listened quietly, intently, to everything he said. There was not a word she did not hear and mark, yet her mind was busy with other thoughts. She had walked and talked with the Mysterious One, the Hidden and Magnificent One, Amun-Ra. He had come to her in the night. He had come to her in the day. She was his Chosen One; she felt it, she knew it. He had told her to stress the name "Amun-Ra": Amun united with Ra in his role of universal and eternal sun, source of light and life; and Ra united with Amun in his role of unseen mystery, of unanswerable question. She would build a temple in the world. It would be Djeser Djeseru – the beautiful home of the beautiful but unseen God – and it would rise from the great golden cliffs of the west; and from it she would gaze out across the desert and the green lands to the golden points of the obelisks she would erect in his honour in his temple over the river.

But this temple was not all she meant to do for him. He would be honoured above all gods by the people in every city in the Two Lands, in every village, in every outlying settlement. From the distant mountains of Nubia to the flat, rich lands of the delta, his name would be above all names.

In the old days the god Amun had been one among many, and the priests who served him no more important than those who served the other gods. But Hatshepsut Khenemet-Amun (Hatshepsut "united with Amun") had a love for him that she did not have for the other gods and a love for Waset that she did not have for other places. Her father had established his capital at Men-nefer, that great and sprawling metropolis in the north, but Hatshepsut spent as little time there as possible. Waset, the cult centre of her favourite god Amun – "the Hidden One", "he who abides in all things" – was the place she most enjoyed, and it was here she spent a great deal of her time.

During the bad old days of the Hyksos rule many temples had fallen into disrepair and ruin. Her father and grandfather had been too busy winning back Egypt for the Egyptians to spend much time on restoration. But this was one of the vows she made to Amun very early in her life. She would restore the temples throughout the land and build new ones, not only for Amun-Ra himself, but for those other great beings who hovered over the world keeping the primeval Chaos at bay.

But to do this she needed strong and trustworthy priests and administrators – men who could plan and organise and make people obey them; men who would be loyal to her and to Amun-Ra and to no one else. Priests she had. Administrators she had. But one man who could combine the qualities needed for both was not so easy to find. She wanted someone who could handle the power she would give him and yet would never turn against her. She wanted him to fear Amun-Ra. She remembered how one of the men who had been carrying her chair that morning had stumbled and the chair had tipped dangerously to one side. She had caught the look of terror in the clumsy man's eyes as she looked at him. That was fear! But it was not the kind she wanted.

Had her god sent her this man, Hapuseneb?

Gravely she studied his features – studied the way he moved his hands, his shoulders, his eyes. Everything about him was strong and sure. He respected her as woman and as a great power in the land – but he did not cringe before her.

"Ah, Holy One," she whispered, though her lips did not move. "Give me a sign if this man would be pleasing to you."

Hapuseneb stopped talking. He began to feel strange – as though everything around him was suddenly distant, as though every sound and movement in the world had stopped. He looked into her eyes and knew she felt it too.

As far as she was concerned, Amun-Ra had spoken. The sun's rays were coming from directly behind him, illuminating his head.

"Hapuseneb," she said confidently. "I have a task for you."

She told him about her vision, and he listened as quietly as she had listened to him. When he was a young lad he had spent time in the temple. His father had intended that he should train for the priesthood, seeing that he did not enjoy farming. For several years he had served alternately three months behind the great mud-brick walls of the temple, and three months out in the fields. It was in the temple he had shown his aptitude for writing and for numbers, for organising, and for planning. But he had found the atmosphere claustrophobic, the daily routine boring. He had been glad to get out. Could he face it again? Could he sit poring over scripts in the Per Ankh, the House of Life? Could he face those hard-eyed examiners yet again? Did she know about that hot still day when he sat cross-legged before the three chief prophets and was questioned from the time the sun came up until the sun went down, answering every one of their questions so well that at the end it had seemed a foregone conclusion that he would stay with the priesthood forever. And yet the thought had filled him with dismay and revulsion. Why had he studied so hard? Why had he answered so brilliantly? Because he wanted to succeed. Because, at whatever he did, he wanted to excel.

He sighed. He had known even then, when he was arguing with his father all those years ago, that the Temple would get him in the end!

But her vision of what he would do as First Prophet of Amun-Ra was very different from what he remembered of the daily routine as a boy apprentice. His would not be the duty to sweep the floor and spread fresh rushes, to chant the holy words from dawn to dusk, from dusk to dawn. Other men would be trusted with the routine purification rites, the supplications, the tedious ceremonies. The Temple priesthood acted as surrogates for the whole population. They held the dialogue with the god on behalf of the people. They alone interpreted the god's words to the people – even to the Pharaoh.

Hapuseneb's eyes narrowed as he thought what it would mean to be in a position to interpret the god's words to the Pharaoh.

Hatshepsut smiled, and he suddenly became aware of her eyes looking into his heart. She knew him. She knew what he was thinking. She would never be easily deceived. Nor, he thought, would he want to deceive her. If he became what she wanted him to be, he would surely have a status in the land that would satisfy even his ambitious nature.

He bowed his head slightly – but not too much.

She hesitated.

She had him – but was he what she wanted? She could sense that he was not as spiritual as she had hoped. Userhet was more spiritual – but he was getting old and had never had a stomach for administration. Under him the temples of Amun-Ra would quietly go about their business as they had under Aa-kheper-ka-Ra, her father. She wanted something more for her favourite god.

Amun-Ra had given her a sign. The Mysterious One no doubt knew things about Hapuseneb that she did not know. She appointed him High Priest, First Prophet of Amun-Ra, without further investigation.

CHAPTER 4

Senmut and his brother Senmen had been introduced into the royal household by their uncle, one of the old Pharaoh's scribes, who had stayed on after his death to serve his successor, Aa-kheper-en-Ra.

Senmut's first professional appointment was as confidential scribe to the young King. He was young also and eager to advance. He worked long hours to please his master and he soon noticed the contempt Hatshepsut, the Queen, had for her husband, and the frustration the Pharaoh suffered in consequence of this. He was turning more and more to minor wives, and to Ast in particular, and the children born to them were soon occupying the royal nursery. Hatshepsut herself became pregnant, though Senmut wondered how the coupling had taken place with so much antipathy between them.

At first the Queen did not take any particular notice of the young scribe, associating him with her husband's entourage – but he, from the start, was aware of her provocative sexuality and was fascinated by her. Intelligent and fast-thinking himself, he recognised the same qualities in her, and admired them.

It was at Ipet-Esut that their eyes first met. The King was with Ineni, his father's faithful architect, planning an extension to Per-Amun, the Temple of Amun. Senmut was present to record the decisions that were made, and the Queen wandered by almost casually on her way to consult the High Priest about the arrangements for the Opet festival. Their eyes met, and she was shocked. The dark intensity of his gaze, the admiration, the desire were unmistakable. She was used to admiration – and indeed expected it – but she was not used to such boldness. She continued on her way, annoyed.

But she could not forget him, and after this she noticed him often.

Hatshepsut had been inconsolable when her father died, and she mourned a long time, while her brother-husband gave her no support. He had always resented that she had so obviously been their father's favourite and that she had been taken on the royal progress through the Two Lands to be introduced to the priesthood, and not himself. Father and daughter had always been close, sharing jokes, enjoying time together, while he and the other children of the royal household were kept with their mothers, their nurses and their tutors, hardly seeing the royal visage from one month's end to another.

The day she met Senmut was perhaps the first day Hatshepsut's sorrow and loss of her father began to ease. Their paths crossed frequently and her haughty disdain for his obvious attraction to her gave way to tolerance and eventually, because she was lonely and she noticed that his mind was one of the few at court that could match hers, to friendship. It was this friendship that perhaps more than anything else gave her back her zest for life.

At this time Senmut had several good friends, young men like himself with intelligence and ambition. They saw in Hatshepsut a stronger prospect for advancement than in the petulant and ailing King. She became the centre of a group of admiring— but not sycophantic – companions. They talked freely to her and she talked freely to them. Those were good times when everything seemed possible.

Later, when Aa-kheper-en-Ra died and Hatshepsut became Regent for her infant stepson-nephew, Men-kheper-Ra, nearly all of the old companions were given positions of privilege and power. Senmut was made the tutor and guardian of her daughter Neferure, and Chief Steward of the royal household, in charge of all the formal occasions. Nehsi, with Nubian connections but educated at the Egyptian court, was put in charge of the household accounts. Thutiy became Chief Confidential Scribe.

When Senmut was a young man, before he came to the court, he had spent some years in the North in the House of Life at Men-nefer, the great building attached to the Temple of Ptah that housed the archives of ancient texts, where scholars and scribes studied, copied and memorised. Near the city of White Walls was the great funerary complex of King Djoser, one of the ancient kings who had ruled more than a thousand years before. It stood in the desert, and only priests were authorised to walk its silent corridors and gaze upon the great stepped pyramid that Imhotep had designed, the prototype for all the pyramids of the Two Lands. Hooded cobras, immortal in stone, guarded its sacred precincts.

For more than a thousand years the mortuary priests had chanted their prayers and spells for the dead king, and the place held his presence still. Deep underground in corridors tiled in turquoise, the king eternally paced out the boundaries of his kingdom as he had done at his jubilee. Through a spyhole in a small chamber attached to the side of the pyramid at ground level, a statue of the king enthroned gazed out impassively, watching the world go by, century after century, accepting the offerings of men born generations after he had first ruled the Two Lands.

Outside the high walls of the Djoser funerary monuments, other burials had taken place – later than his, but still ancient to Senmut and his contemporaries. This place more than any other in the Two Lands fascinated Senmut.

Senmut, when he arrived at the archives of the Temple of Ptah, was the youngest of the scribe apprentices. He had a mind infinitely curious, always exploring new possibilities but never neglecting what he called the durable thread that held all things together.

He approached his studies with such fervour and understood the most obscure references so quickly that his mentors soon stood back and let him have his head. There were some texts that had so baffled generations of scribe masters that they no longer expected them to be deciphered. Senmut teased at them in his sleeping cell at night by the light of a small flickering bowl lamp. When the oil gave out he would lie awake in the dark, seeing the figures of the text still dancing before his eyes. Sometimes he woke with a feeling of euphoria; something had suddenly made sense. But more often than not he woke as frustrated as he had been the night before – the secret the ciphers held still tightly locked away.

It was here, in these great libraries of texts, that Senmut first began to admire Imhotep – architect, vizier, treasurer, seal-bearer to the great King Djoser. Later this admiration became almost an obsession. The wisdom book associated with him had been copied many times since Imhotep's day, and everyone knew that errors must inevitably have occurred. No one alive had ever seen the original and no one knew even whether it still existed. As long as anyone could remember, the House of Life had only had the copies, some of them from a time that must have been very close to Imhotep's own lifetime, but none in the great man's own hand. Senmut wanted more than anything in the world to find this original text. He believed Imhotep had been buried near his pharaoh and friend, King Djoser – and that if he found the tomb he would find the original book of Imhotep buried with him.

One night, after a particularly frustrating time trying to unravel the scribal errors in the great man's text, Senmut went for a long walk in the desert. A full moon silvered the tops of the dunes and illumined the imposing and magnificent stone pyramid that reached in gigantic steps to the sky, echoing the first mound of earth that rose from the waters of Chaos. He looked back from the summit of a small hill at the orderly complex of stone buildings – the high and gleaming boundary walls and the cluster of smaller and later pyramids, of chapels and processional ways, that huddled as close as they could get to this extraordinary and sacred place. Ceaselessly the desert tried to bury the man-made structures in sand; ceaselessly man dug and pushed and swept the sand away.

"I will find your book, my Lord Imhotep," he vowed. "And we will no longer be satisfied with half forgotten truths – but have your own words clear and unequivocal."

CHAPTER 5

One of the first things Hatshepsut did when she became Pharaoh was to plan two obelisks to the sun at the Temple of Amun at Ipet-Esut. She wanted to reinforce the vow she had made to Amun that he would be glorified more than ever in his dual image of Amun-Ra. Later, much later, she was to erect two more obelisks in this temple, but the first two, slightly less tall and impressive than the later pair, were always closer to her heart because of the circumstances that surrounded their erection.

She decided to go herself to the great granite quarries of the South at Suan to choose the stone for them. The journey would serve to remind the southern towns of her position as Pharaoh. Northwards from Waset she was a more familiar figure, her journeys to Mennefer and the delta being more frequent.

She chose to take Senmut with her, and it was during this time that their relationship was at its most beautiful and tranquil. There were periods as the royal barge sailed slowly and majestically south that they felt that somehow they had slipped the tether of time and were free to run wild in an idyllic country, invisible to everyone else. Discretely the servants and the crew went about their business, and if they ever noticed or gossiped about what they saw and heard, they were careful that no hint of it would reach the lovers or the outside world.

The first important stop was at Iuny on the west bank. Hatshepsut would rather not have visited the cult centre of Montu, a war god, but she was too new in her role as Pharaoh to dare to antagonise any important faction in the land. The priests, bowing low, requested the bounty of the Pharaoh for the restoration and extension of their temple. She did not refuse, but her gifts were not generous, and it was not until the reign of the next Pharaoh that the temple was to be properly extended and restored.

From Iuny they crossed the river to Djerty, still under the hawk eye of Montu. Here Hatshepsut was prepared to spend a little more time and ingratiate herself with the priests of Montu's temple in order to get a glimpse of the famous treasure given to the god by Pharaoh Amenemhet the Second about four centuries earlier. She had always been particularly interested in this king, for it was said he had mounted an expedition to Punt, a fabled distant land beyond Nubia that she herself had yearned to visit.

The sanctuary of Montu had received two chests of priceless silver treasure. Though gold was plentiful from Nubia, silver was not readily available in Egypt, and had to be imported from distant lands, from the Keftiu on the Island of the Bulls in the Great Green Ocean, and from the North and East through the traders at Kepel and the lands conquered by her father. Lapis lazuli was also very difficult to obtain and came from the wild mountain regions far to the east. These chests contained ingots and chains, necklaces and bowls of silver, and lapis lazuli in quantities she had never dreamed of.

The priests were obviously uneasy at unsealing the storeroom beneath the altar, but Pharaoh's command could not be disobeyed. Only after many wearisome rituals, during which Senmut wondered if their access to the treasure would be denied, did the High Priest finally start to break seal after seal and reveal the chests. When they were opened, Hatshepsut and Senmut gasped at the beauty and the variety of the objects inside, some inherited by the King from ancient times, some brought from countries almost inaccessible and almost unknown.

Hatshepsut reached out her hand to lift a necklace, tempted to try it on. The High Priest stepped forward at once and stretched out a warning hand.

"Your Majesty," he whispered urgently. "Do not touch. The treasure is guarded by a most fearsome spell."

Hatshepsut hesitated. It was so beautiful. More beautiful than anything she had ever seen. She looked up at the statue of the god standing guard over it. He was hawk-headed like Horus, but so very different in mien. She could feel his eyes on her – wary, cold, malevolent. In her plan for the Two Lands under her rule there was very little thought given to war and conquest. She wanted to stabilise the country within its borders and leave the outside world alone as much as she could. If she antagonised Montu now, would she be attacked, her country invaded and devastated as it had been by the hated Hyksos? Amun had helped her father and grandfather in their wars, but she never thought of him as a war god. All he was doing was helping to restore order and peace to the Two Lands by driving the barbarians out. Montu delighted in war for its own sake.

She withdrew her hand.

The priest, who had held his breath while she had her hand outstretched, gave an almost imperceptible sigh of relief.

She had brought a silver rhyton with fluted sides from the Island of the Bulls, and she handed it to the priest so that he could place it among the other objects. "Perhaps," she thought, "a gift from a peaceful pharaoh, crafted by a peaceful people, will help to temper the blood lust of this god." She made a silent prayer for peace in her time.

She stepped back and turned to go, Senmut close behind her. She was glad to get back onto the royal barge and sip cool wine behind the curtains of her cabin, soon leaving the noisy crowds and the malevolent eyes of the war god well behind.

Their next stop was much more to her taste. Their pace was leisurely, but eventually they arrived at the Place of the Two Hills, a small, pleasant town on the west bank, known chiefly for the Per-Hathor, or House of Hathor, that had been there since very ancient times. There were temples to Hathor – the great mother goddess of love and fertility – throughout Khemet, but this one became Hatshepsut's favourite. It was built on top of the eastern hill, with the little town nestling at its foot. The rocky west hill was honeycombed with tombs from the very early dynasties. "The two hills," Hatshepsut thought, "life and death."

They chose to visit the temple in the cool of the early morning. Hatshepsut refused her golden carrying chair and the company of her attendants, to walk alone with Senmut up the winding path. The garden that had been planted around the Per-Hathor seemed neglected, and the first thing Hatshepsut did was to order that it should be restored and extended.

"Make a bower for her," she said. "She should be surrounded by lush green and colourful flowers." She was pleased to see that the tamarisk and sycamore trees that clustered close around the outer walls looked healthy enough.

The view from the doorway was breathtaking – the little town, the green flood plain, the river, silver-blue, with an island like an emerald. Beyond that, as always in Khemet, was the tawny red desert.

In the first court there was a lily pond with lotus in bloom. Hatshepsut smiled and stooped down to trail her fingers in the cool water.

It was a little temple with only a few priestesses, each giving the impression of being there for love instead of for professional reasons. A very old woman who had been the High Priestess since her youth, her face a map of smiling wrinkles, took delight in performing the dawn ceremonies for the Pharaoh. Hatshepsut herself lifted the incense to the nose of the lovely goddess and said a fervent prayer or two. Senmut watched her, standing well back, his presence only tolerated because Pharaoh had requested it. She was so beautiful – as beautiful as the goddess herself – lifting her arms and her eyes to the serene and gentle face of the divine Lady. From Hathor's womb had come the teeming millions of the earth. At her breasts kings had sucked. Her temple was full of music and light. Hatshepsut lifted a golden sistrum and shook it. The young priestesses gathered behind her shook theirs too, and a slow and graceful dance followed to the soft sound of the sistrum, the sound that this day more than any other reminded him of seeds rattling in a seed pod.

He wished he could take Hatshepsut in his arms at this very moment and make love to her before the altar of Hathor. It would not seem a sacrilege, but a dedication. But her face was so rapt, so intensely concentrating on the words of the hymns she was now chanting, he did not dare.

Later, when the sun was high and hot and they were back on the boat, their lovemaking was more passionate than it had ever been before, as though Hathor had given them her blessing, and any reservation they might have had about the propriety of their relationship was gone. It seemed to him, as they lay quietly afterwards, Hatshepsut's face had the same rapt expression it had had at the height of the ceremony in the temple. He did not speak about it, but he was sure she had felt then the same desire as he had, and their lovemaking now was a kind of sacrament, binding them together forever, performed for Hathor.

Softly he touched her body outside and in with his fingers and his mouth. They had not parted after the first lovemaking, and the second flowed out of the first, like nectar out of a flower. The third and the fourth followed as naturally. Never had either felt such pleasure so deeply and so easily.

When sleep came it seemed that even then there was no parting, but dreams that continued their union.

The next part of the journey passed without their noticing. The green plains of the west bank and the desert on the east slid by. Sometimes they emerged from their cabin and stared up at the great dome of the sky ablaze with stars. Sometimes they listened to the singing from the banks as they passed small villages without stopping. Sometimes they heard and saw nothing but each other.

At Iunyt they had to stop. It was a big cult centre for Khnum, the god who was believed to fashion the bodies and the personal souls of the kings on his potter's wheel, and then breathe the life force into their nostrils. Here Khnum shared a temple with the goddess Neith of the shield and the crossed arrows, and Heka, the goddess of magical power. Hatshepsut was already beginning to plan the reliefs for her great temple at Serui and intended to include a sequence in which her divine birth would be depicted. Senmut spent time sketching some of the scenes from the temple of Khnum to use in his design, while she performed the rituals expected of Pharaoh. This place was not as magical for them as Per-Hathor had been, and the visit was short.

They had quite a long break from the river at the twin towns of Nekheb and Nekhen, the first on the east bank and the second on the west. "The Red Mound" as it was known, was a very important cult centre, the home of Nekhbet, "the White One of Nekhen", the vulture goddess, who had come to be the symbol for Upper Egypt. Wadjet, the cobra goddess, was the symbol for Lower Egypt. These two goddesses were known as "the Two Ladies" and every pharaoh had to have one of his five major titles connected with them. Nekhbet assisted at all the royal births and was carved in relief, holding the circle of eternity, her wings spread out in protection over nearly every temple.

The town was surrounded by sagging mud-brick walls and the temple itself was in very bad repair. While she was there Hatshepsut arranged for its proper restoration, and Senmut drew up the plans and promised to return to supervise the more complicated parts of its construction.

They were told of a small ruined temple to Hathor and Nekhbet in the desert mountains to the east, and took a day's ride on mules to visit it. They passed through silent valleys where the blank eyes of rock-cut tombs from the early dynasties stared down at them, and occasional shrines to Horus crumbled on high pinnacles of rock. Above them in the royal-blue sky, the god himself circled ceaselessly on golden wings.

The temple they sought was no more than a ruined chapel; most of the Hathor columns with the goddess's woman face and soft cow ears were fallen, the combined shrine of Nekhbet and Hathor open to the sky, the ceiling slabs long since fallen and lying on the ground smashed to pieces and half-covered with sand.

Hatshepsut and Senmut sat close together on the warm stone of a fallen column and stared silently at the ruined reliefs, the magic symbols no longer magic, the holy place no longer holy. Then Senmut drew in the sand how he would rebuild it, and Hatshepsut picked some dried grasses that had managed to take root in this rocky wilderness, and placed them on the cracked altar.

A shadow passed over them, and they both looked up. A vulture had come to rest on one of the rocky outcrops and was watching them. Hatshepsut gave a little shiver and took Senmut's hand.

"They're never far away, the gods," she whispered.

He kissed her forehead, but this time chastely. This was Hathor's place as well as Nekhbet's, but somehow the vulture's presence was stern and forbidding. Although they were alone here, unlike at the Per-Hathor, he did not feel like making love under her gaze.

At Djeba Mesen, Hathor's great love, Horus, was worshipped in a temple raised above the flood plain. Here again restoration work was planned. The temple was small, but it had two statues of Horus of smooth grey granite simply and exquisitely carved, crowned with the double crown of Khemet. Around the walls were reliefs depicting Horus sacrificing his eyes to save Osiris from the evil rages of Set. The Horus eyes, sun and moon, had become symbols of awareness in the deepest and most sacred sense, and his sacrifice had shown that evil can and will be defeated. The resurrection of Osiris – like the green shoot growing from the buried grain – gave hope of regeneration and eternal life.

Not long after Mesen the river narrowed alarmingly and the desert marched beside it, often in the shape of huge and towering sandstone cliffs. The place was known as the Place of Rowing, and the crew had to work hard to get the boat through. The rock faces on both sides of the river were covered with prayers, commemorative pieces and names. It was a wonder that anyone could have reached those inaccessible places to make any kind of mark.

While they were in this area the royal party visited the sandstone quarries from which most of the stone for the temples of Khemet had been taken. They spent some days with the quarry master, while Senmut chose the stone he needed for the work Hatshepsut had set him, and she gave her approval. She did not know as much about stone as he, but there was an occasional piece she spotted that she particularly wanted for its colour and its striations. He explained to her that sandstone had to be laid down in a building in conformity with the bedding plane of the rock as it lay in the natural state, or it would weather badly. She was interested in everything, and sprang from rock to rock, enjoying every moment of it.

At last it was time to leave, and there was one more major centre to visit before they approached their destination.

Nubt, on a promontory at a bend in the river, overlooked wide green plains and the curving silver waters of the Nile. Khnum had another temple here, shared this time with Sobek, the crocodile god, and Horus. The feature that interested Senmut most was an extraordinarily deep well, shown to him by a priest who claimed that what could be seen at the bottom of it was no ordinary water, but the original primeval liquid from which all life had sprung, pure as it was at the Beginning.

Hatshepsut performed her duties as usual, but seemed in a hurry to leave. She made the boatman pull in to the bank upstream from the town and the temple. There she and Senmut walked through fields of barley and lay beneath blossoming fruit trees to make love like two young peasants.

"How I wish this journey would never end," she sighed. It was as though, having fretted all her life for power and pomp and ceremony, she was already tired of it and yearning for a simpler life away from the court and all her responsibilities. Senmut held her when she wanted to be held and let her go when she wanted to be let go. They were deeply in harmony with each other and with the rhythm of the ageless river and the land that cupped it between its two hands.

Suan was a garrison and trade town, taking up most of the southern part of a large island in the Nile. Huge grey rocks looking remarkably like elephants stood around in the water, marked with the flood lines of the river. The red granite that was so sought after by all the pharaohs for their pyramids and temples and statues created a great hard ridge between Nubia and Khemet. The waters of the river foamed up to a frenzy over the rocky and uneven bed it created, giving the impression that the Nile itself was bubbling up from the underworld.

Khnum was the god in charge, this time accompanied by the goddesses Satet and Anuket. There were marked steps to measure the water level, dedicated to Hapi, the androgynous Nile god, which gave information of vital importance to the whole country. The height of the waters here could mean plenty or famine the whole length of the land.

The town itself was full of soldiers to guard the frontier between Nubia and Khemet, and others who came in with the columns of pack animals and traders from all over the region. The desert behind the granite quarries was rich in minerals – amethyst for jewellery, copper-malachite and lead-galena for eye cosmetic, granite, quartzite, diorite, steatite for statues and monuments, copper and tin for bronze. South of the town in the great mountainous regions of Nubia there was more gold than anyone could measure. Many languages were spoken, and even those known to Senmut and Hatshepsut they found difficult to understand when spoken by the locals. This was rough country, and the isolated communities had developed some strange dialects.

Senmut went by himself to the quarries. He was well known there and was soon drinking beer with the quarrymen. It felt strange to be far away from Hatshepsut's side with a group of working men again. The journey began to feel like a beautiful dream, insubstantial and easily dismissed as unreal. Everywhere he heard the hard ring of chisel on stone, the cracking roar as big chunks were levered off, and the shouts and whistles of the men.

He enjoyed his work, but he was glad to get back to the island town, wash the quarry dust off his skin and climb into bed with his lover.

When Hatshepsut had attended to all the necessary civil and religious matters, and had chosen the ivory and gold and lion skins she wanted to take back with her, she went with him to the quarry.

Work was stopped at once so that there would be no stone dust to choke her or flying chippings to endanger her eyes. He took her to the area where the best granite was found and suggested which parts would yield suitable pieces for the obelisks. She walked among the giant blocks of stone silently, indicating that she wanted to be alone. She laid her hands on the cliff and meditated. These obelisks must be perfect. They must come virginal from the mountain, flawless, intact. They would be her statement to her god. They would be the outward form of her vow.

She chose the exact pieces she wanted, and at sunset they returned to the river, in time to see the waters blood-red as Atum sank beneath the rim of the western desert. It was nightfall and the jackals were howling before they stepped once more onto the boat that was to ferry them across the river.

Those early years were very good for both Hatshepsut and Senmut. Stimulating discussion of ideas, plans for new building, lovemaking – all seemed perfect. Men-kheper-Ra was no threat, and the Two Lands were totally behind her. When she sat in the great hall, she sat alone and gave judgements and listened to petitions. She was wise and sensible, and earned everyone's respect.

But as Men-kheper-Ra grew older, some said she would have difficulty in keeping the double crown to herself. Some began to think their fortunes would rise higher if they supported the young prince.

Ast bided her time.

CHAPTER 6

The wind tugged at the heavy ropes and the huge pegs that held them to the ground. The tent had been pitched against a rocky cliff as soon as the approach of the storm was called by the outrider. Boulders had been rolled over the edges of the outer covering of tar-soaked skins, but still the wind, blasting at the fabric, fought to rip it up, working at the smallest weaknesses, striving to reach the frail and frightened humans sheltering within.

Inside the royal tent only one showed no sign of fear. Angrily, impatiently, Hatshepsut strode to and fro, to and fro. Her entourage, cowering together, watched her as, head up and shoulders squared, eyes sparkling dangerously, she dared the fearsome storm god, Set, marauder and dweller in the desert, to invade her territory. She believed that somewhere beyond the darkness of the swirling sand the eyes of Amun-Ra could see what was happening to his daughter, and he would not let her die. Not here, not now. Had he not lifted her up so that she was Pharaoh of this mighty land? Had he not asked things of her that as yet she had not had time to bring about?

Her adolescent daughter, Neferure, was afraid. Hatshepsut could feel it, but the girl knew how to conduct herself as the heir to the throne should, and pretended a calm she did not feel. She sat upright on her ebony chair, with her hands folded neatly in her lap and her lids lowered so that no one could read if there was fear in her eyes or not. Hatshepsut, looking at her, remembered that it was always difficult to tell what Neferure was thinking. Sometimes she was glad of this, sometimes she regretted it.

Hatshepsut wished that Senmut were with them. There had been unavoidable delays in starting, and he had gone on ahead. They were to meet where the east-west desert route crossed the north-south one. But this was still many hours ahead, and meanwhile the storm might have struck him before it reached her. The tents he was using were not as heavy and durable as hers and would be more vulnerable.

She could see the lips of her companions moving with their prayers, but she could not hear their voices against the shrieking and wailing of the wind. She could see their hands clutching amulets, fear almost a palpable presence among them.

She suddenly rounded on them.

"Stand up!" she shouted. "Face him out. There's nothing he wants more than to see you crawl and cower. Am I not Pharaoh? Am I not the female Horus of pure gold, the daughter of Amun-Ra?" She raised her fist and shook it at the side of the tent that was bulging inwards from the force of the wind. "His wrath is nothing to my wrath! His power is nothing to my power!"

For a moment her people thought she was going to open the tent flap and challenge him eye to eye, and they trembled – though now they stood and ceased their whining and their gibbering. Many wondered if she could indeed quell the storm with the sheer power of her will. All knew that the small, slender body housed a mighty spirit. They began to be less afraid. Was the roaring of the wind and the rasping of the sand against the skins of the outer walls lessening? Had the lamp flame stopped guttering and spluttering? Even the murk of fine sand that had managed somehow to penetrate the air inside the royal tent seemed to have begun to settle.

Fiercely Hatshepsut held her ground, visualising herself outside the tent, standing on a pinnacle of rock raging back at the storm, commanding the dark god to lay his weapons down, to prostrate himself to the daughter of Amun-Ra. She felt excited, exhilarated, unafraid. There was nothing she could not do with her Divine Father's help. There was nothing she could not achieve.

It was as though she stood on a pinnacle high above the storm. She could see the angry red clouds of sand billowing from horizon to horizon, darkening the land, but above her the sky was pure and clear, the hot eye of the sun staring down.

The dust clouds were already subsiding. She could sense it. She knew it.

"He is leaving," she said to her companions.

Now there was no doubt. The howling was not so close. They could hear the sound retreating into the distance until it was no more than a faint, insubstantial, lonely sigh. The tent walls were no longer heaving and shuddering, but sagging inertly, weighed down by the weight of the sand that had fallen on them.

Inside the royal tent there was total silence. Everyone stood still, listening, hardly daring to believe that they had come safely out of the desert's rage.

And then they were sure and fell down at her feet, calling out her names of power and glory. Hatshepsut, Maat-ka-Ra, had outfaced the desert storm. She was indeed Divine Pharaoh of the Two Lands, the right hand of Amun-Ra.

She looked across their heads and met the eyes of Neferure. The girl was looking directly into her own eyes. Was it fear she read there?

Fear – not of the storm but of her mother? Almost at once the princess lowered her eyes again and bowed. Hatshepsut sighed. She loved her daughter passionately, but always there was a distance between them . . . something deep inside the girl blocking the passage of her love. No matter what she did she could not break it down. She bit her lip. She suspected Senmut alone had the girl's devotion. Busy as she was, she ought to have made more time to be with her.

Impatiently she indicated that they should rise, and began to issue sharp commands that the tent flap should be forced open and the digging out should begin. She was anxious to see what damage had been done to the rest of the tents and the animals, most of which had been tethered between rocks out in the open.

The rest of the day was spent digging away sand and counting the cost of the storm. Several goats and packhorses were dead, and three slaves. On the whole, they had escaped lightly from the desert's anger. Hatshepsut was impatient to move on, but was forced to bide her time and pass the night where they were. The landscape had changed dramatically since the day before and the guides had to study the stars to plot their course. Dunes were where there had been no dunes, and bare, jagged skeletons of rock showed where before there had been smooth mounds of sand.

Hatshepsut slept heavily for a while after the evening meal, but at about midnight she woke and went out of the tent. To the left, beyond the row of tethered animals, she could see a small group of guides and drovers consulting together and occasionally pointing at the sky. So still and clear was the desert air now, she could hear their voices though they were barely whispering. She walked away, unobserved. The left eye of Horus, never sleeping, shone down over the desolate wastes. It gave her enough light to climb a rocky knoll, the encampment and the whispering men now out of sight. The knoll continued towards the east in a long spur. She walked its length, anxious to get as far away as she could from her companions.

She looked at the desert. In many ways, though she feared its dangers, she was fascinated by it. She could understand Set's rages, for she herself had uncontrollable anger from time to time.

Something in her reached out this night towards the desert prince, the violent and passionate strength of Set. He was always the dark god, the feared one. Yet on the barque of Ra he stood at the prow, with his spear protecting the mighty one from his enemies.

"Will you protect me?" she whispered, shivering, afraid to say his name, yet desiring him.

Something was forming in the desert before her. Something potent . . . numinous . . . supernatural . . .

It seemed to her she could see the giant figure of Set the god – man-bodied, animal-headed, silhouetted against the silver of an almost full moon. She felt strange, as though she were weightless . . . as though she were in silence . . . as though she were other than herself.

She stepped forward to the very edge of the rocky ridge on which she was standing, reaching out her arms yearningly towards him, longing to know, once and for all, the truth about him.

He was motionless before her, as tall as the rocky hill on which she stood. The moonlight was behind him. She could not see his eyes though she knew they were on a level with her own.

Her heart was beating fast. Now she was afraid as she had not been in the storm. Yet still she reached out her arms.

"Speak to me," she whispered. "I have to know you. I am Pharaoh. I have to know all things."

"You do know me," a voice replied that could have been within her or could have been without.

"I do not know if you are an illusion or reality. Let me touch your hand."

She was trembling, but she was determined she would not leave this ridge until she knew what she wanted to know.

"You cannot touch my hand."

"Why?"

No answer.

"One day . . . will I?"

"You cannot touch my hand."

"Why?" she almost shouted, becoming angry. "Because you are not there? Because you are dreamed up in my own mind? Because you are *nothing* – less than nothing!"

"Because I will destroy you."

"I am Pharaoh," she said fiercely, "the daughter of the greatest of all gods – the Invisible One, Amun-Ra."

"Farewell, daughter of Amun-Ra." His voice was faint and growing fainter every moment . . . the figure was fading . . . but even in the last syllable she could hear the mockery.

He had gone – and she did not know for sure whether he had been there or not. Tears of frustration streamed from her eyes. How long must she endure half-truth, illusion and deception? When would she see with eyes of eternal fire? When would she know that which Is, from that which Is Not? Amun-Ra had promised – but not delivered.

The desert felt really empty now. She was cold and lonely and depressed. She began to walk back to the camp and stumbled and stubbed her toes more than once on the rocks before she came at last to the shelter of her tent. She crept in without being noticed and wearily drew the rugs over her head.

The next morning the caravan set off again. They were heading for the amethyst mines, the official reason being that Pharaoh wanted to inspect the work and conditions personally, as the miners had recently petitioned her in some desperation. It was not strictly necessary that she should go herself – a high official would have served as well – but she saw it as an opportunity to get away from the constant strain of intrigue and whispering at court, a chance to be with the two people she loved most in the world, Senmut and her daughter, and a chance to meet the desert face to face, a challenge she always found exciting and stimulating.

Neferure had not been pleased at first with the decision that she should accompany the party. She was a girl who liked the luxuries and comforts of the palace and hated travelling. But two things made the journey worthwhile. One was that Senmut would be going, and the second was that she would escape at least for a while the drudgery of studying to read and write. She was tired of the little figures she was expected to draw on slivers of smooth stone. When she was Pharaoh she was determined she would have scribes to do this work for her – so why should she waste her time learning to do it herself? Her mother said it was because a pharaoh could trust no one – not even a confidential scribe – and should be able to read anything and everything that was written, and hear everything that was said. Hatshepsut pored over plans with Senmut and the other architects and argued about details that only a master in the trade should understand. Was there anyone in the world with as much energy as her mother? Neferure sighed. Hatshepsut had ambitions for her daughter that her daughter did not share. She was not at all sure she wanted to be Pharaoh in the way her mother was. She would much rather be like her grandmother, Aah-mes, the woman in the background, the Great Royal Wife, her sole concern to bring children into the world and look beautiful at all the public ceremonies.

When she was very young, her mother had been more fun to be with. Hatshepsut, Senmut and she had sometimes picnicked together in a place remote from the formality of the court. There were even evenings when her mother had come to her bedchamber, dismissed the nurse, and sat at the foot of her bed telling her stories, sometimes showing such tenderness that long after she had left the room the child could still feel the warmth and comfort of her arms around her.

Senmut had been more fun in those days too. It was before he grew too busy to spend time with her. How she loved him! When he tried to teach her something, it was a pleasure to learn. With him each hieroglyph had a story to it – often more than one. She felt the mystery of them, the magic of them. She felt she was exploring the invisible realms and the signs she made were the keys to open the doors to them. But now with her new tutor the signs were dead. She learned them off by heart and resented the time she had to spend at them. She also resented the time she had to spend clearing up the equipment at the end of each lesson. The slates on which the raw pigments had been ground had to be washed thoroughly, as did the little dishes in which she had mixed the pigments with oil or water. If the reeds had worn out, she was made to cut the ends and chew the reed again to make the fibrous brush for use next time. She was sure the servants should do this, but he insisted that she should do it herself. The wooden palette and the cakes of ink had to be carefully placed in the box – everything in its proper place before he would let her rise. Even the knots to hold the whole thing together for carrying had to be tied and retied until they were correct. And then to end it all, the prayer to Djehuti had to be said. If anything was skimped or shoddily done she would have to start again.

She tired of hearing how noble the scribes' profession was and how the traditional method of doing things was the only proper way. Senmut had cut corners. Senmut had made signs sing. He had even invented a few new ones and taught them to her, swearing her to secrecy, saying they would be a private code between them and no one else must know about them – not even her mother.

"When either of us is in trouble," he had said conspiratorially to her one day when she was still wearing the sidelock of youth and sitting cross-legged at his feet, "we can send a message to each other using these signs. When either of us gets such a message we must come to the other's rescue at once. We will swear it."

"I swear it!" she had cried, envisaging all kinds of adventurous situations in which she would send a secret message to Senmut, but never once foreseeing a time when she would send one and he would not come.

Senmut and his party were at the meeting place, waiting anxiously to see if the Pharaoh's entourage had weathered the storm they had seen in the distance, but had not had to suffer themselves.

For the first time since they had left home Neferure's reserve broke down and she jumped from her chair and ran straight into the arms of her guardian and protector, her tutor, her friend, Senmut,

"Superior of Superiors, Chief of Chiefs and Overseer of all Pharaoh's works throughout the Two Lands". He grinned and swung her round in his arms. At fourteen she was already slightly taller than her mother, but she was slender and no weight at all. Over her head his eyes met Hatshepsut's. But this the girl did not see.

The miners were all lined up for the royal visit, clean and neat and orderly. There was no sign of the truculence and disaffection, the resentment and brooding violence that had been such a feature of the past months. The foreman, Pawero, who had been trying to deal with the rebellious workforce and knew if something was not done soon his life would not be worth a jar of chickpeas, was relieved beyond measure when the lookout spotted the approaching caravan of pack mules and horses. It was unusual for Pharaoh to travel far into the desert in answer to a complaint from the miners, and the men were nervous. Either their grievances would be attended to or their lives would be in danger – but either way things would not go on as they had before. The shifts were too long, and there was too little food and too little water. No one liked the foreman. He expected too much and was too ready to mete out punishment for the most minor of offences. The men knew that their rations were cut so that his might be increased.

When it was time for those who had been there longest to return to their families, they carried with them secret instructions to petition Pharaoh and a slate containing the mark of every man on the site except the foreman and his officers.

Pawero had known nothing of the petition until he received a message that Pharaoh herself was coming to inspect the mines. In his rage at the miners action, he thought up the most extreme punishments for the ringleaders – but Nu, his second in command, pointed out that the better policy would be to alleviate the miners' sufferings at once so that when Pharaoh arrived she would see that there was no substance to their complaints.

"There is no reason why, when she has gone, you should not punish them," he said.

"That Kenna will wish he'd never been born by the time I'm through with him," muttered Pawero. He saw the sense of the plan, but it was difficult to hold in check the hatred he felt for the miners' leader, a big and ungainly man, a bearded giant, who had stirred the men up to this. Physically Pawero was afraid of him, being himself of much smaller build, but he knew he had the cunning, the weapons and the power to destroy him as soon as Pharaoh's back was turned.

The foremen in these isolated outposts were Pharaoh's representatives. Any violence against them was not only punished by death but by the worst punishment possible for an Egyptian – the removal of his name from all records and the forbidding of his name to be spoken or written by anyone, ever. Even the gods would not recognise someone whose name had been expunged. Without a name, one would fall back into the Void at death, and exist no more. It was the fear of this that kept the men from open rebellion. The foreman's power was bolstered not only by the weight of the state, but by the spells and incantations that were said over him when he took office. These desolate rocks were inhabited by watchful spirits who guarded the chosen one. Nothing the men did to him would pass unnoticed and unpunished. It was Kenna's idea, after one of the young miners had been beaten to death for stealing hungrily from the foreman's store, that their best hope was to petition Pharaoh. Her magic, seeing she was already part god, would outweigh any that Pawero might have. Kenna had seen her once at the festival of Opet, and he had a good feeling about her. "She will listen," he told his fellow workers.

It was with difficulty that Pawero smiled when he announced the news of Pharaoh's visit. He pretended he did not know about the petition and set about improving conditions very carefully, bit by bit, so that it would not look too obvious that he was responding to pressure. Nu was at his side, continually whispering and advising, and the job was done so effectively that by the time Pharaoh's arrival was imminent the miners, no longer so hungry and thirsty and with fewer hours to work, had very little to complain about.

Only Kenna seemed to see through the trick and fear the aftermath.

As the royal caravan slowly wound down the last hill they were all astonished at the size of it. The line of baggage mules seemed to go on forever. Pharaoh's soldiers led the cavalcade and stood fully armed and ready in a semicircle as Pharaoh herself, her chief advisor and her daughter dismounted in front of Pawero. He bowed at once to the ground, "flattening himself into the sand like the worm he is," thought Kenna bitterly. All the men followed suit. The last to go down was Kenna himself, and Hatshepsut's eyes did not miss this. Hatshepsut knew at once who the leader of the miners was, and knew also that he had bowed to her at last, not because it was the traditional and expected thing to do, but because in meeting her eyes he had judged her worthy.

She smiled. Within moments, without a word passing, she had summed up the situation.

She indicated that they might rise, and stood silently while the interminable formal and flattering speeches of greeting were delivered, first by Pawero, then by Nu and several others of Pawero's ruling group. Most of the men bowed their heads like naughty children, ashamed that their little grievances had exposed this beautiful and fragile-looking woman to all the savagery of the eastern desert.

After the speeches, Pharaoh raised her hand and spoke a blessing, committing them, pointedly, to the care of Maat, the great goddess whose feather was weighed against the heart on the day of judgement, the Lady whose main concerns were order and balance, truth and justice.

Hatshepsut then, with Senmut and Neferure, moved into the foreman's tent, and disappeared from sight.

"Now the lies will begin," thought Kenna, but for the first time he had hope. Her eyes were clear and true. She was shrewd and wise, and there was a good chance she would see through Pawero's ruse.

A cheer went up. The men had been told that in honour of Pharaoh's visit there would be a feast, and this day would be marked forever by the erection of a royal stele above the mine. This would draw down the protection of the gods, through the mediumship of the image of Pharaoh carved upon it, more effectively than all the prayers and amulets they had used hitherto.

Some of the men were still uneasy, and came to Kenna to ask what should be done.

"Nothing," he replied. "I will speak to her."

One laughed.

"What? Will you force your way into her presence? You know Pawero has his men everywhere, ready to keep you from her."

"She will ask to speak to me. You will see," he replied confidently.

And with that they had to be content.

The baggage mules were brought forward and unloaded, and there were gasps from dry throats as wine and beer and water by the barrel were lowered to the ground; meats and spices, and even dried fish; cones of salt, beans, bread and honey and baskets of fruit. The miners forgot their grievances and crowded round, chattering and laughing.

Inside the tent the smooth Pawero entertained his royal guests, feeding them with the choicest food from his private store of delicacies and talking about the men as though they were his beloved children. Hatshepsut was told that he was as shocked as she must have been to hear that they were not happy. He had done his best for them, and as soon as it was brought to his attention that they had grievances he had set them to rights. He could not imagine why they felt it necessary to go over his head to her. He mentioned Kenna as a troublemaker.

"Kenna," she said musingly. "The big, dark one?"

"Yes," said Pawero. "A son of Set. Always at the centre of any commotion."

"I was told that several miners died while being beaten."

"Most unfortunate." Pawero shook his head sadly. "Hardened criminals. There was no other way."

"And many deaths by accident."

"You will find, Majesty, that all of them were due to carelessness. I issue warnings. But if the men will not heed them . . ."

"I was told there were faults in the construction of the mine. Dangers that could have been avoided."

"I assure you there is nothing wrong with the mine construction," he said. "I would ask you to inspect it yourself," he crooned, "if it were not that your Majesty is a woman."

Neferure and Senmut looked at each other behind her back with amusement. The foreman could not have said a more provocative thing. Now, nothing would prevent Hatshepsut from examining the mine shafts from top to bottom.

"My chief architect and I will inspect everything while we are here," she said stonily. "I have not come all this way just to sip a cup of wine with you." She looked at the goblet in her hand with some distaste. This was not the sweet wine she was used to. This was almost vinegar.

Pawero grovelled at once and denied that he had implied . . . that he had suggested . . . that it had even crossed his mind . . .

"Enough!" Hatshepsut cut him short imperiously. "I am tired, sir, and as soon as my own tent is ready I intend to rest. At moonrise let the feasting begin."

It would be a full moon this night, the time when there would be festivals in the villages back home. There would be music and dancing and feasting from one end of Khemet to the other. Khonsu, the moon god, the son of Amun and Mut, would walk the sky in all his finery and a thousand thousand of his shrines would be lit with lamps, decorated with white flowers and presented with gifts. Rich lovers would give silver gifts, and poor lovers garlands of white flowers, to their beloveds.

There were no flowers in the desert, but Senmut had brought with him, in the private pouch that never left his side, a ring of silver with white crystal lotus flowers, made by jewellers to his own design.

* * * *

The night had almost half gone when the first eerie glow presaged the rising moon. Outside, in the valley, all the miners were gathered, waiting for the first sign of the god. Most divided their attention between the horizon and the Pharaoh's tent, not sure which of the two divine beings they were looking forward to seeing the most.

Senmut woke Hatshepsut with a kiss. He had not slept with her, because in these hastily erected temporary quarters there was no privacy. Even at this tender moment he was aware that Neferure was nearby and could wake at any moment. Pharaoh's guards were close, warned especially to be alert. They admitted Senmut, but had been given orders to admit no one else.

He knelt beside her for a few moments, watching the rise and fall of her breast, the dark lashes against her golden cheek. He slipped his gift ring on her finger.

It was her forehead he kissed and then, when she stirred and opened her eyes, it was almost more than he could do to restrain himself from touching her lips . . . and throat . . . and . . .

"I had a good dream," she whispered.

He smiled and drew back a little, aware that Neferure was stirring too.

"I dreamed I was in a dark cave deep below the earth, and suddenly the moon rolled in like a great silver ball and illuminated the whole place. I was completely surrounded by gigantic amethyst crystals." She smiled dreamily. "You cannot imagine how beautiful they were! They glowed – the moonlight gleaming through the transparent purple, throwing filaments and ripples of silver light all over the walls and floor and ceiling and on my body . . ." She lifted up her bare arms and looked at them as though she still expected to see the shimmering silver-purple light playing on her skin.

Then she shook her head and sighed.

"Ah well," she said ruefully. "I'm sure it won't be quite like that in the mine."

He looked at the finger on which he had secretly placed the ring. Her eyes followed his and for the first time she saw it. Her face lit up and she flung her arms around his neck. It was she who kissed him now, and never once thought of her daughter, who was awake and watching them with cold and hooded eyes.

A sound at the door made Senmut pull away and stand up suddenly. It was the guards challenging the messenger that had been sent to call Pharaoh to the moon-rising and the feast. Somewhat flushed, Senmut strode to the doorway and told the guards that her

Majesty was awake and would join the festivities shortly. With only one quick backward glance he left the tent.

The moon was vast, and pure gold, as it lifted off the horizon. The multitude of men were all in the shadow of the cliffs, waiting in dead silence: none to be seen or heard. Hatshepsut stood, the crown with Mut's vulture wings clasping her head, a cloak of light blue wool over her shoulders against the desert chill. Nowhere, however remote on earth or among the furthest of the myriad of stars, was beyond the reach of her soaring, powerful attention, her lofty and beneficial love. She thought about the miners, small frail flotsam in the immensity of the universe, yet each with a burning quick of consciousness capable of illuminating all things.

She drew her cloak closer about herself. If a being that was capable of such awareness could flicker out as easily as a candle flame in wind, what was the point of having such potential in the first place?

The huge golden moon flooded the darkness with light and her heart lifted. The ancient and certain cycle of renewal was her answer.

From every throat the song of gratitude and relief rang out. The desert became tumultuous with sound, full of living hope.

Pharaoh lifted her arms in salute to the great being whose present visible form was the moon. His rays shone on Pawero and Kenna alike and glinted off her silver and crystal ring. Her feeling of insecurity had passed. Behind Khonsu, a mighty invisible force drove all things with order, pattern and regularity. Our consciousness is only part of a much greater one that would not, could not, flicker out.

She bowed to the ground before Khonsu as her subjects did before her. She could almost hear her heart beating with the awe she felt. She was chosen to be the channel of this mighty force in this time and this place. She had been marked for it. The golden cobra had been placed over her forehead, and with its eyes she looked into the eyes of the gods.

What she saw dazzled and frightened her. Was she capable of carrying the responsibility this vision gave her? Was she adequate? Was she strong enough? Senmut shifted his position slightly so that his leg inadvertently touched hers. She recoiled like a taut spring. She would accept no distractions, no diversions. At that moment she hated him for bringing her back to her frail and female body. The god was speaking to her – and *he* dared to interrupt.

He felt her sudden deadly anger and drew back in alarm. For an instant, he looked into her eyes and saw his own end.

* * * *

When the moon was fully up and turned to silver, the real celebrations began. The men had had a difficult and bitter time these past months, and had even forgotten in many cases the wonder of the full moon rising. Now the beer flowed freely and many a drunken and ribald song not fit for the ears of the young princess nevertheless reached them.

Kenna remained sober. He drank, but carefully, watching Pharaoh. She glanced at him from time to time, knowing that his eyes never left her, but gave him no indication that he should approach. She was placed well back from the rough miners, and Pawero made sure no one could talk to her but himself and a few chosen officials.

She too drank very little, though now they were serving the good delta wine she had brought with her. Quietly and neatly she drew the veils of polite hypocrisy away from Pawero and led him on to say things he would later very much regret. She smiled and nodded and said very little. Senmut, watching her, knew that in this mood she was as deadly as a cobra. He almost pitied Pawero.

The feasting and celebrations went on beyond sunrise and moonset, and no one was fit for work. Pawero magnanimously declared a holiday. The royal party retired to their luxurious tents, the miners to their hard and dusty bunks. Pawero nursed the father and mother of all headaches and tried to remember what he had said to Pharaoh.

The day after the holiday, Pharaoh announced that she was going to inspect the miners shafts and galleries. There was pandemonium as Pawero despatched people in every direction with instructions. He had been sure she was discouraged from going, and now he tried to arrange that she would be shown only the safest and most accessible of the shafts. The whole thing was so much like an underground labyrinth that he had no fear she would find her way to those places he would rather keep hidden.

The expedition started well. Neferure chose to remain above ground, bored as she was with this desolate place. Hatshepsut was dressed in a male kilt, with hardy leather sandals, a short woollen cloak against the underground cold, and a leather cap fitting closely and protectively around her beautifully shaped head. Senmut, similarly simply dressed for practicality, followed her closely.

The rough-cut stone steps leading down into the earth were dangerously steep, but little earthenware lamps had been placed in niches at intervals and the going was not particularly uncomfortable. As they went deeper, the walls closed in more tightly and the steps became narrower. Pawero turned to Hatshepsut and tried to offer her a helping hand. Even in the dim light of the stone shaft he recoiled at the expression in her eyes. He did not offer again, and he noticed that Senmut did not either.

At the bottom of the shaft, they could stand fairly comfortably in a chamber – and Pawero took the opportunity to make a little speech about the depth and extent of the mine and how many improvements had been made since his predecessor's time.

He led her down one of the corridors that branched off and showed her a working face. She had been right when she said her dream was nothing like the real mine. There seemed to be very little amethyst, and what there was was dirty and chipped. She sighed and asked to be shown another section.

Pawero showed her two more similar faces and then suggested they returned to the surface.

"No," she said. "I want to see it all."

"I think, Majesty, we should really return to the surface. It might be dangerous for you."

"If it is dangerous for me, it is dangerous for the men."

"There are always dangers in mining, Majesty. The men know this and live with it. It is their professional risk. But there is no need for you to expose yourself to it'

"The men are Pharaoh's children, Pawero, even more than they are yours. I want to see these dangers you speak of. I want to see if they are the normal dangers of mining – or if they are more than any miner can reasonably be expected to accept."

The petitioner had told her some horrifying things about the more remote passages, and the roof falls and suffocation that could have been prevented.

Pawero was sweating profusely.

"Every precaution has been taken but . . ."

"I hear not every precaution *has* been taken, sir."

"You have been told lies."

"Ah, Pawero, do you not think Pharaoh with his cobra vision can see who is lying and who is not?"

The expression in her voice made him cold all over. He was shivering and sweating at the same time.

"I tell you, Pawero, no one lies to Pharaoh – and lives."

There was a terrible silence.

"Poor Pawero," though Senmut. He knew she meant what she said. But he himself had lied to her in those early days when he declared a love for her he had not really felt. Had she seen that he was lying? Had she let it pass unpunished because with her cobra vision she knew that it would one day be true? Perhaps she let it pass unpunished because the woman side of her wanted so badly to believe it. Now it was true – and yet he felt more insecure as her lover than he ever had in those early days. His mind began to drift into dangerous waters. What if . . . what if he married Neferure? This would give him the ultimate position in the country he had always wanted and Hatshepsut had refused him. Hatshepsut was training her daughter to be Pharaoh. How suitable that he, who had been the girl's foster father, tutor, companion and friend should stand beside her when she came to the throne. She would need the intelligence and cunning, the powerful allies and friends he could bring with him.

Even Hatshepsut, who doted on her daughter, could see that the girl did not have her own strength and would soon be destroyed by the many court factions opposed to her. It need not be a marriage of the bed. Hatshepsut would still have him to tease and play with when she wanted, but he, as husband to the heir, would have a formal status that would make him less vulnerable to the hot and cold of whim and fancy.

But Pawero's whining and Hatshepsut's stern replies cut across his thoughts.

Hatshepsut had got her way – as she always did – and was calmly walking down a forbidden corridor, Pawero whimpering and protesting at her side.

The low gallery they now entered was almost airless, the lamps barely alight. Among the crouched men at the face, Hatshepsut spotted Kenna.

She commanded that the work should cease at once and everyone follow her to the surface. The men did not even look at Pawero to see if he accepted this or not. Thankfully they crept and slithered out - some wheezing and gasping as though about to expire.

No words were spoken until at last they were standing in the sunlight, Hatshepsut as streaked with dirt as any of them.

Then Kenna stepped forward and placed a rough ball of dusty stone in her hand. She took it and looked at it, puzzled. She noticed that it was cracked like an egg, and with a touch it split open and lay in two halves in her hands. There she saw the cave of her dream, a shining mass of purple crystals encrusting the curved inner walls.

She looked up at him and smiled. Her god had given her a sign. This was the man to trust.

* * * *

57

Pawero was not deprived of his life, but he was deprived of his livelihood. He and Nu were told to leave, and they knew it was unlikely they would ever be employed in any position of responsibility in her service again.

"As long as Hatshepsut is Pharaoh," Pawero thought bitterly, his thoughts turning to the young prince whose place on the throne she had usurped. If Men-kheper-Ra took back the double crown, he would have loyal supporters in men like Pawero and Nu.

Before she left, Pharaoh did one more thing for the miners. She found the place where new wells should be dug.

A small group set off along the valley: Hatshepsut and Neferure and several of the miners. Senmut remained behind at the miners' village to make arrangements for the smooth changeover of power. Hatshepsut had brought three men in her entourage who were capable of replacing the most corrupt of the officials. Senmut carefully selected those among the miners whom he thought would respond well to responsibility. Kenna, of course, was one of the first. Pawero, excluded from the consultations, sourly packed up his belongings.

"Mercy?" he muttered. "We'll see who is shown mercy when Men-kheper-Ra takes the Two Lands into his hands!"

From very ancient times, the pharaoh had been expected to find water in the desert when it was needed. It had been a long time since any had been called to do so, but the wells serving this mine had run dry over the past years and water had to be fetched from a long way away. Every drop had become more precious than silver and its distribution was under the control of the foreman, a source of bitter contention.

Hatshepsut insisted that Neferure should accompany her so that she might learn what had to be done. The girl trailed disconsolately behind, sheathed in fine cotton wraps against the searing heat of the sun, her face showing her distaste at everything to do with the project.

They started at dawn, hoping to have success before the heat became too unbearable; but in case it did, they brought light canopies and couches with them for shade and rest.

Hatshepsut knew enough about the kind of places water was likely to be found not to waste her time on impossible sites. The first four places she picked, though having the potential, brought no reaction from the L-shaped copper rods held loosely and expertly in her hands.

Wearily, as the day grew hotter and hotter, the entourage followed Pharaoh further along the rocky, desolate valley. At last she agreed to the canopies being set up and the precious water jars broached. Thankfully they settled down to rest, the miners stretching out on the sand, Neferure and Hatshepsut side by side on the travelling couch.

"There's no water here, mother," Neferure sulked. "Why do you pretend?"

"I'm not pretending, daughter," Hatshepsut said wearily. "There *is* water. It is just a matter of finding it."

Neferure sighed. She expected a lecture on how one must never assume when one could not see something that it was not there – but, for once, it did not come. Why were they doing this? Surely all this could be done by others. Surely a pharaoh should be resting in a cool room with a goblet of cold wine at the elbow and servants wielding ostrich-feather fans. She looked around them. As far as the eye could see there was rock and sand shimmering in the heat – yellowish, reddish, monotonous, lifeless. They had long since lost sight of the mining village. What if they could not find their way back there, let alone to their distant home? She was exhausted and frightened and bored. Tears began to gather in her eyes. She turned away from her mother, afraid that she would see them and chide her for showing weakness in front of men. "Pharaoh is strong. Pharaoh is god. All look up to him. He cannot waver. He cannot be afraid."

But she had seen her mother weep. She had come running in from play one day when she was small, her eyes dazzled from the sun. She stood still at the entrance to her mother's chamber unnoticed, waiting for her temporary sun-blindness to pass. She heard the most terrible sobs she had ever heard – and then she saw her mother lying diagonally across the bed as though she had flung herself there in her despair, her shoulders shaking.

The child was so shocked she crept out again without making her presence known. *Mothers* did not cry like that – let alone pharaohs! It was on that day, for the first time in her protected and privileged life, that Neferure knew fear and loneliness. Even Senmut did not comfort her when she ran to him for reassurance. His expression was hard and abstracted and he turned away from her impatiently before she could begin to tell him what she had seen.

Her mother was asleep now, her tense body relaxed for once. Neferure allowed the tears to flow, and with them a prayer to all the gods she could think of to take her home as quickly and as safely as possible.

Suddenly Hatshepsut sat up, clear-eyed and eager to be on the move again. Neferure groaned. She had just managed to calm down enough to drift off to sleep with her left thumb in her mouth – another thing her mother told her pharaohs did not do.

Hatshepsut had been shown a valley in her dreams, on the other side of the ridge of hills, and it was here her rods moved decisively, swinging out from the centre as though moved by ghostly hands – and it was here she told them to dig.

"You will move your village to this side of the ridge, and tunnel through to the mine from here. That way you will have water on your doorstep – as much as you want."

Neferure stared at the dry, crackling sand beneath which Hatshepsut had said they would find water. The men were bowing to her and singing praises to the god she was, without any proof that there was actually water there. Neferure's own rods had done nothing. She could never feel the "earth energies" that Hatshepsut and Senmut talked about, never understand what they meant when they called a place to build a temple or raise an obelisk or statue, or even plant a tree, "the will of Maat". The "will of Maat" seemed to refer to the rightness of its being precisely there and nowhere else. She had seen them worrying for days over where to put a statue or a stele and then, when they had decided to settle for one place that seemed no different from any other, they rejoiced as though they had found a lost gold pin in a sand dune. It was true the placing, once it was done, always felt right. She had known her mother to order the pulling down of a building because it interrupted the flow of what she called "Maat's will". On these occasions even Neferure had to agree the building had somehow seemed wrong in its particular location – and had always had a gloomy or uncomfortable atmosphere about it.

But she would never understand the things her mother understood! How would she ever take her place?

Water was found where Hatshepsut had said it would be, though the well shaft had to go deeper than any they had dug before.

It was Hatshepsut's idea that Neferure's visit should be particularly noted on the stele that was to be erected to commemorate their visit, but the wording was Senmut's:

Neferure, beloved of Senmut. May she live as Lady of the Two Lands, Mistress of Upper and Lower Egypt. Beautiful in the sight of Ra.

CHAPTER 7

The Egyptian ships built sturdily of cedar wood turned into the bay, wind filling their sails and the oarsmen using their great oars merely to steer. It seemed that a thousand small canoes were bobbing towards them on the water, and every cliff and rock on shore as far as the eye could see was crowded with black figures watching their approach. The crews were tired and nervous, but the captains were dressed in clean, crisp linen, hair well oiled and dressed, standing in the prow of each ship, ready for whatever the encounter with these foreigners might bring.

This was the first time an official Egyptian expedition had visited the land of Punt since very ancient times. The trade in precious gold, incense and myrrh was usually carried laboriously overland to Nubia, and thence over mountain and desert to Egypt. An occasional adventurous merchant had risked the terrors of the great ocean, but never had the local inhabitants seen a fleet of such huge vessels as were now silently moving in to shore.

The first canoes reached them, looking like so many floating seedpods. Tall black figures stood precariously in their rocking craft, waving their arms and shouting – whether in greeting or in anger it was difficult to tell. Impassively the Egyptian captains continued to stand with their arms folded on their chests, staring straight ahead and delivering short, sharp commands to drive the great ships on. There were well-armed men standing ready – but Pharaoh had demanded that there should be no unnecessary bloodshed.

Senmut was in the first ship of the fleet and, gazing down into the clear aquamarine, noticed that the floor of the bay was shelving deeply towards the beach. The timber keel juddered on the crystal sand and the ship came to a sudden standstill. By the shouting and the waving of arms from the canoes it was clear now that they had been sent out to warn the strangers of this very hazard.

The captain of Senmut's ship was no longer so impassive and was shouting orders and imprecations in equal proportion. The men in the canoes were grinning and laughing, their teeth showing startlingly white in their black faces. They moved round and round the beached ship, their singing and chanting sounding like the whine and buzz of flies around a carcass to the irate captain. Senmut, having grasped that they were in no danger, listened with interest to the rhythmic sounds and felt a thrill of excitement to think that they would soon be ashore in this legendary land.

Was this the place Hatshepsut had seen in her vision? It was as she had described: distant mountains fading blue into blue; forests, green on green; men as black as Nubians, but different in stature and feature; houses built on stilts.

Larger boats were now setting off from the beach, decorated with flowers and leaves. Officials in robes were standing under fluttering canopies.

"This is better," muttered the captain, now content that their reception would be a peaceful and amiable one. Stone anchors were dropped one by one.

The people of Punt had known of their approach for days. Lookouts had been following their progress down the coast, sending fire signals at frequent intervals. Spies had swum out to the ships at night and brought back reports of the fabulous trade goods piled up on the decks. The fleet was deemed to be friendly, but just in case, Perehu, the King of Punt, called up a huge host of warriors, ordering them to remain out of sight. He now waited on the beach to greet the strangers, clad peacefully in cloak and crown of coloured feathers, his grotesquely fat Queen, mother of twelve of his children, standing a few paces behind him. His children, arranged according to size in two rows, were further up the beach. Courtiers in their best finery flanked him, and between him and the place where the strangers would first put foot on this land, crouched the royal shaman, watching with lynx eyes everything that happened. He had already marked the sand secretly with a line of coloured dust. If any one of these foreigners harboured a hostile thought towards his King, he would be destroyed as he stepped across the line. If that failed, his hand was fingering the power charms in his pouch.

Senmut was the first to step over it. The shaman's eyes narrowed as the alien foot scuffed up some of the coloured dust. But nothing happened to him. He stepped forward and greeted the King of Punt as Hatshepsut had instructed him – with a slight inclination of the head while his hand inscribed the sign for eternal life in the air before him.

One by one the captains crossed the shaman's line unharmed. Only one, the fifth, coughed and put his hand to his throat, then fell to the ground, choking. Senmut turned to see what the commotion was. Uneasily his crew stood around him. The physician priest with the fleet stepped forward at once, hastily bringing out some strong-smelling herbs for the man to sniff – but it seemed as though he was too late. The man was almost dead.

Senmut caught an almost imperceptible nod between the King and the shaman. The shaman strode forward and put his hand on the head of the choking man. Several Egyptians moved forward angrily to push him aside, but paused when the choking ceased. The man was not dead, but he seemed very weak and was wheezing badly. As it happened, it was not until he was on board his ship again and turned for home that he recovered his health completely.

But at this time no one suspected witchcraft. If anything, Senmut was grateful to the shaman, barbaric, weird and frightening as he appeared, for his quick attention and the effectiveness of his healing. "I must learn from him," Senmut decided, and he felt elated to think of all that there was to learn from this strange and remote country. He had been doubtful when Hatshepsut told him that Amun-Ra had commanded her to mount this expedition to bring back incense trees for her temple. He had argued against it: "Too far, too dangerous, too expensive." He had told her he did not want to be away from her and the Two Lands for so long. He had suggested that he might not return. But she had been adamant. "Now," he thought, "I'm glad I came – and I know I shall bring back more than incense trees to Khemet."

That night in a smoke-filled clearing in the forest, with the strange reed houses high on stilts behind them, the King of Punt entertained them to a magnificent feast and a display of dancing which, for its sheer power and energy and stirring rhythm, outdid any they had ever witnessed before.

Senmut noted that his men clustered close together. Huge drums were beaten until they were not sure whether the sound was coming from their own hearts or from the earth itself. Dancers, naked apart from feathers in their hair and paint on their bodies and faces, stamped and thundered until the dust flew, mingling with the smoke from the fires and torches to make an eerie fog, out of which figures loomed and into which they disappeared.

Senmut heard the change in the rhythm of the drum beat. It was broken slightly and then accelerated. He found his heart was hammering and he knew that he was afraid. His men were terrified. He could see that. But the King and his wife were sitting peacefully on their great carved chairs, smiling amicably, watching as though what they were witnessing was something commonplace.

Suddenly the air was filled by a high, ululating sound, coming from the throats of hundreds of women who formed a huge circle around the dancers. They seemed to be clutching at each other's hands, trying to keep the circle unbroken, while some unseen force was trying to break it up. Senmut saw that the shaman was in the very centre. He had not noticed him before and could not imagine how he could have missed him. He was such a distinctive figure – skeletally thin, his face a grotesque painted mask, his hair so dressed with scarlet feathers it seemed to stand out around his head like a shining fireball in the muted red glow of the fog. Around his waist he wore a fringe of apron made of human bones.

Senmut's eyes followed the shaman's eyes as he stared at one particular part of the straining, shrieking circle of women. He saw the circle break and the women scatter – and then, into the clearing, came dancing some of the most macabre figures he had ever seen. Whether it was the effect of the fog or whether it was the heady liquor and strange food he had been plied with all evening, Senmut thought that some of the figures were transparent. A chill rippled up his spine and the skin on his arms goose-pimpled. Some of these dancers were not made of flesh and blood . . . some of them were disembodied spirits . . .

The shaman greeted them with wild and savage glee and led them in a sinuous serpent line round and round the clearing. Senmut could see the King and Queen shrink back in their chairs as though even they were afraid of these new visitors. The other dancers, the women, the Egyptians, had all drawn back into the shadows. The drums continued to beat. The other-world beings wove in and out of the firelight, their feet stamping the earth but making no sound, throwing up no dust.

Senmut swallowed hard but did not move. He had the feeling that if he moved he would die, that if anyone of flesh and blood, apart from the shaman and the drummers, moved – they would be dead. No one did. As though turned to stone, the people of Punt and the people of Khemet together watched the ghostly dance in stillness and in silence.

At last, when Senmut felt the tension was at breaking point, the shaman led his extraordinary band out of the clearing and into the huge shadows of the forest beyond the houses.

The drums began to sound a gentler beat, the other dancers began to come back. The women began to sing. But this time the mood was of rejoicing and of gratitude. The ancestors had graced their celebration with their presence. All was well. Gradually the music and the mood calmed down until Senmut's men, as though released from a spell, shifted about and began to talk excitedly and nervously to each other.

* * * *

Over the next few days, Hatshepsut's favourite official, Senmut, her scribe, Thutiy, and the ambassadors she had sent with them, cautiously went about their business.

One of the ambassadors, Pa-an, had been a merchant in his younger days, one of the few who had ventured as far afield as Punt. His boat had been damaged in a storm and he had stayed with these people for more than a year. By the time he left he had a fair understanding of their language. Senmut chose him as his interpreter, though there were many Nubians in the party who could have done the job as well.

Thutiy had been sent to record everything that happened and he followed silently, scarcely uttering a word from one day to the next. Senmut often wondered what he was thinking. He was a young man, but greatly trusted by the Pharaoh. His father had been her father's chief scribe, and as a boy he had followed the old man about as he now followed Senmut. His training had been day and night at the old man's elbow since a very early age.

At night or in the heat of the day when everyone else was resting, Thutiy would be sitting with crossed knees, his hand tirelessly working over a scroll with reed pens, watched intently by a crowd of inquisitive children. He spoke to them only once – and that was to tell them, in answer to their enquiries, that he was making magic. "These signs are magical spells," he explained. "They change into strange and wonderful things when they enter through the eye of the beholder. They have wings, and those who have them in themselves can fly to the ends of the earth . . . to the ends of all the worlds. In these little marks," he said, "lie everything that was and is and shall be. They are strong and powerful magic." The children's eyes opened wide and they took a step or two back from him.

Senmut, who overheard this rare pronouncement from Thutiy, smiled and walked away. Scribes were indeed magicians. They could control everything that happened by influencing the minds of those who could read those little squiggles and scratches. He himself was master of scripts, and proud of it, but he was glad that his sole task was not to record the expedition. There were much more important things he wanted to do.

When Senmut was not with the King and attending to the main business of the expedition, he sought out the shaman, taking the interpreter rather unwillingly along. Pa-an was terrified of the man and clutched his familiar amulets of Amun-Ra and Anubis nervously whenever they were anywhere near him. Senmut was making a point of learning the language as quickly as he could, but it would be some time before he could carry on a full conversation.

The shaman and he were close in many ways, both men who stood alone, very much ahead of their contemporaries. Both had shrewd and subtle minds, Senmut tending towards the rational and logical, the shaman more at home with the inner and deeper levels of consciousness. Senmut had not trained as a priest. He had come to his position in Hatshepsut's service by his sheer natural intelligence and ability. He was looked on as scribe, teacher, architect, advisor – not as a wielder of magical artefacts or caster of spells. But he was interested in everything, and the shaman's powers fascinated him.

In his turn the shaman had noticed Senmut from the very beginning, and not just because he was the leader of the expedition. He knew he was a man of many worlds, a traveller throughout the realms. Senmut himself might not know it yet, but the shaman knew that he would cross thresholds that were barred to the ordinary human being, and master secrets given to few to understand. He knew he would come to him and question him, and he knew he would give the answers.

The shaman lived in a circular hut on stilts well away from the other houses, deep in the forest. To reach him, a guide had led them most of the way. As soon as the hut was within sight, however, the guide squatted on the ground and refused to go any further. Senmut, Pa-an and Thutiy had to go on alone – but not before Senmut had threatened the guide with dire consequences if he dared leave the spot.

Without his paint, the shaman appeared to be a shrivelled old man, his bright, dark eyes sunk deep in their sockets. He greeted them curtly and indicated that they might enter and sit down on the reed matting of his dim, single-chambered domain. Pa-an was sweating profusely and made sure he was as near to the doorway as he could be. Thutiy sat where he could most easily observe the whole chamber, and Senmut sat down cross-legged directly in front of the shaman.

After the polite preliminaries, during which the scribe stared around him, noting the skulls, the human bones, the feathers, the crystals, the shrivelled lizards, the beads, the wooden carvings, the set of drums and many other things, Senmut got straight to the point.

"Tell me," he asked, "those spirit forms we saw – were they really there or was that some kind of illusion you conjured?"

The shaman grinned, and Thutiy noticed that he had no teeth.

"The spirits were there," the old man answered after a long silence. "The forms they took were illusion, but not of my making."

"Whose, then?"

"Of the people. They have pictures in their minds of how the ancestors look and they see these pictures when they feel the ancestors are near."

"But I saw them too. Did I see different forms to everyone else?"

"No. You saw what the others saw because many minds were projecting a single belief-form. It grew strong. It could not be ignored."

"I noticed the drums . . . The beat changed just before the spirit forms appeared."

"The ancestors are in another realm."

"So the drums called them?"

"The drums allowed them to appear to us. The vibrations of the drums matched those of their realm and created a threshold."

"We too believe the ancestors can cross the threshold. But we do not use drums."

"What safeguards do you have to prevent them coming when you do not want them?"

"There are many tests and judgements in the other world before one is given the freedom to come and go. The soul that may come in and out of the tomb does so freely of its own will, but only when it has won that freedom."

The chamber was very silent for a while as the men thought about what had been said. Pa-an wanted to leave. Thutiy wondered if he would remember everything to write it down.

It was Senmut who spoke first.

"Would you teach me the calling of the drums?"

The shaman looked at him intently with his bright little eyes.

"It is dangerous if it is not done properly," he said at last. " If irresponsible people give the call . . ."

"I am not irresponsible."

"I know. But there are mysteries. There are secrets only a shaman should know. You are a man of curiosity, living among men of curiosity. You will take the knowledge as a piece of curious lore to your people. Others will experiment. Some may pick up the beat to use, not believing, not understanding, and use it randomly. Ancestors will come and will not go back. They will enter the hearts of your people and cause mischief. All this is possible."

"I know it. But I will be careful. I will be responsible."

"Why do you want this knowledge? It is not the way of your people."

"There is one with whom I wish to talk."

"An ancestor?"

"Imhotep – a great man. Not my personal ancestor. But a brilliant architect, an understanding teacher . . . a source of great wisdom."

The shaman's eyes seemed to bore into his.

"I could teach you something. But not all. I would not do even this if I did not see you are already a man of knowledge, an initiate well advanced on the path."

Senmut frowned. "I have passed no initiation rites. I have had no priest training."

"The initiation rites that matter are never the ones given in initiation schools. There are many things you do not know about yourself yet, Egyptian."

Senmut was silent. It was true. He felt it. He had felt restless for a long time, as though he knew something important – and yet he could not put it into words, he could not name it. He had been thinking of Imhotep more and more lately. He identified with him, a commoner who had become the favourite of a pharaoh, the wielder of great power with great wisdom. He admired him beyond all others: a man who had lived more than a thousand years earlier, at the time of King Djoser, and yet to whom he felt as close as to his own grandfather; a man who was worshipped as a god by people who did not know a fraction of what he knew.

He looked up at the shaman eagerly. "When can we begin?" he asked.

"Not now. Not today. First you must learn my language."

Senmut looked disappointed. "That will take a long time."

"Not long," the man said. "Our minds already speak."

It was clear that the audience was over. Impatient as he was to start, Senmut rose too, and the three Egyptians left.

The shaman's last words were that Senmut was not to come to this place again and seek him out. When the time was right he would call Senmut – and Senmut would know the time had come and that he was ready.

When the time came, the shaman took Senmut on a journey deep into the interior. Nehsi, the commander of the expedition, protested, saying that it was essential that Hatshepsut's special envoy, the "King's messenger", should stay with the main party. Senmut begged leave of the Puntite King, Perehu.

"My King has seen a vision of your land, my Lord," he told him, "and has instructed me to seek out the special features of the vision. I cannot return to my land, my Lord, if I have not carried out the wishes of my King."

Nehsi glared at Senmut. Was this true? He had heard of no such instructions, but he knew that Senmut had had a long audience with Hatshepsut just before they left and had emerged very thoughtful. Nehsi was not one of those who gossiped about Hatshepsut and Senmut – but he did notice they seemed to have a special relationship. At times he had been jealous. At other times he was relieved that it was Senmut who was the recipient of her unpredictable and sometimes violent moods. He had witnessed more than once how she humiliated Senmut in public, pouring scorn and invective against him, beyond all provocation. There were times when he had seen Senmut, sullen and physically bruised, storming out of her chambers, only to be recalled soon after to be given priceless gifts and honours. On the whole, Nehsi preferred to be an ordinary friend and advisor, and keep a certain distance from Pharaoh's secrets. But he did not like the look of that shaman with his apron of human bones, and he did not like someone as important as Senmut risking the dangers of the interior. He shuddered to think of what Hatshepsut would do if Senmut did not return. But the man was determined, and that meant there was no stopping him.

Senmut set off alone with the shaman, refusing to accept the porters and warriors Perehu offered.

It was no comfort to Nehsi, as he stared angrily after them, to be told through Pa-an that the King had said that because the shaman was so powerful in magic, only the greatest of demons would dare challenge him, and even they would think twice when he was accompanied by such a man as Senmut.

The King and his advisors had been greatly impressed with Senmut. Without a common language, they had still sensed the quality in the man that had brought him from obscure and impoverished beginnings to the right hand of one of the most powerful rulers in the world. Senmut's detractors said it was only because Hatshepsut desired him that he held the position he did. But those who knew him well knew that if Hatshepsut desired him it was because of the man he was. There were handsome men enough around her vying for her favours, and Senmut was not particularly handsome. It was the power of his spirit that made people notice him, love him and follow him. The King of Punt might well be right when he said that Senmut would be a match for any danger and any demon.

They climbed through the beautiful myrrh terraces in the foothills of the high mountains, Senmut's heart stirring to the majestic dignity of the trees. Since the cedars of Kepel he had not seen any tree that moved him more. From these trees came the incense the gods loved, the incense that carried the hearts of mortal men to the gods, the incense that carried their prayers to the timeless regions, to the realms beyond the visible world. As he walked among them and heard the rustling of their leaves in the breeze coming off the mountains, his heart ached for Hatshepsut. How she would have loved to be here. He longed for her so intensely, he almost felt she was there, walking beside him, barefoot as she loved to be when she was communing with her god. She would have run on ahead so that she could be alone. She would have lifted her arms to sing that strange and haunting hymn she always sang when she was happy in the presence of her Lord. He suspected he was the only one who had ever heard it. He had asked her about it one day when he felt confident in her love. It was not in any language he had ever heard.

She had smiled enigmatically, as she often did when she was in that particular mood. "I cannot translate it," she had said. "My father taught it to me." When she said "my father" in that way, he knew she meant the god Amun-Ra and not Aa-kheper-ka-Ra, the Pharaoh, her earthly father.

Hatshepsut could not be with him here in the god's land, Punt, but Senmut could bring her a grove of living incense trees so that she might walk amongst them in her own land in the precincts of Amun's most holy temple.

Beyond the myrrh terraces the terrain was steeper, rougher, more challenging. The heat, even for an Egyptian, was excessive. Sweat poured from him and once or twice even he wondered if he was being wise to follow the shaman so unquestioningly. The man scarcely looked back, but climbed like a mountain goat. Senmut longed to rest, but dared not let the old man out of his sight.

At nightfall they made camp, the shaman circling their fire many times chanting spells and throwing coloured dust into the flames. Senmut, the city dweller, the sophisticated courtier, the ruler of many men, looked around uneasily. The shadows in this country seemed darker than any he had ever encountered before. There were no stars, and a cloud lay between the heavens and the earth.

Senmut was uncomfortable, overtired and filled with doubts. He noticed the shaman removing several human bones from his apron and setting them up like little sentinels to guard the four directions.

When the shaman came at last to squat before the fire beside him, Senmut asked about the bones.

"In my country we would think it sacrilege to use the dead so," he said.

"In mine it is an honour. When a man dies, we give his flesh to the birds that his spirit may fly in the sky and join the gods. His bones remain with us. If he has been an evil or a foolish man, or even just an average man, we bury them in their mother earth, and she takes care of him in her own way. But in the case of a great man, we bargain with her to let us keep some of his strength with us. She makes us a gift of some of his bones. They are potent magic – strong and fearsome magic. No one but the shaman may touch them."

"What would happen if I touched them?" Senmut asked, thinking how strange other people's customs were. The shaman's belief in his relics was strong. Was it his belief that made them effective – or was there something in the bones themselves? His own people went to great lengths to keep the body of the deceased intact, believing that part of its spiritual essence, its ka, would leave forever if there were no physical body to draw it back to earth.

"If you touched them when you were not prepared you would be taking a great risk. Some shadow from the bone might enter you. It might not leave you and you might never again be free of it."

"You touch them."

"I am prepared."

Senmut stood up restlessly. He was tired and he ached in every limb, but he felt like moving away from the fire. It had a strange smell from the powder the shaman had thrown in. He felt like distancing himself from the man – and from the bones.

The shaman raised his hand imperiously, and he stopped.

"Do not cross the lines between the relics," he said, quietly but menacingly. "On the other side of those lines I cannot protect you."

Senmut looked at the bones, the leg bones standing upright, white in the flickering light from the fire. He saw a faint luminous line passing between them, boxing him in.

He sat down again. He felt very strange. He wished he had not come. From the darkness beyond the box created by the bones, he could hear uncanny sounds, whether of animals, or insects, or demons, he was not sure.

"Sleep," the shaman said.

But, Senmut thought, weary as he was, he would never be able to get to sleep. The old man lay down on the ground and shut his eyes. Senmut, squatting beside him, looked at him closely, wishing he understood more than he did. If what the shaman did with the bones worked, and if what his own people did with their deceased worked – where was the truth?

He buried his head on his knees and prayed to Maat – she who guarded the order and the truth of the world, she who kept the balance of all that is, she who understood the heart.

Was she standing there in the firelight? If he lifted his head, would he see her? He felt her presence. He had felt it before when he, as architect, had experienced the inrush of a great design. He had known then she was there helping him, for every line he drew had been in the right place. Without even trying, he had created a beautiful and harmonious plan that he knew would work, for it was true of heart.

But now he was not opening himself to her guidance as an architect; he was questioning the very root from which the order of the world grew.

Was she smiling at him? He could feel her smile.

Ai, she was beautiful – everything in proportion. Upon her head her numinous feather drew his inner eye.

She did not speak. There were no words to say what she said to him, but before she moved away he knew that seeking sincerely, humbly and with love was the only way, and nothing would be found with arrogance and aggression.

He opened his eyes, but there was no one there.

He must have slept because just before dawn Senmut was woken by a fearsome crash of thunder and opened his eyes to see the sky livid with lightning. The shaman slept on. It seemed as though awesome giants were contending for the square of territory marked out by the shaman's relics. Senmut had experienced storms before, but never like this one. The air crackled and hummed, the sky split open, crashed together, and split again.

Then the storm spent itself and an uncanny silence fell.

The sun rose on a beautiful landscape, hills beyond hills fading into mist. They had climbed to the plateau beyond the wall of mountains they had seen from the coastal plain.

The shaman awoke, refreshed, as though this had been a night like any other.

About noon of the third day they reached a place that appeared to have no shadows. The shaman stopped and put down his staff, his bag of power objects, his pouch of food.

"We will rest," he said. "We have arrived."

Senmut looked around. There was nothing to distinguish this place, but if the shaman said they had arrived, he would not ask "where?" Thankfully he sank down onto a boulder and lowered his own burdens to the ground.

He thought they should eat, but the shaman shook his head when he reached for the dried meats in his carrying pouch.

After a brief rest the shaman rose again, picked everything up and indicated that Senmut should follow him. They clambered down the side of a rocky hill and paused again when they reached the flat at the bottom. It was filled with scrubby bushes – this side of the mountain not being as wet as the other. Insects rasped and sang in the heat. Birds screeched into the air from almost under their feet.

The shaman seemed to be looking for something in the bushes. Senmut patiently waited until the man found what he was seeking and called out to him.

Together they heaved back the tough and wiry growth of years, and Senmut was startled to find himself looking into a dark and gaping hole.

Unquestioningly he followed the shaman down into it. For a while they struggled through the darkness, Senmut stubbing his toes and bruising his shoulders on the rough wall of an underground passage. Then, suddenly, it became lighter and he found himself on a narrow path cut deeply into the rock. It ran below the surface of the land between sheer rock walls, but was open to the sky. The light flickered in only intermittently through the thick branches of the bushes that almost formed a roof.

Sometimes the shaman took a side tunnel that led off; sometimes he did not. Senmut walked close to him and did not let his attention wander for a moment. He knew he would never get out of this labyrinth alive if he lost his guide. The walls now were so sheer and high there would be no climbing them. He was glad this was not the rainy side of the mountain. He would not like to be caught here in a flash flood.

At last they reached their destination – a huge chamber at the confluence of three paths. This was not open to the sky, but the shaman fumbled with his fire stones and finally lit some torches and a fire in a small bronze brazier standing at the centre of the chamber. There was a strong smell of incense.

Senmut noticed with relief a group of drums stacked in a corner. He had been puzzled that they had brought no drums with them, though he had specifically asked to be taught the language of the drums for raising the ancestors.

He was desperately hungry now and felt quite faint. But he recognised that this fasting was part of the training and tried not to think of food.

The shaman signed that he should squat down in a particular place and carefully arranged three of the drums before him. He himself sat on the other side of the brazier with three similar drums. There were three entrances to the chamber where the three passages led into it. Through them a faint light found its way. With this and the torchlight he could see reasonably clearly.

The shaman seemed to spend an interminable time scattering his coloured powder around and intoning incomprehensible prayers. Senmut was tense with discomfort, hunger and impatience. And then he remembered Maat's message: no arrogance; no aggression. Search with sincerity, humility and love. He tried to think only of his respect for the shaman and what he had seen him do. He tried to think of Imhotep, whom he admired beyond all other men. "To learn," he whispered, "not for idle curiosity. To learn from him – with sincerity, humility and love."

But somewhere inside him there were other emotions, other motives, that he could not control. He wanted to meet Imhotep face to face so that he, Senmut, would be known as the man who talked with Imhotep. Imhotep's friend. Imhotep's pupil. The man whom Imhotep honoured with his confidences.

Perhaps he had been wrong to come. Perhaps he was not worthy to receive these secrets. He remembered how often he had sought worldly advancement. Even his love for Hatshepsut wavered between passion and ambition. Would he have loved her had she been a peasant girl from his village? Would he have cultivated their love had he not needed her to open the way for him to carry out the schemes and plans his brilliant and restless mind devised?

The shaman had stopped chanting and was looking at him intently.

He nodded. "I am ready."

Worthy or not, he had come all this way and he was not about to go back again without at least trying.

The lesson began.

At first he followed the shaman's lead fumblingly, and then with greater conviction. How long they were there, he had no idea. The light from the doorways dimmed and finally disappeared. They were still drumming when the light reappeared. He could not judge the passing of time. He could no longer feel the hunger and discomfort of his body. He became the drum and spoke with its voice.

Around him the spirits gathered . . . but they were strangers.

"Imhotep," he murmured, ignoring them. Why would he not come, the great soul, the hero of his heart?

One detached itself from the others and stood before him. He was not as Senmut imagined Imhotep to be.

Senmut began to feel ice-cold, as though all his blood were

74

draining away. The vast dim figure was coming closer and closer. His eyes were greedy and cruel. They were not the eyes of Imhotep.

Senmut scrambled backwards, toppling the drums as he did so, and losing his own balance so that he was sprawled on the dusty floor with the giant shadow of the ghost-being towering above him.

The shaman began to beat his drums furiously, his voice rising above the sound, high and weird, part howl, part chant. While still beating the drums with his right hand, he reached into his pouch with his left and brought out a handful of dried leaves. He flung them into the fire. The flames blazed up and, for an instant, Senmut saw the chamber filled with figures – every feature stark and clear. The face of the one leaning over him was the most hideous and evil he had ever seen.

And then it was as though the fire exploded and sparks and burning debris flew all around the room.

Senmut hid his face behind his arm, and when he looked up again the chamber was empty apart from the shaman, who had now left his drums and was standing looking down on him.

The Egyptian looked around the chamber, dazed and bewildered. He began to pick himself off the floor. He had hurt his hip when he fell, the burn on his arm where a spark had caught it was beginning to sting, and he felt sick.

Senmut looked at the shaman angrily. The man's face was hard to read. Had this been a trap? Was the shaman in fact his enemy and trying to implant some evil spirit in him to carry back to Egypt? He did not want to believe it had been his own fault. He had already forgotten that his motives in calling up Imhotep were impure, and that it was he who had insisted that he be given this instruction although the shaman had warned him of the danger.

His legs felt weak. The chamber was unbearably stuffy and the acrid smell of the leaves that had been thrown in the fire made him cough and choke.

He staggered towards the door he thought they had come through, and out into the deep-cut passage. Some light filtered through the branches that had grown over the top. He could think of nothing but getting as far away as he could, and began to run.

"Never again," thought Senmut, "will I allow myself to be in a position when I am not in control of myself. Never again will I risk being taken over by someone else."

His pace had slowed from a run to a walk. He began to feel stronger. Did he really need to speak with Imhotep? Was it not enough that his example was in the world? He, Senmut, was himself. He had his own strengths: his own reason and purpose for being alive. If he tried to do everything Imhotep's way, and not his own, would he not be a lesser man for it? Would he not accomplish a lesser goal?

And then he remembered the shaman and realised he was alone. He stopped short. All thoughts of Imhotep and his own high ideals and aims disappeared.

Was this the path they had taken before?

He began to concentrate on the details of his surroundings – the sheer rock walls, the scattered, flickering light through the leaves high above him. He walked back to the place where he had last noticed a side path, and stood at the crossing – but could not be sure either path was the one he and the shaman had come down.

He was hungry. He was tired. He was lost.

He started to shout, hoping that the sound would carry a long way down the passages. It did, but as it travelled it became distorted: it bounced and changed direction. Even if the shaman heard him he would not be able to pinpoint where he was.

He leant against the wall and looked up at the height he would have to scale if he were to climb out. There seemed to be no footholds, no cracks – nothing to break the smoothness of the walls. And even if he did get out, would he ever find his way back to his comfortable tent and his friends?

He slid down the wall until he was sitting.

He tried to calm himself. He tried to think.

On this same earth, a long way away, was Hatshepsut. He had not wanted to leave her – but she, in one of her moods, had decided that he must go, that they must try to break from each other; that they must try and restore some kind of balance to their relationship. Just before he left, it had been very difficult. It was as though her passion was ungovernable. She was risking everything to have him at her side. The court was whispering, and he could go nowhere but there were nudges and winks. She herself was beginning to lose the fine cutting edge of her judgement in state matters and was impatient of anything that took her away from him. It was after she had made a hasty decision that cost the lives of several people that, in paroxysms of tears, she insisted he went away. The Punt expedition was about ready to go. Everything had been planned to the last detail – a great deal of it by the two of them together in her chamber. But it had never been their intention that he would lead it.

Would he ever see her again? There was no one like her, lady of storm and sunlight. She could whip the desert sand into the air with her anger. She could lay it down again with her tenderness. She could make it flower. She could make it sing. How he missed her when he was away from her a day. How he longed to be away from her when he was with her for much longer. It was as though she were more than one person – strong and sometimes vicious and cruel, and then – almost as the wind changed – so sensitive and kind and thoughtful, so generous and loving, that he could lie on her breast and feel he was a child secure in its mother's arms. But the times that haunted him most were the times when they made love. So vivid was his memory of these that, weary, frightened, hungry as he was, he could feel his body stirring and rising, longing to enter that sweet marvellous place, to feel her skin against his, the hardening of her nipple in his mouth, the flow of her passion enveloping him. Ai, she could make love, that woman! When she was in bed she was not Pharaoh, daughter of Amun-Ra – she was a peasant of the earth.

A pebble dropped, clattering against the rock walls and landing beside him. He jumped, startled out of his intimate and powerful preoccupation. Dazed and bewildered, he could not understand where he was or who the face that appeared belonged to.

Then it came back, and he leapt to his feet and shouted with relief.

The face vanished instantly, and a surge of disappointed anger made him curse the son of Apep that had brought him here. Another pebble clattered down, followed by some twigs and dust. The shaman was back, lowering a long rope of plaited hide. The curses dried on Senmut's lips and he waited anxiously for the rope to reach him. If he got out of this alive, if he got back to Khemet, the first thing he would do would be to take his love in his arms and never let her go.

When the great ships reached Egypt again, more than twelve months later – after they had overcome the hazards of the open ocean and manoeuvred through the narrow canal dug in the twelfth dynasty and only recently cleared by Hatshepsut's army – and finally sailed up the Nile to Waset, where she waited, Senmut's heart was so full of pain and longing for her he could not think how he was going to get through the ceremonies of greeting with dignity and reserve.

They had been away a long time. Only three ships returned of the five that had set off, and many men had died of fever. But they had accomplished what they had set out to do: they had made contact with the Land of Myrrh; they had established a sea route to the southern lands; and they had brought back gifts for their Pharaoh and their god. There were times when none of them had expected to see their own land again. And now, as they worked their way upstream, they sang praises to their gods and threw garlands of exotic southern flowers into the waters of Hapi, chanting a victory hymn to Amun-

Ra. And every day the crowds gathered along the banks of the Nile to see them pass, cheering and shouting.

It was Senmut's idea that they should reach Waset at dawn.

Before first light, the crowds gathered, hundreds and thousands of torches lining the river with fire. Small boats stood off ready to herald them in, boys at the masts keeping a sharp lookout.

When first light broke over the ochre-pink mountains, birds in chattering strings flew out to meet them. Dawn breezes stirred the palm leaves and fluttered the pennants joyfully above the temples.

The sun began to rise behind Waset, behind the eastern mountains. Hatshepsut lifted her arms as the first brilliant rays of Ra's golden energy appeared above the rim of the distant rocks.

The voice goes forth, and the earth is inundated with silence,
for the Sole One came into existence in the sky before the
plains and mountains existed . . . You glorify my spirit, you
make the Osiris of my soul divine. I worship you. Be content,
O Lord of gods, for you are exalted in your firmament, and
your rays over my breast are like the day.

As though it were a signal, the great boats appeared, moving steadily, silently, towards their anchorage. Not a sound was uttered by the crowd. Not a child cried out. Not a bird squawked.

Then, as the sun rose into full view, the humming began. Every throat vibrated to Ra's praise, swelling from a low hum to a high and magnificent chant. In gratitude for the travellers' safe return every voice was raised in praise of Pharaoh's Father, Amun-Ra.

Standing in the prow of the first boat, Senmut had not stopped watching Hatshepsut from the first moment he saw her. She was standing on a raised plinth, like a statue, Mut's vulture crown enclosing her fine head, wings of gold and turquoise over her ears. Her body glowed golden in the dawn light, her smooth limbs barely misted over with fine linen. Golden snake bracelets twisted around her arms and ankles. A wide collar of gold, turquoise and lapis lazuli rose and fell with her breath. She was Divine Pharaoh. She was untouchable – unapproachable. Why had she chosen to appear as woman this morning of all mornings? It would have been easier for him to bear if she had appeared as she often did on state occasions as male Pharaoh, in a king's garments, with a king's false beard strapped to her chin.

On the long journey home he had thought about her incessantly, and he knew that when he left, she had been the one sick with love, and he had been fairly detached. Now, he was desperate with desire for her, and had even been thinking of ways and means to make it possible for them to marry. Part of her torment had been that she dared not acknowledge her love for him publicly, because he was a commoner, and because her hold on the throne was insecure and there were many who resented him and feared the rapidity of his rise to power. But she claimed to be King and not Queen. Kings had wives who were not called "great royal wife". Kings had wives who were commoners. The young Men-kheper-Ra, her stepson-nephew, whose place on the throne she had virtually usurped, was born of a secondary wife. Hatshepsut's own father was not of purely royal blood. Senmut had not pressed the idea of marriage before because he was not sure that he wanted its dangers and its constrictions. But now he was sure. He did not want to settle for Neferure, her daughter. He wanted to override all opposition, all court jealousies and intrigues. He wanted all the world to acknowledge him as Hatshepsut's choice, the beloved of Maat-ka-Ra.

She did not look at him once during the ceremonial greetings, and even avoided his eyes when he was standing right before her.

"It's because we are in public," he thought. "She thinks we are still playing the games we played before. When we are alone . . . then she will look at me. Then she will not be able to hold herself back."

But when the day's duties were done, when the long day of formality and business was finally behind him, and he went to the Queen's chambers, he was barred from her presence by the guards at the door – the same guards who had admitted him a hundred times before.

On his insistence, one of her women was called and sent in to tell the Queen that it was Senmut who sought admission – and that he had a special and private gift he wanted to deliver to her personally.

The message came back quickly. "Pharaoh is tired. She has retired for the night. She will see no visitors."

Senmut looked at the frightened woman. He knew she was not lying – this was what Hatshepsut had said.

Bitterly he turned on his heel and strode away.

Six days went by and Senmut saw nothing of Hatshepsut but the face she was prepared to show to her friends. She never summoned him alone, but always with someone else from the expedition. She was anxious to hear every detail and questioned them again and again, as the official reports did not satisfy her. Several times a day she was down at the quayside watching the unloading.

She was particularly excited about the panther they had brought.

The colour of midnight, with eyes of cold fire, it prowled its cage restlessly, muscles rippling. Senmut watched her watching it and knew that she was identifying with it. He knew more than anyone that burning ambition had put her on the throne, but another side of her hated the formality and restrictions that came with it, and she longed to run free sometimes and shake off her responsibilities and duties as a dog shakes off water from its coat. Senmut had suffered from that dark and powerful restlessness more than once – that prowling hunger for freedom. He suspected their lovemaking was her way of breaking out of her cage – but even as it ended, she was already accepting, and, indeed, welcoming, the bars again. The panther lay in a patch of striped sunlight, asleep – but even so, wary and alert. Senmut smiled. He had been foolish. Distance had made him sentimentalise his relationship with Hatshepsut. He should never have expected her to fling herself into his arms and say conventional things like "I love you" and "I've missed you". Her passions were taken up entirely at the moment by the excitement of what he had brought her.

At her feet he had laid fragrant woods, heaps of myrrh resin, fresh and growing myrrh trees, and ebony, out of which she was already planning to commission a magnificent ebony shrine. There were huge cases of pure ivory, of shells, of green gold from Emu, cinnamon wood, khesyt wood for incense, ihmut incense, sonter incense, eye cosmetic . . . There were apes, monkeys, dogs and mounds of panther skins.

When she had wearied of all this, and the pressures and the anxieties started again, she would seek him out. If he expected more, he was deceiving himself. He forced himself to go about his business and forget his dreams, and, instead of rushing to her side the next time she called, he sent a messenger with an excuse and stayed at her temple helping Thutiy arrange with the stone-scribes where the various inscriptions describing the Punt expedition were to go. How different to the rough and exhausting reality among the heat and flies it sounded in that formal jargon written for posterity.

> I have led them on water and on land, to explore the waters of
> inaccessible places, and I have reached the Myrrh terraces. It
> is a glorious region of God's-Land: it is indeed my place of
> delight. I have made it myself, in order to please my heart,
> together with Mut, Hathor, Wereret, mistress of Punt, the
> mistress "Great in Sorcery", Isis, mistress of all the gods.
> They took myrrh as they wished. They loaded the vessels to
> their hearts' content, with fresh myrrh trees and every good

gift of this country, strangers, southerners of God's-Land. I
conciliated them by love that they might give to thee praise,
because thou art a god, because of thy fame in all the
countries. I know them, I am their wise lord, I am the
Begetter, Amun-Ra; my daughter, who binds the Lords, is the
King Maat-ka-Ra, Hatshepsut. I have begotten her for myself.
I am her father, who set her fear among the Nine Bows, while
they came in peace to all gods.

They have brought all the marvels, every beautiful thing of
God's-Land, for which thy majesty sent them: heaps of gum of
myrrh, and enduring trees bearing fresh myrrh, united in the
festival-hall, to be seen of the lords of the gods. May thy
majesty cause them to grow, before my temple, in order to
delight my heart.

My name is before the gods, thy name is before all the living,
forever. Heaven and earth are flooded with incense: holy
scents are in the Great House. Mayest thou offer them to me,
pure and cleansed. May the divine limbs be fragant and my
statue be made festive with necklaces. My heart is glad
because of thee.

She had written these things herself and given them to Thutiy to
have inscribed. She told them Amun-Ra had given them to her in a
dream. He could believe it. As earthy and devious, ambitious and
worldly as she was, she could also reach great heights of mystic
ecstasy – and who was to say the god did not speak to her?

Senmut himself chose the wording of some of the passages. He
described her as he had seen her, too eager to wait for the formal
count, running her hands through the treasures herself:

. . . the best of myrrh is upon all her limbs, her fragrance is
divine dew, her scent is mingled with Punt, her skin is gilded
with electrum, shining as do the stars in the midst of the
festival-hall, before the whole land. There is rejoicing in all
the people; they give praise to the lord of gods, they laud
Maat-ka-Ra Hatshepsut in her divine qualities, because of the
greatness of the marvels which have happened to her. Never
did the like happen under any gods who were before, since
the beginning. May she be given life, like Ra forever.

On the seventh day she sought him out. She came to his chamber

81

in the west wing of the palace as silently as the panther itself would have done, but when the door was shut and she was beside him she stood almost hesitantly, waiting for him to make the first move. It crossed his mind to play the game she had been playing and pretend indifference – but his heart was hammering too loudly and at that moment he cared nothing for pride or hurt or rejection. Silently he pulled back the fine linen quilt and made a space for her beside him, reaching out to take her in his arms as she climbed in. What a creature of contrasts she was, he thought. Fearsome, murdering panther, and gentle, vulnerable kitten. He trembled slightly as her silky skin touched his, though he told himself again and again to be cool, calm, casual. No words were spoken. Silently their limbs flowed over each other, each touch, each movement from merest fingertip contact to deeper penetration sending shudders of delight throughout. Ah, that it would never end! Never . . . never . . . never . . .

But it was already over, already past.

They lay quietly for a long time enclosed in the afterglow, dreading the return of the ordinary. At last they began to talk, in whispers, though there was no one near enough to overhear them. She did not explain her treatment of him since his return, and he did not ask about it. Instead, they spoke of things that had happened in the time they had been parted. He told her about the experiences he had kept back from the official report, and she, similarly, described her feelings one day when she stood beneath the towering peak of Meretseger, "She Who Loves Silence", in the valley of her father's tomb, watching the men dig her own.

Her mortuary temple was on the far side of the huge stone ridge she was facing, and she planned to have the passage of her tomb dug directly into the rock of the mountain from this side so that her embalmed body might lie close, but unseen, behind Amun's most sacred sanctuary. The tomb and the sanctuary would be in exact alignment with the axis of her temple, which led through a long straight avenue of myrrh trees and sphinxes to the river bank directly opposite Amun's great temple at Ipet-Esut. There she was intending to erect two obelisks tipped with gold, taller even than the ones already there, which would be visible from the top terrace of her mortuary temple and would be a delight to the part of her soul that would dwell there after her death.

"But I don't want to die," she said to Senmut, sitting up suddenly and clasping her knees. "I want to live forever!"

"You will live forever."

"I know. I know," she said impatiently. "But not as Hatshepsut. Not as I am now. I want so much. I want to do so much! I want to feel the evening breeze on my skin. I want to sail the river. I want to make love to you. Nothing will be the same in the Myriad of Years. Nothing will be the same as a bodiless ka no matter how many offerings are put in my tomb."

"And if you come back, as some believe, to live other lives in other times and places? If you have flesh and blood again? If you feel the dawn breeze? If you sail the river again?"

"Will you be there? Will Thutiy? Nehsi? Hapuseneb? All the rest? Will my panther be there? Will we make love?"

Senmut laughed. "I'll never leave you."

Her face suddenly went white and she looked at him as though she had seen a ghost.

"What is it?" he asked, startled.

"You will."

"Will what?"

"You will leave me. You won't be there when I need you."

"I vow—"

"Don't vow, don't – don't . . ."

She was shivering, but she would not let him take her in his arms. She began to weep, and her shoulders were shaking convulsively – but she drew away from him.

"My love, I swear I'll never leave you. Even if I die I will make sure my ka is with your ka." It was at this moment that he decided to dig his own secret tomb beneath her mortuary temple, so that in death his ka would be with hers. "If we walk the earth again, in whatever time, in whatever place, I'll be with you. I swear it."

She looked at him angrily, her face streaked with tears.

"How can you be so sure?" she snapped. "Nothing is sure. Nothing!"

"I am sure of our love. It is strong enough to hold us together, no matter what."

She snorted and jumped out of his bed. She swept her robe up off the floor where she had dropped it and swung it round her shoulders.

"If I as Pharaoh cannot be sure of my future, how can you . . .?"

She used no epithet, but he was suddenly reduced from "Chief Steward, Favourite of the King, Conductor of all his works, Guardian and Mentor of the Princess Neferure, Overseer of the fields of Amun, Overseer of the gardens of Amun, Overseer of the cattle of Amun, Chief Steward of Amun, the Confidant of the King, his Beloved . . ." to a naked man tangled awkwardly in a crumpled quilt.

She walked imperiously to the door, but turned just before she left – and he could see that there was fear and despair in her eyes.

"It's all so short!" she said bitterly. "We've hardly time to find

83

out who we are!" And then she was gone, the wood juddering from the way she slammed the door behind her.

CHAPTER 8

Hapuseneb strode between the pair of great obelisks that flanked the entrance to the Temple of the Sun at Yunu, north of Men-nefer. Hatshepsut had made a particular point of restoring the temples fallen into disrepair and disuse during the time of the Hyksos "who ruled without Ra and did not act by divine command". The desert-dwellers had had their own gods – but they were primitive and savage compared to the sophisticated hierarchies of Khemet. Hatshepsut believed that a land networked with living temples, each in its special place, was a healthy land, a secure land, a dynamic and powerful land. From the wheat growing out of the grain that was sown, to the preservation of life after death, everything was the gift of the gods – and if the gods were happy everything would be in order, everything would work smoothly.

Since she was very young she had heard tales of the cruelties of the Hyksos and how not only the temples and the people but the land itself had suffered at their hands. She was immensely proud of her family for driving them away and her father for establishing strong borders to keep them out. She believed her own task was to reassert the rule of the cosmic law within the country and to encourage the flow of benevolent divine influence through her priesthood to her people. She saw Amun-Ra as the great unifying force behind them all.

Hapuseneb had done his work well as her chosen emissary. Old temples had been restored to the honour of the diverse aspects of the Mystery behind existence. New temples had been built to the one she felt more than any other was vital to the whole.

Hapuseneb encountered no opposition to his programme of extending the worship of Amun-Ra throughout the Two Lands until at Yunu he tried to make the temple of the combined god Amun-Ra larger and more prestigious than the temple of Ra alone. Yunu had traditionally been the home of the cult of the sun god and had enjoyed long centuries of unrivalled power and privilege. The priests of Ra were not happy to accept any diminishing of this prestige.

What had once been only a cult local to Waset had gradually become more and more important as the warrior pharaohs, under the banner of Amun, had driven the Hyksos out and extended the borders of their own empire further and further east towards the Euphrates and further and further south into Kush and Nubia. The god was obviously powerful and a force it would be prudent to have on one's side. In taking the double crown from her stepson-nephew, Men-kheper-Ra, Hatshepsut claimed that her royal mother had been impregnated by Amun, and that she, therefore, was truly the daughter of Amun.

> *He made his form in majesty like that of her husband, Aa-kheper-ka-Ra. He found her sleeping in the beauty of her chamber. She wakened at the fragrance of the god and he took her in his arms and had his desire of her. Then he caused her to see him in his form as a god and she rejoiced at the sight of his beauty. His love passed into her limbs and she was flooded with his divine fragrance. All his scents were of frankincense and myrrh. Then did the king's wife and king's mother Aah-mes, speak in the presence of this great god, Amun, Lord of Waset:*
> *"How great is thy presence, O Lord! Thou hast united me to thee with thy favours – thy dew is in all my limbs." Then did the majesty of this god do all that he desired of her, and at the end he uttered these words:*
> *"Khenemet-Amun-Hatshepsut shall be the name of this my daughter, whom I have placed in thy body. She shall exercise excellent kingship in this whole land. My soul is hers, my treasure and my crown, that she may rule the Two Lands, that she may lead all the living to know that I am I."*

Even before Hatshepsut had the scene celebrating her divine origins carved on the walls of her temple at Serui, she had heralds proclaiming it throughout the land.

But Ra-hotep, the High Priest of the Temple of the Sun, "the Greatest of the Seers", protested at sharing his god's glory with that of the upstart Amun. For millennia, apart from the years under the Hyksos' rule, Yunu had been the supreme religious centre of the Two Lands. Local cults might flourish for the common people, but Yunu was a powerhouse of theological knowledge and training, its great god of light in the three aspects of Kheper at dawn, Ra at noon and Atum in the evening, unchallenged and unchallengeable. Since the earliest days the young heirs to the throne were obliged to serve apprenticeship with the great sun priests and, when they left their fathers donated all kinds of riches to the temple. Hatshepsut herself had studied there, as had Men-kheper-Ra.

Now Hatshepsut was threatening to lessen Pharaoh's bounty. Her favourite god was to receive many of the vast estates, and much of the gold and silver, that Ra-Hotep felt should be coming his way. And here was the High Priest of Amun declaring that Ra in his aspect of Amun, or Amun in his aspect of Ra, was the only Mighty One, the Ancient of Days, the Lord of Lords.

Ra-Hotep was a man in his middle years, heavy in build and with eyebrows startlingly thick and black in contrast to his shining shaved skull. He had laboriously worked his way up to the position of First Prophet of the Sun at Yunu, without benefit of royal relations, and was not at all pleased to find that when he at last reached what he thought would be the primary position of power in the land, second only to the Pharaoh, Hapuseneb was there before him.

Hapuseneb arrived at the Temple of the Sun during the summer solstice, one of the major festivals of the god.

The city, always busy although it was no longer the capital of the Two Lands, was packed to overflowing with enthusiastic pilgrims. The tent city, pitched outside the crumbling walls that had not been restored since Hyksos' times, was almost as large as the permanent one. There were pedlars selling amulets of Ra and Kheper and Atum, and effigies by the thousands were set up in little shrines. The din of excited people shouting and the whine and whistle of flutes and pipes was almost deafening.

Not all would be allowed into the first court of the temple for the ceremony – but a great many would. Ra-hotep and his closest associates turned a blind eye to the bribery that was going on as members of the public tried to persuade the junior priests on guard at the gate to let them in. But Hapuseneb noticed it, and smiled grimly. No doubt it went on everywhere, he thought. Probably even after death people would try it on at the many gates on the Duat – but there it would not benefit them. There the gatekeepers were incorruptible and the only way through was by the honesty and wisdom of the answers they gave to the fearsome questions asked. He must remember to have a word with his own priests. The people must learn that merit, and not bribery, was all that they could safely rely upon.

After a brief ceremony in the outer court for the benefit of the crowd, Ra-hotep, Hapuseneb and certain other priests left for an inner court where the public were not allowed. There they performed more ceremonies of purification – standing still as stone while sweet oils and pure, cool water were poured over their heads. On the walls around them images of the sacred ablutions were painted.

On the door that they were to pass through Hapuseneb read these words:

I am the god who resides in the egg of the first and the last. I am the god who rises from the horizon and swims in the shining sky. Who sends light to illumine all things and whose like is not found among the gods . . .

Silently Ra-hotep broke the clay seal of the door and stepped through, followed only by Hapuseneb.

In this chamber prayers were said to prepare mortals for the encounter with the immortal. Each word had been taken from ancient and well-used texts and was engraved on the stone walls.

To enter the next chamber another seal had to be broken.

Hapuseneb found himself standing before a column of smooth black diorite. Its top was pyramid-shaped except for the very tip, which was hollowed out so that a huge green crystal egg could rest there. The flames of four low braziers illuminated a room that would otherwise have been pitch-dark, their flickering light reflected in the polished black stone so that it appeared that the crystal egg was rising from the flames.

The smell of incense was almost overwhelming.

In spite of the fact that Hapuseneb had entered the temple in a mood very far from the religious – his thoughts almost entirely concentrated on how he could replace Ra-hotep as High Priest with someone who would be more co-operative – he felt a shiver run down his spine.

The huge green crystal seemed to be made of light, and light was streaming from it. Dimly in the shadows the figures painted on the walls seemed to move in a slow and rhythmic dance. He felt dizzy and blinked his eyes against the stinging aromatic smoke. Did he see the folded wings of a golden bird contained within the transparent green crystal egg?

Ra-hotep bowed to the ground, and Hapuseneb found himself following him. He who had never felt the awe that others seemed to feel when faced with sacred images, found himself trembling and thought he heard – no, was sure he heard – the beating of mighty wings in the chamber. He wanted to raise his head and look up, but he could not.

The phoenix, *Lord of the Green Stone*, with eyes fashioned in the Millions of Years, could see into his heart. And he was afraid that what it saw there would condemn him to the Void.

At last the chamber was silent again.

What was this? Some trick of Ra-hotep's? He hoped it was.

Ra-hotep rose. Hapuseneb avoided meeting the sun priest's eyes and hoped that his face was sufficiently mask-like to hide how disturbed and shaken he had been by what he had just experienced.

Ra-hotep glided forward and unsealed the door on the far side, and Hapuseneb followed him out of the chamber. He waited beside the High Priest of the Sun while he took a small piece of damp clay out of a box in a wall niche, fixed it on the lock and impressed it with his seal ring. Hapuseneb noticed how thick and heavy the ring was – so heavy that the bezel looked clumsy. He fingered his own with satisfaction, a slender silver ring with seal stone of lapis lazuli. It had been given him by Hatshepsut herself, and for a moment he fancied he felt her light touch on his hand as she fitted the ring on his finger.

Ra-hotep finished resealing the last door and led Hapuseneb silently through another antechamber where once again they were purified by incense.

At last they came to the huge inner court, open to the sky.

Since they had entered the temple proper the floor of each succeeding chamber had been slightly higher than the last, and this courtyard was raised still higher. It represented the first mound of earth that had risen from the waters of Chaos. A white limestone pyramid, its tip made of polished gold, stood on a platform at the centre.

The light from the crystal egg in the dark chamber had been numinous and mysterious. Here there was a blaze of white light. Here Hapuseneb could see into every corner. Here he felt safer.

The heat was intense, the glare dazzling. Around the outside of the court there was a cool colonnade. He wished they could stay there, but noon was approaching and they had to take up their positions for the solstice ceremony.

There were seven white alabaster steps on each of the four sides of the central pyramid. Two other high priests had entered from the opposite side of the court, and now all four closed in on the symbolic centre of the court.

At the base of the pyramid they paused, exchanging glances to ascertain that each was ready.

The sun was almost at its zenith. Hapuseneb could feel sweat running down his face, his neck, his body. He wondered if he would be able to stand the heat. He wondered if he would be able to concentrate on what he had to do.

The moment had come.

The four high priests – of Ra, of Amun, of Ptah, of Djehuti – stepped up onto the first step.

Four voices intoned the praises of Ra:

"Beautiful is thy brightness on the horizon of the heavens, O Ra!"

On the second step they recalled that he had existed before all else.

On the third they remembered the "Thought of his heart" in which All had been prefigured.

On the fourth they described the coming forth from the Void and the creation of the first day.

On the fifth they praised his wisdom in that he had created day and night so that the dark and light would alternate and a continual dynamic process of renewal would be generated between them.

On the sixth step they bowed silently.

On the seventh they stood up straight and each gazed into one of the four golden triangles covering the apex. They were exactly the correct height for their faces to be reflected.

Hapuseneb stared into the eyes of a stranger. How could he have lived so long with this man and known so little about him? How could he have thought that the busy acts of each day were all that were required of him? In that moment he saw clearly that everything he did, everything he thought or said, had an extension into other realms, and in each of those other realms every act, thought and word had a deeper significance.

He thought about the various festivals of the gods, when the priests acted out the myths. The people looked at the actors and heard what they were saying and saw what they were doing. Some thought that was all there was to see. Others saw that what was happening before them was only the shadow of what was happening beyond the limits of their comprehension. It was no more than a sign at the crossroads pointing out the way.

He had intended to use this ceremony to assert the supremacy of Amun over Ra and the others, but he was suddenly ashamed. He saw his busy activities over the past years in trying to make the priesthood of Amun richer and more powerful than any other in the Two Lands in a different light.

At that moment, for perhaps the first time in his life – unless he counted his experience in the chamber with the green crystal egg – he knew beyond any doubt that he was more than he appeared to be and "the gods" were more than he gave them credit for.

He felt immensely humbled and embarrassed to think that his petty manipulations had been observed by beings who could not be deceived. *They* knew it was not for them, nor for the good of the land, that he had been labouring so hard.

The four "gods" represented here were different aspects of something so extraordinary and mysterious that no representation, no image, no symbol, could ever hope to get anywhere near the truth of it.

He saw something stirring in the gold mirror before him. It was as though his face was breaking up into long threads and streamers of gold which became fluttering, shimmering feathers. It seemed to him that he saw a golden bird lifting up from the burning surface of the metal, spiralling above them until it was united with the sun. Dazed, he stared until his eyes hurt so much he had to shut them.

He felt Ra-hotep's touch on his arm. It was time to leave.

Had he seen the bird? Had he experienced what he thought he had experienced? Was it the trick of a clever magician – or the gift of one of the beings he had just learned to respect?

Hardly aware of what he was doing, he followed the others in the final ritual and found himself once again in the less sacred rooms of the Temple, surrounded by lesser priests.

He took off his clothes and bathed in the sacred lake.

But later at the home of Ra-hotep, sipping wine in the leafy shade of the High Priest's garden, he began to doubt that any of it had happened. He knew how easy it is to make gullible people see things and hear things. No doubt Ra-hotep, like most priests, had a few tricks up his sleeve. He didn't object to that. Was there not a small hidden chamber above the sanctuary at Ipet-Esut for the priest to hide when the god spoke through oracles? But he had thought he, Hapuseneb, man of the world, was beyond falling for tricks.

The sound of wings beating in the sanctuary of the divine egg and the impression of a golden bird flying out of the golden tip of the pyramid could easily have been produced. He was quite ashamed that he had fallen for it. He was no better than his parents, for whom the ancient myths were more real than their everyday lives. But in the court it was his own face he saw in the mirror – and he saw it with the heightened consciousness of his own soul. For that brief moment he saw beyond all shadows and all shams to the certainty of a great purpose beyond the busy actions of individuals, and he wanted to build temples in the Two Lands not for his own gain and his own power but because he saw something of Hatshepsut's vision for them.

But the habitual thinking of a lifetime was not slow in overriding the momentary splendour of that vision. By the third glass of wine, Hapuseneb was aware of the slender and unusual beauty of a young woman —seemingly a particular protégé of Ra-hotep – and was calculating the advantages of taking her to bed before the night was out.

She in her turn noticed the handsome priest and was well aware of his intentions. He attracted her more than any other man she had met since her arrival in Khemet. He had the hard, strong look of a man of action, and yet he was a priest. That he was much older than her attracted rather then repelled her. She had left behind the young man she really loved in the country of her birth, Britain – a country so far away hardly a person in the Two Lands had ever heard of it – and come to Khemet, the land of her father, to train as a priest. Because in her own country there had been a Temple of the Sun, she had chosen to start her training at the Temple of the Sun in Khemet. But there were great differences between the civilisation she had left and the one she had sought out – and she found herself at first, as a foreigner, looked on as some kind of an illiterate savage compared to the sophisticated people of the City of the Sun.

Gradually she had won their respect, quickly adapting to their ways, and learning her lessons at the Temple with extraordinary rapidity. She was already almost indistinguishable from the locals, although what attracted Hapuseneb to her in the first place was the unusual lilt she gave to the pronunciation of his language, and the slight, haunting impression of foreignness, of mystery, about her.

Inevitably the conversation started with questions about her background, but she did not seem eager to talk about it. She mentioned the long journey over land and over sea, but more she would not say. He could see that she did not come from any of the lands with which he was familiar. Someone had whispered to him that she came from "beyond the west wind", and when he taxed her with it she smiled secretively and said that that was a good enough location for her country.

Her name, it seemed, was Anhai.

"But that is a name from Khemet."

"It is not the name my people called me," she said, "but it has associations for me and so I chose it for my new life here."

"What did your people call you?"

"De-va," she said quietly, her eyes staring into the distance, remembering.

"What does it mean?"

"Shining One."

"It fits you. Why did you not retain it?"

"It does not fit," she said; her voice was suddenly sharp and bitter. "I betrayed it. I have to earn it back."

He looked at her with interest.

92

Ra-hotep joined them at this moment.

"I see you have found our beautiful foreigner," he said.

Hapuseneb looked at him irritably. The young woman's expression changed. From the open sincerity of her last remark, she now seemed guarded.

"She is not only beautiful," Ra-hotep continued, looking pointedly at her, "but she has an extraordinary dedication to her studies. She has no time for anything beyond the work of the Temple."

"Is that true?" Hapuseneb asked, amused. He knew he had not been mistaken in catching a glimpse of a desire almost equal to his own when he first accosted her.

She smiled and met his eyes boldly.

"Up to now," she said pointedly.

Ra-hotep caught something of what underlay their remarks and was annoyed. He himself had tried to interest Anhai in other matters and she had rather brusquely ignored him.

"She needs no distractions," he said sharply. "She is about to face a very severe initiation test. She will need all her wits about her."

Anhai reluctantly drew her eyes away from Hapuseneb's and sighed.

"He is right," she said. "It is time I retired. Tomorrow is an important day for me and I must be ready for it."

"Perhaps you will relax more and sleep better if . . ." She laughed and Ra-hotep scowled.

"Goodbye, First Prophet of Amun," she said lightly – and turned on her heel. Both men watched as she crossed the room. She had a swinging grace, a casual sensuous beauty. It was hard to think of her locked deep in the earth, facing the difficult and searching questions of the Assessors, and the very real dangers that lay in the mysterious region of shadows that was neither of one world nor the other.

But Anhai did not turn him away when he came to her chamber that night, though she knew she should. Once or twice she told him he must leave, but when he obediently turned on his side and began to haul himself out of the bed she pulled him back and clung to him as though her life depended on it. Only in the lovemaking did she forget her dread of the trials she had to face, and the regrets of her past. But as soon as the long and exquisite moment of the climax was over, she was already questioning, wondering and doubting again.

Hapuseneb propped his head up on one elbow and looked down at her quizzically.

"Are you sure the path you have chosen is the best one for you?" he asked, smiling.

"No, I'm not sure," she said sharply, turning away from him. "But I've got to try it."

He ran his fingers gently down her back, and she shivered with pleasure. It was a long time since she had felt what she was feeling this night. The spiritual satisfaction she sought in the stern training of the Temple of Ra that had seemed so desirable just a few hours before, seemed very undesirable now. She knew that Hapuseneb was married with children, but there was no reason why she should not give up the priesthood and be a secondary wife. She would live a soft and easy life in a comfortable home with nothing to worry about but food and lovemaking and sleep. As High Priest of Amun he was rich, and she would live in great luxury. She might not even have to give up the priesthood. There were married priests and priestesses. She could have both worlds. She bit her lip, recognising the temptations that had been her undoing before.

This time it was she who left the bed and stood in the pale shaft of moonlight from the window, looking down at him.

"You must go," she said. "I cannot keep my thoughts straight."

He didn't move at once, but lay watching her.

"Go," she said urgently. "Please!"

Slowly he rose and dressed. She never moved – holding herself in check, she watched him, her body still tingling from his touch, still wanting it, still needing it.

When he had gone, she seized the first object that came to hand and smashed it against the wall.

"I will go through with it," she said aloud. "I will!"

Beneath the Temple of the Sun at Yunu were twelve dark chambers representing the twelve dark hours of the night.

Several potent myths told what the sun did when it had passed through the twelve hours of daylight and was seen no more on earth for another twelve hours. One claimed that the sun was swallowed by Nut, the sky goddess, travelled through her body in darkness and, at dawn, was born from her body, refreshed and renewed. Another said that there were twelve caverns in the Underworld through which the sun passed, finding in each a dark and silent world, all life suspended. For the time of its passage through the individual caverns, light and life returned, and all rejoiced – only to fall back into the motionless dust and darkness as soon as it departed for the next cavern.

The *Book of Caverns* was a well-known text, inscribed on papyrus and carved and painted on the walls of coffins and tombs. It was accepted as a description of the Underworld, of the progress of the deceased as he or she accompanied the sun through the caverns of darkness to emerge at last, after many testing experiences, at the dawn of a new life – providing, of course, that the soul had successfully overcome the dangers and passed the tests.

The initiates of the priesthood of the sun, however, were expected to make the journey while still alive in the earth realm. How could they instruct the dead if they themselves did not know the way?

Anhai had already successfully passed through several grades of training. Her determination, her bright and active mind and the experience of her childhood as the daughter of the High Priest of the Temple of the Sun in that far away, cold, north-western land, pushed her forward perhaps more rapidly than the usual candidate.

She was now to face the journey through the twelve caverns.

The day following her night with Hapuseneb was to be spent in preparation – in last-moment instructions from her tutor, and in fasting and purification ceremonies. She wished she had not met Hapuseneb. Since coming to the Two Lands the discipline of her mind had been good. She had accepted that she could never have the lover she had left behind, and she had immersed herself completely in the work of the Temple. She saw no one to stir her blood and was content with a celibate and cerebral life. But those dark eyes had touched her where she would rather not have been touched, and she found that she was longing to make love again when she should have been thinking only deep and spiritual thoughts.

Her tutor sensed her abstraction and warned her that it could be dangerous to enter the caverns in any state other than complete preparedness. He told her horrific tales of men who had failed to face up to what they found in the caverns and had emerged at the end as gibbering idiots never to recover. He suggested that she put off the journey until she was in a better frame of mind.

"No," she said at once. "No!"

Was it beginning again, the tyranny of the flesh, the betrayal of the sacred by the sacrilegious?

At sunset she entered the first of the dark subterranean chambers. The door was unsealed, and then resealed behind her – this time not with a light and easily broken clay seal, but with molten metal which was poured from a crucible and set solid. There could be no retreat. If she died, no one would know until twelve days and twelve nights had passed and she did not emerge at the other end. She was already hungry, but she had been told that this would pass. In certain caverns there would be bread and beer – of which she must eat and drink sparingly, no more than she needed to keep her body alive.

She listened to the footsteps of her instructor climbing the stone steps outside the first of the caverns and heard the clang of the door at the top. Now she was totally alone, in complete silence, and in a darkness so absolute that blindness might have seemed sight in comparison. Her tutor had warned her about this. He had taken her through the texts a hundred times. She knew what to expect – but she knew also that after this first terror, this initial realisation that she was entombed and that there was no way out except by being reborn, everything would be unexpected. Each of the caverns was a hollow cube of stone, with no feature but a door by which to enter and a door by which to leave. What she would encounter had not been placed there by the priest of Ra, but by the god himself. What she would have to face would not necessarily be what another person would have to face. Each was an individual confrontation, unique to the soul of the person undertaking the journey. There were certain ritual words to be said – a certain loose structure of events – but all this could be abandoned if the gods so chose.

In order to steady her nerves she spoke the words she had learned so carefully:

I have come to thee, Unen-Nefer – thou who dost exist eternally. I have come to thee, gods of the caverns, who guide the souls, who judge, who distinguish truth from falsehood.

The darkness began to lift and it seemed to Anhai she was standing before three luminous figures, two male and one female, each holding the long staff that symbolised their power to transmit energy from one realm to another. Their eyes were cold fire and they did not greet her.

She took a step forward as her tutor had instructed and bowed before them.

"My physical body is mine," she intoned, "my ka body is mine, my ba soul is mine, my akh spirit living in eternity is mine, my shadow, my name, my heart —all are mine. My intelligence, my willpower." She named the many aspects of herself the Egyptians believed carried their own separate energies. "But all are in darkness without grace. Grant me access to Ra's light, O Guardians of the Way."

"Why should we grant you access? Why should we let you pass?"

Their voices were hollow and she knew they had no warmth of feeling towards her. She was a stranger who had to prove herself to strangers.

"Because in my heart of hearts I am humble before thee. I am a true seeker and pilgrim. I would have no life but that which I seek here. I am nothing without the light of my Lord."

Suddenly one of the male beings raised his sacred staff and pointed at her, and she reeled back with the pain that shot through her.

"You lie, and your heart does not know truth. You long for pleasures we cannot provide."

She was crouching on the ground, holding her chest where she had taken the full force of his wrath.

"I confess it," she whispered. "I know that I am not pure of heart – but I seek to be. Without light, how will I ever overcome that which is dark in me? How am I to be reborn with the coming of a new day?"

The female being stepped forward.

"I will guide you, daughter – but you must turn around. That which you must face is behind you."

"I want to go forward, not back!" she cried. Had she not suffered enough by clinging to the past? Had she not suffered enough regret?

But the three advanced on her menacingly and she was driven back. She could feel their stern determination and she turned to run, thinking that perhaps by some miracle she could open the door behind her and escape.

But there was no lock, no handle, no way of opening it from this side. She beat at it, shouting for her tutor, crying that she had made a mistake and he was right: she was not ready for the test. But she knew he could not hear her.

In despair she fell to her knees and lay crumpled against the door, sobbing.

The three figures were close behind her. The second male being lifted his staff and lightly tapped the door. Immediately it fell open and she tumbled through it.

She looked up in delight, thinking that they had taken pity on her, and expected to see the flight of steps she had come down with her tutor. But there were no steps. She seemed to be in another chamber, identical to the last. She looked around, startled, and found that the door had shut behind her and she was alone again.

She felt her way round the walls of the chamber, puzzled that she should find herself in another cavern when she was so sure she had come through the door that led outwards to the stairs.

She spent a long time whimpering and feeling the walls and exploring – still hoping that somehow she would find the way out. There were two doors, as there had been in the first chamber, but neither apparently had any means of being opened.

At last she gave up hope of escape and sat down in the middle of the darkness with her head on her knees. "So be it!" she thought. "If I have to go through with it, the sooner I start the sooner I'll finish."

At that moment she heard a faint sound and lifted her head. Towering above her were three figures – two male and one female as before – but she knew these were not the same beings that she had already encountered.

"I have come," she said, chastened and weary, rising to her feet, "to face what is behind me."

These ones were dressed in the robes of her own land and had faces that seemed familiar and yet were not.

Event by event they took her through her past life before she had come to Khemet. She lived again the agony of her mother's death, knowing that she had been responsible for it. She experienced the pain of losing the man she loved and knowing that he would never be hers again. She felt shame at her involvement with the black magic that had almost brought about the destruction of the great temple of which her mother and father were High Priests. One by one the mistakes of her past and their consequences in the lives of others were shown to her. One by one she learned to face the responsibility for them.

She passed through door after door and no longer knew whether she was progressing or going backwards. In each chamber three figures confronted her: one accusing and punishing her; one teaching and encouraging her; one rewarding her by opening the next door when she finally understood what she was meant to understand.

After she had passed through seven of the caverns in this way, she stood on the threshold of the eighth and knew that, painful as it had been, she had won through. It was as though the ghosts of old guilts had been laid and she was free to start a new life in a new way. She had not expected to have to face her past like that. In coming to Khemet, so far from her own land, she had thought to escape it. Her tutor had not warned her. Perhaps he had not known. Perhaps he had led so blameless a life that there had been no dark shadows for him to exorcise when he entered the caverns. But was there anyone who entered who had not something to exorcise? Surely even he . . .? Perhaps he had known but had not told her because the very unexpectedness of the confrontation had helped its effectiveness.

She took a deep breath. In the eighth chamber there was the first of the food and drink. She no longer felt hungry but she knew she had to eat and drink something if she wanted to survive. And she *did* want to survive!

In the eighth cavern she encountered numerous beings, and each had a question for her about the teachings she had been given in the temple. If she answered with the words she had been given by her tutor, she was chastised. If she answered in her own words and showed that she had understood the meaning behind the teaching, she was accepted and allowed to move on. There were beings who carried others on their shoulders, thus showing the dependence of the human realm upon the spirit realm. There were others who were recumbent, face down, their hands upon their brows, rendering humble homage to the divine. Yet others carried offerings.

In the ninth cavern she faced mummiform beings standing amongst a forest of hissing serpents rearing on the points of their tails. She faced bulls. She faced Anubis, Lord of the Necropolis. She passed through danger and conquered fear of death. She understood the fertility of her body was only a shadow of the fertility of her spirit. Nothing would be lost in death, all gained.

In the tenth cavern she met those who belong to the Light – those who grant light in the midst of darkness. A woman poured pure water from a tall, narrow vase over her head and she knew she was purified. She could feel the renewal beginning, the joy, the glory. She had been opposed, but now she was being accepted. She had opposed, but now she accepted.

In the eleventh cavern she walked among the Watchers and the Summoners, listening in silence to the great invocation of those who were already enlightened.

A herald strode before her, driving away any that would stand in her path. A coiled cobra with a woman's head granted her power, and a standing mummiform figure with a ferocious face reminded her one last time that to reach the light one had to endure the darkness.

At last she was in the twelfth chamber, and she trembled at the beauty of it. It was as though she stood on the shore of a great sea and was waiting for the sunrise, knowing that it would come and that when it came it would draw all things into the light – her soul with it; for she was now "justified", and capable of embracing all the manifestations of the divine – and worshipping with understanding.

She passed the final door and she saw the steps leading upwards and a blaze of light coming down from above.

On her hands and knees she crawled up the stairs, so physically weak that she could hardly stand, but spiritually stronger than she had ever been.

Against the light there was a silhouette. It would be the tutor reaching out his hands to her, rejoicing that she had emerged at last like a butterfly from the cocoon.

She could not see his face, but when he took her in his arms she realised it was Hapuseneb and not her tutor. He had been waiting.

CHAPTER 9

One day Hatshepsut returned to the area of Suan, where she had been so idyllically happy with Senmut on the expedition to choose the granite for her first obelisks, but in very different circumstances. In spite of her desire for peace, an incident in Nubia – the massacre of two high Egyptian officials and the small community that served the lonely outpost – demanded a show of military might. As commander of her soldiers she found herself on Sehel Island, south of Suan, waiting to plunge into battle.

Sehel Island was a place of prayers . . . the threshold of the Unknown. Around it the white waters of the first cataract swirled. Beyond it the civilisation of Egypt gave way to the barbarian lands of Nubia and Kush.

Hatshepsut, in full military dress, stood beside one of her men as he carved the words of her supplication to the gods into a huge rounded boulder. This was her first battle and she was at once deadly afraid and very excited. It was as though her senses were heightened in a way not unlike the way they were in the temple when she was close to her god. Was it the closeness of death that gave this edge to her perceptions? It seemed to her the words were already in the rock and the man with the chisel was uncovering them rather than incising them. She felt, as she had felt several times before, that prayer was a tuning-in to what was already there.

She looked around her. In the flat and dusty bowl at the centre of the island, many of her own men were relaxing before what they knew was going to be a gruelling campaign. The rocky, mountainous regions of Nubia were not easy fighting terrain and, although they were confident that the might of Egypt would prevail, as always, not all of them would return. Some were standing before the various prayer boulders, thinking their own thoughts, saying their own prayers. If they had been able to read, the history of their people would have unfolded for them from the inscriptions on those rocks. Since predynastic times this had been a holy island, and captains and commanders, pharaohs and priests, had set their mark upon it, as alert to danger as a dog eating at a lion's kill. These were not the elaborate boastings of men out of harm's way, looking back on and exaggerating their military exploits. These were cries from the heart of men before they knew what was to become of them in that dark and alien country, the Unknown. A thousand years ago, or five thousand; a thousand years into the future, or five thousand – people had felt and would still feel the need for supernatural help, and pray for it.

Hatshepsut's eye fell on a prayer carved so long ago that an ancient earthquake had split the rock in two pieces – the prayer with it. She knelt beside it, tracing with her finger the little figures scratched on the surface representing a language so archaic she could barely decipher it. "Anhai, daughter of Imhotep . . ." she thought she read, but the rest she lost. She was thrilled with excitement. She must tell Senmut. His almost obsessive interest in the ancient sage was well known to her. She wondered if he had ever heard of a daughter.

As she reached the end of the inscription she began to feel strange – and knew that she had touched something that still carried a living charge of magic. What was the story behind it? The ancient hieroglyphs gave her no clue. Perhaps something that had happened in this place, at this rock, had left a trace there for someone sensitive enough to pick it up. She looked round, and it seemed to her everything had eerily changed. Her soldiers were gone and the island was deserted. Most of the rocks were now bare of inscriptions. And then she saw that she was not alone, after all. It seemed to her that on one of the high boulders at the top of the steepest jumble of rocks, a man stood watching the river below him intently.

He was totally still, as though suspended in time – and as she stared at him he seemed to become momentarily more solid. He was tall and well built, young and strong. He was clad in a pleated white garment of archaic style. Suddenly he raised his arm as though acknowledging or greeting someone below him on the river.

As he did so, he disappeared – but whether he had leapt from the rock or had vanished into thin air, she could not tell.

She ran to the east of the island to see what he had been watching. Hundreds and thousands of flowers were washing up against the shore, carried there by the ripples from a boat that was even now disappearing round the headland. Before it did, however, she caught a glimpse of a young woman standing upright in the boat, dressed in a garment of fine gold, scattering blue cornflowers.

Hatshepsut scrambled over the rocks to see further, but the boat had already passed out of sight, leaving its trail of flowers.

She searched the island, but saw no more of the man or the young woman. Frustrated, she returned to the rock she had been studying, convinced that the vision had sprung from something connected with that rock.

As she reached it and touched it once more, she heard a shout and, spinning round, saw that all the men were ready to move out. She was back in the present.

"I'll be back," she whispered to the silent boulder, and straightened up ready to face her men.

She climbed until she stood high on a boulder above their heads. Against the rock her flesh looked very vulnerable. She wore the military kilt, the dagger at the belt, and on her head the commander's cap. Her thin but wiry arm raised a spear above her head and shook it fiercely. Her voice seemed louder, stronger than a woman's. Hardly a man there even remembered she was a woman. They saw Pharaoh – descendant of a line of conqueror kings. They saw Pharaoh – the punitive right arm of Amun-Ra raised against the rebellious Kush.

Though most of Nubia accepted Egyptian rule because it could not do otherwise, there was an underground swell of hate and disaffection waiting all the time for the moment to break free. Successive pharaohs had mounted raids into the country, determined to quell the slightest sign of rebellion, carrying out their missions usually with the utmost efficiency and ferocity. Many a temple wall was decorated with the boasting description of a Nubian campaign, and the lines of bound and hopeless prisoners en route to a life of slavery was a familiar sight in Egypt. A great deal of Egypt's wealth came from Nubia and it was not about to give it up.

Most years the strong Egyptian administration of the country kept the peace. Pharaoh's intelligence service was a well-organised one, and most uprisings were nipped in the bud before they had a chance to develop.

The murder of an entire administrative unit could not go unpunished, however corrupt and unjust it might or might not have been. Even Hatshepsut believed this, though she was not as ready to leap to war as most of her predecessors had been. She knew her hold on her country was a tenuous one and she must always be seen to be doing the expected thing, the strong thing, the right thing.

She had decided to lead this campaign herself, all the more so because Men-kheper-Ra had laughed so uproariously when she suggested it. Senmut and her advisors had more soberly tried to dissuade her, but she was determined to carry out everything that was expected of a pharaoh – at whatever cost to herself.

When she was quite a young child her father had taken her on his hunting expedition into Nubia. She was therefore familiar with the type of terrain they would have to cover. She was also no stranger to killing. At the age of sixteen she had personally felled three lions on one day in the foothills of the very mountains they were about to scale. As Pharaoh, she had ordered men to death, but never plunged the knife in herself. Now she would see. She did not relish it – but it was expected of her.

She spoke to her men in a clear and ringing voice. If she had any inner misgivings, there was no outward sign of them. The men felt confident that Amun-Ra would see them through.

As she finished speaking they raised a shout of approbation.

She looked down on them and knew they would follow her to the ends of the earth and dare any kind of danger for her. She thrilled to the power and forgot everything else.

Hatshepsut and her troops returned to their boats and carefully bypassed the angry waters of the rapids by using the narrow canal cut centuries before, silted up and cleared by her father during his own campaign against the Nubians. This way they could penetrate quite deeply into the vassal territory, disembarking only just before the second cataract.

The Nubians were, of course, aware of their approach. When Hatshepsut's men scouted the banks, they found whole villages totally deserted. The regular rhythmic sound of the oars, and the drumbeat that accompanied them, the high, harsh commands of the captains, the ominous glint of serried ranks of spears – all this must have been reported by breathless runners from community to community.

Hatshepsut knew exactly where they were going. They did not want to waste time by trying to track down frightened villagers. They were out to punish the area where the insurrection had taken place. They might not get the actual culprits, but they would make certain that such men would not be harboured there again.

When it was time to leave the boats, at first it seemed that all was well, and the Egyptians prepared to march towards the south-east. But they had not gone far when they were ambushed.

Suddenly Hatshepsut found herself plunged into the reality of what she had dreaded in her daydreams the past few weeks. For one terrible moment she wondered what would happen to her if she had no supernatural protection at all, but was only a frail being of flesh and blood vulnerable to sudden and painful extinction. The moment passed, and again she was yelling to her men, urging them on to defeat the enemy of her forefathers, "the vile Kush" of the southern mountains.

The campaign lasted almost a full moon, and during that time Hatshepsut grew weary of men's screams as they met their death; she sickened at the piles of hands that were triumphantly put before her at the end of each day. At night, alone in her tent, she twitched convulsively in her sleep. Was there no end to it? Was there even any point to it? When she could not sleep, her active and agile brain devised a dozen ways grievances could be removed, the administration strengthened, and more troops spared for guarding the isolated outposts. She would see that this did not happen again in *her* reign. She wondered why Men-kheper-Ra, so young and still unbearded, enjoyed soldiering so much.

When she had first tried on the pharaonic beard she had not realised fully to what she was committing herself. With a rueful smile she remembered the scene in vivid detail.

She was alone in her chamber. She'd sent her women away and forbidden them to return until she called them. Even Ma-ya, the cat, had been roughly pushed out. It was not the first time she had wanted to avoid the penetrating gaze of those uncompromising topaz eyes. The silver mirror with the lotus handle would be her only witness.

At first she fumbled and almost called Mut-awa, her most trusted maidservant, to help her tie it on – but set her lips and tried again. She'd watched her father and her husband often enough and was determined to get it right. At last it was in place, and with trembling hands she lifted the double crown.

Now she was ready to look at herself in the mirror.

A stranger stared back at her: a boy's face – too young to grow a natural beard – pretending to be a man. In some ways it made her look younger, more vulnerable. She threw the mirror down in exasperation. She had a woman's form, slight and sometimes fragile-looking. Her face was as soft as a flower, and, if she was truthful, she had made use of this external image a great deal to twist her father – and lesser men – to her whim. But now she wanted the world to see her as she felt herself to be: neither man nor woman, but eternal being, divine king, transcending sexual demarcation, human limitation. One by one she took up the symbols of the Pharaoh and looked again. Was it possible the image that stared back at her from the polished metal was changing, growing, deepening, strengthening? Clothed finally in all the trappings of the royal role, she felt herself complete at last. She straightened her back though the crown was heavy. Her eyes gazed steadily back at her, not the eyes of just a woman or of just a man – but the eyes of Pharaoh overshadowed by the ureaus, the fearsome protective cobra, the eyes of someone who walked with gods and would do so again. This is what she believed herself to be, and the power of this belief transformed her external image. Men would tremble and worship her. Her every command would be obeyed.

A slight frown shadowed her smooth brow, a momentary doubt that she was ready for this.

"I must not doubt, I must not waver," she told herself sternly, for she had seen that in the instant that she doubted herself the image in the mirror lost strength and power.

On her return to Khemet after the war with Nubia, the stone-scribes carved her praises on the great southern pylons at Ipet-Esut.

I am satisfied with my victories. Thou hast placed every rebellious land under my sandals. Every land which thy serpent-diadem has bound, bears gifts. Thou hast strengthened the fear of me: their limbs tremble. I have seized them in victory according to thy command. They are my subjects. They come to me doing obeisance, and all countries bow their heads. Horus of Pure Gold, King of Upper and Lower Egypt, Companion and Daughter of Amun-Ra. Maat-ka-Ra, Hatshepsut.

It was a long time before Hatshepsut again thought about that mysterious boulder on Sehel Island. The war had driven it temporarily out of her mind, and her busy life as sovereign of the Two Lands made it difficult for her to return to it, even in thought.

And then something happened to reawaken her curiosity.

At Serui, where she was building her great mortuary temple, the cult of Hathor had been established for a long time. There was a cave in the cliff that since the most ancient and primitive times had been associated with the womb of the Great Mother and, as the centuries rolled by and religious iconography became more developed and elaborate, a shrine had been set up to Hathor. The Great Mother was first symbolised by the image of a cow, and eventually by a woman with cow's ears. When Hatshepsut began to build her temple, Djeser Djeseru, she incorporated the cave and built a stately and magnificent chapel to Hathor over its entrance. It was in this chapel that Senmut had secretly placed an image of himself, obscured in a dark corner behind a door, in gratitude to Hathor and in memory of the lovemaking he and the Pharaoh had experienced on that journey to choose the obelisks so many years before. On the walls of the courtyard, Hatshepsut had had carved scenes in relief of herself as Pharaoh imbibing milk and spiritual nourishment from the Great Mother.

Hapuseneb asked her if a young protégé of his could be installed as priestess or chantress there, and Hatshepsut agreed.

When Hatshepsut was told her name, it crossed her mind that it was strangely familiar, but she dismissed the twinge of memory as insignificant. The name "Anhai" was not uncommon in the Two Lands. It was only later, when Senmut told her that he had an eerie feeling that the young woman was somehow associated with Imhotep, she suddenly remembered her experience on Sehel Island and the inscription that read: "Anhai, daughter of Imhotep". She told Senmut at once, and together they puzzled about it.

The very next day Senmut accosted Anhai and questioned her about Imhotep. She claimed that she knew nothing more about the great architect and sage than what was common knowledge, but Senmut thought she looked uneasy at the questioning and that she protested her ignorance too much. He established from Hapuseneb that her mother was foreign and she had grown up far from the Two Lands. He enquired about her father and found that he had been a young priest of Ra before he had left Khemet never to return.

Senmut's suspicions grew when he noticed the young woman seemed to be deliberately avoiding him. He reported this to Hatshepsut, and the Pharaoh immediately summoned Anhai to her palace on the west bank at Waset.

Apart from the many large, formal palaces Hatshepsut's husband had built for her and those inherited from her parents and grandparents, Senmut had built her a small private one at the beginning of the green fertile land, beside the long causeway that led from the bay of cliffs where her "Mansion of Millions of Years" was being erected, to the quay opposite Amun's great temple at Ipet-Esut. It was a place she used a lot when she was tired and wanted to get away from matters of state. Not many people were invited to visit her there – and it was more heavily and diligently guarded than any of her other palaces. Although Senmut himself could usually come and go as he pleased, she insisted that she wanted to see Anhai alone, and that he must not intrude.

Anhai was led through the cool corridors of the palace, stepping lightly on the pavement of green-blue tiles. It was as though she were under water in the Great Green Ocean. The walls and floor were all painted with scenes of sea creatures and sea plants, designed by artists who had been on the Punt expedition. Even the light on the ceiling, filtering through narrow slits, seemed to flicker and ripple as it would on water.

There was a pause at the doorway at the end of the corridor, while her guide asked permission for her to enter. She was nervous. She was not sure she had done the right thing to come to the Temple of Hathor at Waset and cut short her training at the Temple of Ra at

Yunu. It was possible Ra-hotep's spies had told him that she had spent the night before her preparation with Hapuseneb, or maybe it was just so obvious he could see it in their eyes, but he had begun to make her feel very uneasy, his sly innuendoes giving way to open suggestions that she should go to bed with him. So she had asked Hapuseneb if he could arrange for her to work at another temple, far from Yunu and Ra-hotep's unwelcome and persistent attention.

On the journey south the landscape had drifted by, richly green and palm-fringed in some places, and precipitous with pink and gold cliffs in others. Hapuseneb had come with her but they had not made love. Without her saying anything, he had understood that some experience in the caverns had changed things between them. They had watched the stars and talked deeply like old friends, and she had withdrawn her arm quickly when his had inadvertently touched hers. Lying on her bunk alone, she had wondered if the disturbance she was suffering by not going to bed with him was not more than if she had.

When they reached Waset, Hapuseneb had almost instantly gone off again on some mission for Pharaoh, and Anhai had been given to the care of the High Priestess of Hathor to train as chantress.

She worked hard because the numerous chants that were used throughout the day and night in the temples were complex. The words were taken from ancient texts and their meaning was sometimes obscure. But whether she understood them or not it was important she used the exact tone and pitch of voice that was expected. A particular resonance of sound could make the invocation of any particular divine influence succeed or fail. Sometimes she despaired of getting it right.

She was startled when Senmut had asked her about Imhotep. It was during one of Hapuseneb's brief visits back to Waset, and she was not in the mood to think of anything but Hapuseneb. She had replied without thinking that she knew nothing more than anyone else. But then certain shadowy memories had begun to stir. When she was a young girl living in a country very different from Khemet, she had had certain dreams, and flashes of what seemed like memories of Khemet from a past life. In that past life she had lived at the court of the great Pharaoh Djoser. Her father, Imhotep, was an honoured man, an architect, philosopher and healer at his court. His name had meant nothing to her when she was a child in that cold northern land, but here in Khemet she never heard his name mentioned without experiencing a twinge of recognition.

Why should Pharaoh, the mighty Hatshepsut Maat-ka-Ra, call her to a private audience? Carefully she straightened the folds of her long skirt and rearranged the Lotus blossom in her hair.

Her guide reappeared and ushered her into the presence of the Pharaoh.

She found herself in a courtyard overflowing with green plants and flowers. Creepers climbed up columns and cascaded down from the roof on all four sides like green and scarlet curtains. There was a pool at the centre.

Hatshepsut was reclining on a couch in the shade of a flowering tamarisk, her limbs oiled and golden, her wig plaited with beads of gold. Golden bands shone on both her arms above the elbows.

"Ah," she said pleasantly, as Anhai bowed to the ground before her. "Rise, child. We have no formalities in this garden."

They were alone. The guide had melted away.

Hesitantly, Anhai rose to her feet and stood looking down on the woman who called herself a king. She saw a woman who reminded her of a lioness resting in the shade, ready to spring at any moment, her eyes as golden as those of a lioness, half-hooded with drowsiness, half dangerously awake. She raised a languorous hand to wave Anhai to a cushion at her feet.

The young woman slid down thankfully. Her legs were trembling.

For a long time there was silence between them, Anhai wondering if she should speak, and if so, what she should say, and Hatshepsut studying the face of the young woman. "So this is Hapuseneb's latest fancy," she thought. She saw that she was beautiful and still very young. She saw also that the young woman had suffered and matured beyond her years. She was no lightweight chantress, the daughter of a privileged family, passing the time before marriage by serving a few years in the temple, as so many of them were these days. She would like to find a place for her in her own entourage – but she did not want her too close to Senmut. He swore that he had interest in the chantress only because of her mysterious connection with Imhotep – and she believed him. Beautiful as the girl was, who would take her to bed if they could have Hatshepsut herself? Nevertheless . . .

"They tell me your name is Anhai." Hatshepsut spoke at last.

"Yes, Majesty," was the almost inaudible reply.

"They tell me also that it was not always your name. Why did you choose it?"

Anhai swallowed nervously. Names were very important to the people of this land. How could she begin to explain the long and complicated reasons for her choice?

The golden eyes bored into hers and she knew she had to tell every detail, no matter how difficult it might be to do so.

She tried to describe the flashes of far memory she had had as a child about a past life in the Khemet of ancient times – during the reign of the Pharaoh Djoser. She described her father and said – very hesitantly, with her eyes fixed on the alabaster pavement – that she believed her name had been Anhai and her father's Imhotep. She knew it sounded far-fetched, but . . .

As soon as she reached this point Hatshepsut sat up straight and swung her legs over the side of the couch so that her feet rested beside Anhai's cushion. Anhai looked up, startled, and saw how agitated the Pharaoh was.

"In what place is it recorded that Imhotep had a daughter Anhai? I know of no such place." Her voice was almost angry, almost accusing.

"I know of none," Anhai said humbly.

"And what makes you think it is Imhotep, the architect of the Pharaoh Djoser, who was your father?"

Anhai was silent for a few moments, and then, in a very low voice, described the dreams and visions she had had – including the building of the first mighty building using blocks of cut stone, the stepped pyramid of Sakkara.

"I have no proof," she almost whispered. "It is just that the visions were so vivid and I knew nothing of such things when I had them. My father in this life found me scratching hieroglyphs on pieces of soft stone – though I had no idea of what they were or what they meant."

Hatshepsut stood up and began to walk up and down beside the pool. She became so occupied with her own memories it was almost as though she had forgotten the presence of the girl.

Anhai rose to her feet too, and stood silently beside the cushion, wondering if she had made a terrible mistake to tell what she had told. But soon she was glad she had, for Hatshepsut stopped her restless striding and stood directly in front of her, looking into her eyes.

"Now," she said, "I'll tell *you* a story." And she told Anhai about her experience on Sehel Island, and how the whole thing had come into prominence now because Senmut kept thinking of Imhotep whenever he looked at her, Anhai.

Anhai felt a cold shiver run down her spine. It was one thing to think you might possibly have a memory of a past life, but another to have it confirmed.

"How strange," she thought, "how strange all the events, so apparently disconnected, that have brought me to this point at this time."

"Have you any memory of Sehel Island?" the Pharaoh was

asking. "Can you explain anything of what I experienced: the inscription on the stone, the man on the rock, the woman in the boat, the flowers?"

"Nothing," Anhai said regretfully. "Nothing."

"Think!" Hatshepsut commanded.

Anhai shook her head. "Majesty," she said quietly, "even the memories I have told you about were fleeting and disjointed – and I have hardly thought about them in years."

"I will send you to Sehel Island," Hatshepsut said decisively. "You must go there and look at the inscription. Perhaps it will set the memories in motion again . . ."

"I cannot promise it will work," Anhai said anxiously. "They have always come to me. I have never sought them out."

"This time you will seek them, and we shall see what happens."

Anhai bowed her head.

While Hatshepsut and Anhai were talking, Senmut, consumed by restless curiosity, returned to his work on Djeser Djeseru. He tried to be patient, but it was not easy.

He watched a huge slab of violet sandstone being hauled across from the ruined temple of Mentuhotep, the eleventh dynasty King who had first built his mortuary temple against the great arc of cliffs. The centuries had tumbled some of the edifice and scattered its stones. The King and his family lay tucked up peacefully enough in their tombs and would not miss the periphery blocks needed for the new and magnificent house Hatshepsut was building to eternity close against his northern shoulder.

The new stone, the white limestone from the south, was being brought by barge along the canal from the river. Day after day the oxen patiently toiled along the towpath, dragging the heavy barges as near as they could come to the site. This day as any other day the mountain rang with the sound of hammers and the shouting of the leaders of the work gangs. To the north he could hear some of the groups singing rhythmically as they inched the blocks into place.

Though the temple was still under construction, the Hathor chapel on the second terrace and the sanctuary of Amun-Ra on the third were already in use. The great cedar doors, bound with copper and covered with gold images and ciphers, that separated the most sacred sanctuary area from the noise and dust of the workmen and the gaze of the unpurified, were shut firm.

On both granite doorjambs stood an image of Hatshepsut with sceptre and mace and right arm raised in gesture of greeting and respect. On the one side she wore the crown of Upper Khemet, and on the other side the crown of Lower Khemet. Above her the standard of her ka proclaimed her eternal nature and the timelessness of her love for her god. On the lintel were two images of her kneeling, offering wine to Amun, with her royal stepson-nephew behind her.

On other thick blocks the image of Hatshepsut knelt again, offering to the god in his sanctuary, while beneath her image the words of Djehuti were inscribed:

> *Amun-Ra, the Lord of the Thrones of the Two Lands, when*
> *thou restest in thy building where thy beauties are*
> *worshipped, give Hatshepsut Maat-ka-Ra life, duration and*
> *happiness. She has made for thee this building, fine, very*
> *great, pure and lasting . . .*

The funerary chambers for her father and herself to the south of the Holy of Holies were not yet completed, but on the north side, against the cliff wall, the open chapel to the sun god was frequently used. Hatshepsut had been known to officiate there as priest. Although she believed the great sun god was but one of the many manifestations of Amun, the Hidden One, sometimes it was easier to address them in their separate aspects.

On the great arched lintel inside the sanctuary of Amun-Ra, Hatshepsut and the young prince Men-kheper-Ra knelt before the god enthroned, Hatshepsut on the left offering wine, and Men-kheper-Ra on the right, cakes. Behind them stood their spirit counterparts, honouring the Hidden One throughout eternity. Above them hovered two shimmering, powerful images of the winged sun protected by the royal cobras – the whole scene set among the mysterious and distant stars.

Inside the barrel-vaulted sanctuary itself, Hatshepsut's craftsmen had surpassed themselves. The statue of Amun-Ra waited and watched, a golden image with eyes of lapis lazuli, tall double plumes stiff above his head – the shell into which the spirit of the great god could move at any time.

All around the walls just above floor level, Hatshepsut had insisted that a garden be carved in relief – the image of the garden she had planted on the lower terrace of her temple, but this one to last for all eternity.

Senmut remembered the day they planted the living trees from Punt . . . Hatshepsut was in the garden from dawn to dusk, choosing the site for each planting carefully. Senmut could see she was in one of her moods of heightened awareness, a mood in which she felt she was in direct communication with her god, and he kept in the background, only making sure that everyone jumped to her commands even more quickly than usual.

She went into the inmost sanctuary of her temple before first light, and there in the god's chamber carved into the living mountain, by flickering lamplight she asked for his guidance, and received it.

She knew precisely where each tree pit should be dug and how much rich river silt should be poured into it. She was constantly on the move, making sure that each was prepared exactly as she wanted. When the first was ready she stopped work on all the others so that the gardeners could come and stand in a great circle surrounding those who were manoeuvring the tree into place. Although Senmut had made sure the trees that they brought were young and sturdy and that their roots were well-protected in bags of damp earth during the journey, some were beginning to wilt. Hatshepsut prayed over each one of them and particularly over the ones that seemed to be feeling the strain of the uprooting most. She was determined not to lose a single one. Each tree had four gardeners to carry it to its place. There a rhythmic chanting accompanied the unbinding of its roots and the heaving of the great trunk upwards so that it could slide into the pit. Before the rich silt was finally trampled down, Hatshepsut knelt on the earth beside it, and with her own small hands placed a parcel of amulets against the trunk root, speaking words from an ancient spell prayer to ensure that it would grow strong and tall and yield rich incense to her lord. She then covered the amulets with earth, rose and stood back with shining eyes to watch the final buckets of soil being shaken on. The first drops were from a crystal vase of sacred water poured as a libation by the Pharaoh-Priest, "the god's wife", Hatshepsut Maat-ka-Ra. Only after all these things were done was the command given that work should recommence on the other trees. She stood back beside Senmut, her head lifted. He could see by the expression on her face that she was seeing the tree in its full glory, deeply rooted and thriving, and not as it was now, still weak and drooping from the shock of transplantation.

When all the magical and mystical ceremonies were done, his was the practical task of getting water to the garden. There were already two ornamental pools with fish and ducks and water lilies on either side of the entrance to the ramp that led to the second terrace. To assure that these were always filled with water, he had devised an ingenious series of underground earthenware channels leading from the main irrigation ditch that reached back to the nearest canal and ultimately to the river. To have brought water so far into the desert was an achievement of which Senmut could be particularly proud. If his lady wanted a garden in the desert, she would have a garden in the desert! Men were stationed at intervals along the whole length of the ditch and the canal with buckets and pulleys to raise the water to a higher level. From the second terrace could be seen the green cultivated fields of the flood plain beside the river, ending abruptly as the rust-gold sand of the dead land took over. Men could be seen working on the double row of sphinxes that lined the avenue to the east shimmering in the heat haze, and behind them the thin dark ridges of the newly dug canal banks. In time reeds would grow there and the green land would encroach a little further towards the stark, steep cliffs – but for the moment every precious drop was hard won and needed for the garden.

At the end of the day of planting, Hatshepsut was exhausted – but too tired to sleep. She sent for Senmut and they talked deep into the night. "Was there ever such a temple since the world first began?" she demanded.

"Never," he assured her, smiling, thinking how eager she was to do everything better than anyone else just to prove that she had a right to be where she was. He was glad of her ambition, for it gave him an opportunity to stretch his own wings. Who else had come from such unpromising beginnings and, since the great Imhotep, achieved so much? The close and trusted confidant of a pharaoh was no ordinary thing to be. A chance to realise a dream in stone, a temple that would last and bear witness to his genius for ever, was a rare and marvellous opportunity . . .

But now Senmut prowled the site, growling at his workmen, only occasionally praising what he saw, his mind puzzling about the connection the young woman, Anhai, had with his great hero, Imhotep – wondering what Hatshepsut was saying to her, and what she was saying to Hatshepsut.

CHAPTER 10

Senmut made sure he had to travel south to the quarries at Suan before the month was out, and with him he took Anhai and Hatshepsut's daughter, Neferure.

If Anhai had ever had any doubts that her strange visionary experiences of this land when she was living in her own country were true memories, they were gone now. She "remembered" sailing this great river before. She "remembered" watching these cliffs slide past, these islands emerge. When they reached the Suan area, the huge boulders that rose hunched from the waters like the backs of great grey elephants were very familiar to her.

Senmut, watching her face as they reached Sehel Island, caught the fleeting expression of excited recognition before her feelings of puzzlement and self-doubt took over.

"Have you been here before?" he asked quickly.

"Yes. No . . . I don't know . . ." She fought to pull back an incident lurking at the very rim of her memory like the shadowy form of something just out of range of the eye.

Neferure wondered why she had been brought to this desolate place. She suspected her mother had sent her along as a kind of chaperone for Anhai and Senmut. Or maybe it was because she had been growing too close to one of her mother's handsome captains, Amenemheb. No one was sure quite what Hatshepsut had in mind for her daughter. The most logical and traditional thing would be to marry her to Men-kheper-Ra so that they could rule as Pharaoh and Great Royal Wife, the royal bloodline secure, after Hatshepsut's death. But Hatshepsut never did the expected and traditional thing. She had kept her daughter unmarried long past the royal marriage age. Some thought she was grooming her to rule alone as she herself ruled – but if this was the case, Hatshepsut did not know as much as she should about her daughter. Neferure would never make a good pharaoh. But, like her grandmother, Aah-mes, she would make a good queen. Some feared Hatshepsut would marry her to a powerful commoner, one of her favourites. Bets were taken on whether it would be Senmut or Hapuseneb. But no one entertained the possibility that Hatshepsut would let her daughter marry, for love, a mate of her own choosing. Neferure herself did not expect it, and when she first noticed Amenemheb in Men-kheper-Ra's company she tried to talk herself out of the pounding of her heart and the quick flush that came to her cheeks whenever he looked at her.

He in his turn was not slow to notice the effect he was having on the young princess, and discretely questioned Men-kheper-Ra about the prince's own feelings towards her and if he thought it likely she would one day be his Great Royal Wife. Menk-heper-Ra replied scornfully that he found her pretty but boring, and that he supposed he would have to marry her one day.

Amenemheb knew that if he was to make anything of a relationship with Neferure it would have to be secret. He contrived to meet her in the palace garden one day and hint that he loved her – but added that he knew a liaison was impossible. He then left it up to her to work out what could be done about it. If she married Men-kheper-Ra as a political act, but really loved him, Amenemheb, there would be no end to the advantages he could milk from the situation. But Men-kheper-Ra must first be installed as sole Pharaoh.

Neferure was in turmoil. Up to now she had loved only Senmut and had thought that no future would make her happier than if she were given to him in marriage, old as he was. But Amenemheb was young. His dark and flashing eyes promised her things she had not even dreamed of with Senmut. She loved her mentor, but now she realised it wasn't the love of the body, and if she married him her body would never know satisfaction.

Senmut had been hinting that he would ask her mother for her, and she had led him to believe that she would be very happy with the arrangement. And now? How could she break his heart? She thought it was for love of her he wanted the marriage not because he sought to reinforce his already considerable power in the Two Lands. A few months ago she would have been excited and delighted about this trip. But now it put her in an awkward position. When Senmut took her arm in the old familiar way to point out a kingfisher or heron, she moved away from him and tried to show him by such little movements that things had changed between them.

Senmut noticed nothing. All his thoughts were on the possibility of Anhai being Imhotep's daughter.

Sages taught that there were several different destinations for the traveller after death. Some were almost immediately united with the divine in the highest realms. Others had further journeying to do, further tests and trials, further choices and decisions in a realm that was neither earth nor heaven. Only after passing through these could they progress onward and upward. If they failed these tests and trials, they ceased to exist as separate individuals and fell back into the

Void. But some sages taught another destination. The traveller returned to earth, not as a disembodied ka to fly in and out of the tomb, but as an apparently totally new person in a different time and place, born in bodily form of man and woman in the normal way, but carrying the soul of someone who had died and lived before. This was called "reincarnation", and it intrigued Senmut more than any of the other possibilities.

He even wondered if he might be the reborn soul of Imhotep himself, and that was why in Punt, when he had tried to raise the sage's spirit form, he could not do so. But if he was, it disappointed and frustrated him that he could remember nothing. What was the point of being reborn, if you didn't carry memories over from the past life to help you in this? It was true he had risen swiftly and unexpectedly to a powerful position, and it was not only because Hatshepsut desired him. He had always felt that "someone" was helping him, perhaps the god Djehuti, with whom both he and Imhotep had a particular rapport. But might not the alternative explanation be that deep inside he was somehow still carrying Imhotep's knowledge, though on the surface he had apparently forgotten it?

One thing bothered him with this theory. Imhotep was obviously an enlightened being, judging by his achievements on the earth plane at the time of King Djoser – so why had he not ascended at once at death to the higher realms?

"Perhaps," Hatshepsut had suggested when they discussed it, "it is because Imhotep chose to come back to earth, believing he still had something left to do here."

Senmut hoped that through Anhai he would be able to experience a proper recall of his past life as Imhotep. He had not wanted to bring Neferure, but Hatshepsut had insisted. He had not broached the subject of their marriage yet, and he was sure it was a twinge of jealous anxiety about the beautiful Anhai that made Hatshepsut send her daughter, her deputy, her eyes, to watch over them. She knew Neferure's hero worship was so strong she would never let Senmut out of her sight and allow him to be alone with the foreigner.

Impatiently he got through the work he had to do at the granite quarries in connection with the second two obelisks Hatshepsut had requested, and hurried the two young women further south to the island where Hatshepsut had seen the inscription. He was disappointed, but not surprised, that Anhai had no more than a twinge of recognition when she first saw the place. He hoped that her memory would fully return when she saw the inscription.

It was hot and Neferure was grumbling at the flies and burning sand underfoot. She couldn't understand why she was expected to walk like a commoner and not be carried in a chair like the princess she was. Senmut insisted on their coming alone to the island. She wished she had not come. The joy of being with Senmut was no longer so intense. He even seemed less interested in her than before. It was not that Anhai attracted him. Neferure could detect no sexual energy between them, but the foreigner absorbed all his attention. He scarcely took his eyes off her face.

Neferure could not see the point of the expedition. As far as she was concerned, whatever happened after death was best dealt with then. She had no wish to know who she had been before or who she would be in the future. The present was quite enough for her to cope with. She dreaded the thought of all those trials she would have to go through in the Other World, and she would rather hear nothing about them.

Look at him, she thought, bounding along like a young buck! For the first time in her life Neferure saw Senmut as ageing, as thickset, as not as handsome as he should be. Amenemheb was so firm and strong and beautiful! Ah, but so unobtainable! Her mother might conceivably consent to her marriage with Senmut instead of to Men-kheper-Ra for political reasons, but never to Amenemheb. She sought out a shady patch beneath a cliff of piled boulders and settled down to wait for the others. She had had quite enough discomfort for one day, and had some dreaming to do.

It took them some time to find the right boulder, in spite of Hatshepsut's instructions.

It was Anhai who found it at last, and Senmut took this as a good sign. At first he watched her closely as she stood staring down at the inscription, and then he forgot her as he too gazed at it. He wanted so badly to experience something, to remember something. But nothing happened. The hot sun blazed off the surface of the stone, and the ancient inscription was so faint it was almost impossible to see. "Anhai, daughter of Imhotep . . ." was there as Hatshepsut had said it would be, but there was something else there that Hatshepsut had not been able to read. Perhaps all those years with the archaic languages of the early dynasties in the archives at the Temple of Ptah at Men-nefer would help him now. Senmut frowned as he stared at the signs, moving his head so that the angle of light would change and give a better image. He thought he deciphered the words "for safe return". This was not so very different from what was inscribed on the other rocks on this frontier island, for nearly everyone who stopped here long enough to carve a prayer was on a dangerous journey and wanted a safe return. He was disappointed – until he looked up and saw that Anhai's eyes were streaming with tears. Something was stirring at last. If only he could feel it too.

"What is it?" he urged. "Speak to me. Tell me everything you are feeling. Don't be afraid. Speak."

She sank to the ground and sat beside the boulder with her arms around her knees and her head sunk on her arms, sobbing and rocking like a very young child.

"What do you remember?" Senmut insisted impatiently. He was deadly afraid of driving the memory away by intruding – but he had to know!

"It is just sorrow I feel," she said. "The sorrow of parting . . ."

Senmut frowned. He had heard the story of how she had left the Two Lands in the ancient days with her lover. But he could not see that she would have left from this place. It was far, far from the Great Green Ocean she must have sailed upon to reach that distant and alien land.

She shook her head. "I didn't carve these words," she said quietly, her weeping done. "It is my father's pain I am feeling here."

Imhotep himself! Senmut put his hand on the images and tried to will the memory of carving them into his mind. Perhaps he, as Imhotep, had come south to the granite quarries, as he himself frequently did, as architect and supervisor of Hatshepsut's building projects. Perhaps he, as Imhotep, had come to this holy island to weave a spell to draw Anhai back. Senmut shivered with excitement. If Imhotep, master of mystery and magic, had arranged to draw her back to this spot, he would certainly have arranged to be present at the same time. Senmut felt more convinced than ever that he was the great man himself, reborn.

But what was this? Anhai had risen and was looking at someone over his shoulder, standing beside him. He spun round, but could see no one.

Why? Why? He who wanted so much to have transcendental experiences and had trained and prepared himself for years was never granted them. Hatshepsut, now Anhai, seemed to have them with extraordinary ease, while he, with all his intellect, his creative talent, his arcane knowledge, could never make them happen.

She had moved closer to where she had apparently seen someone. Her back was to him and he could not see her face. It seemed to him a long time passed as he waited impatiently for her to tell him what was happening. But he held himself in check and made no move and said no word.

At last she turned to him, and her face was transfigured with joy.

"I spoke with my father," she said in a low and awed voice.

"Imhotep?"

"Yes," she whispered.

"What did he say?" Senmut tried to keep the disappointment out of his voice. He knew now he could not have been Imhotep. Imhotep had materialised separate from himself. He felt ashamed that he had tried to claim identity with a being who was more of a god than a man.

She smiled sympathetically, looking into his eyes.

"He sent greetings to you," she said. "He thanked you for carving this rock for him. He thanked you for your loyalty to him all these years."

"Loyalty?" Senmut sounded dazed.

"It seems you were a favourite apprentice of his. You worked on many building projects with him; he entrusted you and the woman you loved with the casting of this spell to bring me back. You were the young man Hatshepsut saw in her vision, and your beloved was the young girl in the boat casting flowers around the island to seal the spell so that it couldn't be taken up and misused by someone else. It was a gentle spell – a calling of the heart. I was not compelled to come, but I came."

Anhai turned her head and looked across the hot sand to where Neferure was resting in the shade.

"The Princess Neferure was your beloved in that ancient life."

Senmut was silent. He was not surprised. There had always been something between them since he first held her in his arms as a young infant, and Hatshepsut, seeing the tenderness of his expression, had appointed him her guardian and tutor. How strange this play within a play . . . this constant ebb and flow of time, the same shells rattling on the beach as each breaker washed them in again . . .

He knew Anhai was telling him the truth. His old restless desire to be Imhotep was gone. He knew who he was and he knew who he had been – and he was content. Many people claimed to have been great and famous people because they remembered glimmerings of the time in which such heroes and heroines had lived. Would not the ordinary people who now lived in Hatshepsut's Khemet remember the great events of her reign more readily than the small and mundane events of their own lives?

"Has he gone?" Senmut cried. "There were so many things I wanted to ask him!"

Anhai looked different somehow. Older. Wiser.

"Now we have made the contact, we will not lose it," she said confidently.

"Will it be only in this place?"

"I'm not sure."

She didn't finish. Neferure came running towards them.

"I had the most extraordinary experience," she cried. "I am sure I wasn't asleep, and yet suddenly it seemed as though the river was full of flowers."

Senmut and Anhai looked at each other and smiled. But neither felt that it would be right to tell Neferure what had occurred. Somehow – though she had been a part of the original event – they both felt she would not now understand.

CHAPTER 11

Men-kheper-Ra spent very little time in the south at Waset. He found his aunt-stepmother Hatshepsut to be a dangerous and difficult woman. He never knew where he was with her. One moment she treated him like a close and beloved relative, and another like a suspected traitor; one moment like a man, and another like a child. Sometimes he thought of her as an inspired visionary, and at others as a ruthless manipulator of men's lives. His friend Amenemheb believed that the visions were self-induced because of her overweening ambition.

"Anyone can say they have spoken with the god," the cynical young man said. "She is always alone when it happens. Either she has been supping on the milk of the sycamore fig and genuinely believes that her hallucinations are religious verities, or she quite deliberately chooses to fake and lie." Amenemheb was taking his life in his hands speaking about the Pharaoh as he did, but he was relying on his long and close friendship. He was the son of one of the high nobles who had served Hatshepsut's husband. At the moment, Men-kheper-Ra seemed powerless to assert his rights, but it would not always be so, and when he was Pharaoh in real practical terms, Amenemheb was determined to be there at his right hand.

Men-kheper-Ra had several close friends who were certain that one day Hatshepsut would either relinquish power under pressure from strong nobles on the side of her stepson-nephew – or would be eliminated. It was not easy to assassinate a pharaoh, but it was possible.

It seemed to his ambitious friends, and his equally ambitious mother, Men-kheper-Ra was too sanguine about the flagrant usurpation of his rights by Hatshepsut. Perhaps he had been too young to rule when his father died, but he was older now – a strong and vigorous soldier, a virile and likeable young man. If he lacked anything it was his patience with diplomacy and the slow machinations of intrigue. If he could have stormed the palace he would have done it. But to manoeuvre secretly, to spy on people, to bribe people, to find his own way among a swamp of shifting and uncertain loyalties – that was not his style.

When he was fourteen a bid to place him fair and square on the throne had almost succeeded . . .

It took place in the great hall of cedar columns the architect Ineni had erected for his grandfather at the Temple of Amun in Ipet-Esut. Behind the huge wooden doorway inscribed in gold: *Amun, mighty in strength,* with its leaf of Asiatic copper on which the shadow of Min was modelled in gold, one of the major ceremonies of the sacred year was in progress. Hatshepsut had made her private obeisance and sacrifice to the god in the inner sanctuary, and he was now being carried in procession in his golden boat around the temple – torches flickering, chanters chanting, incense burning.

The priest who had planned this dramatic challenge to her sovereignty had made sure that Men-kheper-Ra was present this day in his capacity as trainee "god's servant".

All was going as usual when suddenly the statue of Amun and his boat began to shake violently and then move wildly about the hall as though seeking something. Apparently the four priests carrying it were unable to control it.

It passed Hatshepsut, who was standing in her golden robes with the blue crown on her head, and came to rest at last before the young prince, Men-kheper-Ra. The implication was that Men-kheper-Ra was the rightful king.

Those who were in on the trick fell down at once to worship him, while those who were not, looked uneasily from Hatshepsut to her nephew, not knowing whom it would be most advantageous to support.

In the confusion, those who had planned the incident might well have won the day – had Men-kheper-Ra not hesitated and Hatshepsut not acted so decisively.

In an instant she stepped forward and confronted the god.

"Tell me, my father," she said haughtily, "am I not Hatshepsut Khenemet-Amun, she who unites herself with Amun, the first of the nobles? King of the North and South, Maat-ka-Ra, Son of the Sun, the Female Horus of Pure Gold, Bestower of Years, Goddess of Risings, Conqueror of Lands, Vivifier of Hearts, Chief Spouse of Amun, the Mighty One? Am I not," she continued, "The Lord of East and West, the daughter of thy heart whom thou lovest before all others?"

As her titles rolled through the great hall in a voice of authority, those who supported her were strengthened by the sheer power of her conviction that she was indeed Pharaoh, the daughter of Amun-Ra, the Chosen One. Men-kheper-Ra hung his head, and the priests who had tried to shift the balance of power in his favour were lost.

Silently supporters of Hatshepsut moved forward and took the golden barque from them, and the whole procession moved on its way as though nothing had happened. It passed through the door called "Amun, mighty in strength" and through the pylon of gleaming white stone, beneath the fluttering flags and between the granite obelisks with the golden tips erected by Hatshepsut's father and between which the sun was seen to rise each morning. It wound out through the gardens of the temple, past the sacred lake and down the causeway to the river. The people crowding the river bank to catch a glimpse of the procession as Amun left to visit his consort Mut at the southern temple had no idea that a struggle for power had just been fought, and Hatshepsut's mind, as she walked so sedately and reverently beside the barque, was seething with plans to prevent any such thing ever happening again.

But when Men-kheper-Ra finally came to the throne he would have his own version of the event carved on the walls of the temple, and this time there would be another ending to the story.

It was on one of his military training exercises in the desert that Men-kheper-Ra finally decided to accept what help he could from his friends and take back what was rightfully his.

They had received intelligence that tribute had not been coming in as it should from an area his grandfather had conquered in the east, beyond the Bitter Lakes, and he and his friends, hot and excited from a practice chariot charge, were in the mood to test themselves on a real battlefield. But Pharaoh had said she would deal with the situation diplomatically, and no troops need be sent to the area.

"If you were King," the young captain Amenemheb said angrily, "no one would dare hold back tribute. Foreigners jeer at us for having a woman in charge. No other country would tolerate such a thing."

Men-kheper-Ra, equally annoyed, rubbed down his horse more roughly than he intended, and the beast trampled nervously and whinnied.

"Sh-sh-ssh," he hushed, and moderated his action. The horse calmed down.

He had always known that the time would come when he would take back the throne. He had procrastinated so long partly because he was enjoying the vigorous life of a soldier and the escape from what he regarded as imprisoning protocol and boring state affairs, and partly because Hatshepsut's spies had him and his supporters boxed in so well they couldn't make a move without her being instantly aware of it and making a countermove.

The two young men handed their horses over to the grooms, and, on Amenemheb's suggestion strolled away from the practice ground towards the low hill that overlooked it. They climbed silently and stood for a while at the top. They could see the straight tracks the chariot wheels had made in the sand, and the others of their company gathering at the long, low building to the east where there would be food and beer for the young men who had been working at the exercises since sunup.

They both knew they could not reveal what was in their minds in the presence of anyone else. These were Hatshepsut's soldiers, though the young prince, Men-kheper-Ra, was ostensibly their commander. He worked hard, drank hard and played hard – and his rapport with his men was exceptional.

"If you asked them" – Amenemheb spoke first – quietly – "you know they would follow you."

Men-kheper-Ra nodded, but said nothing. He could feel it again, that feeling he hated, a kind of rising desperation to be a real king and to have ultimate power. He had it from time to time, but it always went away when he said to himself "one day" . . . "just a little longer" . . . It was so much more comfortable to stay as he was. He had seen Hatshepsut exhausted from long hours spent poring over despatches, records and texts. He could read, but he felt he had better ways to spend his time. He would enjoy having power over people's lives, but he would not enjoy the meticulous attention to detail that Hatshepsut seemed to consider essential for a ruler.

Sometimes, impatiently, he felt he would have made a better pharaoh than she; but at others, he wondered. He often did things impetuously that afterwards he regretted. She always seemed to know exactly what she was doing, and why.

"If you leave it too long," Amenemheb continued, "the empire will be lost. Your aunt does not care to maintain your father's frontiers."

"She fought well in Nubia," Men-kheper-Ra said hesitantly.

"Yes, she did," Amenemheb agreed grudgingly. "But one battle is not enough. That was years ago. If a show of force is not constantly maintained, the bright edge of power blunts like an old sword."

Men-kheper-Ra picked up a small chip of rock and flung it with all his might into the sky. They both watched it as it spun against the blue and started to fall in the direction of Hatshepsut's distant palace. It would not reach it, of course, because the building was miles away shimmering in the heat haze – but for a moment everything seemed possible.

"A few of us would like to meet to talk with you," Amenemheb said.

"Who? Who would like to meet and talk with me?" Men-kheper-Ra asked tersely. He felt that this time – this time he was ready.

There had been other times, other suggestions, other plots. Some good men had mysteriously disappeared, and the talking had stopped. But this time – this time he felt it would be different.

Amenemheb paused. How far should he go? Had he already gone too far?

Men-kheper-Ra turned and looked at him intently. Amenemheb swallowed. Had he misjudged the moment?

"Set the meeting," the prince said "I'll be there."

"It should be away from here."

"Of course."

"I suggest Yunu. The priests of Ra would give us protection. I hear they are not pleased to take second place to Amun."

"I don't want to get involved in temple politics. I need the priests of Amun on my side."

"We will not get involved. It is just a place. A safe place."

"To talk?"

"To talk."

"No more than that?"

"No more than that."

"Then arrange it."

Amenemheb bowed his head. Usually the two young men were full of jokes and jibes. They were good friends, and a soldier's camaraderie bound them together. But they both knew that something had changed between them. They had taken a step from which there would be no going back. Amenemheb had staked his future on a throw, and he would win either great power in the land – or death.

Ra-hotep welcomed the meeting Amenemheb suggested. As far as he was concerned, Hatshepsut was obsessed by Amun and was set to destroy the age-old balance of the hegemony of the gods.

Ra-hotep did not believe any more than any other thinking priest did that the gods were up there in the sky with jackal and ibis and falcon heads, wearing feathered crowns and sun disks . . . He knew the images of the gods were only signposts pointing beyond themselves to a deeper, intangible and inexpressible reality. He knew the danger of having anthropomorphic images often led to the image being mistaken for the reality. But he knew that in not having images there was also a danger – the danger of forgetting that there *was* a deeper, intangible and inexpressible reality behind the one people could see and touch.

As guardians and interpreters of these images, Ra-hotep and his colleagues enjoyed a privileged and a very comfortable position, particularly as the sun image had always been of primary importance. Anything that threatened that position worried him. He resented that more wealth was going to the temples of Amun-Ra these days than was coming to the temples of Ra alone – and he feared even more of his privileges might be whittled away in the future by Hatshepsut. "That a woman should choose to wear a beard and dress like a man is against nature," he said. "And when you start defying natural law, you start a process that can only lead to chaos."

Amenemheb's uncle was a priest of Ra, and it was he who brought the young captain to Ra-hotep to request permission for the meeting. Nothing was said about its purpose – but Ra-hotep was no fool.

They knew it was impossible for Men-kheper-Ra to go anywhere without Hatshepsut knowing of his movements. There was no open hostility between the two of them, but she kept a close watch on him just the same.

It was agreed that Men-kheper-Ra should make no secret of his visit. He asked his step-mother if he could be the royal representative this year at the great Festival of Sopdt, that was soon to take place.

The festival celebrated the heliacal rising of the brightest star in the heavens. Each year when it rose at the same time as the sun, the life-giving floods came to the Two Lands. Then it was indeed Khemet, the Black Land, for when the floods subsided, they left behind them the rich black alluvial mud that made the country the grain-house of the world.

The festival was a very important one, and there was not a temple in the land that did not greet the star at this time, that did not praise it and sacrifice to it. The major centre had always been the Temple of the Sun at Yunu, for it was the combination of the two divine beings, Ra and Sopdt, that triggered the phenomenon that sustained the earth. The Pharaoh almost invariably took the major role in the ceremony.

But this year Hatshepsut had her reasons for wanting to stay where she was at Waset, and agreed for once that Men-kheper-Ra should take her place at Yunu.

Hatshepsut was pregnant with Senmut's child. She and her physician knew it, and her two most trusted women, but no one else – not even Senmut.

When she first discovered it she had been very excited, but very soon the difficulties of the situation began to present themselves.

That she felt sick almost continually was the least of her worries. She believed that her grip on the Two Lands would easily slip away if she appeared as anything less than the great male-female divine being she had built herself up to be. She also feared that Senmut might acquire more power than she was prepared to grant him if he was known to be the father of her child, and that the other great nobles on whose support she relied might be jealous and swing against her. Men-kheper-Ra's supporters would certainly fear that Senmut would be made consort, and act immediately to unseat her.

Hatshepsut decided to abort the child. Her trusted physician-priest took the readings of the heavens that were necessary for such a hazardous and far-reaching act, and told her that for maximum protection she should do it at dawn on the day of the Festival of Sopdt.

"As Sopdt pulls the Nile floods into the Two Lands, so will it wash out what is in your womb."

The physician and Hatshepsut never mentioned the child in her womb, but spoke always as though it was some unnatural "thing" that had got in there by mistake.

She could not afford to allow her people to know what was happening, nor even to know that she was ill. Having taken the throne by force of personality and held it in the same way, she had always to appear strong, beautiful and capable. She had to make a public appearance at the festival, so the deed must be done before the rising – in spite of what the physician-priest had told her. She would have to accept the consequences.

She arranged with the physician and the two women that they should be with her in her private chambers in the palace closest to the temple of Ipet-Esut, where the nearest ceremony was to be. She would have preferred to be in her favourite palace on the west bank, but it was too far away. She was to be carried to the temple on a golden chair immediately the abortion was done. She would stand to greet the great star in its rising between the golden tipped obelisks when it was time to do so, as though nothing had happened.

The physician warned her that the pain would be extreme and that she would be bleeding.

"I do not think, Majesty, that you will be able to carry out the ritual."

"Your task is to do what I have asked of you, and mine is to rule this land," she said coldly. "I do not interfere in your work. Do not interfere in mine."

He and the two women looked at each other but said no more.

They made the preparations carefully. They performed the operation.

Hatshepsut did not cry out once, but her face was ash-white and very drawn when they came to paint on her cosmetics for the ceremony.

Normally she would wear male attire for such a ceremony – but this time the only concession she made to what had just happened to her was to wear female garb. When she stood between the great obelisks and raised her arms, layer after layer of filmy linen hid her body. Her face, painted like a mask, showed no sign of pain. Her voice as she led the chant of praise did not waver.

Senmut was celebrating the festival at Suan in the south, where the first signs of the flood would appear. The people believed that there was a huge hole somewhere in that area from which the waters welled up at the command of Sopdt. Priests announced when the first fractional increase in river height was recorded, and then thousands of people would shout and dance for joy. Their livelihood depended on the yearly rising and they were ready with praise for their Pharaoh, who so ruled with Maat that the cosmic order was beautifully maintained.

Senmut, Anhai and Neferure watched the rising of Sopdt and the Sun together – Pharaoh's daughter leading the ritual chant in the south as her mother did at Ipet-Esut, and her cousin-step-brother did at Yunu.

Anhai said her own prayers to the divinity of her childhood, wondering if ceremonies were going on at this very moment in the Temple of the Sun at home —and wondering about her present-life father and if his heart had healed since the death of her mother, Kyra.

So much had happened since she had come to his ancestral land. What would he say if she told him she had spoken with Imhotep, who was as great a hero to him as he was to Senmut? What did she feel about it herself? She had always known that she had lived millennia before in this land. She had even known that Imhotep had been her father – but until that moment on Sehel Island she had not known the significance of it. She had not known what was expected of her by the great beings of the Shining Realms because of this relationship. She had been through all she had been through – the waste of years waiting between worlds for a love that was no longer hers; and the rebellion against her present-life parents and the greed that had made her the apprentice of a sorceress whose one ambition was to destroy the Temple so important to her people. In all this she had thought she was free to make her own choices, make her own mistakes. And yet here she was, with this feeling of inevitability, this knowledge that she had been called to this place and given a task.

She had not been able to tell Senmut all that Imhotep had said to her, for at the time she herself did not grasp it fully. It seemed to her he had started a train of thought in her that continued after the actual vision of him had disappeared. She was to found a centre of healing in his name. She who had spent the first part of this life helping the forces of destruction was now to spend the second part in dedication to the positive good of those around her. It was not exactly a penance, but it was a making good.

As she stood beside Senmut, a step or two behind Neferure, and watched the green-cool first light of a Nile dawn, she should have felt elation and peace. As the great star rose just ahead of the sun the sky was on the move with birds – great strings of them rose from the dark islands and winged away towards the growing light. Silver fish leapt. A sigh of awe rose like a breeze from the thousands of people gathered there.

But Anhai felt a twinge of apprehension. She could not see that Hatshepsut's eyes were dark with pain and that the paint on her face was running with sweat, but she felt that the river might not rise as soon as it should this year. The cosmic order – the beautiful balance of Nature – had somehow been mocked.

In the north, at Yunu, Men-kheper-Ra stood in the Temple of the Sun with his arms raised, leading the chant, as were his cousin-sister and his aunt-stepmother at the different key points in the land. But behind the beautiful and ancient words he spoke, his mind was busy with other thoughts.

The meeting had taken place the night before, the conspirators arriving secretly in the night after elaborate security precautions by Ra-hotep. They had left before dawn and would not appear at the festival celebrations. Hatshepsut must not know that any of Men-kheper-Ra's friends and supporters were present at this time in this place.

It had been Ra-hotep's suggestion at the meeting that the matter should be left in his hands. He implied that he had already taken certain steps that would be helpful to them.

"Hatshepsut has spies planted everywhere among your friends so that you cannot make a move without her knowing," the High Priest of the Sun said. "But I am not under suspicion. If the priests of the Sun choose to support you rather than your aunt, and if the secret of their support is well kept . . ."

Men-kheper-Ra's face lightened.

"Do you think that will be possible?"

Ra-hotep pursed his lips.

"Shall I say – not impossible?"

"But will they all follow you?"

"No, not all. I must be careful. There are some I can think of at this very moment who are disaffected by the rise of the power of the priests of Amun. There are others I will have to woo. It were better, Majesty, if you and your friends knew no more than you know now. When the situation calls for it, you will be informed. But then there must be no hesitation." He looked hard at the young prince.

Men-kheper-Ra flushed with embarrassment.

"I was a boy then," he said. "I will not hesitate again."

"Good," Ra-hotep said. "It is agreed?"

"How long will we have to wait?" asked Amenemheb impatiently.

"As long as need be," replied Ra-hotep sharply.

"Wouldn't it be quicker if the army . . ."

"Do you want the deaths of thousands?"

"No. But . . ."

"With my plan there will be no need for bloodshed," the High Priest said.

"I'm prepared to leave it to Ra-hotep," Men-kheper-Ra agreed at once. "I would not enjoy fighting my own people. We need our strength for our enemies. When I am Pharaoh in truth instead of just in name, I shall extend the empire beyond even the dreams of my grandfather."

"Careful you won't be too old to throw a spear by then," muttered Amenemheb. Men-kheper-Ra did not hear him, but Ra-hotep did. "That young man is reckless," he thought. "He could ruin everything if I don't watch him."

Hatshepsut passed several days and nights after the festival tossing and turning with a high fever.

She had not expected the foetus to look so human. Nor had she expected it to be a boy. If she had known, would she have done as she had done? As the dark night closed in on her and the sweat poured from her, she did not think that she would make the same decision again.

At first she was angry. Not with herself, but with Senmut, and then with the whole male population for being able to make love so easily and without having to face the consequences. Her anger turned to hatred and, as she lay, she cursed all the men she had ever known. She even turned her anger on her father, whom she had deeply loved, for giving her the aspirations of a man without the body to make the most of them. She cursed her husband, whom she had never loved but to whom she had dutifully submitted. She cursed Men-kheper-Ra. That he existed at all had caused her endless problems. Even now she knew that if she relaxed her tight rein on the Two Lands for an instant, the people, who had seemed to worship her, would think nothing of trampling her underfoot and raising him up – the male prince, the mighty male king!

Amun himself was always depicted as male. Why had he deserted her? Typical! When a woman needed help most, the male god was nowhere to be seen!

She had not asked his permission to abort the child. For every other decision she had turned to him for help, but for this one – this very difficult one – she had not trusted him enough. Was this why he was punishing her? The pain was almost unbearable, the fever dangerously high. Would he go so far as to take her life because she had defied him? She knew he would have told her not to do what she had done. It was against Maat. Destiny had given her another royal child, and she had thrown it away with the garbage. She had not even been able to give it proper burial – for if she had, someone would have found out about it and used the information against her.

It seemed to her Amun-Ra himself was standing in the room beside her. He had given her the child and she had refused it. For the first time in her life she wished she were an ordinary woman and every decision she made were not fraught with so many far-reaching repercussions.

She began to shout at him.

"Why should I feel guilty? Why should I? Do you think I am a slave? Less than a slave? I am led like a leopard on a golden chain. I cannot step where I want to step, or sleep where I want to sleep."

"Ah, daughter, you have asked for this. You have pleaded for power. You have walked the night, paced the colonnades of the day, your shadow at your feet, your shadow at your back, your shadow going before. I have heard your cry. I have listened and I have said, my daughter, if it is your wish to play the leopard, then here is my golden chain that you do not destroy my flock. You bowed your head. You took my chain willingly around your neck."

"Have I not done all that you asked me, time after time?" she said. "I did not want to carry this particular burden, and I am punished like a slave."

"There is no slavery like the slavery of power," he said. *"You asked for power. You have power. You cannot have freedom too."*

"I will break your chain around my neck. I will give up the power.

I will leave the golden throne and give the double crown to the boy who slavers for it, to the woman who stands at his side and is sick for want of it. Anything to free me from this pain, free me from this guilt!"

"And will you give up the crown?" His voice was sceptical.

"What have I become? A walking crown? Have I no legs, no arms, no breasts, no thighs? I will be as much Hatshepsut if I wear no crown!"

"Give it up then, my daughter," he said quietly. *"Be no more my chosen one."*

"I will give it up! I *have* given it up. From this moment on I walk where I want to walk and love whom I want to love."

She felt something change. She could no longer see or feel his presence.

She was frightened, and she was alone. That which had sustained her all these years was gone; the subtle and invisible elixir that had infused every moment of her life with significance had somehow leaked away, and her body that had been sensitive to the faintest influence, her mind capable of making sense of the most complex juxtapositions and relationships, her heart tuned like a fine lute to the breath of the gods – all, all were numb and dull. Even the ring on her hand seemed like base metal instead of gold.

"Forgive me," she cried. "Having known the closeness of your heart to my heart, if you withdraw from me I will walk in the shade and die for lack of the sun. Forgive me! If you do not, I will lift wine to my lips and taste only red dust."

But there was no answer. If he heard her, he gave no sign.

And then – and then she saw that there was someone else in the room, a tall young man, a stranger. He was there and not there. She could see him and yet not see him.

She sensed that he was not of the same order as the gods. He was human, and yet as she looked at him she could see the faint outlines of her cabinet of ivory and ebony that was behind him.

"Who are you?" she asked, but her throat was dry and in her heart she already knew.

His eyes were hard and bitter.

"I am your son," he said coldly.

"You have no name," she whispered, shivering. "You cannot exist."

"I have a name," he said.

"I gave you none!"

"In your agony you cursed me. You gave me a name."

She shuddered.

"What name?" She brought the words out with difficulty. She was more afraid now than she had ever been.

He smiled knowingly, but did not reply. His image began to fade.

"What name?" she screamed.

But he had gone and she was left sinking back onto the bed, wringing wet with sweat, yet shivering with cold.

The door burst open and her two women came running in. They had heard her scream.

"Majesty, what is it?"

She was sobbing and shaking. She clung to their arms.

"Don't leave me! Why did you leave me? Night and day you should be with me."

"Yes. Yes, Majesty. Everything is all right. We are here. We will not leave you."

"Fetch the physician," one whispered to the other.

"What are you whispering?" Hatshepsut shrieked. "What are you saying?"

"Nothing. Nothing, Majesty. We think we should fetch the physician. That's all we were saying."

"Fetch him then – one of you. The other stay." Her fingers were biting into an arm of each and would not let go. "But before you go, tell me – tell me something . . ."

"What, Majesty?" The women were frightened. They had never seen her like this, almost like a child gibbering with fear.

"When – when it was happening what did I say?"

"Nothing."

"You lie! What did I say?"

The two women looked at each other in terrified bewilderment.

"You said nothing, Majesty. You did not cry out once.

"You lie! You lie! You *lie!*" she shouted furiously, and started to hit out at them, her face distorted and ugly with weeping and rage.

One broke free and ran out of the room; the other took blow after blow, twisting and turning in trying to break the Pharaoh's grip. Hatshepsut fell off the bed, and the two women were rolling on the floor when the physician at last came rushing in. He took one look at the scene and took something out of the box he was carrying. He held it for a moment in the flame of the brazier and then waved it, smoking, back and forth over their heads.

At last, spent and exhausted, Hatshepsut fell back.

Fresh clothes and bed linen were brought. Cool, perfumed water washed away the tears and sweat. Medicines were sipped, and finally the great lady fell asleep, curled on her side, without a headrest, like a child.

CHAPTER 12

When Senmut, Anhai and Neferure returned from Suan and Sehel Island they found a shadow on Hatshepsut's face that had not been there before.

Senmut was called before the assembled officials of her administration to give his report on the cutting out of the two giant obelisks she had ordered, the second, and larger, pair she planned to erect to her god in his temple at Ipet-Esut. Senmut reported that the fleet of little boats was ready to start the towing and the rollers were already in place for rolling the granite monoliths down the quayside and on to the huge barges that would bear them north to Amun's city. By the time the rising waters of the Nile had gathered enough force for the operation, the obelisks would be in place, securely lashed down on the barges, and the ceremonies to obtain the god's protection completed.

The work had been rushed and the men were exhausted. Slaves and freemen, skilled and unskilled, had been driven almost beyond endurance to finish the project in time for the inundation. No obelisks had ever been cut so quickly. No obelisks had ever been so tall and heavy.

The first two had been erected many years before as a visible sign of her vow to promote Amun-Ra above all other gods. These two were a kind of confirmation that it had been done and that she should reap her reward in the "myriad of years" by living forever at the side of her god, no matter what other mistakes she had made.

She herself composed the inscriptions that were to be carved into the sides and on the pyramid at the apex. On one she would inscribe:

She made a monument for her father Amun – two obelisks of enduring granite from the south, their upper parts, being of electrum of the best of all lands, seen on the two sides of the river. Their rays flood the two lands when the sun-disk rises between them at its appearance on the horizon of heaven. I have done this with a loving heart for my father Amun after I entered unto his secret image. I slept not and I turned not from what he ordered until it was complete. I have paid attention to the city of the Lord of the Universe – for this city is the horizon of heaven upon earth, the place of ascent and the sacred Eye of the Lord.

I was sitting in the palace and I remembered the One who created me: my heart directed me to make for him two obelisks of electrum, that their pyramids might mingle with the sky from the pillared hall between the great pylons of my earthly father, Aa-kheper-ka-Ra. Each would be of one block of enduring granite without joint or flaw. My majesty began work on them in Year 15, second month of winter, day 1, making swift time in cutting them from the mountain.

I acted in this way with love and respect as a king does for his god. Let no man say it is boasting when I say that I have used the finest quality of gilded electrum measured by the sack like grain. Let them rather say: "How like her it is, she who is truthful to her father." The god Amun, Lord of the Thrones of the Two Lands, knows it in me that I am his daughter in very truth, who glorifies him.

On the other she would inscribe:

I am the beloved of His Majesty, Amun-Ra, who placed the kingship of Khemet, the deserts and all foreign lands under my sandals. My southern border is at the region of Punt . . . My eastern border at the marshes of Asia . . . My western border at the edge of the horizon . . . From all these places I have brought gifts for my Lord: incense from Punt, turquoise from Sinai, tribute from Libya.

Since her illness after the abortion she had had a feeling of urgency, as though time were running out for her. When Senmut brought the news that the obelisks were ready for the journey – but that the river was slower to rise this year than in other years – she was alarmed. She wanted them to be raised. She wanted them carved and in place, gleaming in the sun. She wanted to be back in Amun-Ra's favour again. She wanted to be his chosen one, no matter what it cost.

She ordered sacrifices to Hapi, the Nile god, to be increased throughout the Two Lands. Osiris, the god of regeneration and fertility; Amun, the breath of life; Ra, the giver of light; Hathor, the mother – each and every aspect of the Great Mystery Whose Name Was Unknown, was to be petitioned and bribed. She herself would make a secret sacrifice – a vow that would change her life. She lay face down in the sanctuary of Amun and vowed she would take no man to her bed again if Amun would but restore her to his favour.

The great god made no immediate sign, but Hatshepsut left the temple feeling that she had done all she could to placate him, and if he did not accept her sacrifice she did not know what more she could do.

She sent for Senmut and Anhai together.

Both entered the small audience chamber, the walls painted almost entirely with lotus flowers and water scenes. A pool in the centre of the floor, catching the light from a rectangular gap in the ceiling, contained living fish swimming among living blue lotus flowers. As in her temple, the eternal image was mirrored from the temporal. They bowed low before her chair of ebony and gold. Senmut tried to catch her eye for a personal message, but she carefully avoided looking at him. Her face was as masklike as it was for public occasions and he could read nothing there of the woman's love for him or whether she had missed him or not. He noted that she was thinner than when he had last seen her, and the body that had always looked as though it was taut and poised for action now had a certain slackness about it.

She drew Anhai forward with a gesture of her hand, and indicated that she should stand and tell her tale.

She listened without comment to the whole story.

When it was done she said only: "And where do you envisage this healing sanctuary?"

Anhai hesitated. She knew where she wanted it to be, but whether Hatshepsut would grant her such an important piece of land and build what she wanted on it, she hardly dared hope. Should she ask outright, she wondered, or leave it to the Pharaoh to suggest the best and most obvious place.

"I'm not sure, Majesty," she said diffidently.

Hatshepsut looked at her thoughtfully, and then at Senmut. She would not go to bed with Senmut again, but that did not mean she wanted to hand him over to someone else. This young woman had a vibrancy and an energy she remembered she herself had had in her youth, in fact she herself had had until very recently. She would build her sanctuary, but it must be far from Waset, far from Senmut. But where? If she put it too far in the desert, those who were seeking healing would never be able to visit it. Perhaps an island where her spies could monitor who crossed over to it, and how often. Sehel Island. That would be the perfect place, the place where Imhotep himself had crossed over from the Other Realms to speak with his daughter.

"It shall be on Sehel Island," she said decisively.

Anhai smiled, and bowed her head.

"Djehuti and Imhotep should be the patron gods of the sanctuary, Majesty," Senmut broke in.

"And Hathor," Anhai said quietly.

"And Hathor," Hatshepsut agreed. For a moment the old fire flickered in her eyes as they met those of Senmut. The memory of Per-Hathor was in both their hearts, but Hatshepsut could not afford to let it linger there.

"The location has the blessing of Maat," she said formally. "I can feel it is part of the divine intention. I will give you all the support you need, Anhai, daughter of Imhotep."

Anhai bowed to the ground.

"I am grateful, Majesty."

When she rose she could see Senmut was frowning. He couldn't understand why Hatshepsut was being so cold towards him. Why was he out of favour? Was it something he had done or not done, or was it just one of her unaccountable moods? As the strain of holding the Two Lands under her control increased, she was becoming more and more unpredictable. More than ever she needed her friends, yet she was in danger of driving them away with her moodiness.

He was still frowning when he left, dismissed at the same time as Anhai, without a personal word or a further glance.

Neferure returned to Waset eager to see Amenemheb again, only to find that he was in the north, at Men-nefer. She was determined to visit him, but it would not be easy to do so without making her mother suspicious. It had always seemed to her that nothing could be hidden from Hatshepsut. That golden cobra on her forehead had eyes that could see through walls and mountains, over deserts and oceans. She wouldn't be surprised if her mother could see directly into the Duat and knew all that was to be and all that had already been since the beginning of time.

She did not know to whom to turn to for help. Men-kheper-Ra was a possible future husband and could not be approached about his friend. She could not travel about the country just as she pleased. Wherever she went, an entourage went too. Those few moments she had had sitting in the shade on Sehel Island numbered among the very few she had had to herself at any time in her life.

And then she thought of Anhai – a stranger, a foreigner. What were the politics of Khemet to her? She was young, though not as young as Neferure. The princess had seen the way Anhai had looked at Hapuseneb. She would surely understand.

Anhai had scarcely returned to her duties at the Temple of Hathor when she was summoned to the private chamber of the princess. Anhai regarded the girl as sweet and pretty and very, very young. When she looked at her she saw herself at that age, wilful and full of smouldering impatience to be counted as grown-up, and prepared to do anything to further her own wishes, however much it harmed others. But Neferure did not have as strong a personality as Anhai, and perhaps she would not wreak as much havoc.

Neferure did not come to the point right away.

She called for the servants to bring cool drinks and sweet-meats and reminisced about the Sopdt ceremony at Suan. She asked if Anhai was happy now that she was back in Waset.

"I hear you'll be going back to Sehel Island soon," she said. "Won't you find it very dull down there so far from everyone?"

"I expect I'll soon have company. There are always people who need healing."

"But sick people!" Neferure said, wrinkling up her nose.

Anhai smiled. She might once have felt the same.

"I wondered if you would like to accompany me to Men-nefer before you go?" Neferure asked.

At her home in Haylken, Deva/Anhai had used psychic means to manifest material luxuries and had caused a great deal of suffering. Now she would use psychic and spiritual means to transform fear into confidence, sorrow into joy, sickness into health. It was as though she had been playing at life all those years before, and had only just discovered who she really was and what she wanted and needed for the fulfilment of her destiny. But there was one thing that still troubled her: her relationship with Hapuseneb. He was at this moment at Men-nefer. Was she being given a chance to tie up this loose thread before she started to weave the new pattern?

"Why do you ask that, my lady?" she asked quietly.

Neferure flushed slightly. "I would like to go myself," she said, "but I cannot travel without good reason."

"What reason would I have to go, my lady? I too have my duties here at Waset, and much to do to prepare for my healing sanctuary on Sehel Island."

"It is said that Imhotep is the son of Ptah, and Men-nefer is Ptah's home. Would it not be important for you to go there before you make any decisions about your sanctuary?"

Anhai smiled. Yes, she had heard that legend. But Imhotep had been her father in that ancient former life, flesh and blood like herself. He was no god or son of a god. But behind all legends there are unexpected hidden truths. Perhaps to know more about Imhotep she should know more about Ptah.

"Have we not become good friends since our journey to the south?" Neferure appealed. "Have you not fired me with a longing to learn all about the Mysteries of Ptah?"

"My lady, forgive me, but you wouldn't be asking me this if you had your mother's approval to visit Men-nefer."

Neferure pouted. She toyed with defiance for a moment, wondering if she should not demand, as princess, that the commoner, Anhai, should obey her. But she came down at last on the side of friendly appeal. She told Anhai of her love for Amenemheb and how much she wanted to see him again before she was married off to someone her mother chose for political reasons.

"He is a fine man," she insisted. "He has noble blood and will be general of all the army one day."

"Then surely your mother would approve of your seeing him? She might even approve of your marrying him."

Neferure shook her head.

"Have you asked her?"

"You know my mother," Neferure said, suddenly bitterly. "She is Pharaoh. She sees only what is good for the country, not what is good for her daughter. Men-kheper-Ra is the co-regent and not Amenemheb."

"But . . ."

"She sent me south with you and Senmut so that I would be parted from him."

Anhai looked troubled. She had sympathy for the girl, but she had a lot to lose if Hatshepsut should be angry with her.

"If I asked permission to take you with me to the Temple of Ptah because you wanted to study some of the teachings, *would* you study them?"

Neferure hesitated.

"I could not take you unless you were genuinely interested in the teachings."

"I'll do anything you say," Neferure agreed hastily.

Anhai knew she was stepping on to a slippery path and feared the consequences, but Neferure's big eyes were so appealing and she knew how desperately strong the pull of desire could be. "When I get there I'll hand the whole problem over to Hapuseneb," she thought. "He'll know what to do for the best."

Hapuseneb had spent more time than he wished at Men-nefer. He missed Anhai and he missed the stimulating, surprising company of Hatshepsut. There was always something going on at Waset, though in a sense it was only a small provincial town compared to the administrative capital of the Two Lands, Men-nefer.

He lived in great luxury, in a big house set in a large garden well away from the narrow dusty streets and teeming government buildings. He had affection for his wife and children, but saw little of them. Most of his time was spent going through reports and issuing orders. People found a number of ingenious ways to get out of paying the tithes due to the Temple, and he needed his experience as a vizier to outwit them. Sometimes he longed to be what his title claimed for him: "First Servant of God in the House of Amun", and leave the haggling over properties and dues to others. But then, when he spent more than a few days in the Temple environs and was drawn into the unchanging routine of preparation and purification, of sacrifice and supplication, of ritual clothing and unclothing, he was bored.

The transcendent experience he had had at the summer solstice in the Temple of the Sun was not repeated and, as time passed, he began to doubt more and more that it had ever happened. He stood before the statue of Amun-Ra and looked into the unmoving eyes of lapis lazuli and prayed that he would hear the god speak to him, as Hatshepsut claimed he did to her. But nothing happened. Anhai had told him that he was being unreasonable. "The statue will not speak with stone lips," she had said. "It is in your heart that you will hear his voice."

"But I hear many voices in my heart," he had complained. "How am I to know if it is genuinely the god or not?"

"You will know," she had said confidently.

Hapuseneb sat beside the pool in the courtyard of his house and pondered the sacred epithets about Amun-Ra.

Hidden of aspect, Mysterious of form. He who protects all other gods with his shadow. Creator and Procreator. Kem-atef: the serpent who sloughs his skin: who has no beginning and no end. He who abides in all things. Who was in the infinity, the nothingness, the nowhere and the dark. He who was born of the self-laid golden egg, and is now in the infinity, the all, the everywhere and the light.

At that moment a young serving lad appeared, walking slowly around the pool, and presented him with a leaf from a persea tree. Hapuseneb smiled. The leaf was a message that had been prearranged with Anhai; when either of them needed the other, a persea leaf would be sent. The tree was sacred to the god Djehuti, for on its leaves he wrote the names of the pharaohs to last for a myriad of years. There were two planted at the entrance gate to Hatshepsut's temple, Djeser Djeseru, and it was thought that in the Duat, the Tree of Life was a mystical form of the persea tree here on earth.

"Who gave you this?" he asked the lad.

"A woman in the clothes of a chantress of Hathor, my lord, standing at the gate."

"Is she still at the gate?"

"No, my lord. She told me she had business with the god Ptah."

Hapuseneb indicated that the boy was dismissed, and sat for a while after he had left, quietly thinking.

Then he stood up and made his way unhurriedly to where high whitewashed walls enclosed the ancient Temple of Ptah. He greeted the Gate Keepers with the words that would allow him entrance to the holy precincts. He was well known in the city and a frequent visitor to the temple, and the guards hardly waited for him to finish before they stepped back to admit him.

He found her in the first courtyard, speaking to one of the priests. She was dressed in simple pleated linen garments, with no adornments, but her beauty, as always, was astonishing. Her face had a glow about it he did not remember. She turned to smile at him, and behind the unmistakable pleasure she showed at his arrival, he could see that something had changed her. She seemed more sure of herself, happier. He had respected her wish to be friends and not lovers, believing that she would change her mind in the end. He knew her desire for him was as strong as his for her. Was this the moment of surrender? But when he looked into her eyes he knew it was not. She had experienced the something that distinguished the merely existing from the truly living. She had true freedom.

Whether the priest she was talking to melted away or walked away he had no idea, he saw only her.

"I did not expect you," he said.

"Forgive me, my Lord, there was no time to send a message. My decision to come was very sudden."

"And what decided you?"

Before she could reply they were joined by the First Prophet of Ptah himself, Ptah-mes, and there was no chance for private conversation.

After greeting Hapuseneb rather coldly, for he too, like Ra-hotep, resented having to take second place to Amun in his own city, he led his two visitors towards the priests' quarters that flanked the temple proper, and settled them down in a pleasant, light chamber with goblets of cooling white wine.

Anhai then told them that she intended to found a healing sanctuary on the island of Sehel in the name of Imhotep, and had come to the threshold of the House of Ptah to learn what she could about father and son.

Hapuseneb lay back in his leather chair with his long legs stretched out before him, sipping his wine and listening, watching the faces of both his companions. Ptah-mes was very excited about the idea of the sanctuary and generously offered any help he could towards its establishment.

"Thank you, my lord. The Pharaoh herself is making arrangements for the construction of the physical building – but it would be a great help if, while I am here, I could have access to your library of texts and wisdom books."

Ptah-mes nodded at once.

"Of course," he said enthusiastically. "If I were a younger man I would gladly join you on your island." He looked across at Hapuseneb, for the first time with a smile. "Sometimes we get lost under the burdens of our office and long for a simpler time when we were closer to our god."

Hapuseneb stood up.

"Speaking of the burdens of office," he said, but gave no indication that he agreed with the sentiment pronounced by Ptah-mes. "I must be going." He then looked at Anhai, who had also risen at once to her feet. "I trust you will visit me at the Temple of Amun-Ra one day while you are here," he said formally. "The King of kings is also a great healer and would be glad to be associated with your project."

"I had not heard that Amun was a healer," Ptah-mes said sharply. "I always thought him more of a warrior. Did he not lead the great Aa-kheper-ka-Ra and his father and grandfather into battle?"

"The Hidden One is the breath of life," Hapuseneb said drily. "He has many aspects."

"It will be a simple sanctuary, my lords," Anhai said hastily. "All gods will be welcome, but Imhotep himself will preside." She told them that she had been inspired by a vision of Imhotep himself, but not that she believed she was the actual daughter of the great sage reborn.

"All gods will bless your work, my child," Ptah-mes said quietly. "I am sure of it. And none will want to change the mandate you have been given." He looked hard at Hapuseneb, who smiled and took his leave with a slight, almost mocking bow. It amused him that the priests of the other gods of the Two Lands were so nervous of his power.

When he had left, shown out by a servant summoned by Ptah-mes, the old man turned to Anhai.

"Come," he said, "I will introduce you at once to the Keeper of the Records and the Priest of the House of Life. I hope," and here the old man hesitated, "I hope you will be able to run your sanctuary without any undue interference."

Anhai guessed what he meant. She smiled.

"My little sanctuary will not be big and important enough to attract any 'undue interference'," she said.

"Healing sanctuaries attract rich gifts and donations, and others might desire to share in the wealth."

"I have seen what such wealth can do," she said. "I'll be careful to take only the bare minimum we need for the proper running of it – no more. There will be no wealth to entice the predators."

"You will refuse to accept rich gifts?"

"I will suggest they are given where they are more needed, in our name, if that is the only way the donor will be satisfied."

He looked at her with respect. She was a young woman, with foreign blood in her veins, but she had extraordinary strength. He could believe that she would run the place as she said she would. Good fortune to her! He had been idealistic like that when he was young, but had forgotten those ideals more often than not since he had grown comfortable as High Priest of Ptah.

When Hapuseneb and Anhai next met there were angry words spoken between them. She had underestimated his personal loyalty to Hatshepsut, and he was very angry that she had jeopardised the future of the Two Lands for the sake of a passing romance.

"Amenemheb and Neferure are not children," she said sharply.

"Amenemheb certainly is not, and the very fact that he has encouraged this to go on shows his irresponsible, possibly treasonable attitude to the throne. And you know as well as I do that Neferure is no more than a sweet and vulnerable child."

"She is of marriageable age. Her mother considers her capable of being Pharaoh."

Hapuseneb rose from his chair and strode about the room.

"I thought you had more sense than this," he said. "Why are you deliberately shutting your mind to the very real danger of the situation?"

"From what Neferure says" – Anhai's voice sounded a little less confident – "Amenemheb is a nobleman who has a brilliant career ahead of him. I can't see that he would be so unsuitable."

"He has a brilliant career in the army – as Men-kheper-Ra's right hand, not as a rival to the prince! Can you not see how this will affect Men-kheper-Ra?"

"He doesn't care for Neferure. I've seen how he looks at her."

"What has caring got to do with it? This is power. This is politics."

"Well, I think it is shameful that Neferure has no choice in the matter and her happiness is to be sacrificed for power, for politics!"

Hapuseneb did not reply to her last impassioned cry. Without even glancing back at her he strode out of the room and slammed the door behind him.

She was hurt and upset, shaken and angry.

The next thing she knew was that Amenemheb was sent off suddenly to Kepel, and Neferure was accompanied back to Waset by Hapuseneb himself. She did not see him again before he left. All her messages were ignored, all her attempts to see him frustrated.

She forced herself to stop thinking about him, and busied herself with learning all she could about Imhotep and Ptah. The memories she had of those ancient days as Imhotep's daughter were so fleeting and incomplete they could not be trusted.

Ptah-mes told her that it was believed Imhotep had written all his wisdom down in one great book, but that no one had ever been able to locate it. There were references to it and quotations from it in many of the old texts, but whether these were handed down by word of mouth from Imhotep's lifetime or actual quotations from a book that was known and read afterwards it was difficult to tell.

"The King's architect, Senmut, has been searching for it for years," he told her. "If anyone could find it, it would be he."

Anhai smiled. She knew of Senmut's obsession. She was grateful for it because it had taken her to Sehel Island to meet her destiny.

She told Ptah-mes she would like to read the texts that quoted from it, and settled down in the House of Life among the papyri and the quiet rustling of the other scribes.

Because of her determination to forget Hapuseneb and prepare herself for the great task Imhotep had set her, she spent longer at her research than perhaps was sensible. When the daylight shafting through the high window slits faded, she lit the lamps and continued alone when the others had left to go to bed.

Late on the third night, the full moon shone directly through one of the windows onto the back of her head. She could feel its light almost like a physical touch. As the shadow her head cast on the scroll she was reading passed, the moon's eerie light illuminated the text. It was as though the focus of her eyes had changed, and images

145

and glyphs that appeared to be important the moment before, now receded and others came into prominence. With the altered emphasis, a different meaning emerged.

The moon moved on and the light returned to normal. Before she could forget what she had seen she wrote it down. Then she looked at what she had written. It now meant nothing to her, but she knew that it could not be meaningless. Djehuti, the moon god, had passed by, the ancient friend of Imhotep, the god of wisdom, of scribes, of healing. It was he who had given her the message, and it would have been pointless for him to do so if he was not intending to give her the key to understand it.

She was suddenly aware of her own weariness. She felt too tired to rise and make her way back to her quarters. With a sigh she put her head down on her arms on the table and dropped off to sleep where she was.

She was not aware that a figure had entered the great hall of records and was standing silently behind her, looking down at her.

When she woke as the first light came streaming through the windows, she was relaxed and refreshed. She had had no dreams that she could remember, and she felt bright, cheerful and ready for anything.

"Senmut will know!" was her first thought.

She left the House of Life and stepped lightly out into the garden. A long streamer of birds floated above her, and she could hear children calling from the priests' married quarters. Somewhere, far away, someone was singing a hymn to the god of the dawn.

The wounds in her heart had healed, and she was ready for the future.

Senmut came north as soon as Anhai's messenger reached him. He was glad to leave Waset. He had taken the opportunity of Hatshepsut's rage at Neferure's escapade to suggest that one way of keeping her safe would be for him to marry her. He had said it lightly, as though he had only just thought of it. When Neferure was a child, everyone had remarked on the beautiful and tender relationship between them, and Hatshepsut knew more than anyone that that relationship was one of the most precious in Neferure's life. If anyone could make Neferure behave sensibly it would be Senmut. She ignored the suggestion of the marriage between them, but suggested at once that he should take the young princess aside and spell out her responsibilities to her.

Since he had first conceived the idea of marriage to Neferure he had been waiting for the opportunity to suggest it to Hatshepsut. He was disappointed that it had not been taken seriously, but not really surprised. The seed of the idea had been sown, however, and he did not give up hope that it might one day take root.

He went to see Neferure in the private chamber to which she had retreated since her unwilling return with Hapuseneb.

At first she refused to see even him, but finally, when he sent in a message written in the secret code they had once agreed to use in times of dire emergency, she allowed him in.

She ran to him at once, as she had always done when she was a child, and he took her on his knee and rocked her gently as he had done then.

He tried to tell her that her passion for Amenemheb would pass and that Pharaoh had to consider what was best for the country as a whole. He tried to tell her that it was worth giving up her freedom for the priceless privileges she had as royal heir, but his voice carried no conviction.

"When you die," he said, "as Pharaoh you will become part of the pattern of the imperishable stars. You will look down with your shining eyes and know that you have had, and are having, an influence on everything that happens on earth."

"I don't want that. I don't care about that. I'll give it all up – everything, everything! I don't want a life after death. I want this life, here, now, with Amenemheb!"

"That is easily said, my dear, but later when—"

She climbed off his lap, her face tear-stained and angry.

"You are no better than Hapuseneb and my mother. I'll never forgive Anhai for telling Hapuseneb. Never! And now you too are turning against me."

"Little kitten, you know I am not!"

"You are, and I want you to leave. You and your secret messages! I'll never come to you when you need me, no matter how many codewords you use!"

"Princess . . ."

"Leave!" she commanded.

He stood looking at her for a moment, and knew that while she was in this mood it would be useless to reason with her.

He left.

Anhai impatiently awaited Senmut's arrival.

She had not wasted her time, but her concentration was not as good as it had been. She was sure Senmut would know what the cipher message meant. For some reason she had shown it to no one else, not even Ptah-mes, who had been so kind in extending every help she needed.

She scarcely allowed him time to rest and refresh himself after his journey before she hurried him to the House of Life. She showed him the text she had been reading, and she showed him the glyphs that had been picked out for her. She told him she was afraid that she had misinterpreted the whole incident and that it had all just been a trick played on her by her overtired mind.

Senmut studied what she showed him carefully, his face giving very little away. Then, after what seemed an intolerable length of time, he looked up at her – and she knew by his expression that she had not been mistaken.

"I can't say for sure until I have tested it out," he said, trying to keep the growing excitement out of his voice. "But I think we might have been told where Imhotep is buried and, with him, his wisdom book."

"But if it is buried with him," she said, disappointed, "we'll never be able to read it." She knew with what curses tombs were sealed, and with what anathema tomb robbers were regarded.

Senmut's face had become the face of a stranger, his eyes dark and secretive. She could see that he would do everything in his power to get the book, and face any consequences.

She did not know what to do. She too would give almost anything to read the book, but would she be prepared to rob a tomb?

"But if we were not meant to have it," she thought, "why were we told where it was?"

She decided to let a night's sleep pass between the problem and her decision. If they were meant to go after it, surely she would be given a sign.

That night she tossed and turned as Ra passed cavern after cavern in the Underworld, and the wide striding stars encompassed the heavens.

Just before dawn, clear thoughts came to her as though fed into her mind by someone else. They were meant to read the book, but not to steal it from the tomb. She knew it was possible to leave the body and "spirit travel" because she had seen her parents do it as part of their priestly work. Her mother had drilled into her a hundred times that "the body is the least of our realities". "Don't live in the body alone, or you will waste so much of your potential as a spiritual and eternal being," she used to say. Suddenly Anhai knew there would be a way to visit the tomb of Imhotep and read the book without desecrating it. She could not wait to tell Senmut.

But when she went to find him at the house of Ptah-mes, she was told that he had not been there the night before, and that no one could tell her where to find him.

Her heart sank, surely she was not too late.

She rushed from place to place where she thought he might be, but no one had seen him.

By midday she had no doubt that he had gone to find the tomb and that he would not hesitate to enter it and remove the precious book. Anxiously she went back to her private chamber, thinking that she would try to contact him on another level. She took out the little box in which she kept her most precious possessions.

After she arrived in Khemet she discarded just about everything that she had brought with her. She had taken on new clothes and a new identity during the long and hazardous journey over land and over sea. She was deeply scarred by regret for what she had done in her homeland and was desperate to make amends. She knew that the only way she could make some good come out of the death of her mother would be for her to become what her mother had always wanted her to be. The vision of Imhotep was now giving her that opportunity. If his grave was entered and the elaborate system of magical protection broken, she would be responsible yet again for the destruction of something important and good.

She brought out the box with trembling hands. Why was it that even when she was trying to do good she still ended up doing something bad. She should never have told Senmut!

The box contained one of her mother's sacred crystals. For the first time since she had left her distant home, she took it out of its tiny box of yew wood and knew that she had to use it.

Tenderly she lifted it and unwrapped it from its soft nest of dried moss. As the scent of the moss that had grown on the moors of her damp homeland pervaded her nostrils, she swallowed a lump in her throat. Strange, when she was there she had longed to be here, and now she was here, she longed to be there. It was as though she belonged nowhere. Did one ever? she wondered. Was not the sense of homeland, for which people killed, but one of the many false images they clung to to give them bravado against the Unknown?

She shivered. It was beginning. The crystal was speaking to her – or, rather, causing her to hear her own Higher Self, the eternal part of her being, without the usual distortions and distractions of her lesser, temporary self.

She had never realised how beautiful the crystal was. It had six perfect facets at each end, and fitted her hand as though it had been designed for it. Within it she could see what looked like a phantom crystal, and within that another, smaller one. The exquisite object was actually three crystals in one.

She stroked its cool sides, gazing and gazing into its depths – and as she did so, her breathing became deep and regular and her whole body relaxed.

It seemed to her the crystal was showing her that her life on this earth at this time contained within it the life of a different place and time, which in its turn contained the life of yet another place and time. The memories of all were preserved, but seen only phantom-like within the outer one.

And then it seemed to her it was showing her other things as well. She had the feeling that the longer she gazed at the crystal the more messages it would bring her. She saw it now as the symbol of the ka, the astral or ethereal body, containing within it the ba, the long-lived personal soul, which, in its turn, contained the akh or khu, the eternal spirit, which was the seed or germ from which the others had grown – its essential nature giving shape and meaning to the others.

She felt confident now that she had so entered into the mood engendered by the crystal that she would be able to reach out and see whatever she wanted to see. She thought about the night she had received the message by moonlight. She knew now she had not been wrong to tell Senmut. She had been given the message because she was psychically sensitive enough to receive it – but she was not knowledgeable enough about the ancient scripts to be able to interpret it. Senmut's long, hard training had given him the skill to translate the ancient ciphers. She needed his skills, and he needed hers.

"But if he is going to commit sacrilege with the knowledge," Anhai asked the crystal, "why was he trusted with it?"

"You are given knowledge. You are given opportunity. What you do with them is your responsibility. We do not judge you to see if you are capable of handling what we give you, for more often than not someone who seems completely unsuitable suddenly finds the strength in themselves to do great deeds, and someone who had seemed the perfect choice fails to meet the challenge."

Senmut had told her about trying to raise Imhotep's soul-figure with drumming on that expedition to Punt, and how disastrously wrong it had gone. Now the miraculous had happened and he had been given the location of Imhotep's tomb, she could not blame him for wanting to use the information.

She began to feel strange, as though she were floating off from herself. A twinge of fear almost brought her down again, but she managed to master it, and the sensation continued.

If anyone had come into the room at that moment, they would have seen a young woman holding a crystal out before her and gazing into it with extraordinary intensity. But as far as Anhai was concerned, she had left the room and was floating above the great complex of buildings associated with King Djoser's funerary enclosure in the desert.

And then somehow she was beneath the earth, travelling along a corridor, an underground tunnel. She knew there was no light, and yet she could see as though there were. Without passing through any door, she found herself in a tomb chamber, the walls glowing with symbolic pictures of the afterlife, the colours as vivid as though they had been painted yesterday.

Resting on the heavy stone lid of the sarcophagus was a package wrapped and rewrapped in dry and brittle persea leaves. She knew this was the book they were seeking, and the excitement she felt at that moment almost broke her concentration on the crystal and lost her the experience.

She understood she must not touch it or unwrap it, but try to probe it with the eyes of her ka. She almost despaired. How could she do that? Having come this far, had she the skill to do what had to be done?

She directed the tip of the crystal in her hand towards the package. At that moment it seemed to her filaments of light crackled around the package, enveloping it completely.

She began to understand Imhotep's teaching and she knew she would be able to do justice to his trust in her. She had finally shed the skin of her irresponsible youth, and knew what she had to do and how to do it.

At that moment the scene before her faded and she was back in her chamber. She sat down on the edge of her bed, exhausted and shaken. The crystal in her hand had become burning hot and she dropped it onto the surface of the alabaster table beside her. There was a terrible sound and, horrified, she saw that the tabletop had split in two and gone crashing to the floor. Trembling with anxiety, she scrabbled among the jumble of cosmetic jars, mirrors, flowers and vases, desperately looking for the crystal.

She found it at last – intact. It was cool again, and not even chipped.

Thankfully and very, very nervously, she wrapped it in the moss and returned it to the box of yew wood.

* * * *

Meanwhile Senmut had, as she suspected, gone to search out Imhotep's tomb.

When he first read the instructions he thought he had misunderstood that Imhotep's tomb was in the royal funerary complex of King Djoser. So he, Senmut, was not the first commoner to aspire to being buried with his king.

The fact that he was the Pharaoh's close associate and a very high official in the Two Lands gave Senmut access to Djoser's closely guarded enclosure. He claimed to have Pharaoh's instructions to inspect the area thoroughly in order to make a report on possible repairs and restorations.

He walked round the complex with the High Priest, commenting on various things that needed attention, and then announced that he was going to inspect the underground shafts and tunnels. He could see this made the High Priest uneasy, but with the Pharaoh's seal presented to him he could not refuse. He excused himself for a few moments while he went to find a rope ladder, a torch and some tools.

Senmut wandered over to the towering stepped pyramid Imhotep had built for his king, the first mound, the sacred ground which had emerged from the primeval ocean of consciousness. What a concept! What a mighty innovation! Senmut's heart raced to think how this must have looked to Imhotep's contemporaries. Nothing like it had ever been done before. Nothing like it had ever been seen before. For a moment Senmut felt the same thrill he must have felt that day centuries before, when he had stood beside his master and seen the work of years come to magnificent fruition.

He noticed he was standing beside the serdab, the chamber in which the statue of the king looked out upon the world. He stepped forward to look in through the two small holes. There was the statue of Djoser, as he expected: strong, fierce, powerful, gazing out from the world of the dead.

His eyes looked directly into those of Senmut, and Senmut felt his gaze like a bolt of lightning pass through his body. He reeled back.

He knew magical ceremonies were always performed on such statues to make them capable of housing the ka of the king whenever it chose to return to earth, but Senmut had never experienced so directly and so terrifyingly the reality of such magic.

He felt he had been warned – he must not enter Imhotep's tomb; he must not remove the book.

At that moment the High Priest returned and Senmut, still half dazed, followed him to the area where the entrance to the underground labyrinth of corridors lay. It had been carefully disguised, the secret of its location passed by word of mouth from high priest to high priest since the earliest times.

They worked together to prise the heavy slabs of stone up, and when the shaft was finally opened, Senmut told his companion to leave him alone to inspect the tunnels, and to make sure that everyone else was kept well away from the site. The man was not at all sorry to be spared further involvement in what he considered to be a dubious and dangerous activity, and retreated at once.

As Senmut climbed down into the shaft on the papyrus-rope ladder provided for him, his heart was pounding unnaturally fast. He believed King Djoser himself had forbidden him to do what he was about to do, and yet his desire was so strong he could not bring himself to stop. He tried to persuade himself that it had been his own imagination and his own feelings of doubt and guilt that had given him that experience at the serdab. He knew that priests and superstitious people believed that statues of cold stone could see and speak – but he did not. No, not he! He repeated this to himself several times.

At the bottom of the shaft, he stood in a corridor with walls shimmering like turquoise-coloured water in the light of the torch he held above his head. The rock was lined with thousands upon thousands of little faience tiles.

Carefully he checked the inscriptions and the reliefs. He passed the striding figure of King Djoser, depicted at the time of his jubilee marking the boundaries of his kingdom. He passed the guardian cobras and the procession of the gods. He followed all the signs Anhai had been given until he came at last to the place, after many twists and turns, he knew to be the one he was looking for.

He found that someone had been there before him. This part of the corridor had suffered heavy damage. Many of the facing tiles had fallen or been pulled off and several blocks of stone removed from the walls. Dust and debris almost blocked the passage. Shaking with anxiety that the precious book was already gone he scrambled over the rubble and raised his torch to peer into the darkness beyond the hole in the wall. Dimly he could see a small chamber with several broken statues lying scattered on the floor. He tugged at a block of stone feverishly until the cavity was wide enough for him to climb through. He was sweating profusely and his hands and arms were scratched and bleeding.

Once inside he could see that the chamber was no more than an antechamber to the main tomb. He stumbled through the door cavity in the opposite side, stooping low to avoid the lintel. Why had he been given the secret ciphers that would lead him to this place if he were not meant to have the book? He began to whisper prayers to Djehuti and to his hero Imhotep himself. He had been led step by step. He was linked closely to Imhotep. His finding of the book must have been intended. It must have been planned.

He stood at last in the burial chamber itself. The coffin had been broken into and the quartzite lid lay fragmented on the floor. All the grave goods of the great sage that had not been stolen lay scattered about. Muttering to himself like a madman Senmut searched the chamber, turning over pieces of broken furniture, empty chests, shattered oil and wine jars – in his agitation not remembering that he was handling objects that Imhotep himself had handled, and that at any other time he would have been in ecstasy enough just to have found what he had found. Occasionally the flickering light of his torch illuminated the paintings on the walls and gave him a moment's pause. If only – if only he had time to study them – but he dare not be too long. The atmosphere was oppressive, the air stale, and his torch would not last forever. Above ground no doubt the High Priest was waiting for his return.

He was almost turning to leave in despair when he noticed a dark object lying in the corner that he had not examined. He had no hope – but he lowered the torch to see it more clearly.

He gasped. It was what he was looking for! The thieves who had picked the tomb clean of all its gold and jewels, its valuable unguents and talismans, had thrown aside with scorn the most precious object of all — the Wisdom Book of Imhotep, wrapped in persea leaves.

With trembling hands Senmut lifted it up and hurried from the chamber.

All the way back, stumbling along the dim corridors, his torch almost burned out, his mind was racing, trying to imagine what was written on the scrolls, trying to imagine the fuss that would be made of him for having found the book of Imhotep. He would be its sole guardian. It was more than likely he would be the only person who could read it because of his knowledge of ancient scripts. The finding of it was the turning point of his life, and whatever had happened to him before was nothing to what was to happen to him in the future.

He clambered up the last ladder, his breath coming in gasps. He dreaded that someone would be waiting at the top, but there was no one.

The last few rungs of the ladder seemed impossibly difficult. He had a horrible feeling that he might fall back down the shaft to his death, losing the book to whoever came to haul his body out.

With a tremendous effort, he reached the top of the ladder safely, ascertained that no one was waiting for him there and placed the precious package ahead of him on the ground so that he would have both hands for the last heave.

He was out of the shaft at last and lay for a moment, panting, face down on the ground.

At last he was recovered enough to rise and look at what he had brought up from the tomb.

He stretched out his bruised and bleeding hand to take it up once more – and found to his horror that his hand passed right through it.

He stared, appalled. Whether it was from the contact with the cold, crisp night air, or whether it was from some ancient spell, the package had turned to dust!

Shaking uncontrollably, Senmut searched through the dust with his fingers, hoping against hope that it was only the wrapping that had disintegrated.

But there was nothing there but fine, ash-like grey dust. Not a single figure, not a single hieroglyph of the greatest book in the world was preserved.

CHAPTER 13

The inundation came, but tardily. The great river rose and swelled at last and overflowed its banks. The life-giving black silt was on the move.

Hatshepsut thanked her father Amun-Ra by giving vast donations of land to his temples, land that supported crops and people and villages, goats and cattle and geese. The priests of Amun-Ra could draw on more resources of manpower and produce than any other in the Two Lands, with the exception of the Pharaoh herself.

Until the waters came, Hatshepsut had been morose and tetchy. Every day she went from Amun's temple on the east bank to her own, rapidly growing, personal mortuary temple on the west bank. Supplicants to the throne were barely listened to. Most of them were dealt with by Hapuseneb.

He did not know what was bothering her, but suspected that it was something more than annoyance with her daughter. That the inundation was delayed seemed the obvious answer, but he caught a look of fear in her eyes sometimes that made him think it was more even than this. Her women told him that she was sleeping badly. Even if they had not, he could see it in her face. She took to using cosmetics heavily, a thing she had never done before except on state occasions when it was important her face should become an impassive pharaonic mask.

At a time when Neferure most needed someone to talk to and comfort her, to advise her and gentle her out of her heartbreak, she had no one. Senmut was away in the north at Men-nefer. Hatshepsut was preoccupied with some grim problem of her own. Her women and her old nurse had been told that she must not be allowed to leave the palace, and that her movements were to be watched at all times.

Her nurse would have listened, but Neferure chose not to confide in her. "What would such an old woman know about our kind of loving!" she thought. She forgot, as most young people forget, and most old people too, that in order to be old one must also once have been young.

She barely left her room, and when food was brought to her she scarcely touched it. Every day she asked if a letter had come for her. But no letter came.

In the east, Amenemheb had little idea of the situation at Waset. He had been suddenly summoned and sent urgently to Kepel to put down an insurrection. But when he and his men arrived after the long sea journey from the delta, they found the great market city full of merchants as usual and no sign of any trouble. Keftiu from the Island of the Bulls in the Great Green Ocean were trading their rhytons containing sacred oils. Silver and cypress wood and wine were exchanged for turquoise-coloured faience, ivory and gold and ostrich eggs . . . From the distant and mysterious mountains of the far east, the traders in precious lapis lazuli were driving hard bargains with the representatives of the kings of neighbouring states. Every succeeding pharaoh demanded rare lapis lazuli for the holy statues, and every vassal ruler wanted as much of the valuable stone as he could get, to use in bribing and bargaining and sweetening relations with the mighty overlord and neighbour. Horses from the eastern and northern plains stamped up the dust impatiently in their stables; cattle lowed in their pens; donkeys brayed on every street. Amenemheb walked through the market and heard the shouting and the laughing and the busy hum of barter trade and began to realise that he had been sent *away* from Men-nefer – not *to* Kepel.

He and Neferure had spent several warm and secret nights. She had been a virgin when he first took her in his arms and her wide-eyed trust and adoration had almost made him hesitate. But he had put aside his scruples for the pleasure of the moment.

Afterwards, as she lay crying, overwrought by all that had happened, his thoughts were already far away on the consequences this liaison might have for his career.

Now, as he sat in the fort overlooking the city, he could see the tall columns of the huge Temple of Hathor erected here to protect the Egyptians against the spells of foreigners, and wondered if any god or goddess would be able to protect him against the wrath of Hatshepsut and Men-kheper-Ra now that his affair with the princess was probably common knowledge. He spent a long time dictating a letter through a scribe to Men-kheper-Ra.

It was a masterpiece of diplomacy, mentioning Neferure nowhere, but hinting that scandalous rumours were abroad about him, spread by their "mutual enemy" (no name) and that he, the prince, his lord, his friend, was not to believe them. He remained the true Pharaoh's loyal and devoted subject. He knew the ambiguity of the last line would be appreciated by Men-kheper-Ra.

The messenger left at top speed, spurred on by offers of great wealth on his return with a reply from the prince – and terror of the punishments that would be inflicted if he brought no such reply.

Neferure waited in vain for some word, some sign. She was sure he would find a way of communicating with her, though she knew a straight letter was out of the question. All her communications were being intercepted, and no letters of hers left the palace without first being read.

She grew paler and thinner as the days went by.

At last, weak and ill, she wrote a message to Senmut in the secret code she had told him she would never use again.

Hatshepsut was informed about her daughter's deteriorating health and paid her a brief visit. She was shocked to see how thin Neferure was, and spent her time ordering her favourite dishes and insisting that she eat them.

She told her Amenemheb was not being punished, nor would he be if he stayed away. "You are both young, and I can understand how such a romance developed. But you are old enough now to understand our lives are not our own. Our position demands sacrifice if we are to maintain the good relationship between the gods and Khemet. See how late the inundation has come. We have to be so careful . . ." Her voice trailed away as she returned to her own thoughts and anxieties, but Neferure interpreted her words as meaning that the Two Lands had almost been plunged into the horrors of famine because of her own rebellious act. She turned her face to the wall and large tears ran down her cheeks.

Her mother rose, unaware of the true despair in her daughter's heart. She had never understood how very different Neferure was from herself.

"You have had time to mourn your lost love," she said briskly. "I have given you time. But now you must stop. You must take your place again. You must eat. You must grow strong. You must face the world. I want no more of this hiding in your room and sulking."

Pharaoh swept out of the room without a backward glance.

The old nurse moved forward anxiously and tried to take the girl in her arms, but Neferure pulled away.

Hatshepsut had her own troubles. With the coming of the inundation, she felt it was possible that Amun-Ra had forgiven her, but every night the young man with the dark and smouldering eyes who claimed to be her son, appeared in her chamber. He never spoke. When she demanded that he leave her alone, he smiled. When she tried to reason with him and asked him to explain his presence, he smiled. She pleaded. She even wept. But always he smiled that cold, cold smile and then faded away.

She went to Amun-Ra and asked what she must do.

But he too did not reply.

She neglected her official duties, and Hapuseneb became a tower of strength by deputising for her on every possible occasion. There may have been whispers at this arrangement, but he soon quelled them with a glare of his hard, black eyes. On the whole, the people respected him, but feared him. He was a more formidable man than Senmut, and less predictable.

The only thing Hatshepsut seemed to be still interested in was the arrival of her obelisks from the south. She believed in her heart that when they rose in their full glory in his House of Millions of Years, and when the praise-poems were carved on them and the electrum covering gleamed in the sunlight, surely then her father, Amun-Ra, would fully forgive her and rejoice with her.

She was often to be seen gazing out over the river towards the south, straining to catch the first glimpse of the barges bearing the granite monoliths.

Something of her old vivacity returned as soon as they were drawn up at the docks. Impatiently she went aboard as the first wooden gangplank was lowered, not waiting for the rich royal carpet to be laid for her sandalled feet. She stroked the smooth sides of the crystalline pink granite and traced with her fingers some of the praises to her lord she had ordered to be carved.

A throne had accompanied the barges, placed high on deck, with ostrich feather fans at its side waving in the moving air as though fanning an invisible majesty. This was to show that her ka had accompanied the obelisks on their journey from the mountain out of which they had been cut and would be with them to the moment of their erection. Only when the images of herself and her ka before Amun-Ra were cut into the rock of the small crowning pyramid would the throne and the fans leave the site.

The crew cheered as she took her place in full physical majesty on the throne. And then, in it, she was lifted high and carried triumphantly from barge to barge to inspect all that they had brought with them. Some said later that they had seen tears in her eyes when she looked at the obelisks, but this was only whispered, for pharaohs were supposed to be above ordinary human emotions.

Day after day she sat at the quayside on the throne that had accompanied the barges, watching the activity. Praise-singers ran up and down the banks, waving palm and tamarisk fronds. Crowds of people, some from very far away, pressed as close as they could get behind her guards to see what they could of the great event and the woman who had caused it to happen. The priests of Amun-Ra, hundreds of them of every rank, dressed in their best robes of office, passed up and down, up and down, covering the obelisks in clouds of incense.

With the river high, it was possible to manoeuvre the two giants quite near to the temple. Then they had to be taken overland; thousands of men pulling and heaving were employed with ropes and rollers.

Hatshepsut on her throne accompanied them every inch of the way.

The whole activity of placing the obelisks, carving them and erecting them took many weeks, and in all that time Hatshepsut showed no interest in anything else. Hapuseneb virtually ran the country, and Neferure, forgotten, grew weaker and weaker.

Hatshepsut had grown hardened to the presence of her phantom son and chose to ignore him. Her obelisks were nearly ready to be raised; and she believed that when they were, his unwelcome presence would cease. She would be back in Amun-Ra's favour, and *no one* would be allowed to threaten or discomfort her.

But one night something different happened that really frightened her.

She woke as she always did when her son's ghost appeared. She was about to turn over away from him, as she had grown accustomed to doing, when she noticed that this time there were two figures standing where there was usually only one. Startled, she sat up and had a closer look. This time the young man with the cold and accusing eyes had his arm around a young woman, who was weeping. Hatshepsut's heart gave a lurch.

"Neferure!" she cried, leaping out of bed. But even as she called out, the two figures totally disappeared.

Trembling, she drew on her robes and summoned her women. Together they rushed down the corridors of the palace until they came to Neferure's quarters. There they found Neferure apparently safely asleep in bed.

But Hatshepsut was not satisfied and insisted that she be woken.

With a white face the woman who had been given the task turned to the Pharaoh.

"Majesty," she whispered, "the princess will not wake!"

"What?"

Hatshepsut flung herself forward and turned her daughter over. She had been lying curled up like a very young child, her thumb in her mouth.

She was dead.

Hatshepsut was ashen. The phantom had taken her.

She fell down on the floor beside the girl's bed and took her body in her arms and sobbed and sobbed. The women stood back, clustered together, both horrified and afraid.

What had she done? She had destroyed her two children, the two precious living beings that had been entrusted to her. She had been a good king and her country had benefited in many, many ways during her rule, but her own flesh and blood, her own babies, she had betrayed.

Suddenly her anger turned on Amun-Ra. She had done everything for him! She had made him the most important god in the Two Lands. She had endowed his temples with priceless gifts. She had strengthened his priests above all other priests. One mistake! Just one mistake, and all that was apparently for nothing. He had turned his face from her, and she felt she couldn't win him back though she erected a hundred obelisks and covered them with all the gold in Nubia.

The women were shocked at her unrestrained grief and did not know what to do. None stepped forward to comfort her.

Hatshepsut Maat-ka-Ra, beautiful and powerful Pharaoh of the Two Lands, had no one to turn to in the hour of her despair.

Senmut did not receive Neferure's sad little message as soon as he might have, for, after the experience with the book, he did not return to the city but walked out into the desert.

Now, wandering far from the city of the dead and the city of the living in the hour just before dawn, Senmut shivered, and not only from the chilling air. The ancient spells were indeed strong.

But why? Why? He asked himself this question over and over again. Why be told where the book was to be found and not be allowed to take it?

The more he thought about it the less he understood.

At last, exhausted, he sat down on a rocky knoll and watched the huge red-gold orb of the sunrise directly behind Imhotep's mighty brainchild, the great stepped pyramid of King Djoser. For a long moment the rising sun seemed to rest on the smooth white platform of polished limestone at the top, and the whole structure was suffused with gleaming golden light. Then it lifted off like the first phoenix taking flight from the first mound.

Around him the dark and undulating desert began to shimmer like the primeval ocean.

"O Lord of the Horizon, Falcon of Millions of Years, illuminate my eye with thine Eye. Teach me to see beyond the immeasurable Dark."

Senmut shut his eyes against the strengthening glare of the sun, but through his lids he could still see the blaze of glory, a disk-shaped hole of raging fire: the Eye that saw into his heart.

Senmut kneeled down in the sand and lowered himself face forward until his forehead felt the cool desert beneath it. Still the after-image of that disk of fire stayed with him. He could not shut it out. It burned into him. It consumed him.

He knew what he had done wrong. He had sought the book to satisfy his own curiosity and to give himself glory. He had thought that when he found it, it would be *his,* to use as he liked.

Djoser, with his cobra vision, had seen that while gazing into his eyes.

Imhotep had seen that as he carried the book away.

Where was there to hide from his shame?

Senmut did not know how he was ever to rise to his feet again.

He had been seen, not as the great and skilled viceroy and sage, the champion and companion of the Pharaoh, the creator of beautiful and eternal buildings, but as he was in his heart . . .

At last, when the heat of the sun on his back became too much to bear, he dragged himself to his feet and stood gazing out into the western desert that had no limit. He felt like walking out into it and never returning. He had had within his grasp what he had sought all his life, and he had failed it and lost it – not only for himself but for all mankind.

Putting one foot after the other, he began to walk. He did not know where he was going and he did not care. The sun rose higher – Kheper-Ra in its full divinity. Sweat poured from his skin, and his eyes burned as he strained to see through the heat haze ahead of him.

Did he see figures? Was there a procession coming towards him through the flickering and shimmering air?

He stood still, blinking, trying to clear his vision.

In the forefront was Ptah, the Creator of manifest form, with his close-fitting skullcap, beside him his consort, Sekhmet, the Destroyer, with the fearsome head of a lioness, her eyes red with rage. He had offended against the cosmic order – and he would suffer for it.

"I am suffering for it," he whispered with a dry and parched throat. His lips were cracked, his stomach and head aching with hunger and thirst.

Behind these two were others: Amun, with his tall plumed crown

162

and his consort, Mut, lion-faced, vulture-crowned. Hathor and Horus, Khnum and Neith, Isis and Osiris, Nepthys and Set. Djehuti and Seshat . . . The procession stretched to the horizon, and all the myriad of gods were there in their male and female aspects, the great spirits who hovered over the world and played their role in the immense unfolding drama of each and every human soul.

Senmut fell to his knees and pleaded for forgiveness. Tears streamed down his dusty cheeks, and his throat constricted with the words that were choking him yet could not be said.

It seemed to him Sekhmet reached him first, and he fell into her darkness like a lost soul into the Void. No man could have regretted more what he had done. No man could have pleaded more desperately for a second chance.

He opened his eyes. He looked up into the impassive and curious face of a sand-dweller, a Bedouin. Behind him his tribe were gathered, waiting to see if the stranger would live or die. They had already searched for his valuables and found Pharaoh's seal ring. Was it they who had approached him through the heat haze?

His head was shaded and he was given water from a goatskin bag. Weakly he sat up and was propped against some baggage. He looked from face to face. These were a people who lived outside civilisation as he knew it. They were a people always on the move, fading into the distant deserts as soon as anyone tried to tax them and make them settle, emerging sometimes to trade the furs of the desert animals and the carpets richly woven from the wool of their flocks dyed with colours no city-dweller had access to.

They were a rough and mysterious people, their ancestors different from the orderly and law-abiding Egyptians, their gods savage and uncouth. Yet their women wore jewellery a queen might be pleased to wear – crystals drilled through, pieces of ostrich shell and bone, all linked together with beads of gold. So much gold! They were ragged, and poor, yet gold was swinging from their hair and their ears. Gold was coiled around their wrists, arms, fingers and necks.

The sand-dwellers had always known where to find gold and turquoise and amethyst. It was their trading which had first alerted pharaohs and officials to seek out the best areas for mining.

Senmut had not come in close contact with them before, though with his interest in languages, he had learned a little of their speech once. He used it now.

He was welcomed and given food. It was not often they came across a river-dweller who had taken the trouble to learn their language.

163

Senmut stayed with the sand-dwellers for some time, moving with them, camping with them, learning their ways. He found comfort in the fact that the complexities of his life were reduced to the minimum – walking in the cool of the morning and evening, raising the black woollen tents at night, striking them at dawn. He learned to hunt for his food. He learned to go without drink for extraordinary lengths of time. He learned to listen to their stories and sing their songs. He learned and learned and learned, but told them nothing about himself. It was as though Senmut had died and the man who was with them, clad like one of them, had newly sprung from the desert the day they found him. They wondered if he was a criminal escaping retribution, but did not question him. They watched as his clumsy attempts to live their life gradually gave way to skill and facility.

It was when he brought down a fierce lioness single-handed and received their enthusiastic approbation that he decided he was ready to return to the river. He looked at the animal's golden coat and its once magnificent and powerful limbs lying flaccid and helpless, and he knew the life of the hunter was not for him. For the first time he missed the life of the river-dwellers. It was good that he had lived so close to the elements for so long. In the old life he had forgotten how physical life could be, how insecure and primitive. But here he had almost forgotten how subtle and complex and interesting the life of the mind could be. He needed both.

He told the sand-dwellers he was leaving them.

They did not try to dissuade him, but gave him gifts and made speeches of farewell.

At the very last their chief held out to him Hatshepsut's seal ring. Nothing had ever been said about their taking it.

CHAPTER 14

Hatshepsut and her husband had had no more children, but the great Se-quenen-Ra and Aah-hetep, who had founded the dynasty, had had other children besides Nefertari and Ahmose, and through one of them, in direct bloodline, Hatshepsut found her heir, Meryt-Ra.

She now took the young princess into closer contact with the royal household and began to groom her for her role. She even went so far as to add her own name, Hatshepsut, to the girl's. She would never take Neferure's place, for, now that her daughter was dead, Hatshepsut realised just how much she had loved her. But she was determined that when she herself died, someone would rule Egypt with the true royal blood flowing in their veins.

She had intended Neferure to be Pharaoh like herself, but now regretted very much how hard she had driven the girl to satisfy her own ambitions. She would not make the same mistake with Meryt-Ra. She was sure the girl would make an adequate queen, but she did not have the drive of will necessary to rule a country. Hatshepsut Maat-ka-Ra decided to bow to the inevitable and settle for marrying the princess to Men-kheper-Ra.

In the moments of her deepest despair after Neferure's death she thought of stepping back from the position she had created for herself and letting Men-kheper-Ra have his head. She had had many good years of power and had achieved an enormous amount in the Two Lands. She knew there was whispering and manoeuvring for her overthrow among Men-kheper-Ra's supporters. She felt no guilt about what she had done, but she was suddenly very, very tired.

When Senmut returned to Waset, lean and brown from his desert sojourn, he found her in this mood. He expected rage because he had been away so long and so mysteriously, but he was not subjected to it. She was at her lowest ebb and needed a friend.

The news of Neferure's death devastated him. With tears in his eyes, he clutched her little note pleading for him to come to her at once. He had failed her. Once again he had failed.

But this time regret strengthened rather than weakened him. What

165

was done could not be undone, but perhaps something could be salvaged from the ruins for the future.

He listened to Hatshepsut's words of despair and agreed with her that it would be a good time to give up the throne. He suggested they marry and retire from public life to one of her numerous estates.

"Let Men-kheper-Ra take the strain of kingship. You have suffered it enough."

He took her in his arms and stroked her silken skin. She did not respond to him as she once would have done, but neither did she draw away.

She said nothing while he talked on and on about how much he loved her and how, as private nobles, they would enjoy a wonderful life together. His own ambitions for power had died in the refining furnace of the desert, and he genuinely saw them as a happily retired couple, walking in shady gardens, talking over old times.

Whether she was accepting what he was saying, or whether she was indeed listening at all, he could not tell. He held her and stroked her as he had done Neferure a hundred times, as a kindly foster-father and friend – not as a lover.

He left her when at last she fell asleep. He laid her down tenderly on her red cedar-wood bed, Wadjet the cobra watching over her, coiled in golden image around each of the bull's-foot legs so that no harm could rise up to her from the earth, and hovering over her on the uprights so that no evil could befall her from above.

But Hapuseneb was not so eager for Hatshepsut to give up the throne, and he and others of her close circle met to discuss the situation and how they would deal with it if she went ahead with Senmut's suggestion.

Senmut himself believed that she was ready for the great renunciation he proposed, confusing his change of heart in the desert with her temporary mood of despair. He told Hapuseneb in confidence in order to enlist his help, and then left the court to make preparations for their retirement to her estates near Suan.

Hapuseneb wasted no time in asking for an audience, and was shown into the antechamber of her private quarters.

Hatshepsut was thin and drawn, as though she had neither slept nor eaten for some time, as indeed she had not. She was haunted night after night by the spectre she believed to be her son, who seemed not to be content with what he had already done, but was waiting, gloatingly, for another opportunity to hurt her. Amun-Ra had ceased to communicate with her, and she felt desperately alone. The guilt of how she had misunderstood and neglected her daughter and deprived her son of life never left her.

Hapuseneb's shrewd dark eyes bored into hers. Was she indeed contemplating a step that no pharaoh had ever taken before and would be a disastrous precedent for the future? If the King was divine, Amun-chosen and Amun-protected, how could he just give up his kingship as though it were any ordinary office? How could the people be expected to believe the Pharaoh's position was sacred and unchallengeable if it was subject to whim and pique like any other? "This is what comes of having a woman pharaoh!" he thought bitterly.

When Hatshepsut had taken the double crown, he had been hostile to the idea of a woman ruling; but she had proved herself strong and able and had given him a rank apparently second only to herself. Only Senmut was in a comparable position.

Since Senmut's departure, Hatshepsut had stayed close to her chambers. She was in a daze, dreaming of the quiet ease of a private life away from the pressures and tensions of the life she knew. It was tempting, and yet, and yet . . .

As soon as she saw Hapuseneb she knew she would not leave. Pharaoh could not step down. Pharaoh could not follow a private dream. Senmut was irresponsible even to think it!

All this passed between Hapuseneb and Hatshepsut before a word was spoken.

"I heard your Majesty was not well," were the first words he said.

She had entered with shoulders drooping and her mouth down at the edges. He could see her straightening her back even as he looked at her as though the Djed column of Osiris had been inserted into it and was giving her strength.

She lifted her chin and looked him straight in the eye.

"My women shouldn't gossip," she said. "I am well."

"It is a long time since your Majesty has been seen."

"Even pharaohs need time to themselves sometimes," she said haughtily.

"But if the sun doesn't rise, Maat is no more."

"Do you dare to reprimand me?" she asked sharply, something of the old spark returning to her eyes.

He bowed low.

"No, Majesty. I do not dare."

She contemplated the top of his head. She knew he was not a man who enjoyed bowing so low. And she knew he was a man she greatly respected. He was right: she was endangering Maat, the Cosmic Order, by her weakness and self-pity. It would not happen again.

"Rise," she said quietly, "I know you. I'm sure you have nothing in mind but the good of your Pharaoh."

He rose, and there was a silence between them for a while. Both stood facing each other, both suddenly aware of their closeness, yet neither wanting to make the first move away from the other.

It was she who turned at last and walked back towards the door through which she had come.

Just before she left, she looked back over her shoulder.

"I'd be glad if you would accompany me to Djeser Djeseru," she said formally. The moment of intimacy passed, but was not forgotten. "I hear the whole of the third terrace is complete at last."

How could she have contemplated giving up Djeser Djeseru, her Mansion of Millions of Years, built for a pharaoh, to house a pharaoh, to ensure a pharaoh would live forever and walk freely with the gods among the Imperishable Stars? Would Men-kheper-Ra not have taken it over and toppled her Osirian statues and erased her name?

Ah, how listening to Senmut had nearly destroyed her! She would not listen to him again.

Senmut went straight to Sehel Island before he went to Hatshepsut's southern palace. Whether he would tell Anhai what had happened with the book or not, he was not sure.

"I will tell her everything," he decided at one moment. "I owe it to her." But the next he had changed his mind and thought it would be best if the secret of his appalling deed died with him.

The temple was already almost complete on the island, and only a few craftsmen were left to paint the texts on the walls and finish the fine polishing of the statues of Imhotep, Djehuti and Hathor that were to be its focus.

Anhai had a suite of rooms leading out into a small garden through one door, and into the healing area of the temple through another, where the dreaming cells and crystal rooms were already established.

She took Senmut at once on a tour of inspection and gave no indication that she thought his behaviour in Men-nefer had been at all odd. Neither of them referred to it, but Senmut had an increasingly uneasy feeling that she did, in fact, know what had happened.

"Crystals?" he said in astonishment as she led him into one of the rooms. There was a low couch and a chair beside it at the centre, but all around the walls were narrow tables loaded with the most amazing crystals he had ever seen.

"Crystals were used in ancient times for healing," she said quietly. "And I don't see why they should not be used again."

"Do you know how to use them?" he asked, surprised.

"Yes," she said.

"Where did you learn this?"

"Partly from my parents before I came to the Two Lands, and partly from . . ." She hesitated. He looked at her intently, knowing in his bones what she was going to say. "Imhotep," she finished.

He wanted to question her further, but he was afraid his own fiasco would have to be confessed.

He walked across to the south wall and picked up an enormous transparent quartz crystal the size of an ostrich egg. The facets were sharp, as though they had been artificially cut, and the matrix was perfect. He held it up to the light and turned it slowly round, staring into the beauty of it. Would it be so terrible if he told her what had happened? If anyone understood it would be her. He would tell her about the desert too, and how he had changed, and how he and Hatshepsut would retire and marry. He felt calm, as though whatever had happened or would happen was part of a pattern, an order, greater than he or Anhai or Hatshepsut could possibly know about.

She was beside him, smiling.

"Crystals heal when the heart tunes into them," she said. "They are so much part of Maat's beautiful order. Nearly all illness is because the heart is out of order, out of tune with Maat. To get back into tune puts you into a mood where the natural healing capacity of your body can function, nothing is preventing it, nothing is blocking it. Your mind gives way to your heart. Your heart gives way to your soul. Your soul gives way to your spirit. Your spirit gives way to *that which knows.*"

Senmut put the crystal down and turned to Anhai.

"I can believe it," he said. "I am already better for having entered this room. And now I feel myself strong enough to tell you something."

"About the book?"

"About the book." He met her eyes. "You know?"

She nodded.

"How?"

"I have seen it," she said, "without entering the tomb. It was not necessary to enter physically. I looked for you to tell you, but you had already left."

"You've seen the book? You know what was in it?" There was mounting excitement in his voice.

"I think so."

"You think so!" he cried. "Don't you know?"

"I *believe* so," she corrected herself.

169

He shook his head impatiently.

"I need to *know* what was in it!"

"What was in the book cannot be easily spoken as we stand here. I do not know myself exactly the words used on the papyrus. But I know its teaching will unfold for me as I do my work in this place. I have been in its presence, and its presence has entered my deepest consciousness. I know the teaching of my mother Kyra in my heart in the same way, and both will come to me surely, gradually, if I let them, each complementing the other, each completing the other. It is as though the two together comprise a key I can use now, but which I was not capable of using before, even if I had had it in my possession."

Senmut wondered whether, if he stayed with Anhai and worked with her on the island, he would learn all that Imhotep had to teach. But he believed now it was not his destiny to know what was in the book at this time. Perhaps one day he would be ready to know it in the way Anhai knew it. Until then he must be content to do what he could do and do well: design and build harmonious and beautiful structures worthy of a pharaoh and a god. He would make Hatshepsut's southern palace a place where he and she could live together with Maat.

If he tarried any longer on Sehel Island the work would never be done. He decided to leave at once.

Some months later the servants in the great palace at Waset exchanged glances, amused, as Senmut strode past them. His face and neck were red with anger and they could see a vein pulsing on his forehead. They all knew where he had been, though all pretended they did not.

"This time she has gone too far," he was thinking. "This time I shall not let it pass."

As he stormed through the cool tiled passages of the palace, he saw nothing of the decorative designs of palm and tamarisk. He saw only her face as he burst into her room against the guards' restraining arms. Thinking about it now, he was not sure the guards had not deliberately let him through. They had given in too easily. He was sure, in retrospect, that he detected something in their eyes that should have warned him. They were new men, not the old familiar ones who had known him well for years. He had worked hard and fast to make her southern palace beautiful for her and had returned to Waset, his heart full of hope and love, to find everything changed.

As he burst out of the shady palace into the blinding white heat of the sunlight he relived the shock of seeing her in bed with another man, Hapuseneb. This was something he would never have envisaged in all the years he had known them both. He knew she had given Hapuseneb more power than any high priest had ever had before, extending his estates and his jurisdiction beyond the usual cult areas of Amun to the whole country, north and south, but he had thought she was doing this in order to honour her beloved god, not because she desired his High Priest.

All who knew Hatshepsut knew that her position was becoming more precarious by the day as her nephew grew less interested in spending his time in foreign garrison towns looking after the empire, and more interested in playing power politics at home. Was her intimacy with Hapuseneb part of a cunning game she was playing to hold the throne? Having lifted the local god of Amun above the heads of all the other gods in the Two Lands, and having given his priests in general, and Hapuseneb in particular, unprecedented riches and power, was it not but shrewd good sense to bind him to her with something more than political loyalty?

Senmut's rage almost subsided. He could understand that. He remembered her, half-raised on one elbow, looking directly into his eyes as he burst in – as though she was expecting him, as though this was a deliberate confrontation. Was there regret in her eyes, a plea for forgiveness?

Could he forgive her this time? Could he ignore what he had seen?

He pressed his lips together, remembering Hapuseneb's hooded eyes, his relaxed and comfortable naked body.

Was everyone laughing at him as he stormed from the palace? He had not missed the sly, amused glances, the crude nudges of the palace servants.

How much of his life had he given up to her? His brother had warned him time and again to find an alternative to the wayward Queen. But who could love any other woman, once he had loved Hatshepsut? He had taken other women to bed but, always, Hatshepsut spoiled it for him.

There were times when he almost hated her god Amun. She made him the excuse for everything. Amun-Ra "commanded" her. Amun-Ra "advised" her. Amun-Ra "revealed" to her. There was no doubt that she communicated in some mystical way with the Hidden One. He, who had very few mystical intuitions or transcendent communications, found it difficult sometimes to accept the major changes she made in her life and in the lives of those around her based on nothing more than a message from Amun-Ra, a message no one else had witnessed. No doubt Amun-Ra had instructed her to drop him in favour of Hapuseneb, he thought bitterly. Had she not written on her obelisk:

> *Behold, I worked under His direction. He was my leader. I was unable to think out a plan for work without his prompting.*

Hapuseneb was the chief of the four First Prophets of Amun-Ra and should as such be a very holy man. But Senmut knew that he was not. His interest in his position was political. He had been an able vizier before, and he was an able administrative high priest now. There was nothing that went on in Amun-Ra's vast estates that he did not control. If "Amun-Ra" had advised Hatshepsut to take his High Priest to bed, Senmut believed it had been arranged in some way, for political purposes. But this did not comfort him. His own was not a political love – it was his life. She should not play with it like this.

He desperately needed to make a gesture of defiance – an assertion of independence. And he wanted her to notice it!

A short while later the gardeners at Djeser Djeseru were startled to witness an unscheduled procession passing along the avenue of sphinxes, between the sacred persea trees and through the gate of the lower terrace. Many of them downed tools and moved towards the causeway, curious to see what was going on.

Senmut strode ahead, and behind him came a small column of priests almost running to keep up with him, the leader carrying an extraordinary object. It was a statue of Amun of the kind that usually emphasised a large erect phallus to indicate his role as creator-force. His sacred symbol, the ram, had been chosen for its strong procreative activities.

Those who were nearest could see at once that the image had been crudely castrated.

The procession, looking neither to the left nor the right, mounted the first causeway at once, between the lion balustrades.

As they reached the second causeway with the serpent balustrades, several more workers joined the small crowd that was now following the procession.

Between the great granite doorjambs boasting of Amun's potency as Bull of the Two Lands, and Hatshepsut's role as "the Great God's Wife", the heavy cedar door swung open to Senmut's imperious knock. Behind it in the colonnaded court, the priests of Amun were hastily gathering, confused by the unexpected arrival of a procession.

Senmut was the King's confidant and favourite and could not be turned away, but had he the right to break in like this? What was he carrying? They gasped as they took in the blasphemous nature of what he was bringing into the Holy of Holies.

Some retreated hastily into the cult rooms and returned with burning incense to fumigate and purify the intruders. Others tried to remonstrate with Senmut and block his passage to the door of the sanctuary itself. No one entered there but the sovereign and the highest of the priests.

Senmut drew the bolts before he could be prevented and stormed into the dark and secret place. The light from the third court now blazed in.

He had seized the statue from the leader of his procession. He entered the forbidden chamber alone and shook the disfigured image furiously before the perfect golden form of Hatshepsut's god.

"Amun," he shouted. "Father-husband of Hatshepsut Maat-ka-Ra! Beware she does not castrate you too!"

But before he could say more he was seized from behind and dragged out of the sanctuary. Just before the great door was slammed behind him and he was pulled and pushed to the ground, he thought he caught the eye of Amun, and read there a cold and merciless message.

The story of Senmut's extraordinary action spread like wildfire, and Hatshepsut could not have ignored it even if she had wanted to. She and her god had been insulted, and the least punishment should be death. But she had loved Senmut for a long time and, although she was very angry with him now, she could not forget that. She stood on the terrace of her official palace on the east bank, looking over the river – the mysterious, silver-blue, deep and abiding flow that kept her country alive.

She had wanted to teach him a lesson for assuming that he had exclusive rights over her, that he could presume to unseat a pharaoh and make her a woman like any other. There were many reasons she had taken Hapuseneb to her bed, but that was certainly one of them.

Now she wished she had not done it. Not only had she lost the greatest love of her life, but she had broken her vow to Amun-Ra. What would become of her?

Was Senmut mad, or possessed?

His long sojourn in the desert had been the beginning. Had he been called there by the dark and subtle desert god Set? Had he been taken over, influenced in some way, to destroy her? Had her enemies cast spells?

The sun was setting and she could hear the hum of prayers from everywhere in the city. The dark was coming and everyone was afraid. They were praying for the return of Ra. The mountains where the body of her earth-father, Aa-kheper-ka-Ra, lay, were already black, silhouetted against an increasingly crimson sky. How inexorably the dark came!

She shivered. Somehow the joy, the excitement of being Pharaoh was not as great as it used to be. She felt in her bones the best years were over and she was being drawn down, sucked down, into the night.

The whole sky was suffused in a red glow, and silence had fallen, as though all the praying had stopped and the world was waiting for something momentous to happen.

It was Hapuseneb's suggestion that he, as First Prophet of Amun-Ra, should be the one to pronounce sentence on Senmut. He pointed out that as it was the sanctuary of Amun-Ra that had been desecrated and her in her role as Great God's Wife who had been insulted, it was only fitting that as defender of her and her god he should take on the responsibility.

In former years Hatshepsut would not have even considered the suggestion. To step down as judge in favour of one of her officials would have been unthinkable. But Hatshepsut was not as clear-thinking as she used to be. She could not bring herself to face Senmut. She could not bring herself to condemn him. She turned her face to the wall and Hapuseneb took her place.

The High Priest of Amun-Ra showed no mercy. To keep his power intact he could not allow anyone, however important, to storm uninvited into the sacred precincts and insult his god and his king. Senmut was condemned to death.

"She will come to me," Senmut thought. "She will have to make a show of punishing me, but she will forgive me." At least he was not in a dark and stinking cell, but in his own chambers, albeit heavily guarded.

A bird was sitting on a palm frond out in the garden, the sun behind it throwing its shadow on his wall, high up near the ceiling. He stood on the chest made of ebony heavily inlaid with ivory, a priceless gift from Hatshepsut, and reached up to the bird's shadow until it lay on his hand. For the first time a chill touched his heart. What if she did not come? What if the execution was carried out?

The bird in the tree was moving; it was warm and vital, soft and feathery and full of song, but he could feel nothing on his hand except a coldness where the bird's shadow prevented the beam of sunlight reaching his flesh.

He climbed down hastily and sat on the edge of his bed with his head in his hands. What had he done and why had he done it? It was not only personal pique and spite; somewhere deep inside him he knew that something had gone wrong, not only with their own relationship but with her relationship to her country and her god. If she came to him he would tell her that. He would tell her he had not done what he had done for jealousy, but as a gesture to save her, to shock her into looking at herself and her actions more closely.

He stood up and paced the chamber. But the jealousy was there – a dull ache. What right had he to point the finger at her? What right, after all the mistakes he had made? She would do anything for worldly power, and he the same for intellectual power. Two of a kind, he thought. No wonder they understood and loved each other so much.

He heard steps in the corridor outside and spun round, expectantly watching the door. She had come! He knew she would. He would say nothing. There would be no need.

The door was unbarred. He heard the clink of the guards' spear-shafts as they stamped their salute on the floor.

The door swung open.

It was not Hatshepsut.

It was his executioner.

Senmut was buried without ceremony, not in his official tomb that had been prepared high in the desert cliffs above the tomb of his humble parents, but in some obscure and undistinguished pit. No prayer-spells guided him through the Duat. No images of food were provided to feed him through eternity. He was on his own to find his way, or be lost. Most of his statues were ritually defaced, his nose and mouth smashed in so that he could not draw the breath of life or continue to communicate with those still earth-living after his death. Hapuseneb was prepared to have all mention of him erased from every record so that he not only would not exist in the future, but would apparently never have existed.

Senmut's friends managed secretly to preserve enough mention of him, enough intact images of him, so that he would not suffer this fate. Hatshepsut herself, shocked by how extreme Hapuseneb's punishment had been, called a halt to the erasures before they were complete.

* * * *

As soon as Senmut's fall from grace was known, Hatshepsut was told about the personal tomb he had been tunnelling under her mortuary temple. She went at once to visit it.

The entrance was well outside the sacred ground of the temple, but the tunnel was dug under the perimeter wall and his tomb chamber carved out as close as he could get it to the axis line that ran from Hatshepsut's own tomb, through Amun's sanctuary, through the temple and along the avenue of sphinxes that led with such direct intention towards Ipet-Esut and the exact place where Hatshepsut had erected her two giant obelisks.

The Pharaoh stood alone in the first chamber among the piles of chippings not yet cleared away from the excavation of two further and unfinished chambers. She gazed at the complex astronomical ceiling.

He had not been content to have the usual vague representations of the stars by the thousand, but had drawn on his knowledge of the ancient star charts he had studied at Men-nefer to produce a great panorama of the moving heavens, part literal, part mythological, in every section of which his respect for Hatshepsut was clearly visible. A representation of her secret spirit name, several times repeated, showed her as a major protagonist in the great drama of challenge and conflict acted out eternally between good and evil, order and chaos, creation and destruction.

He might have suffered moments of serious doubt in his life and he might not always have respected the gods as deeply and consistently as he should, but here it was clear that he had come to terms with a truth that could not be expressed in isolated images; it needed a dramatic and sweeping presentation of motion and dynamic interaction – a truth that gleamed for a moment as she stared at the ceiling, but was almost immediately lost because her mind was too small to grasp it.

Beneath it he had written:

Having penetrated besides all the writings of the divine prophets, I was ignorant of nothing that has happened since the beginning of time.

She lowered the torch and sighed. In a lesser man that would have been an arrogant boast, in Senmut it was a statement of fact. She would miss him.

Companion greatly beloved, Keeper of the palace, Keeper of the heart of the King, making content the Lady of both lands, making all things come to pass for the spirit of her Majesty.

Soon after that she forced herself to visit Amun's sanctuary. Since "the incident" she had avoided it, and all the purification ceremonies had been undertaken by Hapuseneb.

She bowed low before her god.

"My Lord, my Father," she said humbly. "Forgive him. It was I who drove him to it. Forgive me. Let me see him again. Let him live again. Let us meet in the Millions of Years."

There was no answer.

She looked up.

The statue with the blue eyes of sacred stone stood rigid and upright in his golden barque like a painted doll.

She heard a movement behind her and spun round.

It was Hapuseneb. How long had he been there? Had he heard her prayer?

His face was impassive – a priest's face.

She rose and stood aside while the High Priest moved forward and shook the smoke of aromatic incense over her and over the god's statue – the same incense that Senmut had brought her from "the god's land", the land of Punt.

CHAPTER 15

Anhai gathered her community of healers around her on the island. She covered the sandy surface with rich black earth and irrigated it until it burgeoned and bloomed.

Hatshepsut herself paid it a visit, bringing with her as a gift a young frankincense tree. This became the centrepiece of a circular maze garden. Healing herbs flourished in its shade, and hardy flowering shrubs constituted a colourful wall around the outside. Those who sought healing on the island could walk slowly during the cool hours of dawn on the labyrinthine paths in this garden, winding in and out until they reached the sacred tree, where they rested, their backs leaning against it, drawing strength, as it drew strength, from the earth in which it was rooted and from the sun that poured down beneficent rays on its crown.

When Hatshepsut first took Hapuseneb as her lover, the ghost that had been troubling her all but disappeared. Whether it was the solid, down-to-earth nature of Hapuseneb or the sheer formidable strength of his personality that kept the spectre at bay, she could not say, but night after night, curled in his arms, she had a respite from its icy and accusing stare.

But now, lying alone, unsleeping, staring at the ceiling, a small night-light burning beside her bed, she knew the phantom had returned. She faced the wall, but knowing he was there and not being able to see him frightened her so much she turned to confront him.

As though his dark soul had fed on this latest horror, he seemed larger than before, darker, his eyes more penetrating, his hatred more intense. He did not have Senmut at his side, as he had had Neferure on the night of her death, but she knew he was gloating over her suffering; over her regret.

She picked up a little alabaster bowl from the table beside her bed and threw it at him with all her might. It passed right through him. He laughed – and moved nearer.

She threw another object and another. But each time the object passed through him he seemed to grow larger and move nearer, until he was towering over her and she was ice-cold with terror.

He leant down towards her. She tried to pull away. She tried to leave the bed and run from the room, but she found her limbs would not obey her. It was as though her own body had deserted her. She tried to call for the help of her father Amun-Ra, but a hard shell seemed to be around her heart, preventing any out-reaching towards the divine realms – a carapace of fear and guilt and hate, but most of all, despair.

"I am finished," she thought, almost with resignation. To continue a life without Senmut, without her dream for Neferure, without her self-respect and without her relationship with Amun-Ra . . .

She dreaded the spectre's icy touch, yet almost welcomed it. What would it be like, death?

But she did not die.

Suddenly he was gone. She was alone.

She pulled herself together sufficiently to consult her physician – the only one, apart from the two women who had helped her that fatal day, she told about the haunting.

The physician advised certain spells of exorcism and Hatshepsut carried out his instructions to the letter. But it did no good.

Even when she could not see him, she felt the phantom's presence. It was then she decided to go to Sehel Island and see what the daughter of Imhotep could do.

In some chambers of the healing sanctuary there were statues of the gods Imhotep, Djehuti and Hathor, each with a little hollow carved out of the stone at its feet. Sacred water was poured over them, to absorb the energy of the god who inhabited the statue, and this was administered to the patients when necessary.

When Hatshepsut arrived for her healing, the first thing that Anhai did was to give her a drink of the potent liquid energised by all three of the sanctuary gods, and then she led her to a small sacred pool. There, secluded behind rocks and a reed screen, Anhai and the great Pharaoh immersed themselves completely, symbolically washing off any contamination that might be clinging to them from their worldly lives. Emerging as though fresh from the waters of the womb, they made their way along a path lined with young sycamore saplings sacred to Hathor, to the buildings of the healing sanctuary.

The next step was to lay Hatshepsut to rest on a couch beside a small central table in the first chamber of healing: the dream chamber.

She had been given a light meal of carefully chosen ingredients and was feeling physically comfortable, but a little apprehensive. She had heard Anhai's methods left no secrets in the heart. On the other hand, she knew she might lose the precious double crown if she did not return to her full strength and vigour. She was no longer sure her will was strong enough to sustain the protective psychic shield around her that was so essential to a ruling monarch. She had even grown to doubt her own links with divinity.

The table beside the couch was of olive wood. It had four legs and beneath it four bricks were placed one above the other, each inscribed with two names: Amun and Mut, Ptah and Sekhmet, Horus and Hathor, Djehuti and Seshat – the male/female aspects of four potent spirit forces.

In front of the table was a silver censer in which burned olive wood charcoal and little balls of mixed goose fat and myrrh. Over the table was a fine white linen cloth covering certain objects Anhai did not permit Hatshepsut to see.

Anhai lit the censer carefully, whispering a prayer for the protection of herself and the Pharaoh as she did so.

She assured herself that Hatshepsut was lying comfortably, composed for sleep, and then she left her alone.

Hatshepsut wondered what dreams would come to her that night. Anhai was a strong but calming presence. She had confidence in her. For the first time in a long while she did not dread going to sleep. If anyone could drive the dark shadows away it would be this young woman.

At first she could not sleep because she was curious to know what lay under the cloth on the table. But it was clear Anhai did not want her to touch anything in the room or move from the couch, so she tried to restrain herself. At last, the darkness, her own weariness and the strange, hypnotic scent of the olive, myrrh and goose fat had its effect and she drifted off to sleep.

She found herself on a river in a boat, floating with the current towards the great ocean. Everything was fair and fine. Distant mountains, pink in the sun-haze, slid past; palm trees, cornfields, mud-brick houses . . . It was her land as she had seen it all her life. The only thing that was different was that she did not seem to be the Pharaoh, but an ordinary woman.

The river became narrower, the boat bobbing dangerously as it passed swiftly between high and rocky cliffs. She clung to the sides and looked apprehensively around her. The cliffs cut out the sunlight and it was chilly in the shadows. She wished she had oars so that she would have some control over the boat.

At last she burst out of the narrow constricting channel into the sunlight. The river broadened and calmed. Now there were no familiar habitations on either side, but from time to time there were tall, more than life-size figures standing on the banks and watching her. She believed them to be the gods.

Jagged rocks now appeared in the river. The water was no longer as smooth and benign as it had been before the narrowing of the cliff passage. She was in danger of being wrecked. "Why don't they help me?" she thought almost angrily. But she could not bring herself to call out to them for help.

She searched about in the bottom of the boat to see if there was anything she could use as an oar, but the craft was bare and empty. Something knocked against the side, and when she looked up she saw it was a piece of palm wood. She tried to catch it but the swift water had already carried it past. But if there had been one piece of driftwood, there was a good chance there would be others. She watched intently for her opportunity.

At last she found a plank, presumably broken off from a wrecked boat, and managed to alter her course sufficiently to avoid an enormous rock that suddenly loomed up ahead.

"You see," she said triumphantly to the impassive figures still watching her from the bank, "I don't need your help after all."

But in looking up to make her point, she found that they were nearer than before and she could see them more clearly. Her heart missed a beat as she realised they were not the gods after all, but duplicated versions of her familiar spectre.

She hit an impediment just under the surface with a sickening thud. Her frail craft splintered into a hundred pieces instantly and she was flung into the turbulent white water of a series of rapids that passed through a second narrow channel between cliffs.

Now she was fighting for her life as she was tossed and buffeted, dragged and thrust in the powerful coils of the river. She thought for a moment that she saw the malevolent eyes of the serpent Apep, the enemy of existence, waiting to swallow her into the endless void of its repulsive stomach, and fought with even greater determination to stay alive. Around her, strings of silver bubbles swirled; muscular ropes of liquid energy wound around her neck and almost choked her. The river roared and the boulders rolling along its inhospitable bed rumbled ominously.

Fearfully she looked up and felt that the solid black sides of the gorge were leaning over her as "he" had leant over her the night of Senmut's death.

She screamed and woke, sweating, in the dream chamber on Sehel Island, the charcoal almost burned away in the censer. Merciful light was pouring through the high windows.

The door opened and Anhai was beside her at once.

Later, when she was calmer, Anhai crossed the room and extinguished the last glowing embers of the charcoal. She lifted the white cloth and folded it neatly. From beneath it she took three pebbles, which she then presented to the woman on the couch.

Hatshepsut sat up and held them in her hand, looking at them, puzzled. Three ordinary stones of the earth: one white, one black and one grey – the grey made up of the crystals of the other two. They were river-worn to egg shape.

Anhai offered no explanation but said that Hatshepsut should keep them.

After the dream, the two women walked in the garden. From time to time Hatshepsut caught sight of other figures flitting about the corridors and chambers of the sanctuary, but it was Anhai herself who attended to every aspect of her healing.

The sun had risen but the air was not yet too hot to bear. Anhai encouraged Hatshepsut to tell her about her dream as they walked, and drew detail after detail out of her. Hatshepsut found herself talking to Anhai as she had not talked to anyone in her life before. Anhai listened and said nothing.

She heard about Hatshepsut's love for Senmut and how she could not have endured those early years of struggle to establish herself without his encouragement and help. But Anhai noticed that when Hatshepsut spoke of more recent times her feelings for Senmut were ambiguous. She still loved him, but there were signs that she had begun to resent his influence on her, and the fact that he knew so many of her innermost thoughts and fears.

Anhai could see that there were many things Hatshepsut was not prepared to tell her, but, warned by the fate of Senmut, she was careful not to probe too deeply. If she needed to know about something that Hatshepsut wanted to keep secret, she would have to find out by means other than direct confrontation. She suspected it was a sense of guilt that was festering in the Pharaoh's heart and drawing the colour from her cheeks and the flesh from her bones. It was a sense of guilt that had held her back from calling on the gods for help in her dream – and that made her later prefer to doubt their existence rather than to accept their criticism.

The next part of the treatment took place in the crystal room. Imhotep and Djehuti presided over the whole sanctuary, but Hathor, the goddess of crystals and minerals, "Our Lady of Turquoise", presided over the crystal room.

The Great King laid herself down on the couch without demur

while Anhai carefully selected the appropriate stones from the tables around the room. She explained as she was doing so that she could not say one particular crystal would always cure one particular malady, and another would always cure a second. Their effect was more subtle than that, and each had to be chosen intuitively by the healer to suit the person seeking healing.

The next step was to hold a slender amethyst crystal suspended on a silver chain above the Pharaoh and quietly, contemplatively, move it from toe to crown of head and back again, watching intently as the pendulum swung, apparently of its own volition, either sunwise or anti-sunwise, each movement registering some significant imbalance or unusual eddy in the life flow of the woman lying beneath it.

Anhai knew nothing of the abortion Hatshepsut had had, but when she held the pendulum over the region of her womb the swing against the sun was so violent it almost left her hand. Quietly she moved on and made no comment, but for a moment she caught Hatshepsut's eyes and knew that she had seen the violence of the swing and knew what it signified.

Anhai put the amethyst pendulum aside, and began to place a wall of quartz crystals around the figure on the couch. As she laid each one down she asked a particular spirit-god for protection. She knew the crystals in themselves could not protect from malevolent influences, but by their shimmering beauty each would be a reminder of the ancient, marvellous splendour of the natural universe, complex and subtle, physical and yet numinous. That, with the help of the gods, would provide the courage and strength to ward off any baleful effects from the dark forces.

Anhai believed that if visualising something terrifying could result in an actual physical effect – for example, sweat and nausea – visualising something harmonious and beautiful could also result in a physical effect – such as calm and wellbeing, conditions necessary for self-healing. She knew that very few cases of disease were due to baleful influences from without – most were brought about by fear and guilt and anger from within. The word, after all, indicated a "lack of ease". All these emotions could trigger harmful secretions in the body. Her task was to stop this process and reverse it by encouraging the natural healthy energies of the body to flow uninterrupted.

After the protective prayers and their accompanying crystals were in place, Anhai put the symbols of the great spirits upon Hatshepsut's body, each carefully chosen and precisely placed.

On her forehead she placed a triangle: Atum at the apex, the great He-She who produced the first impulse towards existence. Below that, Ptah and Sekhmet, who had "thought" the world and could as easily destroy it. These were carved out of amethyst, the crystal for deep and mystical understanding. On each cheek, beneath the eyes, she placed the Eyes of Horus made of lapis lazuli, white calcite and jet – the all-seeing eyes of the Falcon. On either side of the mouth she placed Djehuti and Seshat in turquoise, to ensure that the words she spoke would be wise ones. On her heart rested Ra in the form of Kheper, the scarab, the transformer, in green nephrite. On her breasts were Hathor and Isis, the mothers, in warm rose quartz. On either side of her body, level with her heart, Anhai placed Amun and Mut in red jasper to keep the life's blood flowing through her veins. She had already laid small images of Geb, the earth god, along the couch to coincide with her backbone, and the Djed column of Osiris.

On her womb, Heket, the frog-headed goddess of birth and rebirth kept guard, in bloodstone. And between her legs, protecting the southern entrance to her body, Bes in flint and Tawaret in chert.

Between her feet she set the shen, the symbol of completeness, the knotted rope that would hold all together. And beneath the soles of her feet there were two coiled cobras of black obsidian with eyes of topaz, fiercely preventing any malevolent influences entering her from the earth.

Finally, above the centre of her skull, Anhai placed a perfect rock crystal sphere. "That which is beyond all forms of the gods is formless," she said. "The nearest we can get to imagining it is as the all-embracing sphere."

A shaft of sunlight came through the high window slit at that moment and illuminated the crystal sphere with brilliant and blinding light. Anhai stepped back, startled. But as suddenly as it had come, it was gone.

She put both her hands on either side of Hatshepsut's head, at the temples, and smiled.

"You have been favoured," she said softly. "The gods are with you."

As she said it she knew it was true. She could feel them all around her, as though their passive and invisible presence had been given life and animation by the rays of light that had shot out from the crystal sphere.

Hatshepsut was aware of it, too. At last she had the feeling that the gods were real, that she was not alone. She shuddered to remember how hopeless and despairing she had been lately. She had forgotten the universe with its swirling stars, its vortices of energy, its vast and purposeful millions of living beings. She had forgotten that, in spite of that vastness, each minute individual had somehow, paradoxically, the same significance as the Whole, and that each was as much responsible for the cosmic order as any god.

She could feel Anhai's warm hands becoming even warmer on her temples. She could feel energy pouring into her. She felt renewed, revitalised, as strong and determined as she used to be. She had done wrong on three counts, and each deed had passed into the Whole and altered it – had become part of it.

For the first time she told Anhai about the abortion of Senmut's son and how he had been haunting her.

Anhai listened quietly. So that was it. She had felt the shadow, but had not properly understood its cause.

She asked Hatshepsut if she would like to speak with her son.

Hatshepsut looked up at the young woman in surprise – and some alarm.

"Here," Anhai said, "with all this protection around you, he cannot harm you."

"You'll not leave me?"

"No. I'll not leave you."

"It won't do any good. He's determined to hate me."

"You were responsible for the beginning of his hate. You could be responsible for its ending. Did you not say you cursed him?"

Hatshepsut was silent. She had cursed him, and she had cursed his father. Was there nothing that could stay hidden?

"I will try," she said reluctantly.

Anhai opened a little box of yew wood and took out her mother's very special crystal. She held it just above Hatshepsut's forehead and prayed for help in this matter.

The room became very silent.

Suddenly Anhai noticed Hatshepsut trembling and, as every moment passed, the trembling became more violent.

Quietly and competently Anhai adjusted the crystals surrounding her patient and replaced those that were being displaced. She could see that Hatshepsut was having an encounter with someone she herself could not see.

Courageously she went into the Silence and joined her.

Now she could see the phantom that had been haunting the Pharaoh, and she knew at once what had happened. Hatshepsut's physical body still lay on the couch protected by the crystals, but her astral body was crouched and cowering in the corner of the room in dread of the figure that loomed over her.

Anhai stepped between the two astral figures. "Come," she said, reaching out her hands to the woman. "You must stand up. You must face him. He is your son. He needs your help. Give him love, commend him to the gods. He was left vulnerable and naked. A dark force looking for a vehicle to use against you found him and is using him. He needs you to set him free. Come – be strong."

Hatshepsut was sobbing, drawing back.

"I cannot – cannot look at him!"

She had not been able to look at Senmut either as the sentence of death was passed. She who had always been so strong and just was bowed to the ground with shame.

"Come," Anhai insisted. "Come. Look up. Ask for his forgiveness. Give him love. Commend him to the gods."

"I cannot," sobbed Hatshepsut. But Anhai put a firm hand under her chin and forced her head up.

"Pray for him. Give him strength. Give him dignity. Give him life."

Hatshepsut's eyes met the eyes of her son and she too could see that he was struggling against a dark force that was determined to possess him.

She reached out her hands. She named him with a blessing, and cried to all the gods she knew to take his soul into their care. She fought for his release as a lioness fights for her cub.

The young man screamed and writhed, while darkness burned around him like fire.

Suddenly it was over.

With tears running down her cheeks, Hatshepsut watched her son stand up tall and straight. His eyes were clear and calm, looking into hers with sorrow, not resentment.

With wings of golden light Horus enfolded him and lifted him away from them.

The room was empty once more, apart from themselves. They were both exhausted and for a long while too shaken to move. Then Hatshepsut without warning began to rise from the couch. Anhai rushed forward to remove the crystals and the images before they were sent flying on to the floor.

"Wait," she cried. "Majesty, please wait. It is bad to come back too suddenly without the proper ritual." She started putting the crystals into a silver bowl of clear water for cleansing.

But Hatshepsut would not listen. She was already up, impatiently handing Anhai the pieces that had not yet fallen.

"You know what I think?" Hatshepsut said fiercely, her eyes sparking. "I think I know who was responsible for using that poor child to destroy me!"

Without a backward glance, as though Anhai and Sehel Island were already forgotten, she strode out of the room.

The island was galvanised into action. Her servants and attendants, who had been having a pleasant lazy time, were suddenly running hither and thither to gather her things and themselves together.

Anhai stood on the terrace of her sanctuary and watched her go.

As though only remembering her when she was on the water, Hatshepsut turned and raised an imperious hand in farewell to Anhai.

She was Pharaoh again, in full vigour.

CHAPTER 16

As soon as she returned to Waset, Hatshepsut was overwhelmed by pharaonic duties. Nehsi, Thutiy, Hapuseneb and the others had held the fort well in her absence, but they could only do so much. There was a murmuring, a restlessness, under the surface, in their own hearts and around them in the court, the town and the country – a feeling that Pharaoh's eye was sleeping, that her attention was wandering. Her closest associates had been deeply shaken by the death of Senmut. It marked for them the end of the golden age. They withdrew their trust from Hapuseneb, who had been closely involved with them in all their previous councils. No longer did they feel they could freely exchange ideas, discuss projects, advise, comment. He was no longer one of them. They were sure he had engineered the fall of Senmut in some way, for his own purposes. Very little was private in the Pharaoh's life, and it was now common knowledge that Hapuseneb had taken Senmut's place in her bed.

They had all noticed the change in her. At first they had put it down to the sadness caused by Neferure's death – but it seemed more than that. For the first time, they, her closest friends and advisers, who had brought her through so many difficult and dangerous times, felt excluded, afraid. If she could turn her back on Senmut and allow Hapuseneb to sentence him to death, she was not the same woman they had known and loved. Who would be next? They became cautious and circumspect to such an extent that they were no use as advisers and counsellors any more. They told her what she wanted to hear and not what she needed to hear.

But on her return from Sehel Island she made a point of being seen to take control again. She knew that her withdrawal from public life had made her people anxious and strengthened Men-kheper-Ra's hand. She made decisions, pronounced decrees, answered petitions with all her old fire. But in her eyes there was an expression of cold wariness that had not been there before. Someone was using black magic against her, and she knew it had to be someone of formidable skill.

Hapuseneb no longer shared her bed. There were no angry words between them – just a silent understanding that what had once been to their mutual advantage was no longer so.

Men-kheper-Ra was in the east at Kepel at this time. She believed that whatever was being done was being done in his name, but did not suspect him personally. This was not his style. It was more likely to be his mother, though she was probably not capable of such an impressive degree of skill. Hatshepsut decided to ask Djehuti and Seshat which of the smiling, bowing priests around her was capable of magic on this scale.

She made a private visit to one of the small chapels in the garden of her palace at Waset, telling the priest that she wanted to be alone with the god and goddess. He was an old man who had been close to her father and had always had great affection for her.

She asked him for the silver bowl that was used for divination, and he placed it between the statues of Djehuti and Seshat, filled it with clear water, and bowed himself out. He understood she was not to be disturbed, no matter what occurred or who ordered it.

The polished bowl was wide and shallow, and the still, clear water in it almost invisible.

She opened the small ebony box she had brought with her and from it drew a number of persea leaves, which had been inscribed with individual hieroglyphs. Carefully she placed the leaves on the water, the glyphs showing. They floated on the surface and she waited patiently until the ripples had passed and the leaves lay absolutely still.

She then composed herself, calming her mind carefully and patiently. When her own thoughts were as still as the leaves on the water, she bowed down before the statues of Djehuti and Seshat and spoke the words of the divination prayer-spell and the question she wanted answered. Her voice, enunciating each word distinctly, sounded very loud in the chamber, though she did not think that she was speaking above a whisper. It seemed to her she was in a vast hollow space and her words were echoing around her, circling like birds.

She had her eyes shut and her head bowed, but she felt a breath of air moving in the room as though a door had been opened or the gods had breathed out. She longed to look up, but dared not. She wanted to do nothing that would break the enchanted moment.

She knew she was not alone. But she knew also that no one of flesh and blood was there, apart from herself.

She was grateful to Anhai, for Anhai had given her back the capacity to communicate with the gods.

She waited until she could no longer feel the stirring of the air, no longer feel the presences, and then – cautiously and humbly – she rose to her feet.

She looked into the silver bowl. The leaves had moved from their original positions. Most were clustered round the edges; only a few were left in the centre – and they spelled out "Mut-awa". It was the name of one of the women who had attended her during the abortion.

She was shocked. She would never have suspected her of disloyalty, nor of having the skill to perform such sophisticated magic.

She stood staring at the name for a long time and then decided that Mut-awa alone could not be responsible for what had happened. She had been used by someone else, and Mut-awa's only part in it was that she could not keep a secret. She wondered if she had been threatened or bribed.

She decided to ask Djehuti and Seshat once more. Last time her question had been loosely worded. This time she would be precise. She wanted the name of the actual magician-priest who had used her son so cruelly and so effectively against her.

She stirred the leaves around so that they no longer spelled anything, and then, as patiently as before, waited for the water to be completely still.

She bowed down and said her incantation and asked her question, and then remained, head down, in attitude of humble prayer. This time the god's breath seemed a long time coming.

She repeated the prayer-spell and the question three times. And then she felt it – the stirring of air, the almost imperceptible change of atmosphere in the room.

She had the name. It lay before her. "Men-soneb" – a priest of Amun recently come from Khemnu.

Well, he was finished. His name would be obliterated forever. Angrily she smashed her fist into the water. Her golden bracelets glittered ominously as she scooped up the leaves and threw them to burn in the brazier.

As she turned to go she remembered who had given her the name. She bowed quickly to Djehuti and Seshat, Master and Mistress of Names and Naming, Guardians of the records of Millions of Years. Through tight and angry lips, she promised them that justice would be done to those who misused the powers that were given by the gods. Then she left the chapel with a firm and purposive step.

The first thing Hatshepsut did was to confront Mut-awa.

She dismissed all her attendants and called only Mut-awa to her chambers. The woman came quickly and cheerfully, showing no sign of anxious guilt or apprehension.

Hatshepsut set her to fetching and laying out clothes, but she did not seem to be able to find one that pleased the Pharaoh. Mut-awa's cheerfulness soon faded as she was sent scurrying hither and thither for the garments, only to be told irritably that they were not what Hatshepsut had in mind. It was clear that her mistress was in a strange and perverse mood. As soon as she recommended something, Hatshepsut dismissed it with scorn, and if she advised against it, it seemed that was the one thing the Pharaoh wanted to wear.

Hatshepsut was tense and angry, but she was also playing a game with her maid, trying to rattle her so that she would not find is so easy to dissemble when finally the important questions were asked.

But Mut-awa, though becoming increasingly uncomfortable under Hatshepsut's unreasonable treatment, showed nothing but puzzled patience and loyalty.

At last Hatshepsut stopped the game and confronted the woman outright with the accusation that she had betrayed the secret entrusted to her.

Mut-awa was shocked and indignant. Never! Never had she let slip a word!

Hatshepsut persisted, and said some harsh and unkind things.

Tears came to Mut-awa's eyes, but she swore on all the gods, and finally on her mother's grave, that she had not breathed a word.

Hatshepsut paused, for the first time doubting that the oracle had been right; she knew the seriousness of such an oath to Mut-awa.

Hatshepsut paced the room restlessly for a while, thinking.

Mut-awa was crumpled on the floor, weeping.

Suddenly Hatshepsut rounded on her.

"Do you know a priest of Amun called Men-soneb?" she demanded, glaring into her eyes.

Mut-awa gasped.

"Majesty," she said, trembling, "you know he is my husband."

"Your husband?" shouted Hatshepsut in astonishment. Mut-awa was a woman of middle age with very little physical attractiveness. She had never been married, never had any life but one of close personal service to Hatshepsut, first as young princess and then as Pharaoh. But earlier this year Mut-awa had come to her and asked her blessing on her marriage. Hatshepsut at the time had been preoccupied, and, apart from being delighted for her maidservant, for whom she had great affection, she had scarcely taken any notice. She remembered vaguely giving instructions for generous wedding gifts – but then she had forgotten about it. Mut-awa had continued to attend her faithfully and well, as though there had been no change in her life.

Looking intently into the face of her old servant, Hatshepsut knew that Mut-awa had not knowingly betrayed her trust. She had been used by her magician husband. Her anger subsided. She stooped down and took the woman by the arms and raised her to her feet.

"Forgive me," she said. "I should not have doubted you."

"But why, Majesty? Why? Has Men-soneb displeased your Majesty?"

Hatshepsut looked at her. She could see the pain there, the fear that a shadow was about to engulf her life. Mut-awa knew something about Men-soneb that made her fearful.

"Tell me about your husband, Mut-awa," Hatshepsut said gently, drawing the woman down to sit beside her on the couch.

Mut-awa's shoulders drooped. Her hands were in her lap, folding and unfolding nervously. Her tears had stopped flowing, but she kept her head down so that her mistress could not see the growing terror in her eyes. She was remembering . . .

"He – he is much younger than me, Majesty," she said at last in a low, broken voice. "Very handsome." She looked up suddenly, her eyes brimming with tears again. "I'm sure he wouldn't . . ."

"Hush, my dear. I'm accusing him of nothing. How did you meet him? Who are his parents?"

It became clearer and clearer to both of them as Mut-awa talked that the handsome young priest of Amun who had seemed so instantly enamoured of her and asked her to marry him within days of their first meeting could well have had an ulterior motive.

Mut-awa told Hatshepsut, falteringly, that since the first days of blissful union he had been very cold towards her and, in fact, she had seen very little of him. "When I am here with you he always seems to be off duty, but when I am free to go home he is busy at the temple."

"Had he been long at the temple here, when you met him?"

"No. He had come from Khemnu that week."

Hatshepsut put her arm around the woman's shoulders.

"My poor Mut-awa," she said.

"What has he done, Majesty? What has happened?"

Hatshepsut would not tell her. She wanted to see him – and she did not want Mut-awa to get to him first and warn him. She thought of having him killed summarily, before he could do any more harm, but she was afraid his powers in magic might be so great that he could create a spectre of himself to haunt her forever.

She called the guard from the corridor and told him to keep Mut-awa in the room.

Mut-awa was shocked.

"It is for your own good, my dear," she said. "I want to speak with Men-soneb alone. You must not worry. It may be that I am as wrong about him as I was wrong about you."

"Whatever he has done," pleaded Mut-awa, "he is young. He may have been foolish. Please, Majesty – whatever he has done, I'm sure —"

"Whatever he has done," said Hatshepsut, "I will not judge hastily or unfairly. For your sake, if for nothing else, he will have the benefit of any doubt, however small."

With that she turned on her heel and left the room, Mut-awa's eyes gazing after her in despair.

Hatshepsut was angry with herself that she had not paid more attention to her close attendant's marriage. She was also angry that her officials had not investigated the man. It was unbelievable that they had let such an obvious enemy through the net. One of Men-kheper-Ra's spies married to her close confidential attendant! She tightened her lips and wondered whom she should dismiss from office in disgrace, and whom she should condemn to those fearful Nubian prisons she had hardly used since taking the double crown.

But perhaps Men-soneb had somehow blinded them by magical means. He was obviously capable of it. What then? Should she lose more of her best men for something that was not their fault?

But nothing could be decided until she had taken the measure of Men-soneb. She sent for him to attend her in the throne room. Then she called for the double crown. Surprised, the Master of the Royal Vestments clothed her in suitable robes and placed the outward and visible sign of Pharaoh's powerful magic on her head.

When Men-soneb arrived the area was surrounded by guards but the throne room itself was empty apart from Pharaoh, in full regalia, seated on the throne.

She saw before her a handsome young man bowing at each step as he slowly crossed the vast expanse of floor. He came at last to lie prostrate before the steps that led up to the lion throne. He was in the panther skin dress of a "sem" priest, and Hatshepsut knew by that that he was high up in the Amun priesthood. The "sem" priest must be well versed in magic, for it was he who touched the embalmed mouths of kings, of royal and divine statues, with an instrument of iron fallen from the stars, to give them speech. She had been present at many "opening of the mouth" ceremonies and knew how impressive and awe-inspiring they could be. But she had not seen this young man before.

Although as he entered he looked unexceptionable, as he approached she could feel waves of dark and powerful energy

193

emanating from him. Had she been foolish to attempt to confront him alone?

"I am not alone," she whispered. "I am Pharaoh and all the gods are with me. On my head is the double crown, surmounted by the double uraeus, the cobra goddess, Weret-Hekau, Great-in-Magic."

She now had no doubt that he was the one who had created the spectre that had entered her son.

She hastily began to erect protective symbols around herself.

In the air above her she visualised the winged sun disk that was carved above every temple entrance. She "saw" it in a blaze of golden glory – the two cobras curled around the burning sun, spitting protective fire. The wings of the golden falcon spread, shimmering, on either side, as they kept the image hovering where she had placed it. On either side of her she visualised Amun-Ra and Mut and, between them and the sun disk, she visualised beams of dazzling white light. She, on her throne, was placed directly on the light beam that ran between the two gods and was thus contained in a triangle of light linking herself, the great spirits, Amun and Mut, and the winged disk.

She felt she was no longer operating as her ordinary self capable of making mistakes like any other human being, but as her greater "Self", in tune with her higher consciousness and capable of achievements that would reverberate throughout many realms.

She commanded him to rise.

He rose.

She wondered how Mut-awa could have loved him. His expression was cold and arrogant and as hard as black diamond. She could see that he knew why she had called him here; there would be no element of surprise to give her the advantage.

She did not look him in the eyes, but addressed herself icily to a point just above his head.

"Men-soneb, I believe you have been misusing your skills as priest."

"I, Majesty?" he said with mocking, exaggerated innocence.

"Don't play games with me, sir. I know and you know what you have done."

He was silent.

She could feel him willing her to look at him. She knew instinctively that if she did she would be lost. She continued to stare just above his head, but she could feel the beads of sweat beginning to gather under her heavy crown and trickle down her forehead. It seemed to her that her neck would break with the weight of the crown. She had never felt it so heavy.

"It is sorcery," warned Amun at her side. "Keep your head up. Do not look into his eyes."

"I see you, sir, for what you are. You thought to destroy me with the phantom you created."

"I created no phantom, Majesty," he said smoothly.

"I can and will destroy you, sir, but first I am going to make sure you are powerless."

"Majesty," he crooned. "It was not I but you yourself who created the phantom."

The shock put her off guard, and for an instant she met his eyes. A fearful pain shot through her heart, and her limbs seemed to grow numb. With a tremendous effort she pulled away her eyes, and, sweating and shivering, stared desperately at the image of Horus on the opposite wall.

"You lie," she ground out from between clenched teeth.

"No, Majesty. Look into your heart. Was there not guilt there the night you first saw the phantom? Was there not fear?"

She stood up, gripping the arms of her throne.

"You created it. *You* sustained it! *You* seek to destroy me!" she screamed.

He said nothing, but she could feel his will pulling her eyes back to his.

In desperation she called out for the help of Sekhmet, whose image was carved upon her throne.

Suddenly a flash of blue-white light seemed to come from the winged disk and like a bolt of lightning, shoot down directly at her, entering the top of her head and then bursting out in two separate beams from her eyes straight into the eyes of the priest before her.

He shrieked as the light entered his body. Within moments there was nothing left of him but a coil of black smoke rising from a heap of what looked like black and greasy ropes lying smouldering on the floor.

She could not believe what had happened and stared at the place where he had been.

Even as she stared the ropes seemed to move and she saw that they were not ropes at all but black serpents, some already slithering across the floor to make their escape. Knowing what that would mean, she scrambled down the steps, the crown falling with a crash to the ground. She beat at the snakes with the royal crook and flail, screaming as she did so for the guards.

Within moments of the men entering it seemed as though all the snakes were slain.

But were they?

Shaking, she sat on the steps of the throne looking anxiously for any movement from the scattered fragments.

If just one had escaped . . .

CHAPTER 17

Mut-awa was told that her husband, accused of spreading rumours about the Pharaoh, had been ordered to leave the Two Lands and never return. Hatshepsut, seeing the woman's reaction to this, thought it prudent to retire her from her service. She could not risk having someone so closely associated with her who was nursing any kind of resentment. She saw that Mut-awa was well rewarded for her long service and tried to persuade her that if Men-soneb had truly loved her or been half the man she thought he was, he would have taken her with him.

The name of Ast had not been written in the silver bowl, but Hatshepsut would not give up the idea that Men-kheper-Ra's mother was behind the whole thing. She fretted so much over what to do about the matter it became almost an obsession.

Of all her husband's women, Ast was the only one Hatshepsut really disliked. The others she scarcely noticed. Some of them had been brought to his "House of Women" virtually as hostages to keep their fathers, rulers of neighbouring states, under control. Others were bartered by their fathers for gold and exquisite furniture. Some were the daughters of local noblemen whose loyalty the King wanted to ensure. Some had taken the fancy of the King. Ast was the only one, Hatshepsut felt, who had been personally chosen by Aa-kheper-en-Ra because he genuinely loved her. This in itself Hatshepsut would not have resented, for her own relationship was, after all, only a political one; but the woman would not retire, as the others had done, into comfortable obscurity. She still kept an entourage worthy of a queen, and interfered whenever she could in matters of state.

Nothing could be proved against her, but it was clear the lavish parties she constantly threw in her part of the palace provided a good meeting ground for the disaffected friends of her son.

Not for the first time, Hatshepsut considered what she might do to get rid of Ast. But, as before, she always came up against the problem that if she did anything too openly hostile she might precipitate a rebellion by forcing Men-kheper-Ra to take action in defence of his mother.

But this time she was determined not to let her go unpunished. The spectre had almost destroyed her by destroying her peace of mind, and the confrontation with Men-soneb had nearly ended in her annihilation. What would Ast try next?

Ast was lounging in her garden, recovering from a night of heavy drinking, when one of her attendants came running up in a state of agitation to tell her that the Pharaoh had arrived unexpectedly.

Even before the words were out, Hatshepsut was approaching along the path.

Ast did not move, but watched her – as a cat watches a mouse – the whole length of the garden path. Then, when the Pharaoh was standing right in front of her looking down at her with suppressed fury, Ast rose deliberately slowly and, equally slowly, bowed.

Hatshepsut tightened her lips. If Aa-kheper-en-Ra could see her now! The woman used to be beautiful, but in the last few years she had eaten too much and drunk too much and lived an indolent and unhealthy life. She looked much older than Hatshepsut, although she was the same age. Her once slender body was bulging everywhere and her face was unpleasantly puffy. Festering resentment and bitterness had dimmed the sparkle of her eyes, and her smile, though frequent, was now rarely from the heart.

"Such an honour," she said sarcastically. "Hatshepsut spares a moment from her busy life!" Ast never acknowledged that Hatshepsut was Pharaoh and refused to call her "Majesty".

"I think you know why I have come," Hatshepsut said coldly.

"Surely not to gloat over a woman who should be Great King's Mother, but is treated no better than a commoner."

"To see a woman who is known to misuse magic, and a woman who is known to plot against her Pharaoh."

"You'll find no such woman here."

"Certainly none that will succeed."

Ast narrowed her eyes, cat-like, but said nothing.

"I believe Men-soneb, the magician, was one of your friends."

"Men-soneb, the magician?" Ast asked with mock innocence. "I have *many* friends," she added, stressing the word "many".

"He was a priest of Amun-Ra."

"Ah, well," Ast interrupted quickly. "A priest of Amun-Ra! He would have been one of your Hapuseneb's friends."

Hatshepsut did not miss the emphasis on the word "your".

"He was no friend of Hapuseneb."

"But Hapuseneb as High Priest must have chosen him for the temple."

"Hapuseneb has thousands of priests and officials under him. It would be easy for an unscrupulous person, in a privileged position, to slip someone in . . ."

"If that is so, I suggest you dismiss Hapuseneb, for surely he cannot be relied upon to perform his duties satisfactorily if he doesn't even have control over who is appointed priest in his own temples."

Hatshepsut bit her lip.

"I didn't come here to argue with you, Ast. I know you, and I know what you are capable of. I came here to warn you . . ."

"Warn me?" Ast's lip curled.

"Yes," snapped Hatshepsut, holding her temper in check as best she could. Ast's attendants had materialised everywhere in the garden and the whole conversation was being witnessed by a dozen or more pairs of eyes and ears. She could feel the anger in her boiling up to danger point and she knew that she could easily forget the dignity a pharaoh should have at all times, and be provoked into hitting the woman in her sneering, smiling face. "Warn you that you have at last gone too far and I can no longer tolerate your tricks. I am giving orders for you to be moved out of here, out of this palace, out of my life."

Ast's expression of mocking superiority faltered for a moment. She was clearly shocked.

"Out? Where to?"

"Out of the country. Away. As far away as we have vassal states."

"My son . . ."

"Your son will understand no pharaoh can allow the practitioners of malevolent magic against their person to go unpunished. He will be grateful that I have been so lenient."

"What malevolent magic? What are you talking about?"

"You know!" snapped Hatshepsut. "You know very well what I am talking about! But because you are the mother of Men-kheper-Ra you will be sent on a long visit to a comfortable and interesting city where you may see your son whenever he chooses to visit you. Kepel – that is the city."

Ast's complacency had vanished.

"That is a foreign city!" she gasped.

"You will not find it too foreign. There are many from our own country there. The Temple of Hathor is said to be the best in the world. You should count yourself lucky that that is where I have chosen to send you."

"In exile?"

"Not in exile. On an extended visit."

"When may I return?"

"When I have seen that you no longer plot and scheme against me."

"I do not plot and scheme now."

"Maybe not, but I'm not convinced of it."

"My son will not like this."

"Why? You will be nearer him. He is more often in Kepel and the east than he is in the Two Lands."

It was Ast's turn to be silent with rage. Plot and scheme! "This woman has no idea of what I am capable!" she thought. "She will not be on the throne another year from this day!" she vowed.

Hatshepsut turned her back on Ast and walked away, regally and confidently. She felt she had been firm but merciful. It might have been safer to have her secretly killed, but she already had too much blood on her hands and did not intend to add to it.

It was not the end of Hatshepsut's reign that year as Ast vowed – but it was the beginning of the end.

When Pharaoh saw Hapuseneb again they were both in the north, in the administrative capital of the Two Lands – Men-nefer. Hatshepsut was never as happy there as she was in Waset, the religious capital and her family home, but she knew that part of the year had to be passed there whether she liked it or not.

She encountered Hapuseneb for the first time in months in the Temple of Amun-Ra. They had not been lovers since the time Senmut saw them together, and they met now only formally as Pharaoh and High Priest. Not even an intimate or personal glance passed between them as the long and elaborate ritual of cleansing and clothing and feeding the statue of the god took place – the ritual that ensured that when the spirit of the Great Being decided to visit this man-made image, it would be as ready to receive him as they could make it.

When the ceremony was over, Hatshepsut retired to the palace and Hapuseneb came to visit her there. She accepted him in the state chambers, not in her private ones. Ast had sown a tiny seed of doubt in her mind when she pointed out that Hapuseneb must have been responsible for appointing Men-soneb. Later she mused on the fact that the phantom never appeared when Hapuseneb was with her. She had left the judging of Senmut to him, and although she knew what the sentence should officially be, it disappointed her that he had not found a way round it and had been so hasty administering it. Was it really necessary to destroy his tomb, his name and everything about him so quickly and heartlessly? Had she been unwise to give the High Priest of Amun-Ra so much power? Would it one day be to Pharaoh's disadvantage?

"Majesty," he said, bowing low.

So here he was at last in flesh and blood – tall, lean and strong, an impressive figure of a man with or without the magnificent robes of his office. She had thought about him a lot in his absence, remembering their nights together – partly missing them, partly resenting them.

"Hapuseneb."

What should they say to each other, these two with so much to say?

"I am told that your Majesty has stopped work on Djeser Djeseru," the High Priest said at last, stiffly.

"That is so."

"The walls of the north colonnade in the lower terrace cry out for inscription."

"It is not in my heart to inscribe them."

"You have no image of the sacred tree. Djehuti waits to write your names upon the leaves of eternity in vain."

"He will write them on the living tree. My names will live forever."

"But future generations will say Djeser Djeseru is not perfect. It is not complete."

"My life is not perfect, Hapuseneb. My life is not complete."

Silence fell between them once again.

"No woman since the beginning of time has had so much," he said at last. "Why are you not satisfied?"

She looked at him coldly.

"No priest since the beginning of time has had so much, Hapuseneb. Why are *you* not satisfied?" she countered.

"Majesty?"

"I speak of your envy of Senmut, and the haste with which you tried to despatch him to the Void."

"He insulted the divine Pharaoh and the divinity himself. I did no more than my duty."

She stood up and paced the room restlessly, like a caged panther.

"I might have wished to forgive him, but you gave me no time."

"If forgiveness needs time, it is not forgiveness," the priest said.

She looked at him quickly. So he had read the wisdom texts in the temple archives after all. How dared he quote them at her! She pressed her lips tightly together. She could feel herself losing control. She thought of dismissing him from office, but knew that she had no one who could take his place. If she weakened the position of the priests of Amun-Ra now, she would weaken her own position. She pulled herself together and began to question him about the appointment of Men-soneb without telling him any of the details of what had happened.

201

He told her that he only knew he was a promising and talented young priest appointed by the Second Prophet of Amun-Ra at Ipet-Esut while he himself was away from the city.

"Surely all such major appointments should be made by you?"

"They usually are, but sometimes it is not possible. If I recall, the priest who formerly filled that place died suddenly, and Men-soneb was chosen in haste to fill an urgent gap while I was away."

"When you returned to Waset, did you not check on him?"

"What has he done to displease your Majesty?"

"Answer my question."

"I did. He seemed competent and carried high recommendation from the High Priest of Amun-Ra at Khemnu. If he displeases you I will dismiss him."

"He is already dismissed."

"May I ask . . ."

"No, you may not. You should keep a closer check on your priests, Hapuseneb, or I will find someone else who will."

It was Hapuseneb's turn to force himself to keep his temper.

"If your Majesty does not trust my judgement and if your Majesty finds it in her heart to dismiss my priests without consulting me, I think it were better your Majesty *did* find someone else to take my place."

The two eyed each other with hostility for a few tense moments, but both had too much to lose to let it go further.

"You are Pharaoh's right hand, Hapuseneb. I don't want to lose you. But the priests of Amun-Ra are my priests, and if I decide one has to go you must accept it."

Hapuseneb bowed. "I apologise, Majesty," he said, his voice respectful but not humble.

She smiled. "I forgive you – immediately," she said. He laughed, and as suddenly as it had come, their enmity was gone.

"Ah, Hapuseneb, I too am sorry. It was my place to make the decision about Senmut, and I failed to do so. And Men-soneb proved to be too clever for many people."

"I will have his appointment even more thoroughly investigated, Majesty."

"Do so, Hapuseneb, and check back into his past and all who have been close to him. I'm particularly interested in any connections he might have had with Ast."

Ast? He had wondered why Ast had gone so suddenly to live in Kepel. It was clear Hatshepsut had no intention of explaining what Men-soneb had done to cause her displeasure. If it was something treasonable against the Pharaoh and the state, he and all her officials would have known all about it instantly. That she was keeping it so secret implied that it was probably something private. Could Men-soneb have been one of her lovers? Married as he was to one of her women servants, he would have had easy access to the private chambers of the palace, and after Senmut's death and her rejection of himself, who knew what misery might have caused her to do. Although Hapuseneb still had the powers of a High Priest of Amun-Ra, and was the right arm of Hatshepsut, the Pharaoh, he knew he had lost a great deal by losing his place beside Hatshepsut, the woman. He had destroyed Senmut, not through envy, as many believed, but because he sensed that a shadow had appeared in Senmut's heart that would destroy them all by weakening Hatshepsut. If he was losing control of the appointment and dismissal of his own priests, Hapuseneb realised he might lose everything. He must retrieve the situation as quickly as he could by bringing her the information she wanted. Khemnu was where he would begin.

Khemnu was more or less halfway between Men-nefer and Waset, a prosperous city built on a broad fertile plain bordering the Great River. It was called "the City of Eight" because it was believed that it was there that Amun-kem-atef, "he who has completed his moment", in the form of a sacred snake, had given birth to the first eight great gods, male and female pairs representing the primordial abyss, infinity, darkness and hidden power. It had then become the cult centre of the god Djehuti, the thrice great, with extensive parkland given over to the care of sacred ibis and baboons. The Holy of Holies housed part of the shell of the sacred cosmic egg from which the sun god was believed to have emerged in the "island of flames".

Men-soneb had been a priest at the new Temple of Amun-Ra erected since Hatshepsut had come to power, but Hapuseneb started his enquiries among the older priests at the Temple of Djehuti erected during the twelfth dynasty. There was one particular man he had known all his life, in fact who had trained with him as a child. He knew he could trust him absolutely.

He put his first questions about Men-soneb as they sat comfortably on the terrace of the old man's lush green garden, watching the sun sinking slowly behind the palm trees that fringed the river. The wine they sipped was cool and refreshing, as was the light breeze that had arisen among the tamarisk branches. From the direction of the sacred park there was a cacophony of sound as thousands upon thousands of sacred ibis flew in to settle for the night on every available branch and twig. Somewhere baboons were barking, the savage sounds mingling strangely with the smooth and elegant chanting of the evening prayers.

"Men-soneb?" said Hapuseneb's friend thoughtfully. "What do you want to know about him?"

"Anything. His parents. His training. His friends. His private interests."

"I met the young man only infrequently. I didn't like him much."

"Why not?"

The old man shook his head. "I don't know. He had a secretive, dark look. I wondered if he was more interested in the personal use of magic than in the work of the Temple."

Hapuseneb took a long cool draught of wine. Hatshepsut had spoken about the young priest with a certain amount of fear as well as distaste.

Neb-ty, the High Priest of the Temple of Amun-Ra, was not much more helpful. Men-soneb had been born and brought up in Khemnu and had made exceptional progress in his training, soon reaching quite a high position in the hierarchy.

"Why did he go to Waset?"

Neb-ty shrugged. "It is a place to which any priest of Amun-Ra longs to go."

Hapuseneb could not disagree with that. He smiled. This quiet provincial town was full of old people, ibis and baboons. Waset had Hatshepsut, and wherever Hatshepsut was, there was life.

Hapuseneb spoke to Men-soneb's parents, who were anxious about their son, not having heard from him for some time. Hapuseneb understood that he had been a headstrong and difficult boy, but "only because he was so anxious to learn everything there was to learn so that he could serve his Pharaoh", his mother said hastily, trying to counteract the impression her husband was giving that their son had been troublesome.

He seemed to have had no close friends. The most consistent emotion he seemed to rouse in people was fear – though no one could give an instance when they had been harmed by him.

"It was just that he seemed to have a sort of power," one fellow student admitted. "We felt that if we crossed him in any way he would put a terrible curse on us."

"Did you ever hear of a time when he actually cursed someone and they suffered for it?"

"No."

At last one of the junior priests at the Temple of Amun-Ra told Hapuseneb something he wanted to hear. When Ra-hotep of the Temple of the Sun at Yunu had visited recently, he had spent some time talking privately to Men-soneb.

"It is probably he who made Men-soneb restless. Soon after Ra-hotep left, Men-soneb pestered Neb-ty to be allowed to go to Waset."

Hapuseneb left for Yunu the next day.

Ra-hotep was not pleased to hear that Hapuseneb had been enquiring about Men-soneb. He knew a great deal on the subject – about which he would rather not be questioned.

Finding that Ra-hotep managed time and again to avoid him, Hapuseneb grew even more suspicious.

After the second day looked as though it would be as frustrating as the first, Hapuseneb determined to get the better of Ra-hotep and strode into his presence without appointment or announcement, just as he was emerging from his last ablutions of the day in the sacred lake.

"The man is like a great hippo wallowing in a water hole," Hapuseneb thought irritably. "Who does he think he is to keep the First Priest of Amun-Ra waiting?"

He positioned himself between the man and his robes, and the other priests withdrew hastily at an imperious nod from him, knowing that they were no match for Pharaoh's right hand.

Ra-hotep looked at Hapuseneb, and then at his clothes.

"Forgive me," Hapuseneb said smoothly, "but my time here is short and there seemed to be no other way to see you. The First Prophet of the Sun appears to be busier than anyone else in the Two Lands."

Ra-hotep remained half-covered by the water, watching Hapuseneb warily and with dislike. He said nothing.

Hapuseneb towered above him, amused.

"I was interested in a conversation you had with one of my young priests, Men-soneb, in Khemnu."

"I have had many conversations. Why should I remember this one?"

"You will remember this one," Hapuseneb said confidently.

Ra-hotep's skin was beginning to wrinkle in the water. He longed to get out, but he did not want to lose more dignity than he already had.

"I remember nothing about a young priest called Men-soneb."

"Would you not remember after more reflection if your life depended on it?" said Hapuseneb, as though he were half-joking; but the menace in his voice was unmistakable.

Ra-hotep rose from the water, fat and dripping, more like a hippo than ever. But hippos in the Two Lands were not figures of fun. They were violent and dangerous beasts if aroused. The female hippo might be represented as a helpful goddess connected with childbirth and fertility, but the male was depicted on many a temple wall as the enemy of order, to be fought and speared by the young king in his role of Horus, the avenger and protector.

Not all priests went naked into the sacred lake, but Hapuseneb had heard that it was the habit of Ra-hotep at the end of the day. He and Hatshepsut had laughed together over the imagined sight, but he could not help respecting Ra-hotep now for the way he retrieved his clothes, and the dignified and unhurried way he robed himself. The advantage he had had was lost as Ra-hotep swept off towards the building, with Hapuseneb having to hurry to keep up with him.

Later, no matter how hard Hapuseneb probed and questioned, the High Priest of the Sun managed to keep his counsel on what he had really said to Men-soneb and whether he had seen him before or since.

Hapuseneb was more and more convinced that a magician's skills had been used against Hatshepsut. Because of this he decided to use a magician's skills against Ra-hotep. But he knew he must be careful; he had not forgotten his extraordinary experiences in the Temple of the Sun at the summer solstice. If those had been magic tricks, Ra-hotep must be a most formidable magician himself. If they were not, but genuine religious manifestations, Ra-hotep must be close to the sun god's heart and under his protection.

Hapuseneb himself had not much training in the use of magic, so he took the advice of some of his own priests at the Temple of Amun-Ra, and sent for an old man living in the western desert.

The old sorcerer was as crisp and skeletal as a sand-dried corpse, his eyes sunk so deep into their sockets that Hapuseneb could not be sure if they were looking his way or not.

As soon as he saw him he regretted that he had summoned him. He had managed without the use of sorcery very successfully, and he wondered what had made him change his mind now. It annoyed him that Ra-hotep could hold out against any amount of skilful interrogation, and his suspicion that he was meddling in dangerous and treasonable activities was growing rapidly. He would be pleased to give Hatshepsut not only the information she had requested, but the details of a plot against her.

"I want to see the thoughts in a man's heart," he told the sorcerer. "I want to find out hidden things."

The skull-head nodded, the bony fingers locked and unlocked.

"What method do you use?" Hapuseneb asked, already regretting his decision.

"What method does my Lord desire?"

"I don't care about the method. I care about the results."

"The dream method is best, but that could be dangerous. There are some who have not returned from a spell-cast dream."

"Do you dream, or I?"

"You, my Lord. The animal entrails are safer, but do not give so much detail."

"Use the dream method," Hapuseneb said decisively. "Let's get to it!" he added impatiently.

The sorcerer looked around the bare chamber. They were in one of the least used rooms of the temple, built as a storeroom but at the moment empty. There was no natural light, and an oil lamp flickered dismally from a niche on the wall.

"I need a brazier for burning herbs, and I need a couch for my Lord to lie upon."

Hapuseneb opened the door and called out for these to be provided. The servants who brought them scuttled away from the place fast, made nervous by the ghoulish appearance of the sorcerer and the look of stern determination on the High Priest's face. It was strange he had not used the oracles provided by his own priests. Did he not trust them?

While Hapuseneb lay down stiffly on the couch, every muscle tense, the sorcerer wrote some almost indecipherable glyphs on a small strip of papyrus and then threw it into the flame burning in the brazier. He watched intently as the papyrus caught fire, some of the glyphs disappearing at once, others curling up and blackening slowly, some still visible as the last remnants finally turned to ash. The flame burned green as the sorcerer threw some leaves he had carefully selected from some little bags in the filthy pouch he wore over his thigh.

Hapuseneb grew rapidly drowsy. His limbs relaxed and his head fell sideways. He was asleep.

Hapuseneb's dream took him to the bottom of a lake where he fought for his life among the mud and clinging waterweeds. Through the murky liquid he could see the approach of a huge dark form and feared that it was a crocodile. As a child he had had a narrow escape from such a beast, and whenever he had a frightening dream, there was always a crocodile in it somewhere. His mother had taught him to pray to Sobek, the god always depicted in the form of a crocodile. "No one can defend you against him, except himself," she had said. How could he fight the creature? His darkness seemed to go on forever and his own arms were caught in the weeds, preventing him reaching the knife at his belt.

At that point he woke with a start, and sat up angrily.

"What kind of a dream was that?" he demanded. "It told me nothing."

"It told you that what you suspected is true. You are facing a greater evil than you set out to challenge. You cannot fight it."

"What am I to do then?" Hapuseneb was impressed that the man seemed to know what he had dreamed about, and his disappointment and anger subsided somewhat.

"You can use it against itself."

Hapuseneb frowned. The man's words echoed his mother's, and struck him as significant. But, in practical terms, what did it mean?

"What you have told me so far," he said irritably, "I could have thought up for myself. I didn't need a sorcerer to come from the desert to work his fancy tricks for this!"

The man began to cackle with laughter.

"If you could have thought of it yourself, my Lord, why didn't you?" he wheezed.

Hapuseneb stood up angrily and strode towards the door. He was as much annoyed with himself as he was with the man. He had always done his own thinking and made his own decisions. Why had he resorted to this ridiculous method? The man had told him nothing he really wanted to know.

But at the door he swung round and looked at him once more. It had been interesting how well the man's comments had fitted his dream, without his having told him anything about it. Perhaps he had been too hasty. Perhaps he should give him more time. He was tempted to ask him more questions, perhaps to delve into the future. Could Hatshepsut hold power forever – or would she fall to the plots of Ra-hotep and Ast.

He stepped back into the room. The old man was packing away the little bags of herbs he had taken out of his pouch, muttering and cackling to himself. His back was to the High Priest. Hapuseneb put his large hand on the skeletal shoulder and swung him round to face him.

"Old man," he said, trying to see into his eyes. "We're not finished yet." The eyes gleamed out of the dark sockets for a moment as though illuminated from within, and then went dull.

"I can tell you no more," the sorcerer said sullenly.

"You can and will," snapped Hapuseneb.

The old man shook his head. Hapuseneb tightened his hand on his shoulder. It was like holding a brittle stick. A little more pressure and the bones would snap.

"You have seen something more. Tell me about it."

"It will do you no good."

"Tell me."

"I see names chiselled out. I see other names carved in the empty spaces."

"What names chiselled out? What names carved?"

The old man did not answer and Hapuseneb shook him violently. The figure went limp. His eyes closed.

Horrified, Hapuseneb took his hand away from his shoulder and as he did so the sorcerer sank to the floor and lay without movement. He was dead.

Kneeling beside him Hapuseneb noticed the track of a snake in the dust of the floor, and on the dead man's heel there were two neat incisions. Puzzled, Hapuseneb looked round the starkly furnished room. There was now no sign of the snake, nor anywhere it could be hiding.

Hatshepsut was being carried in her golden chair from one part of Waset to another. Respectful crowds were bowing all along her route. She was tired. She missed Senmut, she thought, and she missed the old days. Everything seemed so much more effort now. She idly moved the film of curtain aside and stared out at the people in the street. One man was standing upright behind the bent figures of the others. One man was looking into her eyes.

She went white.

It was Men-soneb.

She dropped the curtain at once and then decided to call her guards and have him arrested. She drew the curtain aside again quickly.

But he was no longer there.

CHAPTER 18

Hatshepsut now barely left the palace on the west bank at Waset. If she did it was to visit her temple Djeser Djeseru. She had always been restless and moody, but these days too many of her moods were listless and brooding. She walked among the frankincense trees on the lower terrace and was angry if anyone approached her. Sometimes coming upon her unexpectedly, they would hear her talking to herself like a mad woman.

Hapuseneb was sent for and arrived back as soon as he could.

Ra-hotep was still managing to avoid all efforts to prove that he was implicated in any plot, but Hapuseneb had no doubt that there was a very dangerous situation building up. He had learned that the powerful priests of the sun would side with Men-kheper-Ra when he chose to wrest power from his stepmother-aunt, and that this time would not be far off. Without the backing of the priests of Ra, the attempt would probably fail, but with it, it would certainly succeed. There had been conspiracies before, but each time they had come to nothing because Hatshepsut's officials had picked off the plotters one by one and left Men-kheper-Ra isolated and powerless. But this time things had gone too far. Ra-hotep, with extraordinary cunning, had created a huge groundswell in favour of the young prince among his own priests, not only at Yunu but throughout the Two Lands.

Hapuseneb paced his quarters beside the Temple of Amun-Ra and wrestled with the dilemma, and then, just before Thutiy's message arrived begging him to return to Waset, Hapuseneb had an idea that might swing, once and for all, the balance of power in favour of Hatshepsut. Hapuseneb had remembered that there was something Ra-hotep and the priests of Ra wanted very badly. If Hapuseneb could succeed in getting it into his own hands, he would at last have the means of manipulating Ra-hotep. It was perfect! A matter of using him against himself as the old sorcerer had suggested.

Ra-hotep wanted the fragment of eggshell that was at Khemnu – the relic that was believed to have been part of the cosmic egg out of which the sun god had burst in primordial times. The priests of the sun had always wanted it at Yunu, but the priests of Khemnu would never part with it. Such a prestigious relic drew pilgrims bearing gifts from far and wide. It was the one thing that assured Khemnu a rich revenue and a measure of real power. In ages past, wars had been fought between the nomes for its possession. Yunu had the gold-topped obelisks, the egg of green crystal, the priceless altar of white and gold, and many other treasures of great importance connected with the sun god, but it did not have the actual eggshell from which the god was hatched.

Hapuseneb had seen it many times, and it certainly was very strange. Although only a fragment, it was easy to see that, complete, the egg it came from would be gigantic. It was of stone, curved like an eggshell and lined with crystals of gleaming white and shimmering gold.

Hapuseneb was not sure how he was to get the eggshell away from Khemnu, but he was determined to try. If Hatshepsut could present it as a gift to the great Temple of the Sun at Yunu, it might just change the situation. The gratitude of the priests of Ra would surely be hers forever.

But not a whisper of this must be heard. If it was, the priests at Khemnu would have no trouble in hiding the eggshell as they had done on several occasions before. No one must know about it but the Pharaoh and himself.

He hurried back to Waset, not only in response to Thutiy's call, but in order to put his proposal to Hatshepsut and prepare for the delicate task ahead.

Hapuseneb requested an audience with the Pharaoh as soon as he reached Waset, and reported at once all that he had found out and all that he suspected.

She listened to what he had to say about Ra-hotep calmly, but went white when he told her that the old sorcerer had suddenly dropped dead from what was apparently a snakebite, just as Hapuseneb felt he was about to give him the names of the conspirators.

She rose from her chair and paced the room. Hapuseneb watched her in silence, hoping that she would trust him enough now to tell him what was troubling her. He had noticed that it was always the mention of Men-soneb's name that fixed her attention. She seemed hardly concerned that her position as Pharaoh was in real jeopardy from Men-kheper-Ra and the priests of Ra.

At last she sat down again and described the haunting to which she had been subjected and the horrifying moment when Men-soneb had dissolved into a heap of wriggling snakes. Hapuseneb had never seen her so agitated as when she described her concern that some, or at least one, might have got away.

"I was so sure he was dead," she said. "Yet whenever I go into the city I see him."

"Surely you have had him arrested?"

"I see him, but he can never be found. It is as though he doesn't exist."

"I will find him," he said firmly. Did this mean her own guards were in the pay of Ra-hotep? Was there no one to be trusted?

He thought back on all those years she had ruled the Two Lands as a great pharaoh should, and the network of magnificent temples she had either raised or restored, through which benefits from the gods could pour into the country. She had brought peace and a quiet prosperity to the people, and freedom from foreign wars. How unfair it was that as soon as she was sad and troubled, everyone was so quick to desert her, forgetting all the good she had done. He knew in his heart that even he had considered joining Men-kheper-Ra's faction, knowing that there the power of the future lay. But there had been too much between them, and he owed her loyalty. Though she was no longer the dynamic and beautiful young woman she had been when he first joined her service, her visions were still worth more than anything the young prince could offer. Her desire had been to create lasting beauty and harmonious communications between all the realms of being. She was indeed Maat-ka-Ra, the spirit of order and light, the daughter of Amun-Ra, the true energy of life.

He realised at that moment that the ambitions he had had all his life were nothing to what he felt now for Hatshepsut. He loved her, not as a means to sexual gratification or as a ladder to his own power and success, but as a being who had been chosen for a mighty task and would have succeeded in it, had she not been so torn between the human and the divine. "At least she tried," he thought. And then he knew he wanted her to succeed, more than anything in the world. He would stand by her and help her to climb back to strength.

He told her about his plan for giving the sacred eggshell to the Temple of Ra at Yunu.

"It should always have been there," he said. "You would be doing no more than restoring it to its rightful place."

But she was no fool and could see at once the advantages of the plan and the very considerable disadvantages. She might buy the loyalty of one group of priests by forfeiting the loyalty of another. Hapuseneb reminded her that the priests of Ra were more powerful than the priests of Djehuti, and that Yunu was a greater centre than Khemnu.

He could see that she was hesitating.

"I'm afraid you have no choice," he said regretfully, and spelled out again the dangerous situation she was in.

Something of the old fire returned to her eyes. "There is always choice," she said. "And it will be my decision, Hapuseneb, and not yours."

He bowed his head, acknowledging her authority. Indeed, he was relieved to see her assert it again.

He took his leave, but turned at the door.

"It is your decision, Majesty," he said, "but there is very little time . . ."

She gestured impatiently that he should leave her alone.

The decision was made at Djeser Djeseru. She prostrated herself in the inner sanctuary before the statue of Amun-Ra in its ebony and ivory shrine.

She waited for a long time for a sign, trying to go into the Silence, where in happier times she had communicated with the great Spirit, but she found she could not lose one insistent image: Men-soneb. She was haunted by memories of his face as the phantom in her chamber, as the priest in her throne room, as the man-in-the-crowd in the busy streets of the city. It seemed to her the sanctuary of Amun-Ra was crawling with snakes. She lifted her head and looked round in terror. The paving stones were clear. The beautiful lamps Senmut had designed burned steadily, illuminating the exquisite statue of the god in his golden barque and the rich, jewelled colours of the painted reliefs on the walls. The scent of the incense from Punt was strong and heady.

She pondered for the thousandth time Men-soneb's accusations that she herself had been responsible for the spectre that haunted her. The latest revelation of Hapuseneb would appear to give the lie to this accusation. Men-soneb had surely been used by Ra-hotep to undermine and weaken her. Should she give the precious relic of the sacred egg into the hands of such a criminal, even to save her own skin?

She had let her daughter down by being too busy to take the trouble to understand her. She had let Senmut down by choosing worldly power over personal fulfilment and love. She had let her son down by denying him life because it would interfere with her own ambitions. She had taken Hapuseneb to her bed when she had vowed to her god that she would not lie with a man again, and for reasons that were unworthy. In each case she had wronged people she should have loved because of her obsession to be Pharaoh and to have unencumbered power. But more than any of this she, as female, had taken sole power, excluding the male. On the mundane level she had no qualms that she had done the right thing, but in a much deeper and subtler sense she had destroyed the age-old balance, the male-female partnership, that had always kept the Two Lands in harmony with Maat.

Hatshepsut fingered the bracelet on her arm, the one Amun had asked for all those years ago. She rose to her feet, standing before her god, turning the silver and turquoise circlet round and round. Was it too late to undo what she had done? Was it too late to make the choice he had offered her? She had tried to have the best of both worlds – and in many instances she had succeeded. But in some crucial ones she had not. She felt she was ready now to make the full commitment she had been so unwilling to make as a young girl. Let Men-kheper-Ra have the double crown to himself. She would be Hatshepsut Khenemet-Amun, Hatshepsut "United-to-Amun", in truth.

When she had made her last obeisance and left the sanctuary, her earthly father's bracelet remained on the top step of the shrine.

Quietly she walked through the colonnaded court of the upper terrace with its scenes of Amun-Ra in magnificent procession, passed through the great doors to the second terrace, where Senmut had had inscribed the story of her expedition to Punt and the scenes of her divine conception and birth.

She paused in the shade of the garden on the lower terrace, listening to the birds singing in the branches of the trees and the fish splashing in the pool. She drew a deep breath and, with it, the strength to do what she had decided to do.

Hapuseneb was shocked when Hatshepsut told him that she was not going to rob Khemnu to bribe the priests of Ra. He noticed that there was something very different about her, but he could not quite grasp what it was. She had a kind of calm strength that she had not had before. Even at the time of her greatest power, her strength had always been restless, almost violent.

He tried to persuade her to change her mind, but she would not listen. She gave no reasons, nor did she offer any suggestions as to how they were going to avert disaster by other means. She seemed very quiet and content, as though an old and troublesome ghost had been laid to rest.

He had been trying to locate Men-soneb, but could find no trace of him. As she said, it was as though he did not exist.

Something had to be done, and he decided to do it without her permission. She was clearly not in control of herself or her kingdom at the moment. Her calmness might well be because she had not understood the implications of what he had been trying to tell her.

He would go to Khemnu and see what he could do on her behalf. He had her seal ring and the considerable powers she had given him. Who was to challenge him if he claimed to be acting in the name of Pharaoh?

He boldly strode into the temple housing the sacred eggshell, and boldly carried it out. The only one who saw him was a junior priest, who was puzzled but not alarmed. Hapuseneb was known to him by sight – indeed, he had seen him in company with his own High Priest very recently – and he would not have presumed to question such an august official's right to do anything he wished. Thinking the relic was being taken for some ritual purpose, he mentioned it to no one and slept a comfortable and dreamless sleep, while the precious object was already on its way north in Hapuseneb's boat.

Late the next day, as Hapuseneb stood on deck, he noticed that the sky to the west was growing unaccountably dark. It was the season of storms and he was not unduly worried, though a little concerned they should make port before the wind rose too high. He spoke to the captain, who was calling all his men out to man the oars.

They were in a section of the river where the desert came down almost to the water's edge and sand dunes were piled against the hills. The captain pointed out several rock chasms that might well serve as funnels through which the wind could tear down on them and wreak havoc with their sails.

They went downstream as fast as they could, but it was not long before not only the dark overtook them, but the wind. It burst suddenly through from the high desert and came screaming and shrieking at them as though it were a host of angry and vengeful demons determined to destroy them.

Hapuseneb clutched the large parcel wrapped in doeskin he had brought with him from Khemnu and braced himself against the wall of his flimsy cabin. The boat rocked and juddered. He heard the captain shouting, the men's terrified yells. How suddenly the storm had come! How strangely it seemed to single out their boat! Hapuseneb found himself praying to Hatshepsut's god, not the ritual prayers he had said a hundred, hundred times, but prayers of his own making – explaining, apologising, pleading for mercy like any superstitious peasant.

"I took it to save Hatshepsut. I took it to save your chosen one," he shouted, as he was flung from one side of the cabin to the other. The thin wall splintered as he crashed into it and he went sliding out onto the deck, where there was pandemonium. The river had been lashed up into waves almost like the ocean. The air was a wall of violent sand driving into his eyes. He saw one man swept overboard and another stunned as the boom hit him on the side of the head. He crawled back to the comparative shelter of the cabin, still holding his precious cargo. He had never experienced such a storm on the river. They could no longer see the banks, let alone the hills beyond them. It was as though the whole desert had risen up and was bent on burying the Two Lands so deep no one would ever be able to find it. Amulets of every description on hairy chests were being clutched. Prayers to every god in the world were being yelled or whispered or sobbed.

Could it have been the stealing of the sacred eggshell? Hapuseneb wondered. Could it possibly have been? All around him men were questioning their souls. All around him men were wondering about their lives and fearing their deaths.

There was a sickening crash as the boat cracked open against a rock the steersman had not been able to avoid. Hapuseneb was only vaguely aware in the confusion that the captain was tugging at his arm and telling him to jump and make for the bank.

"We're sinking fast," he shouted. "Come, my Lord."

Still tightly gripping his parcel, which meant he only had one arm free for swimming, Hapuseneb leapt into the river. The water seemed to suck him down. A shattered plank hit him in the face and darkness flooded into his head. His hands, now limp, lost their hold on the great eggshell of Khemnu, which spiralled to the bottom of the Nile and settled into the mud of the river bed, the mud that already held so many secrets and would, no doubt, hold so many more.

Hapuseneb, Hatshepsut's right arm, was washed up onshore and later found with many of the crew – dead.

On Sehel Island there was no breath of air moving, no sign that to the north the desert was being whipped up into a frenzy by a storm wind fiercer than anyone living at that time had ever experienced, but Anhai felt a perturbation in her heart as though dark forces were on the move. She woke, startled, from a deep sleep, knowing that she had dreamed something important, but unable to remember what it was. After lying for a while on her back, staring at the ceiling and trying to recall the shadowy filaments of the dream, she arose, drawing a robe around her shoulders. She stepped out into the night and paced in the garden, wondering why she felt so disturbed and frightened when all about her was lying peacefully in the starlight.

She found her way to the centre of her maze and sat on the bench with her back to Hatshepsut's frankincense tree.

"What is it?" she whispered. She tried to see images of Hathor, Djehuti and Imhotep, the guardians of her sanctuary, but strangely, this night they felt like aliens to her. She had so identified with the mythic symbols of Khemet, her ancient home, it had become second nature to her to call on them for help. But this night they did not come to her. It crossed her mind that the gods of Khemet were angry and withholding their support. "Nonsense," she told herself. But then she remembered the story that was told of how Atum, the Creator, had once been so angry with the beings of the world for the evil they were committing, he unleashed a destructive force which all but wiped out every living thing. The force became uncontrollable and Atum, whose anger meanwhile had abated, had to resort to trickery to bring about the end of the slaughter. Anhai seemed to remember that he flooded the land with red-coloured beer, and the fearsome goddess of destruction lapped up so much of it, believing it to be blood, that she became drunk and incapable of continuing her grisly task. What had always horrified Anhai about the story was that the destructive force was said to be his life-giving daughter Hathor, who somehow became, or was transformed into, the powerful lioness goddess of destruction, Sekhmet. It had taken Anhai some time to grasp the significance of the transformation.

She could not shake the feeling that something bad was happening or about to happen, although there was no sign of it around her. Everything was going well in her personal life. The healing sanctuary had become an active centre for good. There had been some miracles on the spot, but mostly people left so changed in their attitude to their lives that they themselves brought about their own healing when they returned to their homes. There was every reason for Anhai to feel happy and satisfied; none for her to feel depressed and anxious.

In the darkness, her heart returned to her mother Kyra. How comforting it had been as a child to reach up her arms when she was afraid and to be held by her mother, close against her loving breast. How stupid she had been to drift away from her and cause her so much pain. How she longed to make it up to her. In the healing work she was doing she felt she had finally paid her debt. But did Kyra know? Had the ka of her mother seen what she was doing? If only she was here now to comfort her, to tell her not to be afraid, to give her that sense of conviction she herself had had so unshakeably: that no matter what happened, deep down, the core of things was good and could be reached and drawn upon for strength.

A slight breeze rustled the leaves of the frankincense tree, and a beautiful scent wafted towards her. Anhai frowned. It was different from the usual scent of the herb garden. Strong and sweet, it was the scent of spring flowers from a meadow in her lost northern home.

Her heart lifted. Surely Kyra was here? Surely this was a sign?

But, as suddenly as it had come, it went – and Anhai doubled up with a terrible pain in her head. She held her temples and rocked to and fro in agony. What now? "O Nameless One, what now?" she sobbed. The feeling of foreboding and oppression increased a hundredfold. "No," she cried. "No! No! No!" And then it seemed to her she was caught up in a huge sandstorm, the air raging all around her. For a moment, through the flying sand, she caught a glimpse of a boat on the river, buffeted and tossed and finally smashed to pieces. She saw Hapuseneb struggling, Hapuseneb dying. "No!" she sobbed. She had loved him. Not as she had loved Isar in her youth, but enough to feel his death a painful loss.

But she felt Hapuseneb's death was not the sole cause of the shadow that was darkening her heart. There was something more. Something worse. The Khemet she had known was being destroyed . . . Hatshepsut blown away . . . the temples of love buried under sand, and the temples of war and retribution standing clear.

And then she thought of her beautiful island, her sanctuary of peace. What of it?

She saw a boat drawing up at the little quay. She saw Ra-hotep's great bulk. She knew her time and the time of all who had supported Hatshepsut and Hapuseneb was over. Darkness was coming. Darkness was even coming to her island.

The pain and the vision ceased. Anhai sat in the still garden and looked around her. Everything was as it always had been. Nothing had changed. Nothing had happened.

She stood up and paced about in agitation. Was this a true vision or a spell fed by some malignant person who resented her in some way. Ra-hotep himself, perhaps? He had been very angry when she went off with Hapuseneb, and she knew he was capable of strong magic. Men-soneb, who had persecuted Hatshepsut – was it he?

"I need to know," she whispered. "Kyra, you were here, I know. I need you." She thought of Kyra's triple crystal and wished she had it with her. But her visualisation of it was so strong in that moment of yearning she found that it was with her, to all intents and purposes. It was her strongest link with her mother.

"Beautiful mother, whom I have wronged," she whispered, and her image of Kyra manifested, but somehow Kyra had some of the features of Hathor, the All-Mother, the earth-womb, the beautiful lady of turquoise and sycamore. She stood before her in the garden.

"You have had a true vision, my daughter," Hathor's voice, Kyra's voice, said.

"What am I to do," she cried, agitated, "if Ra-hotep comes to my island and spoils everything I have been working for?"

"Ra-hotep must not come to your island."

"But I saw him, and you said the vision was a true one."

"The true island of healing you have founded is not the sand and rock of this place, but in your heart. You must not let him enter the true island. You must take it away. You must leave, that it might survive this time of darkness."

"Where am I to go?"

"That is your decision. But wherever it is, you must take your island with you. You must never let it go, and you must never let it fail to do its work."

Anhai was trembling.

The figure of Hathor-Kyra had gone. She knew she was alone.

Her decision!

She looked around her and wept to think this green and blossoming sanctuary she had worked so hard to create would return to desert and cease to be. But if what she had seen came to pass, would it not be better to leave and start up somewhere else than have it taken over and run in the way she knew Ra-hotep would run it, for his own glory and to increase his own wealth?

She walked down to the river and stared for a long time at the water surging over the rocks, eagerly thrusting its way north to the great ocean over which she had come to learn humility and wisdom. She wanted to go back; she wanted to go home. Light would come to this land again, of that she was sure. But not now. Not immediately. Should she stay and try to bring it back in her own small way, or leave to bring what she had learned to her mother's people in that other, distant land?

The dawn light was beginning to creep over the sky. The first birds were calling. She was pulled both ways.

She stepped into the river and purified herself, then lifted her arms to the rising sun.

It seemed in that moment it was not Kheper or Ra or Atum, but the Nameless One of Kyra's distant home. The hymn that came to her lips was one she had learned as a child in the Temple of the Sun at Haylken.

She would go home, and everywhere she stopped on that long, long journey she would found a sanctuary of healing. The journey might take a lifetime, but she wanted to be buried with her mother and the friends of her childhood. She had laid the ghost of Egypt in her life, as she had laid the ghost of her guilt in her homeland. She was ready to take up, with a clear heart, the threads of her future.

When Ra-hotep came, he would not find her here.

The storm was not confined to the area where Hapuseneb had made his last bid to save his Pharaoh. It raged for hundreds of miles across the country and even battered at the doors of Waset, though in the green city they did not have to contend with swirling sand to the same extent. The western mountains, where Meretseger guarded the valley of Hatshepsut's father's tomb, seemed to be smoking as the plumes of sand spun around the peaks and crags. The trees on her lower terrace at Djeser Djeseru wrestled with the wind, bending with the strain.

Hatshepsut watched the storm from her western palace, her eyes deeply meditative.

"Rage on," she whispered, "great god of storms. I met you once and I outfaced you. Are you come to test me again?" Had Amun-Ra sent him to see if she was as resolute in her faith as she had been before she started to put worldly power before love?

Day after day the storm lashed the Two Lands. No one had ever known it last so long. In Set's season one could expect a storm of one or two days' duration, sometimes three. But this time the count went on and on . . . ten, fifteen, twenty . . . and there was still no sign of it abating. Whole villages had been buried in the sand, temples with them. In other areas, villages and temples long since lost and forgotten emerged. In the cities, day after day the ceaseless battle to keep the sand and dust out of the houses was wearisome. To venture out in search of food was a hazardous and uncomfortable undertaking.

No boats moved on the river. No news, no messages, came or left. Hatshepsut paced the dusty corridors of her palace like the panther Senmut had brought her from Punt, settling to nothing, only pausing from time to time to stare out with red-rimmed eyes at the sand building up in drifts against her beautiful temple.

One day her servants could not find her and ran about the palace, seeking and calling. She had chosen to take the burden of the storm onto her own shoulders, and had gone out to meet Set for the good of the Two Lands.

* * * *

Swathed in fine linen against the abrasive action of the flying sand grains, and bent almost double against the force of the wind, she began to climb the rocky slopes to the north of Djeser Djeseru. Sometimes the firm limestone supported her, but mostly she slipped and slid on the broken slivers of shale, the same shale that had given the excavators of her tomb such trouble. Her plan of having her tomb tunnel dug in a straight line through the mountain had had to be abandoned in the end because of the friable nature of the layer of shale the workmen encountered. The long tunnel had to veer off the true so that it did not in fact lie directly behind the sanctuary of Amun as she had hoped it would. Remembering this now, she smiled wryly to herself. "Like my life," she thought.

She leant against an outcrop of hard limestone among the shale and drew breath. She had climbed this ridge many times and rejoiced at the view across the plain to the river and beyond it to the sprawling town of Waset, punctuated by the high pylons of the temples with their tall flagpoles of red cedar wood bearing fluttering pennants. How many times had she looked with satisfaction on the gold gleaming from the tips of the obelisks and the winged sun-disks above the gateways? How many times had she watched the white sails in their slow and graceful dance on the river, the flocks of wild geese flying home across the water, the peasants tilling the fields with their slow, lumbering oxen?

But now she could see nothing. She turned her face to the rock and wondered if she had the strength to do what she had to do. For two decans Set had raged at the Two Lands. In the long memory of Egypt this had hardly ever happened before. When the first decan passed she had already begun to believe that this was no ordinary storm. Pharaoh had become weak. Pharaoh had been more concerned with herself than with her land. The vacuum left by the withdrawal of her attention, her strength, was being filled by the enemy of Life. Her promise to Amun-Ra had come too late. She had already damaged the subtle web of interconnection between the divine and the human, the web that protected and sustained the land. It might now take more than the sacrifice of her bracelet to undo what she had done.

But she would fight Set. She would drive him out, and when he was gone she would work to renew the sacred web.

When she had done that and the Two Lands were safe again, then she would hand over to Men-kheper-Ra and Meryt-Ra-Hatshepsut, his wife.

She forced herself to leave the relatively protective rock and face the driving gusts of sand once more. She climbed and slipped back, and climbed again, determined this time not to weaken.

At last she stood where she could look Set in the eye. She stood straight, every muscle in her body tensed to keep her upright against the blasts of his hot breath.

"I am Set, who can raise a tumult of storm in the horizon of the sky, like one whose will is destruction. Daughter of Amun-Ra – we meet again!"

"For the last time, Lord of the Desert Winds. My Land is not for you. Withdraw into your own domain."

He laughed, and as he did so the wind howled louder than ever. Three trees at Djeser Djeseru were blown down, their roots ripped from the earth, Hatshepsut's magical, protective foundation deposits exposed to the dark raging of the god.

Amun-Ra in his sanctuary stood silently watching his daughter, not listening to the desperate supplications of the priests grovelling at his feet.

She staggered, but regained her balance.

"I know you, dark god," she cried. "You are as close to me as my own heart."

"Then you will never defeat me."

"On the contrary," she said, suddenly understanding something for the first time. "It is because you are in my heart I can defeat you!"

He rose up above her on his wings of storm. He glared at her with fiery eyes. He roared at her with his thunderous voice.

But she was no longer afraid.

She closed her eyes, and in the middle of the whirlwind she saw another figure reaching out his arms for her. Amun-Ra, her father, come to fetch his daughter home.

The beleaguered people of Waset and throughout the Two Lands paused with what they were doing and looked up, listening. Dared they hope the storm had passed at last? An uneasy silence had fallen on the land. The sun blazed down from a brilliant blue sky as though nothing had happened. They went to their windows. They went to their doors. They rushed out into the streets, shouting to their neighbours. The wind had dropped. The sand had settled.

Then the rejoicing began – the singing and the dancing, the kissing and the hugging.

After that, more soberly, they counted the cost of the storm and began to rebuild broken walls and smashed silos. They mourned relatives and friends who were not there to greet the return of the sun, and they buried dead animals.

Men-kheper-Ra, who had been in Kepel with his mother, returned hastily to the Two Lands, from his royal boat surveying with horror the devastated farmlands along the riverbanks. Palm trunks like fallen columns of ancient temples lay everywhere.

News was beginning to circulate again, and with it the rumour that the Pharaoh was dead.

Amenemheb and Ra-hotep both accompanied the prince to Men-nefer, and from there the decree went out that Men-kheper-Ra, son of Aa-kheper-en-Ra, grandson of Aa-kheper-ka-Ra, was taking his rightful place as sole Pharaoh of the Two Lands. He claimed the titles: "Strong bull arising in Waset", "Enduring in kingship like Ra in his heaven", "Powerful of Strength, Holy of Diadems", "King of Upper and Lower Egypt, Men-kheper-Ra, the form of Ra remains", "Son of Ra", "Beautiful of Forms", "Beloved of Hathor, lady of the turquoise", "Djehuti-mes the third". His followers called him also "Brandisher of Arms" and "Lord of Action", and identified him with Montu, the war god of Iuny and Djerty.

With ruthless efficiency all who had been close to Hatshepsut were relieved of their offices, exiled or assassinated.

By the time he reached Waset, the country had swung completely in his favour, and crowds ran along the banks, singing his praises as they had once sung Hatshepsut's. Somehow he was associated with the return of the sun, and Hatshepsut with the storm. Her great deeds were forgotten, her name reviled.

CHAPTER 19

As the fog caused by the wind-blown sand settled, Hatshepsut found herself facing the regions of the Duat: the fields of reeds, the sacred lakes, the fiery pits, the gates guarded by interrogators – all that she had seen depicted in the funerary texts. All that she had been taught she would one day have to face.

She knelt down and placed her forehead on the ground as she had done many times in the sanctuary of Amun-Ra, but her limbs felt like air and there was no solidity beneath her.

I am noble. I am a spirit. I am ready. O all you gods and all you spirits, prepare a path for me.

The old words of the spell in the Book of Coming Forth By Day flowed from her heart as though they had been waiting all her life for this moment.

O Lords of Eternity, Founders of Everlasting! This heart belongs to one whose names are great, whose words are mighty. Treat the deeds and thoughts of this heart with understanding and mercy.

She had thought to enter the Duat as Pharaoh, but suddenly she was a being like any other, her elaborate crowns and her luxurious clothes were gone, and what she had done and not done was standing in silent witness like a cloud behind her. In her hand were the three river-worn pebbles Anhai had given her, one black, one white, one grey. She had come from darkness and she was reaching towards the light, but her life on earth had been a mingling of the two. The grey pebble was her life, a mixture of good and evil. On earth she might boast and bluff, but here only the truth would serve. She laid the pebbles down. They had taught her what Anhai had intended.

It seemed to her that she was now rising and her limbs were almost as solid as they had been on earth. She could see her sandalled feet, she could feel the soft, plain linen of her dress.

"Strange," she thought, holding out her hands before her, looking at them in wonderment.

Two figures appeared, one on each side of her, and she turned to look at them. Both were larger than she was.

Each held in one hand the sceptres that distinguished them as gods, and the ankh that was the sign of eternal life. With the other they each took hold of one of her arms and led her forward. Horus and Hathor; one with the piercing golden eyes of the far-seeing falcon, the other with the burnished sun-disk between the golden horns of the celestial cow, the great nurturing mother of the earth – two aspects of the One.

As they journeyed she saw many things that reminded her of earth – marshlands with rushes and papyrus, fields of wheat, lakes of lotus blossom – but whether they were really there or whether they were the forms manifested by her own longing, she could not tell.

At first the way was easy and pleasant, but then it seemed she had to face a series of tests. There was a burning fiery lake she had to cross, balancing on a bridge as narrow as a spear shaft. She was told she would be lost if she wavered or looked back or down, and she would be lost if she stood still. She would be safe only if she walked forward steadily and courageously with her heart pure.

"I have come to you," she murmured, *"my soul behind me and authority before me. O Hathor, Lady of the Two Lands, establish my magic power for me, that by means of it I may recall what I have forgotten, and know what I have always known."*

She stepped forward.

She had called on Hathor, the Lady of Love, and she was suddenly ashamed. Had she ever loved anyone more than herself? She thought of Senmut, Neferure and her son. She had failed in love more than in anything else. Why should Hathor help her? She almost slipped and fell into the raging fire.

And then she thought about the Nameless One, *"the Great God, the Self-created, the Lord of Life, who has created the secret Lords of Eternity, whose forms are hidden, whose shrines are secret, whose place is unknown"*. The same Great God who had created other radiant beings to encircle the firmament, and still more – the gods who are on the earth, who inhabit the west and the east, the north and the south. It seemed to her she could see the hierarchy of mighty spirit forces, known and unknown, reaching upwards in magnificent splendour, and she knew that her father Amun, even united with the sun as Amun-Ra, was by no means the highest of the high. In all this careful order and design, surely there was provision for forgiveness if the heart was truly contrite, if it had learned from its mistakes and was ready to change?

As she stepped off the bridge onto the green land, Amun-Ra was there to greet her.

"You have remembered what you have always known. You have understood it for the first time. Pass on to the Field of Rushes."

As though dreaming, Hatshepsut moved on and found herself among rushes so tall she believed she would be lost forever. She saw a mound rising from the swamp and struggled thankfully towards it through the clinging mud. But it was inhabited by demons who drove her off. She struggled on. Another mound. Another defeat. At the thirteenth mound she was desperate with thirst, but the water that flowed there was fire. Fifteen mounds in all she came upon, some with crocodiles, some with dangerous cobras named "Destruction".

A few of the mounds she managed to climb, and from these she could survey the marshland and see which way she had to go.

As she emerged from the Field of Rushes she was greeted by Djehuti. She bowed low at his feet.

"O you whose heart has never known falsehood, expel my evil," she pleaded. *"Give me new stone on which to carve my story."*

He smiled and lifted her.

"I have thrown off for you the earth which was on your flesh," he said. "Raise yourself that you may see the Book of the Sacred Words, and I will set your feet on the horizon at the place your soul desires."

From the Book of Sacred Words she learned how she was to answer the Gate Keepers of twenty-one gates, and the Forty-Two Assessors of the court of Osiris.

She stood at last before Osiris, the Lord of Resurrection, and her heart was placed on the scales against Maat's feather, the feather of cosmic order and truth. Trembling, she watched the golden pans move up, move down, as though they would never settle.

Amun-Ra stepped forward from the shadows and spoke for her. He told how she had restored the temples of Egypt, how she had brought incense from the land of Punt that the sacred scent might delight the nostrils of the gods, how the Two Lands had been at peace during her reign, and how she had ruled with truth and justice.

"Mostly," Hatshepsut added silently. "But there are things I would change if I had a second chance."

Osiris looked into her eyes as though he had read her thoughts. And then Mut stepped forward, the consort of Amun. How often had Hatshepsut worn the vulture crown of Mut, the folded golden wings around her head, the strong and far-seeing eyes above the forehead.

"My Lord, Foremost of the Westerners, Judge of the Dead," the great goddess said, and everyone in the hall turned to listen. There was a coldness in her eyes and Hatshepsut trembled. Had she offended her? She had supervised the rituals that took Amun to the temple of Mut at all the festivals so that the great couple could be

together; she had honoured their son Khonsu, a moon god, in his own temple at Ipet-Esut; and the three, father, mother and son, featured together in temples throughout the land. But she had never felt love for Mut as she had for Amun. Mut had always seemed so stern to her, standing behind Amun when he offered the scimitar of war, known sometimes as "Mistress of the Nine Bows", the nine enemies of Khemet.

"My husband Amun loves this child of the earth above all others," she continued. *"And has brought her safely through every danger and every trial. But is it just that she should stand before you declaiming innocence when she has all but destroyed the rule of Maat in her land?"*

"Speak, Lady."

"The Nameless One in the Void was neither male nor female, but alone. Movement and change and evolution were introduced as the One chose to become Two. Male energy and female energy were created to be complementary – eternally in opposition, yet eternally dependent on each other. Since the Two Lands came into being, King and Queen have kept the ancient order, the essential balance. This child of earth took the throne alone and ruled without balance."

"In my own body I represented the two forces," Hatshepsut protested. "I wore the male beard. I ruled as man, yet in my nature I was woman. Surely the union of the two in one echoes more closely the Order behind the order?"

"When the Two were One, there was the Void. Nothing moved. Nothing happened. Nothing changed."

"I – I did not rule alone." Hatshepsut was beginning to be very frightened. In her dreams sometimes she had stood before hard-faced accusers who had taxed her with this very crime. "My counsellors were male."

"They were not equal. They were subordinate."

"Many kings have ruled, keeping their great royal wives subordinate," Hatshepsut said defensively.

"No one who rules alone, without Maat, stands before Osiris justified."

Amun stepped forward.

"Wife," he said, *"Hatshepsut did not rule alone. I ruled at her side. The balance of male energy and female energy was well kept, as was the balance of earth energy and divine energy."*

The great god and the great goddess faced each other, male and female, perfectly balanced. Around them the silence and the stillness was absolute. Nothing moved. Nothing stirred.

At last Amun bowed his head as though he acknowledged that

Mut had spoken truth, and with that minute movement it seemed as though the whole universe had started up again, whirling and whirring, fighting and loving.

Djehuti stepped forward now and raised his hand.

"I think we can all agree that Mut is right in that the interaction of male and female energy is needed for the evolution of all things, but Amun has demonstrated that movement and action and change can only come about if, within that overall balance, there is a continual give and take – one stepping down, the other rising, one rising, the other stepping down."

Suddenly the hall was full of laughter and Amun and Mut kissed.

"But what about me?" thought Hatshepsut desperately. It was almost as though she had been forgotten. To herself she had justified the taking of the throne a hundred times. She had never admitted once that it had been wrong. She knew she had benefited the land. She knew she had been a good pharaoh. Now she was not so sure it had been enough. Now she did not know if her action would be found acceptable to the gods. Would it not be ironic if she was refused her place with the gods among the stars? If she was truthful with herself, one of her reasons for becoming Pharaoh was because she wanted to be raised up after death. She wanted to sail in Ra's mighty golden boat across the heavens as Pharaoh "justified" and "true of voice", powerful and remembered forever.

She looked at the scales in despair. The pans had come to rest. They were almost evenly balanced, but not quite. Would she be flung into the Void and cease to be? She had never been so afraid, so doubtful of herself and what she had done.

It was as though a million years passed as she waited for the verdict. And then Osiris smiled and she knew she would be saved. Divine mercy had tempered divine justice.

Look at me, rejoice over me, for behold I am on high! I have come into being. A shape has been provided for me. The path is open to me towards the Imperishable Stars.

But then Djehuti stepped forward and held up his hand. *"Follow me,"* he said. Hatshepsut hesitated. The floor was strewn with lotus blossom, the flower of renewal and rebirth – but the expression in his eyes told her that not everything was settled yet. She followed the god until she came to an empty hall where there were three doors. She knew that her future lay through one of them. She read the first inscription.

This is the way of the Great Illuminator who shines forth from the Void, who is greatly feared. Power of Powers, Mighty and Majestic. This is the way of Union with the One; of assumption into the Highest.

The door had three bolts. She looked at them and knew that it was beyond her present strength or skill to draw them. Though she had dreamed of passing through this door, she was not yet ready to do so.

She turned her attention to what was written above the second door, which had two bolts.

This is the way of Horus, he who flies high among the stars, yet returns to earth as spirit to guide and help those who have no wings.

Above the third door was written:

This is the way of Osiris: the renewal of life upon earth, the continual cycle of life – the seed, the plant, the fruit, the death, the seed, the plant, the fruit, the death . . .

She noticed that on this door there was only one bolt. She had often dreamed of being a shining spirit among the gods and the stars forever. But now she was not sure. She wanted to be Hatshepsut again. She longed to lie with Senmut, talking as they used to talk. She longed to walk among the rustling trees at Djeser Djeseru. She did not want to leave the earth.

If she chose the second door she could stay close to earth, her ka passing in and out of her tomb and her mortuary temple, no one seeing, no one knowing, guiding the fortunes of her people still. But she would not feel the cool of the evening breeze over the river. She would not feel a man's arms around her.

Perhaps the path of reincarnation would be best. But what if she did not meet her daughter and her son and her lover again? What if they had not passed through the tests or, if they had chosen a different door? What if she walked on earth again in flesh and blood, alone?

She hovered between the second and the third door in an agony of indecision.

At last she put her hand on one of the bolts of the Horus door. Through this one she would have no physical body but she would be able to pass in and out of her tomb, still taking an active part in the lives of her people. Had not flesh brought her suffering and pain?

Had it not brought her frustration and failure? She would be happier without it.

Djehuti restrained her with a touch of the arm.

"Wait. See what there is to see before you make your decision."

He touched the door with two fingers. Through two holes that appeared where his fingers had touched she could look through the door onto the world that she had known. She saw her temple, Djeser Djeseru. But why were there so many workmen busy there? She had left it very nearly completed.

Puzzled, she strained to see more clearly. Men-kheper-Ra was directing the work, and beside him stood Men-soneb in the robes of the High Priest of Amun-Ra. She could hear the ringing of hammers and chisels on stone. Why were they working on the reliefs that were already complete?

And then she saw what they were doing and she had never known such anger and despair. They were hacking out her name. They were mutilating her image wherever it appeared. She was being removed from the memory of the earth. The great temple she had built was being changed so that future generations would think it had been the work of Men-kheper-Ra and his father and his grandfather. It would be as though she had never been, and Hatshepsut-who-had-never-been could no longer take any part in the life of her people. They could not call her to their assistance, because she had no name to call. Without a name, without the proper ceremonies and the images, her ka, the earth soul personal to Hatshepsut, was being prevented from entering the earth realm again.

She was furious and pulled at the top bolt of the door with all her might. It gave only tardily after a struggle. She pursed her lips together. She would show that spawn of Set, that faeces of a dog! She seized the second bolt, but it would not draw. Swearing and cursing, she tugged and pushed and did everything in her power to dislodge it.

Djehuti touched the door again and the two spyholes disappeared. His face was grave.

She was convinced it was because Men-kheper-Ra had destroyed her name and her images and had not performed the correct ceremonies at her funeral that she was being denied access to the world.

"Your ambition and anger, your self-will and self-love are still very active, daughter of Amun," Djehuti said. *"If you choose this door now, you will be no more than a troubled and troublesome shade, caught between realms."*

"Give me another chance," she cried. "I didn't know I was still on trial."

"It is when you do not realise you are on trial that you are more on trial than ever," he replied.

"It is unfair!" she said angrily.

"Unfair or not, it is the way. But I will not stop you going through the second door if you are sure that is what you want."

She turned her back on the second door and on Djehuti. What games were they playing with her, these gods?

"There is a third door," Djehuti said quietly. *"You are destined for the stars, favourite of Amun. Do not waste your time on anger and vengeance – they lead nowhere but to sorrow. Start again with a clear heart and try to achieve a higher and more worthy state. Try for freedom between the realms – not imprisonment."*

"But what trick will there be to this door?" she thought bitterly. "Is there no end to tests and trials and humiliation?"

He touched the third door as he had the second and she looked through the two spyholes. She saw a world very different from the one she knew. It was alien and frightening, but it was a world of solid things and living beings of flesh and blood. But where were Senmut, Neferure and her son?

"You must not look over your shoulder," Djehuti said quietly. *"If it is the will of Maat that you meet again, it will happen."*

"Will I recognise them?"

"You might or you might not."

She frowned, suddenly impatient with all the imponderables of this world-between-worlds. Should she take her chances and try once more to reach beyond herself towards the Imperishable Stars?

She took hold of the bolt and it seemed to her that she and the door were melting, dissolving into mist – her familiar shape was changing and she was taking on other forms, other dreams, other memories . . .

She heard a name called – but it was a stranger's name . . .

Chronology

A brief chronological summary of reigns and events in ancient Egyptian history relevant to the reader of this novel. The dates are drawn in main from John Baines and Jaromir Málek, *Atlas of Ancient Egypt* (Phaidon, Oxford, 1980).

Outside Egypt between 3000BC and 2000BC the ancient Maltese temples were built, as were Stonehenge, West Kennet Long Barrow, Silbury Hill and Avebury in Britain. The Cycladic and Minoan civilizations flourished in Crete and the Eastern Mediterranean islands. Mohenjo-Daro in India and Sumer in the Middle East reached their peak.

In Egypt before 3000BC, historians speak of the 'Pre-dynastic Period'.

EGYPT: EARLY DYNASTIC PERIOD
———— 2920-2770BC ————
DYNASTIES 1, 2, 3

Dynasty 3:

King Djoser 2630-2611BC. King Djoser's great architect and sage, Imhotep, designed and built the first major stone building in the world - the first pyramid - the Step Pyramid of Sakkara. Imhotep later became deified and associated with the Greek god of healing, Asclepius.

EGYPT: OLD KINGDOM
———— 2575-2134BC ————
DYNASTIES 4, 5, 6, 7, 8

Dynasty 4:

Khufu (Cheops) 2551-2528BC
Khephren 2520-2494BC
Menkaure (Mycerinus) 2490-2472BC. These were the builders of the Great Pyramids in Giza. Many others were built during the period of the Old Kingdom.

Dynasty 5:

Unas (Wenis) 2356-2323BC. 'The Pyramid Texts' were inscribed on the inner walls of his pyramid at Sakkara for the first time. They were wonderful poems and spells designed to help and guide the deceased through the otherworld.

Dynasty 6:
This ended with the long reign of Pepi II after which Egypt seemed to sink into a decline.

EGYPT: FIRST INTERMEDIATE PERIOD
——— 2150-2040BC ———
DYNASTIES 9, 10

Central power broken. Warring local rulers. A period of uncertainty and violence.

EGYPT: MIDDLE KINGDOM
——— 2040-1640BC ———
DYNASTIES 11, 12, 13, 14

Dynasty 11:

The unification of the Two Lands, North and South, under several kings called Mentuhotep 2061-2010BC. One built his mortuary temple and tomb at Deir el Bahri next to which, much later, in the eighteenth dynasty, Hatshepsut built hers. The seat of power was established at Waset (Greek name: Thebes. Modern: Luxor/Karnak). The later eighteenth dynasty kings looked back to this period as a great one and emulated it whenever they could. At this time an expedition was sent to Punt on the Horn of Africa. Later Hatshepsut sent her own expedition there.

EGYPT: SECOND INTERMEDIATE PERIOD
——— 1640-1532BC ———
DYNASTIES 15, 16, 17

The Hyksos invaded from the Middle East, bringing with them the horse and the chariot. Their capital was at Avaris in the delta. For the Egyptians it was a dark age.

By the end of the period Theban princes led a revolt against them and drove them out of the country establishing their own right to rule the Two Lands.

Ta'o I and Ta'o II (Sequenenre) and Kamose 1555-1550BC led the rebellion and established the next dynasty. Ta'o II had a very strong and long-lived wife, Aah-hetep I.

EGYPT: THE NEW KINGDOM
——— 1550-1070BC ———
DYNASTIES 18, 19, 20

The eighteenth dynasty and the early part of the nineteenth is often thought to be the high point of Egyptian civilization. Egypt was strong internally and by conquering neighbouring states established an empire whose tribute made Egypt rich. Pyramids were no longer in fashion and the kings dug deep into rocky cliffs to hide their tombs. Magnificent temples were built.

Dynasty 18:

Ahmose c.1550-1525BC.

Amenhotep I c.1525-1504BC.

Thutmosis I (Aa-kheper-ka-Ra) c.1504-1492BC. Warrior king who extended the frontiers of the empire and consolidated power with diplomatic marriages.

Thutmosis II (Aa-kheper-en-Ra) c.1492-1479BC. (Son of Thutmosis I and lesser wife Mutnofre). He married his sister who bore him a daughter, Hatshepsut. When he died after a short reign, his son by a non-royal wife was still a young child. His sister-widow, Hatshepsut, was made regent for the boy. She decided to take the throne for herself and became pharaoh, taking male titles and wearing male attire.

Hatshepsut I (Maat-ka-Ra) c.1473-1458BC. Female pharaoh.

Thutmosis III (Men-kheper-Ra) c.1479-1425BC. No one knows how he took over power from his stepmother-aunt, Hatshepsut, but when he did he reigned a long time and was a very strong warrior king. He obliterated her name and her image wherever he could.

Amenhotep II c.1427-1401BC.

Thutmosis IV c.1401-1391BC.

Amenhotep III (Neb-maat-Ra) c.1391-1353BC. Long-lived, rich and powerful. Chose as his Great Royal Wife and mother of his heir, a non-royal lady, Tiye.

Amenhotep IV/Akhenaten c.1353-1335BC (Wa-en-Ra). Moved his capital from Thebes and Memphis to a completely new site called Akhetaten (now Tel el Amarna). Overthrew the traditional religion of Egypt and concentrated all religious aspiration on the one god symbolized by the disc of the sun emitting rays which held out the sign for eternal life: the Aten. His wife, the famous and beautiful Nefertiti, was given equal status. They had six daughters.

*Smenkhkare c.*1335-1333BC.

*Tutankhamun c.*1333-1323BC.

*Ay c.*1323-1319BC.

*Horembeb c.*1319-1307BC. Horemheb, a commoner, reinstated the priests of Amun as a great power and turned the country against the memory of Akhenaten and his religion. He died childless and appointed his general, Rameses, as the next pharaoh on his death.

Dynasty 19:

The nineteenth dynasty with the Rameside kings now begins. By the end of this dynasty Egypt is invaded again and again and its greatest period is past.

All dates are approximate.

Place Names

The place names appearing in this book are followed by their modern equivalents:

Djeber Mesen (Appollinopolis) - Edfu

Djerty (Tuphum) - Tod

Djeser Djeseru (Djeser-menu) - Hatshepsut's Temple at Deir el Bahri

Ipet-Esut (Thebes) - Karnak

Ipet-Resut (Thebes) - Luxor

Iuny (Hermonthis) - Armant

Iunyt (Tasenet) - Esna

Keftiu (The Island of the Bulls) - Crete

Kepel (Byblos) - Jbail

Khemet (The Two Lands, Black Land) - Egypt

Khemnu (Hermopolis) - Ashmunein

Kheny - Gebel Silsila

Men-nefer (Menufer) - Memphis

Nekheb and Nekhen - Kom el Ahmar

Nubt (Ombos) - Kom Ombo

Per Hathor - Gebelein

Punt - Probably northern Somaliland, near Djibouti

Serui - Deir el Bahri

Suan - Assuan, Aswan

Waset (Thebes) - Luxor

Yunu (Heliopolis, 'On' in the Bible) - now buried under a NE suburb of Cairo

Gods and Goddesses

Brief notes on some of the main deified forces mentioned in this novel.

AMMIT
Hybrid monster waiting beside the scales of Maat in the Hall of Osiris to gobble up "unjustified" souls.

AMUN (Amen, Amon)
Primeval god mentioned in the pyramid texts. Later became a powerful local god in the Theban area and a major god in the Egyptian pantheon. Usually depicted as a man holding divine sceptre and ankh with a crown supporting two tall plumes. The name is connected with being hidden, concealed, invisible. "Hidden of Aspect"; "Mysterious of Form"; "He Who abides in all things". His symbolic animals are the ram and the goose. His great temple at present-day Karnak is still impressive.

APEP (Apophis, Apopis)
Appears in the form of a giant snake. Represents "non-existence", the "Void", which to the ancient Egyptians was a state as real as existence. The daily nightly battle between Ra and Apep represents the constant and eternal struggle between existence and non-existence. So far Apep has always been defeated, never destroyed. The possibility that Ra might one day lose is always there. The implication is that we are only held in existence by positive action on the part of our guardian gods against Apep.

DJEHUTI (Djeheuty, Tehuti, Thoth)
"The Silver Aten". The moon springing out of darkness to bring illuminating knowledge and wisdom. Lord of Time. Reckoner of Years. Inventor of writing and protector of scribes. Guardian of the "House of Life", where all the wisdom texts are kept. He wears a crown of the crescent moon supporting the full moon disc. He is represented in two forms: as man-bodied with the head of the sacred ibis, and as baboon. The ibis bird is white and black with a crescent-shaped beak. The baboon was adopted from an already existing god

at his cult centre Khemnu (Hermopolis). Baboon troops greet the dawn with great excitement. This may be why they are associated with sacred matters. The Greeks identified him with their god Hermes, their name "Hermes Trismegistos" coming from an inscription at Esna: "Djehuti the great, the great, the great".

HATHOR

Her name means "mansion of Horus". Her main aspect is life-giving and nurturing motherhood. She and Isis are sometimes interchangeable as mother of Horus, though she is also seen as wife of Horus. Her cult animal is the cow. Pharaoh is often seen in reliefs and paintings as sucking physical nourishment and mystical wisdom from the udders of a celestial cow representing Hathor. Her sacred instrument is the sistrum or rattle. Music and dancing are very important in her cult. She was equated with the beautiful goddess of love, Aphrodite, by the Greeks. A child of Horus and Hathor is Ihy, who personifies joy through music. A well-preserved temple at Denderah is still to be seen.

HORUS

Sky god seen as a falcon with all-seeing eyes, the sun and the moon. The pharaoh is supposed to be Horus on earth. "The eye of Horus" is a very complex concept, one aspect of which rests on the legend of Horus presenting his own eye to his father to give him new life. He has many forms: one is Ra-Harakhti, representing one aspect of the sun. He is sometimes seen as the brother of Set, sometimes as his nephew. In either case both are opposing but complementary sides of a whole – good and evil, light and dark. He is the Egyptian god most readily compared to Christ. As son of Osiris and Isis he completes a sacred trinity, and as husband of Hathor and father of their son Ihy, he completes another. His temple at his cult centre, Edfu, is one of the best-preserved ancient Egyptian temples. It is still standing. The present building was raised much later than the reign of Hatshepsut, Akhenaten or Tutankhamun.

MAAT

Goddess who wears an ostrich feather tied very simply with a ribbon round her head. She personifies the order of the universe working harmoniously with the will of the divine initiator. You will often see a pharaoh presenting an image of her to stress that he rules with Maat – that is, in harmony with the divine and natural laws of the universe. It is against her feather the heart of the deceased is weighed in the Other World.

MUT

Chief wife of Amun at Thebes. Together with their son, Khonsu, she and Amun make up one of the important divine trinities of Egyptian mythology. She wears a vulture head-dress and the hieroglyph for her name is a vulture, but she can also appear as a lioness or cat-headed goddess like Sekhmet in the north. Her name means "mother". The temple of Luxor was primarily dedicated to her.

OSIRIS

King of the Living in the Underworld (known as the "Duat" to the ancient Egyptians). His flesh is often depicted as green as he is the god of regeneration and rebirth. Images of him are often laid flat and filled with Nile silt and planted with barley seed at burials. Such Osiris-shaped trays of rooted and once growing barley plants have been found in tombs. Ra and he are "twin souls", the one reigning "above" the earth, the other "below". It is said he was once a king ruling on earth, destroyed by his jealous brother Set, restored to life just long enough by the magic of his sister-wife Isis for her to conceive their child, Horus, the falcon-headed god. Osiris, Isis, Horus form a divine trinity.

PTAH

One of the major creator-gods of the ancient Egyptians. There is a record of Ptah, self-created, thinking about the cosmos and then speaking it into existence. He is often depicted as a craftsman-creator and plays an important role at the "opening of the mouth" ceremony at funerals. This ritual prepares the mummy or statue   to   house the living ka of the deceased by touching his or her mouth with an adze made of meteoric iron. Ptah's cult centre was at Memphis (Men-nefer). Most of the great blocks from his temple are missing, having been carried away in past centuries to build Cairo.

RA (Re)

George Hart says of him: "Creator sun-god of Heliopolis. Re is the quintessence of all manifestations of the sun-god, permeating the three realms of the sky, earth and Underworld. Hence many deities enhance their own divinity by coalescing with this aspect of the sun-god" – for example, Amun-Ra. In the myth, the sun-god emerges out of the primeval waters on the first mound and as a trinity of force – Kheper (dawn), Ra (noon), and Atum (sunset) – bursts from the cosmic egg, which he/she has somehow laid, into multitudinous life. There are many creation myths in ancient Egypt, none of them logical – but many with a deep mystical integrity and power.

SEKHMET

Consort of Ptah. Lioness goddess of Memphis. "Great of Magic". Associated with destruction, but more often in the sense of making way for creation than destruction for destruction's sake. She has been known to cure pestilence as well as to cause it.

SESHAT

"Foremost in the Library". Usually associated as the female counterpart of Djehuti as they are both concerned with measuring and recording. Seen with a seven-pointed star above her head.

SET

George Hart describes him as a "god of chaotic forces who commands both veneration and hostility". In mythology he is depicted as the murderer of his brother Osiris and the antagonist of Horus, and yet in the solar barque he defends Ra against the even greater menace of an attack by Apep, the ultimate enemy of existence. He is the violent and destructive force on earth, but does not threaten the very existence of the universe as does Apep. Sometimes the energy of such a force as Set can be harnessed and redirected. Traditionally he has come to be identified with "evil" and Horus with "good" in the conflict of good and evil. But, as we all know, nothing is as simple as that. He is associated with the red desert regions and the sand-storms, as opposed to the rich black fertile lands beside the river.

Notes

p.1 – 'May you permit me…' from Spell 15, *The Ancient Egyptian Book of the Dead*, translated by R. O. Faulkner (British Museum Publications, 1985). What we call *The Book of the Dead* was known to the ancient Egyptians as *The Book of Coming Forth by Day* because it consisted of copies of ancient prayers and spells designed to assist the deceased through a series of complicated trials so that he or she might emerge at last, 'justified' and 'true of voice', to be reborn with the sun and live eternally.

p.17 – 'I am the Eternal Spirit…' from Coffin Text 307, quoted by R. T. Rundle Clark in *Myth and Symbol in Ancient Egypt*, Thames & Hudson, 1959.

p.25 – 'Djeser Djeseru: Most splendid…' from J. H. Breasted, *Ancient Records of Egypt*, vol. 2, Russell & Russell, New York, 1962, paragraphs 372—378.

p.60 – 'Neferure, beloved of Senmut…' During her lifetime Hatshepsut bestowed titles on Neferure more suited to a ruler than a princess. There is an inscription in a small temple in Sinai very similar to this. See Donald B. Redford, *History and Chronology of the 18th Dynasty*, University of Toronto Press, 1967, p. 850.

p.78 – 'The voice goes forth…' from Spell 15, *Book of the Dead*.

pp.80-81 – These quotations are from the Punt reliefs inscribed on the walls of Hatshepsut's temple at Deir el Bahri and translated by J. H. Breasted in *Ancient Records of Egypt*, vol. 2.

p.86 – 'He made his form in majesty…' from *Ancient Records*.

p.88 – 'I am the god who resides in the egg…' from Georg Steindorff, *Religion of the Ancient Egyptians*, Putnam, 1905.

p.88 – 'Lord of the Green Stone…' Utterance 301, paragraph 457c, from *The Pyramid Texts* vol. I., translated by S.A.B. Mercer, Longman, 1952.

p.90 – 'Beautiful is thy brightness…' *Religion of the Ancient Egyptians*.

p.96 – 'I have come to thee, Unen-Nefer…' from A. Piankoff and H. Jackquet-Gordon, *The Wandering of the Soul*, Bollingen Series XL:16, Princeton, 1974. Also from Spell 127, *Book of the Dead*.

P.96 – The ancient Egyptians had names for many different aspects or parts of the individual that separated out after death. 'Ka' was a form that we today might call the 'astral' body, the 'ba' one stage more removed from the physical, the 'soul' of the individual. The 'akh' or 'khu' was more abstract still, the eternal essence of the spirit, the highest form of being. To the ancient Egyptians, the 'name', the 'shadow', the 'intelligence', the 'heart', the 'power of will' — all had their own energy and were, in a mysterious sense we don't quite understand, capable of being separate entities after death.

p.106 – 'I am satisfied with my victories...' From Hatshepsut's inscription on the southern pylon at Karnak. Adapted from paragraph 245, *Ancient Records*, vol. 2.

p.112 – 'Amun-Ra the Lord of the Thrones of the Two Lands...' *The Temple of Deir el Bahri*, vol. 5.

pp.135-6 – The texts from Hatshepsut's obelisks from *Ancient Records*, vol. 2, and from Labib Habachi, *The Obelisks of Egypt*, Dent, 1978.

p.141 – 'Hidden of aspect, mysterious of form...' from George Hart, *A Dictionary of Egyptian Gods and Goddesses*, Routledge & Kegan Paul, 198), p. 5. '...in the infinity, the nothingness, the nowhere...' from Spell 76, Coffin Texts, quoted by R. T. Rundle Clark, in *Myth and Symbol*.

p.172 – 'Behold, I worked...' quoted by Wallis Budge, in *Cleopatra's Needle and other Egyptian Obelisks*, The Religious Tract Society, 1926.

p.176 – 'Having penetrated besides...' Senmut's tomb inscription quoted by John Anthony West in *Travellers' Key to Ancient Egypt*, Knopf, New York, 1985, p. 343.

p.180 – Table with four bricks etc. from *Egyptian Magic*.

p.222 – 'I am Set, who can raise a tumult...' from Spell 39, *Book of the Dead*.

p.223 – Men-kheper-Ra's titles from Sir Alan Gardiner, *Egyptian Grammar*, Griffith Institute, 1982, Lesson VII.

Quotations taken from the *Book of the Dead*:

p.224 – 'I am noble...' Spell 9

p.224 – 'O lords of eternity...' Spell 27

p.225 – 'I have come to you...' Spell 107

p.225 – 'The Great God...' Spell 17

p.226 – 'O you whose heart...' Spell 26

p.226 – 'I have thrown off for you...' Spell 170

p.228 – 'Look at me, rejoice...' Spell 180

p.229 – 'This is the way of the Great Illuminator...' Spell 15.

About Moyra Caldecott

Moyra Caldecott was born in Pretoria, South Africa in 1927, and moved to London in 1951. She married Oliver Caldecott and raised three children. She has degrees in English and Philosophy and an M.A. in English Literature.

Moyra Caldecott has earned a reputation as a novelist who writes as vividly about the adventures and experiences to be encountered in the inner realms of the human consciousness as she does about those in the outer physical world. To Moyra, reality is multidimensional.

You can learn more about Moyra Caldecott and her work, and sample some of her writings at www.moyracaldecott.co.uk

For more information about Mushroom Publishing and Bladud Books, please visit www.mushroompublishing.com

Printed in the United States
89632LV00001B/23/A